CRAVING YOU

& You Anthologies

CRAVING YOU

A Spicy Valentine's Day Anthology

Edited by Courtney Umphress

www.andyoupress.com

Cover design by Kerri Odell
Arranged and edited by Courtney Umphress
Typeset by Nicole Frail/Nicole Frail Edits, LLC
Proofread by Nicole Mele

First publication: January 2025

www.nicolefrailbooks.com | @nicolefrailbooks | www.andyoupress.com | @andyoupress

Print ISBN: 978-1-965852-13-2
Ebook ISBN: 978-1-965852-10-1

Contents

Abigail Spencer's Valentine's Day blind date, a cooking class, is about to take an unexpected turn because the chef in charge is the man she spent an unforgettable steamy week with five years ago. Making pasta has never been so complicated or yummy.

Sometimes it takes years to perfect the recipe for true love. Lourdes and Jules have been best friends all their lives, but romance has never been in the cards. When Lo opens a food truck in Jules's town, they find themselves at a crossroads. Will they be able to create something sweet at last?

Niall plans a Valentine's Day picnic to make his relationship with Sam official. The cold seems to ruin his plans, but they find a way to heat things up.

When Sarah's boss, Joe, invites her to Valentine's Day dinner, she's hesitant at first because of past heartbreak. As the night heats up, Sarah finds herself falling for Joe's passionate touch, but can she trust him with her heart?

Vi is hiding not only from her past, but her desires as well. It takes one bite of Nicolas's sweet creations to remind her of everything she craves . . . and has lost.

What happens when the best friend who ran away comes back to the wolf pack and sets everything on fire—family shame, patriarchal traditions, and your heart? A sweet friendship transforms through one night of desire, personal rediscovery, and empowerment.

A reserved chef indulges in a moment of sexual impulsiveness with a stranger. When the subject of her fling emerges as her sous chef for Valentine's Day weekend, sparks fly.

Grace is determined to outmatch her spectacled, gorgeous husband this Valentine's Day. But is she the only one who has secret plans?

Introduction

Courtney Umphress

Thank you for picking up *Craving You: A Spicy Valentine's Day Anthology*! This collection of romantic and spicy stories was published by Nicole Frail Books, a small independent press that specializes in promoting both established and aspiring authors. In this anthology, talented authors in different stages of their writing careers have worked diligently to immerse you in all that is Valentine's Day.

The characters within this eclectic mix of short stories have a variety of approaches to the romantic holiday. While some spend the day bonding with their loved one, others go on first dates, try to focus on their own needs, or take the opportunity to leave behind the friend zone. For some characters, however, Valentine's Day can also shed light on the worst parts of love—painful past breakups, perceived betrayals, and relationships that seem just out of reach.

No matter how each of these stories portray the season of love, sharing meals clearly plays a significant role in developing relationships. Food is a tool for establishing connections, expressing love, and of course, enhancing intimacy, creating shared memories that the couples will remember forever. From working in small-town restaurants to cooking for loved ones to engaging in food play, these characters celebrate the magic food can bring to relationships . . . and the bedroom.

I hope you enjoy this Valentine's Day anthology and that it satisfies your cravings for love, connection, and passion!

MISDIALED LOVE

Misdialed Love
A Recipe for a Rekindled Romance

Ramona Elmes

Chapter 1

ABIGAIL SPENCER STARED AT THE orange-and-white fish as it swam back and forth in the expansive tank next to her work desk. She didn't really care about the fish but found the movement soothing as she pondered how her life had come to this. Tonight, for Valentine's Day, she had a blind date. Who went on a blind date during the holiday of love? She sighed. Apparently, Abigail did. Her colleague and friend Becca walked by and grinned, giving her a thumbs-up.

"You are going to love him. The *Columbia Tribune* named him one of the area's up-and-coming bankers. Perfect marriage material."

While Abigail was pleasantly surprised when she and her polished colleague became friends, she doubted their dating criteria was the same. They both worked at Tidal Technology, in the communication sector. Abigail built and managed the tech for the communication team while Becca was pretty much the face of their group. Their boss, Sal, was a curmudgeon who they both suspected was counting the days until retirement.

"Aren't you the least bit excited?" Becca prodded.

Abigail did really like Becca and knew her matchmaking scheme was out of the goodness of her heart. Still, she didn't care if someone was an up-and-coming banker or marriage material. In truth, what she wanted was to get laid. It had been far too long. Perhaps this date could help her with that.

"I am."

Her friend beamed. "He is going to love you."

Abigail glanced at her reflection in the fish tank. Her blonde curls spiraled around her face and shoulders. Her smiley-face sweater and slacks looked haphazard. She wasn't sure she epitomized a future banker's wife. It didn't matter, she reminded herself. She had plenty of dresses that screamed, *Fuck me, hot banker.* She wouldn't focus on anything further than that.

"Thanks. I do appreciate you setting us up."

Becca sighed. "I wish Stuart and I could join you. Maybe if we stay until tomorrow and—"

"Go out of town with your boyfriend. It is sweet he set something up for you," Abigail insisted.

"It is," Becca said, and then frowned. "If your date turns out to not be great, let me know. Stuart will be in trouble."

A giggle escaped Abigail. "Go give your boyfriend some loving. I'm sure his friend is wonderful and if not, I can manage."

"It's a cooking class at that new hot restaurant, 1796."

"I remember," Abigail said, rolling her eyes.

A tinkle of laughter escaped Becca. "I will stop bothering you."

Abigail's gaze turned doubtful.

"I promise," her friend said before wandering off.

Shaking her head, Abigail attempted to focus on the code she was building for the company website, but her mind wouldn't focus. Sighing, she shut down her computer. She would head home and figure out what to wear.

Later that afternoon, she stood in front of the mirror in her bedroom. She nodded, happy with her chosen outfit. Her curves were molded into a form-fitting red dress with spaghetti straps. The material stopped at about mid-thigh and her girls were pushed up nicely.

Yanking it over her head, Abigail tossed the dress on a chair before kicking off the wedges she wore. She turned back to the mirror and frowned. She would need to dig through her drawer for some sexy panties. Boy shorts and an old bra would not do.

A memory of a man kissing her stomach and explaining all the ways he loved boy shorts flashed in her mind. She sighed, wondering why she was thinking of him. Her brain laughed at her for trying to pretend that she didn't still fantasize about Gabriel. It had been five years since they spent a steamy week together. Five years since she'd bared her body and soul to another human, only for him to disappear.

Still, his jackass behavior didn't stop her body from warming at the vivid flashbacks of him sprinkling kisses down her stomach to the edge of her panties as his fingers sought out what was beneath the fabric. Abigail needed to shower but instead, she went to her nightstand and pulled out her favorite toy before getting comfortable on her bed. Her legs fell open, and she let a memory of Gabriel's touch from long ago satisfy her needs.

Gabriel Donovan hated Valentine's Day, and he shouldn't as a chef and restaurant owner. It was one of the best days of the year for his industry. Hell, his restaurant was fully booked, and the couples' cooking class being held in their community kitchen had no openings. Yes, this holiday was a boon for him, but he still hated the sappy day.

He'd not always been such a grouch but over time, his annoyance with the holiday only grew. Kate, his business partner (and long-ago ex-girlfriend) grinned at him while she patted her baby bump. "I told you to take the day off. We can handle all this."

"You're married. You should," he muttered.

"Spencer has a weekend getaway planned for us starting tomorrow. A babymoon to be exact. Plus, I love working on Valentine's Day and he knows that. Watching all the couples filled with love and hope is a can't-miss."

He made a gagging motion, and she sighed. "Thaw your heart at least for one night. Maybe you will meet someone."

"I would never hit on a 1796 customer."

An amused expression flitted across Kate's face. "You know this whole restaurant, including the name, is rather romantic."

He shook his head. "No. It is a reminder to not lose your head over a woman."

She hit him with a kitchen towel. "I wish your mystery girl hadn't stunted your emotional growth. You would make a good partner for someone. You shouldn't pass on that."

His romantic relationship with Kate had ended because of his inability to open up to her. They stayed together far longer than they should have because neither wanted to give up the friendship. After it was over, they remained close and eventually became business partners. Gabriel had no regrets and wished her and her husband nothing but the best. They were both some of his closest friends.

Josh, one of the servers, stopped by where they stood in the bar area and said, "People for the cooking course are arriving."

They craned their heads to watch people walk into the expansive commercial kitchen space used to host classes and chef's tables. Gabriel was about to turn away when a woman in a tight red dress entered the room. Her spiral curls fell down her back wildly. A familiarness washed over him. It couldn't be. The woman turned and Gabriel stepped further into the wide hallway that led to the cooking space.

Their eyes connected. Hers widened in shock. He was speechless. It was Abigail. After all these years, he couldn't believe they were in the same space again and of all places, his restaurant.

"Gabriel, did you hear me?"

He shook his head, not even glancing Kate's way. Gabriel just continued to stare at the woman who never returned his calls all those years ago. He could still feel her hands on his body. The warmth of her thighs around him. He started to get hard.

"Do you want to be in the community kitchen being used for the class or the dining room kitchen? Why am I even asking? I'm sure it will be hiding out in the dining room kitchen."

"I will focus on the community kitchen," he stated.

A man walked into the hallway blocking Gabriel's view. He let out a low whistle before wrapping Abigail in a hug. Was he . . . her boyfriend? Studying him, Gabriel took in his slick hair, expensive sports coat, and cocky smirk. Anger filled him that this was the type of man the woman he fantasized about for so long chose to be with. He certainly wasn't a chef, especially not a poor one like Gabriel had been when they first met.

"Are you sure? I know you hate all this."

He shook his head. Gabriel would not hide out in his own restaurant. "I've got it."

Kate peered down the hallway, spotting Abigail who was still darting glances at him. "Do you know the blonde?"

If he told Kate that the 1796 girl was here, she would freak out. Instead of answering her, he said, "Let me know if the dining room kitchen gets busy."

He didn't wait for a response but strode down the hallway toward the community kitchen. Toward the woman this entire fucking place was named for.

Chapter 2

ABIGAIL COULDN'T BELIEVE GABRIEL WAS here. What was he doing here and why did he still look so good? The moment she'd spotted his broad shoulders and dark hair she'd known it was him. No man should look that delicious in a black T-shirt and jeans. He had more muscles than she remembered, and he'd had plenty five years ago. She turned around to see if he followed her in and almost stumbled over her date. The man smirked at her as his eyes roamed over her dress that she wore for the sole mission of getting laid.

"Damn. You are one sweet piece."

She grimaced at what she suspected was supposed to be a compliment. What was his name?

"Jefferson likes what he sees."

And he spoke about himself in the third person. Great. The date was not starting well. It had nothing to do with Gabriel, she told herself. Liar, liar. How could someone she hadn't seen in five years disconcert her so much? She blushed remembering the fantasy and orgasm she had earlier.

Jefferson moved to an island and patted the surface for her to follow. She glanced around and still saw no sign of Gabriel. Perhaps he didn't remember her. She doubted it by his expression. All she could hope was he'd left. She studied her date. He wasn't so bad. He was handsome in a suave way and plenty of people referred to themselves in the third person. Yes, she would not focus on the past but the man who happily agreed to spend Valentine's Day with her.

He winked at her, and she smiled back before glancing around the room. All the islands were filling up and the class would start soon. She was happy she still saw no sign of Gabriel. Three women in sky-high heels manned the island in front of Abigail and her date. Jefferson licked his bottom lips as he ogled their asses. Abigail wasn't sure if he was even one-night-stand material. She would make the best of it.

The room started to quiet down as a man made his way to the front. Relief coursed through her that it wasn't Gabriel. He was a chef, after all.

"Hi everyone. I'm Hunter. I wanted to start by saying thank you for spending part of your day of love with the restaurant. Tonight, we will be cooking a decadent pasta dish. Prepare yourself."

The couples giggled. Jefferson winked at her. Hunter grinned, happy the crowd found him entertaining. "You all are extra lucky because not only will you have me to entertain you but one of the owners, Gabriel Donovan, will be assisting me."

Dread filled Abigail. No. No. No.

Gabriel walked in and the room applauded. He nodded his appreciation, scanning the space. Abigail shifted herself, hoping he wouldn't find her behind the three goddesses standing in front of her. He strode back and forth in the front of the room until he spotted her. His eyes burned into her intensely. He definitely remembered her.

He broke contact and smiled at everyone. His eyes lingered slightly on the women in front of her, causing them to giggle. A stab of anger rushed through Abigail, and she hated that she felt anything when it came to Gabriel. This man, after giving her the most amazing week of sex she'd ever experienced, never called. Not once. She should have known when he'd not given her his number.

It didn't matter. She was here with Jefferson. Abigail would focus on him.

"And you two, what is your story?" Gabriel asked, interrupting her thoughts. She didn't realize he'd asked everyone to introduce themselves.

"First date. I need to know if she can cook, right?" Jefferson said.

The women in front of them giggled. Annoyance flashed through Abigail, but she tamped it down. Gabriel frowned but nodded. He glanced at her. She wanted to die or sink into the floor and disappear. Instead, she said, "I guess we'll see."

Gabriel's gaze shifted back to Jefferson. "Perhaps you both will learn something. A woman once told me, long ago, that there was nothing sexier than a man cooking for the woman he was trying to woo."

A blush spread across Abigail's cheeks. She had said that to him, and he'd made fun of her for using the old-fashioned term *wooing*. An image of them laughing about it in bed appeared in her mind. She needed to get a hold of herself. Gabriel was the one who ghosted her. Not the other way around. Abigail wouldn't let him know how he affected her.

She beamed adoringly at Jefferson. "I'm happy to show you my cooking skills."

Did Abigail really like this guy? When he knew her, she hated cooking. Gabriel was struggling with this new version of her. He didn't like it. Preparing a meal was a form of love, not something one did because society deemed it their role.

Unable to continue to watch her beam at Jefferson, he tore his gaze away. She was his past. He wouldn't let her unsettle him. He turned to everyone and smiled. "First, we are going to make our pasta from scratch. In front of you is flour, olive oil, and salt. We are going to make the dough right on the island. Start with the flour and add the wet ingredients into the center. Mix with a fork. Once you start to have a dough-like substance, you can begin kneading it. Hunter and I will walk around to help."

Gabriel wandered around the room, helping out where he could. He stopped at the women in front of Abigail and Jefferson, showing them how to knead the dough. They batted their eyes at him and normally he would have flirted back but having Abigail so close, as much as he hated it, unbalanced him. He glanced back to see her kneading the dough while Jefferson sat on a stool, watching her. Gabriel didn't understand what she saw in him.

He made his way to their island and Jefferson grinned at him. "Don't you think she is doing a good job?"

Gabriel didn't respond but stood behind her and placed his hands on hers. Why he was torturing himself, he didn't know. Perhaps he hoped he would feel nothing, but sparks of attraction bounced between their fingers. He murmured, "You need to push into the dough firmer."

Her breath hitched. Satisfaction surged through him. He intertwined their fingers together and pushed their hands into the dough over and over. Firm and hard. His thumb stroked the side of her hand, and she gasped.

Jefferson cleared his throat. "I think I should try that."

No, Gabriel didn't think so. He reluctantly released Abigail's hands and frowned as Jefferson intertwined his fingers with her. He wanted to deck the man.

"It seems Jefferson is pretty good at this."

Gabriel and Abigail winced at the way he referred to himself. A woman from the giggling trio in front of them glanced back, pouting. "I want to try that."

Gabriel didn't budge, but Abigail's date licked his lips. "I will show you. Abigail doesn't mind."

She flushed but nodded. Gabriel studied her. An energy hummed between them.

"How have you been?" he asked.

She silently stared at him as seconds ticked by but finally said, "Wonderful. Congratulations on this place. All this time I never knew it was owned by you."

Gabriel waited for her to say something about the name, but she didn't. "Thank you. It is my baby." His gaze darted to her date who was still hanging out with the women in front of them. Unable to stop himself, he said, "Your type has changed."

Her eyes flashed. "Yes, for the better."

They stared at each other until Kate appeared at his side. "Everything good in here?"

"Fine," he said, still studying Abigail.

Kate looked at him puzzled before turning to her. "Are you enjoying the class?"

"Very much."

His business partner glanced at him again and then turned back to his long-ago lover. "What is your name?"

Fuck!

"Abigail."

Kate's eyebrows shot up in surprise and she looked back and forth between him and Abigail. He refused to look at her and walked back to the front of the room, joining Hunter.

Hunter clapped, getting everyone's attention. "All right folks. I hope you had fun with the dough. Next, we are going to cut it. Take out the knife shaped like the one I'm holding up."

Gabriel glanced at Kate who was now at the door, motioning for him to join her. He shook his head, but she nodded at him insistently. He sighed. "Hunter, are you good here for a bit?"

Hunter gave a thumbs-up and Gabriel made his way to the hallway. As he stepped out, Kate whispered, "Is that really 1796?"

Chapter 3

ABIGAIL WATCHED GABRIEL STRIDE OUT of the room, both lusting after his firm broad shoulders and wanting to throw something at them. How dare he ask her about her type? He had no right. Jefferson glanced back at her and shockingly flushed. He excused himself from the goddesses and rejoined her.

"Sorry."

She shook her head. "It's fine."

He frowned at her. "Why do I detect you're not feeling the Jefferson?"

A sigh escaped her, and she felt awful because she hadn't been focused on him at all. Damn Gabriel was distracting her.

"Do you know each other?" Jefferson asked.

Her eyes darted to him, surprised. He chuckled. "The way he had his fingers wrapped around yours was of someone who had seen you in your panties."

"We do."

He sighed. "I have the worst luck."

"Can I give you some advice?"

Jefferson laughed. "I need it."

Abigail was going to tell him to stop being so abrasive and referring to himself in the third person but changed her mind. Instead, she said, "Find the person who likes you for you."

His eyes flew to her face. "Really?"

She smiled. "That is what we all want, right?"

Jefferson studied her. "It is, but I'm guessing that isn't you."

She shook her head and then nodded to one of the women in front of them. "She seems to like you."

He frowned. "I can't abandon you."

"No, but you can ask for her number before you leave."

He glanced at the woman whose eyes kept darting back to him. "I think I will but for now let's make that chef jealous."

"You don't have to do that."

Jefferson winked. "But I love that stuff. What happened between the two of you?"

Gabriel walked in just as he asked. What could she say? She'd met Gabriel at a resort in Costa Rica. He was temporarily filling in as one of the chefs, and she was by herself, pondering the next steps in her life. They'd hit it off instantly—mentally, physically, and intellectually. They both swore to figure out how to make a relationship work. Shockingly, Gabriel was from Maryland where she would begin her first job out of college after obtaining her master's. She'd given him her number and waited but his call never came.

She'd thought about calling the resort or finding him on social media but didn't have his last name. Feeling foolish about getting caught up in the moment with Gabriel, she'd decided she wouldn't chase him.

Abigail didn't share all that with Jefferson, even though he was starting to grow on her. Instead, she shrugged and kept it simple. "He ghosted me."

His eyes widened in shock. He glanced at Gabriel. "No way. You are hot."

Abigail smiled at his words, for once finding them endearing. "Thank you."

"Time to make him jealous."

Gabriel waved his hand, trying to get everyone's attention. When the room quieted, he said, "Now that the pasta is done, our next step is to make the dish. The rich and decadent meal we chose for tonight is perfect for a romantic night. We will be making spaghetti alla carbonara."

Jefferson wrapped his arm around Abigail and loudly said, "A perfect start to our decadent night."

Abigail's lips twitched at Jefferson's over-the-top antics. They might not have hit it off as a couple, but she could see a friendship in their future.

Gabriel watched as the couples stirred the ingredients into their pasta. He did his best to make sure his gaze didn't keep swinging back to Abigail. She'd been too much of a distraction and now he had Kate peeking in the door every few minutes. His business partner had been beside herself to discover that the woman the restaurant was named after was here. He frowned, surprised that Abigail hadn't picked up on the name.

A laugh echoed through the room, and he jerked his head up, looking in Abigail's direction. She was laughing as her date dumped half the sauce on the stovetop. They seemed to be warming up to each other. Gabriel didn't like it. Not at all. He reminded himself that it wasn't his place to judge what her preferences were or weren't when it came to a partner. He just knew it wasn't him.

She glanced his way, and their eyes connected. An attraction hummed between the two of them. After all these years, his body still craved her as much as the first time he saw Abigail. He shouldn't be surprised. Gabriel spent many nights remembering his week with her.

Hunter clapped his hands. "Let's take a break while our pasta cooks. Gabriel and I will keep an eye on them. Next is the best part. We get to eat."

He watched Abigail wander out of the room. Kate appeared and he asked, "Can you help Hunter out?"

"Go get your girl!"

He rolled his eyes. "She ghosted me. Don't get your hopes up."

Still, he didn't wait for her to respond. Instead, he followed the path Abigail took. He studied her as she stared at the awards situated at the front of the restaurant. Gabriel wasn't a braggart and had argued with Kate about where to put the things, but he could admit it gave him a great deal of satisfaction to see her perusing them.

He stepped next to her and without turning to him, she said. "You did everything you said you would."

"Sometimes I can't believe it myself."

She turned to him and a soft smile lit her face. He had the urge to brush a curl lying against her cheek behind her ear but stopped himself. Abigail wasn't his but damn it, he wanted her to be.

"I feel completely boring compared to you now," she said.

"Nothing about you could ever be dull."

Abigail frowned at him. "That isn't what you thought five years ago."

Confusion flickered across his face. "I'm not sure what you mean by that."

She turned back to the wall that had photos of him and Kate with the staff, laughing. "It doesn't matter. Your life seems like it turned out just as you imagined."

"Not quite."

"Is your wife a chef as well?" Abigail asked, pointing at the picture.

Gabriel blanched. "Kate is not my wife. We have a history, but she is happily married now. She is my business partner in the restaurant and yes, she is a chef. A damn good one."

"You're single?"

Gabriel nodded and interest appeared in Abigail's eyes but just as quickly it vanished, replaced by a fake politeness. He wanted to kiss the mask away but resisted. Instead, he said, "Have a drink with me after the class?"

"I'm on a date."

He scowled. "You aren't interested in him. There is no way he is getting a second one."

Abigail pursed her lips in annoyance, and he was tempted to kiss her. His fingers itched to pull her against him. She tapped him on the chest with her finger. "Maybe but I would never go on a date with someone who ghosted me like you did."

Before he could respond, she spun on her heel and walked off. What was she talking about? He didn't ghost her. She disappeared from his life. He frowned. Kate stealthily slid up next to him. "I'm assuming it didn't go well."

"Do you have the sign-up info for the class?"

She pulled out her phone. "What are you looking for?"

"What is Abigail's phone number?"

Kate hummed as she searched the list. "There are two Abigails. What is her last name?"

"I don't know."

Her eyes flew to his face as if he were a moron. He sighed. "It was a whole thing. The week we were together, we weren't going to focus on names or anything."

She snorted. "The last four of the first Abigail are 2356."

He shook his head.

"7796."

He closed his eyes. Gabriel really was a fucking idiot.

Kate gasped. "You got the numbers wrong!"

Chapter 4

ABIGAIL DID IT. SHE TURNED him down. She was proud of herself, even if part of her wanted to run back to him and tell him just kidding. The attraction between them was so strong. Just standing next to him, she'd had the desire to lean into him and touch her mouth to his. Her core clenched causing her to sigh. Her body was betraying her.

"I saw he followed you out. How did it go?" Jefferson asked.

"I refused his offer of a drink. How about you? Did you get the goddess's number?"

"I did obtain Sophia's number," he said, and then frowned. "You aren't going to let him explain? What if he was hit by a car and in the hospital?"

She frowned at him skeptically. "This isn't a rom-com."

Jefferson shrugged. "Maybe it is."

Abigail bit her lip. Had she been too rash? Gabriel walked into the room and his eyes found her. His gaze swept over her intently. She flushed. Jefferson laughed. "He doesn't appear to want to ghost you. Actually, he looks like he wants to devour you or eat something."

She smacked him. He winked. "You told me to be myself. Sophia seems to like it."

Sophia glanced back and smiled. Abigail laughed. "You can finish the class with her."

He shook his head. "You are my date, and she wants to finish it with her friend."

Abigail studied Jefferson, feeling guilty about her initial impression of him. "I misjudged you."

He laughed. "I'm still obnoxious. Trust me."

"Can I get everyone's attention?" Hunter said loudly from the front of the room.

The room quieted and he grinned, "Now is the time to enjoy your meal with your partner."

The space descended back into multiple conversations. Jefferson whispered, "He is heading this way."

Abigail would not cave. The man ghosted her. Still, as she watched him walk toward her, her body filled with want. The man was too good-looking. It didn't matter, she silently insisted.

"Can I speak with you after the class?" Gabriel asked.

She pasted a polite smile on her face. "Maybe another time. How about you give me your number and I will give you a call."

"Just five minutes, Abigail."

Jefferson's head swiveled back and forth watching them. She stared at him imploringly. He winked at her and gratefulness filled her.

"I have to head to my gram's. I always bring her a cupcake on Valentine's Day. So, don't turn him down because of me."

Sophia turned and gasped. "You are so sweet."

Abigail was glad Sophia thought so. Personally, she thought he was a big old traitor. He winked at her again and she wanted to dump their pasta over his head. She looked back at Gabriel and begrudgingly said, "I suppose I can stay for another five minutes."

He nodded. "Great, we will talk in my office."

After his departure, she frowned at Jefferson. "You didn't help me at all."

He rolled his eyes. "Someday, you will thank me. That man has something he needs to tell you."

Abigail had no idea what that could be. Nerves filled her stomach. Jefferson scooped up a large bite of pasta, dangling it in her face. "Eat."

She did as he asked. Their pasta actually turned out great. "Very good."

He took a big bite and nodded. "We can go on a double date."

"Don't get your hopes up."

Her gaze turned back to Gabriel, who was talking to another couple. He laughed at something they said. Unfortunately, even though she told Jefferson not to get his hopes up, hers were starting to rise. She tried to push them down. No matter how attracted she was to him, Abigail couldn't fathom them coming back from him ghosting her. Maybe if he was in a coma.

"Stop staring at him. All will be revealed soon. Help me eat this," Jefferson said, dangling a pasta-filled fork in front of her face.

Gabriel guided Abigail to his office. They were both silent and he wondered what she was thinking. He knew, actually. She thought he was a huge ass that never called her. He couldn't believe he'd called and texted the wrong number. When he never got a response, he'd assumed she wasn't interested.

He opened his office door, allowing her to step in first before shutting the door behind them. She frowned. "What did you want to talk about?"

"I wanted to explain why you never heard from me."

She folded her arms, and he was a jackass because his gaze drifted to her breasts that he'd spent a week worshiping in Costa Rica. His cock grew hard as the memories flashed in his mind.

"Were you in a coma?"

"No."

Abigail sighed. "That is the only real justification that would allow me to consider seeing you again."

He didn't blame her at all. Still, Gabriel could fix this. "Do you know why I named my restaurant 1796?"

She shrugged. "It has some type of personal attachment?"

Gabriel stepped closer to her, rubbing one of her blonde curls between his fingers. Her breathing quickened at his closeness. "You could say that. It is the number I called five years ago hoping to hold onto the girl I couldn't forget."

A frown flitted across her face. "I don't understand."

"I called you. More than once, and texted, but I must have misread your handwriting because I thought the last four numbers were 1796."

"The last four are 7796."

"I know that now."

Abigail's eyes widened. "You called me."

"I did."

Abigail glanced around his office and took a step back. Waving her hand, she asked, "Did you name your restaurant after me?"

"I named it after the girl I couldn't forget."

They stared at each other silently. Then a loud laugh escaped Abigail. "All this time I tried to convince myself that I'd made too much of our time together."

"Definitely not."

She stepped closer. "You wanted me?"

"I still want you. I never stopped even when I attempted to move on."

Abigail frowned at him, trying to make sense of his words. His heart and mind screamed at her to give him another chance. She placed her hand on his chest and leaned in for a kiss. It was a brief touching of their lips. A kiss like that would never be enough for Gabriel. He wrapped one arm around her, pulling her flush against his body as his tongue plunged into her mouth. She moaned, pushing her hips into him.

He threaded his other hand through her blonde curls. How many nights had he thought about doing this? Finally, needing to breathe, he broke off the kiss. They stood there breathing heavily. She smirked at him. "You named an entire restaurant after me."

"Don't get a big head."

She grinned at him impishly. "How can I not?" Wrapping her arms around his neck, she said, "If it makes you feel better, I thought of you often."

He nuzzled her neck. "How often?"

She was silent. He groaned. "Come on, make me feel less foolish."

Abigail blushed. "This morning, I used my bedside toy, while I was thinking about you."

"What were you thinking about?"

"I thought about how you used to pull the fabric of my boy shorts to the side and taste me with your tongue."

Gabriel was rock hard now. His fingers skimmed the edge of her dress. She leaned into his touch. Gruffly, he said, "I used to love those boy shorts. Are you wearing them now?"

She shook her head.

His hand stroked her thigh inside her dress. "What, then?"

"Why don't you look for yourself."

He didn't need another fucking minute. He walked her back to his desk and knocked everything off, causing her to giggle before laying her against the surface.

Chapter 5

ABIGAIL'S ASS AND BACK HIT the desk as laughter escaped her. "Excited?"

"You have no idea."

He stepped between her legs and her core clenched. The man hadn't even touched her yet. He ran his fingers down her hips to the edge of her short dress. Lacy red panties peeked out at him as he slowly pulled the hem up. Gabriel groaned.

"That is the most beautiful sight ever." His thumb stroked the lace at the apex of her thighs. "You are already so wet. Is that for me?"

It was. Abigail nodded.

He smirked. "Say it."

"It's for you," she panted.

"I'm so fucking lucky."

He pushed her farther up on the desk and leaned down, pressing his mouth against her panties. His tongue pressed through the fabric, tempting and teasing her. She bucked against his face. "Gabriel."

"I know what you want. Don't worry."

With one tug, he yanked her panties away. Gabriel grinned at her and then did exactly what she wanted. He tasted her, as she threaded her fingers through his hair, rocking her body toward his mouth. She groaned and her pace quickened as his tongue lapped at her. He suck-led the place where all the nerves met, knowing it would drive her wild. Her legs began to shake, and she pressed herself up to him.

He clutched her thighs, holding her up as she rocked into his face. With one more arch, a strangled whimper exploded from her and her rocking became slower and less intense. He ran his hands up and down her inner thighs, causing her to tremble in delight. Her body was al-ways so sensitive to his touch after an orgasm. Only Gabriel's touch.

He stood and stared down at her. Abigail's sated body hummed again, entranced by the ravenous look on his face. Her eyes flicked down to his jeans where his cock strained against the material. She wanted to feel him inside her. Was this madness? They'd only just found each other again. In truth, she didn't care.

"Gabriel, I want you in me."

His face darkened, filling with even more desire, but he hesitated. "I don't have a condom."

"I'm on the pill and haven't been with anyone since my last check-up."

"I haven't either."

They silently stared at each other and finally, Abigail said, "Fuck me."

He leaned down and pressed his mouth to hers. The kiss was filled with so much pent-up emotion and desire. Five years of it. Abigail hadn't been crazy. Whatever was between them was special. Gabriel pulled away and released his cock from his jeans. She arched up as he tugged her across the desk to his body.

In one swift move, he plunged into her, hissing. "You have no idea how often I fantasized about this."

She shook her head. "You are wrong and not alone."

He slowly rocked back and forth, as if basking in the feel of her. An ache started to grow within Abigail again and the rocking became not nearly enough. She needed more. She didn't need to say the words, Gabriel grabbed her hips and pumped into her. She tilted her head back and moaned, arching off the desk.

His movements grew faster and harder, pushing Abigail toward another release. As if sensing she was close, he pushed deeply into her and then rotated his hips, knowing the pressure would drive her crazy. The ache in her spiked intensely. He withdrew and did it again. Her body exploded as he gripped her hips and he furiously pounded into her, chasing his own release. He let out a guttural moan and his thrusts slowed.

Gabriel leaned down and pressed his forehead against hers. "I'm never letting you go again."

She laughed. "You better not. I need more of this."

Gabriel smiled at her as they dressed. Her panties were destroyed, but he stuffed them in his pocket anyways causing her to turn a furious shade of red.

"What are you going to do with those?"

He grinned at her wickedly. "I have plans."

Abigail rolled her eyes.

He nuzzled her neck. "Stay. Sit at the bar or hang out here."

She kissed him but shook her head. "No."

He frowned at her, alarm shooting through him. Did she think this was a one-time thing?

She patted him on his chest. "I expect a proper date from you."

Warmth filled him. "I would like nothing more." He stepped away and grabbed his phone. "This time you are entering it into my contacts."

She beamed at him before taking it and typing in her information. Her phone chimed as she handed it back to him. Abigail glanced at it and said, "I have the famous Gabriel Donovan's number."

"What is your last name?" he asked.

"How stupid were we to share only our first names."

He kissed her. "Very stupid."

"It is Spencer."

He smiled. "It suits you."

Gabriel ran his hands up and down her sides. He wanted her again. He dipped his head, but she stepped out of reach. "I want a proper date."

"Should I pick you up?"

Abigail pondered his question for a moment. "Maybe on the second date but for the first let's meet. I want to be wooed."

A bark of laughter escaped him. "You still like that term."

"I do."

He ran a light kiss across her mouth. "Leave it to me. I will arrange for a car to pick you up. Text me your address."

She started to shake her head, but he pressed his finger to her lips. "I've got one shot at this wooing, let me have this."

"Fine."

Abigail stepped away from him and made her way to the door. He didn't want her to leave. Hell, he wanted her in his bed at his house. "Are you sure you have to go?"

She turned back and grinned at him impishly. "We've waited five years. Another day or two won't hurt you."

"Our date is tomorrow."

She giggled and waved as she walked out. Gabriel had some planning to do. Even though he hadn't told her, Abigail was the woman he wanted to spend the rest of his life with. That meant the wooing had to be perfect.

Epilogue

NERVES SHOT THROUGH ABIGAIL AS she sat in the car. Gabriel had been very secretive about where they were meeting. Hopefully she wasn't overdressed. She'd vamped it up a bit but worn her boy shorts, knowing he loved them so much. The car came to a stop and the driver opened the door. She stepped out and realized she was at a shopping center, standing in front of a small Italian restaurant.

Abigail had no doubt it was a hidden gem. She walked through the door and an older woman at the hostess desk beamed at her. "Are you Abigail?"

"Yes. How did you know?"

"Gabriel told us to look out for you."

This woman must know him well. She wondered if he brought all his dates here. A frown marred her face, and the woman laughed. "Oh, young love is so obvious."

"I'm not young. I'm twenty-eight."

She looked at her amused. "Still young, and no, our Gabriel has never brought anyone here."

Was this woman related to him? "Are you family?"

"Not blood but Gabriel learned to cook and wash dishes here. He started as a dishwasher when he was sixteen."

"You're Rosa! He told me about you many years ago." Abigail explained.

The woman grinned and nodded. They stepped through another doorway and Abigail spied Gabriel sitting in a beautiful courtyard. Twinkle lights were strung everywhere. He appeared to be arranging the dinnerware over and over again.

Rosa giggled. "He does that when he is nervous."

At least Abigail wasn't the only anxious one. As if sensing her thoughts, Rosa said, "You look beautiful. Don't worry, all will be wonderful."

Rosa opened the door for her, and she stepped out. Gabriel stood and they stared at one another, a million emotions running between them. Yes, Rosa was right. Everything would be wonderful. Abigail smiled at the man she thought she would never see again.

"Hi," he said, beaming at her.

"Hello."

About the Author

Since stealing her first romance novel from her mother more than twenty years ago, Ramona Elmes has been all in on the genre. She has two Victorian romance series available on Amazon. If you love drama, steamy moments, and great HEAs, check them out. When not creating ways to entice and torture her characters, she spends her days in Georgia coordinating her family's crazy life, refereeing pets, and daydreaming on her front porch.

You can find Ramona on:

Instagram: @elmes_ramona

You can visit her website at:

www.ramonaelmes.com

DULCE,
POR FIN

Dulce, Por Fin

Tamaya Cruz

Chapter 1: Lourdes

JULES AND I WERE BORN ON the same day, in the same hospital, two rooms apart. My mother and his mother had been best friends since college. They found out on the same day that one would have a boy and one would have a girl.

"Maybe they'll get married one day," Adela had said rubbing her calm belly.

Mama winced, and breathed through another set of my kicks, the outline of my feet like an underground monster beneath her skin. "He'll have to catch her first."

It wasn't as though he didn't try. We'd gone to grade school together and when Belinda Bustos told us all in sixth grade that it was time for us girls to like boys, I chose him. I didn't really know what it meant to have a crush, I just knew he was my friend. We liked the same music and the same movies. We had the same favorite Teenage Mutant Ninja Turtle—Michelangelo because he used nunchucks—and that had been enough.

Unfortunately, Belinda chose Jules, too. She didn't even like the ninja turtles, but it didn't stop her from telling Jules she was going to kiss him at the Valentine's Day dance. When all the girls congregated in the gym by the scoreboard and the boys lingered on the opposite side near the concession stand, Belinda went looking for Jules, her clean, white sneakers gliding along the lacquered wood floor like great white sharks on a hunt.

He was nowhere to be found. He wasn't with the comic book boys chirping over collectors' editions, nor was he with the soccer players comparing jerseys by the door. Belinda ended up kissing Richard Elzinga that afternoon. Now they have three kids and run the San Corazón general store. It suited them, but Julian would never have been satisfied stocking cans of green beans.

As we walked home from the dance, he told me he'd hidden in the basketball coach's office.

"Why?" I asked.

He shrugged. "I guess I just always thought my first kiss would be you."

Chapter 2: Julian

I'D ALWAYS KNOWN LO WAS mine. I never missed a single one of her track meets in high school or college and I cheered her on during every marathon she'd ever run. I was the person she called with good news and the person who listened to her cry when it was bad. I wouldn't have it any other way. She was my rock, too.

After graduation, we drove out of San Corazón in her little white pickup, a Ford I once said was sweet and which all of our friends called Dulce from then on. We packed all the things we thought were important in boxes and piled them high in the bed. Our mothers cried. They always did.

Lo and I were looking forward to starting our new lives. The music was high, the wind blew her long, dark hair around her face, and things were easy in the way most things were when you were young. As she drove, I caught sight of her smile, lifting into her brown eyes, bright with the promise of all that was to come. Yes, she'd always been mine, but it was only then that I realized I loved her.

I still loved her now. She just didn't know it.

We spent nearly a decade in Albuquerque. She racked up the marathon medals and cooking accolades. I rode bikes and got a new tattoo for all the things I wanted to remember. Sometimes I wasn't good at saying what I felt and the ink was my way of reminding myself what mattered. The last one I got was a lily on the back of my hand and I didn't give a fuck who saw it.

After I finished law school and she got her culinary degree, Lo and I both moved out of New Mexico. She went to California to work with some five-star chef she met at a lecture and I moved north for a job at a law firm in Denver. Pining for Lo from a thousand miles away seemed a terrible way to live, so over time, we just saw each other less and less.

When she visited, it was like it had always been. We laughed, we cooked, and I read her case law until she fell asleep in my bed and I made my way to the couch. My heart always ached for more. The timing was just never right—either she had a boyfriend or I had a girlfriend or both. I was single for a while after Lo left. Heartbreak had a way of making you tough and I just didn't have it in me to care.

Then I met Ellie.

Chapter 3: Lourdes

ELLIE MALDONADO.

Long black hair. Perfect body. Ivy League. She was a lawyer, too, just like Jules. She was perfect for him. I guess I had my chance.

Sometimes I think about the only time Jules and I kissed. The day before I left for LA, my friends threw me a going-away dinner party on the private patio of our favorite restaurant. There had been a lot of laughter, a smattering of tears, and a handful of margarita pitchers that seemed like they sprang from a magical well that never ended. It was probably just because Jules smiled at the waitress. He had that effect on people.

He wasn't just handsome with dark skin, black eyes, and perfect abs. He was deliberate and direct; he was kind but reserved, and he made people feel like they mattered. He controlled every room with a quiet assurance, and all you wanted was for him to direct you, too— maybe under his firm hand, with a growl in his chest, slowly convincing you to give in. He was sexy and he didn't even have to try, and I wasn't the only one who thought so.

Soraya, my closest girlfriend, never stopped nudging. One night as she got ready for work in front of the bathroom mirror in our apartment, she'd had enough of my indecision.

"Lo, if you don't do something about this incredibly hot and brilliant guy who obviously loves you, I will." She pulled her wild, rose-red hair in a bun and lifted a brow. "I'm not subtle, either. The last match I made involved a certain local minor league baseball mascot and a hot-air balloon ride. Two years later, the mascot officiated their wedding."

I squinted. "The orange baseball bear?" I asked. "They let him moonlight as matchmaker?"

"He's an alien, not a bear." She looked at me through the reflection, matter-of-factly. "The guy inside the suit is a friend of mine and what the Albuquerque Isotopes don't know won't hurt them."

I wasn't interested in the Extraterrestrial Newlywed Game. "Jules is just a friend. I can't imagine him as more."

"Have you tried?" She closed her eyes, her long feathery lashes fluttered as she drew a picture in her mind. "'Cause I'm doing it right now and, oh my God, his thighs."

I took a long breath and rolled over on her bed. "That's not what I mean. I just . . ." I paused, trying to articulate the complicated feelings I had for Jules. "I just don't know what I would do if it didn't go well. I'd lose him and that would be the worst thing that could ever happen."

She turned away from the mirror to face me. "Worse than never having him at all?"

The night of my farewell dinner, Jules sat next to me. There was a palpable energy between us, different from anything I'd felt before. I chalked it up to my departure. He and I had never lived more than fifteen minutes away from each other since we'd been born. Distance was hard on best friends.

Soraya's words were on my mind, but Jules could never be my boyfriend. We had too much history. He knew all my secrets; all the dreams I had for my life; and all the fears I had that they might never come true. When I told him I was moving to LA, I knew he was disappointed. I could see in his eyes that he wished I would stay, but he knew how important my career was to me. When I told him how scared I was to leave, he hugged me. "Be gentle on LA, Lo," he'd said. "They ain't ready for someone like you."

At dinner, beside me, he nodded politely at my friends' stories of drunken karaoke and the time I almost burned down the apartment building trying to make deep-fried empanadas. Jules tilted his head while the conversation shifted around us, swirling with salt and tequila.

"Were those the empanadas you made for me?" he whispered, a lock of his dark wavy hair falling over his brow. "The time I broke my leg?"

He'd been mountain biking and it was his femur, but he'd been on too many pain meds to remember the specifics. As he came out of anesthesia, he asked if I would make him empanadas filled with mazapán. The Mexican molded sugar candy had always been Jules's weakness, and though I liked them okay, I failed to see how frying them up in pockets of dough might bump their appeal with any significance.

Nevertheless, morphine tended to make a person open to possibilities. "You know how it crumbles the second you take it out of the wrapper?" he chattered under the fluorescent recovery room lights. "A million little sugar crystals barely holding it together in life. That's like us, isn't it, Lo? Like people. We're just trying to make it through life without falling apart." He blinked lazily then laid his head back on the pillow and closed his eyes. "We all need someone to give us a safe place to melt, don't we? Put the candy in an empanada, Lo. It's a million-dollar idea."

Maybe, but I wasn't a dessert chef so, instead, I bought him two boxes of mazapán which he ate immediately while I was getting all his paperwork from the discharge nurse. I hid the wrappers in the trash bin and spilled a full container of cotton balls on top. I made him deep-fried steak empanadas that night as a compromise—prepared sugar-free.

At the long dinner table the night before I left, another piece of the puzzle fit into the collective memory of us. "I didn't know you almost took out an entire building for me."

I shrugged sheepishly. "We had a fire extinguisher. Soraya's hair extensions smelled like smoke for a week, though."

His eyes held mine, reflecting the sparkle of the string lights overhead. "Thank you," he said gently. His long fingers pushed the hair from my brow. "You're my best friend, Lo." There was a pause—long, heavy, hopeful, and sad. We had twenty-seven years of late-night talks between us. Twenty-seven years of heartbreaks and high-fives. Twenty-seven years of firsts and lasts. "I love you."

Chapter 4: Julian

THE NIGHT OF HER GOING-AWAY dinner, I bought Lo a bouquet of lilies. I wore the shirt she gave me for my birthday that year, a short-sleeved button-down she said showed off my biceps. "It will be good for dates," she'd said, running a fingertip along the tattoos on my forearm. She'd looked up at me then and pulled her hand away with a sudden clarity, as if the feeling of her skin against mine burned like ice. "Whoever she is," she corrected herself with a decidedly platonic tap on my ink, "she should want to know what each one of these means to you." Lo had been there for almost all of them. She was my memory outside of my head, my heart outside of my chest.

When she met Chef, I thought I might have lost her for good. He was Colombian with an accent, a six-pack, and two houses. He ran marathons, just like Lo. I hated how perfect he was for her, and if I could have run him down at mile thirteen with my mountain bike, I would have. But I couldn't. She seemed happy and that was all I would let myself want.

He'd moved to California a few months before he asked her to join him. My heart hoped she'd change her mind and stay. Two homes were too hard to keep clean, and visible abs were a dime a dozen, but I knew LA was more than Chef and his real estate. It was her career. It was her life. She had to go.

43

When I told her I loved her, I meant it, but I couldn't tell her all the reasons why until I had her alone. Something had been building between us for years. I'd been afraid to say it until then—afraid the very foundation of our friendship might crumble beneath its weight—but the clear desert sky doesn't care to keep secrets. Perhaps it was the margaritas. Perhaps it was the fear that we might walk out of each other's lives and never be the same. Perhaps it was the mascot of a certain local minor league baseball team who'd just walked into the bar.

It was getting late. Lo said goodbye to everyone else, but the two of us stayed; as always, just us. I swallowed, nervously.

"Thank you for the lilies," she told me. "They're beautiful."

I'd known her favorite flower since the sixth grade. I could have written a book about Lo and filled a whole chapter just with anecdotes about her favorite things. It would be somewhere after the chapter about our long debates over nunchucks and turtles but somewhere before the ending I wanted desperately to write with her. Lo picked up the vase and dragged it across the table toward us. The sound rumbled in my ears louder than I expected, amplified by the echo of blood rushing through every part of my body.

A few feet away in the bar, people tittered and talked. The music was on. The summer wind blew through the lily stems and carried their fragrance between us. I leaned forward. The warmth of her skin was like velvet to my soul and I hadn't even touched her. "I need to tell you something."

Her brows raised and her eyes got round as she sensed the conversation was going to be about more than the fighting styles of underground amphibians. She put her hand on my cheek softly. "What's wrong?"

My jaw stiffened at her touch and I reached up to take her hand in mine. "Lo, we've known each other . . . well, since before we were born. My mom told me she and Nadia used to put their belly buttons together so we could talk like those can phones with the string."

She shook her head. "They were the weirdest ladies in town, weren't they?"

"They still are, but don't tell them I said that." Lo grinned, her expression so familiar and safe that I went on. "Anyway, I've felt like this for a long time, I just didn't know how to tell you. We were friends and we had our own lives. Boyfriends, girlfriends." My heart was in my throat. "You seem happy with this chef. He treats you well?"

She nodded, her eyes full and I dropped my gaze to our hands, clasped in my lap.

"I don't want to upend your plans, Lo. If you think you have a future with him, I would never come between you, but you're leaving and I just . . ." My voice trailed, unsure, but I couldn't let her go without her knowing. "I just need to tell you how I feel. You and me . . . I think we'd be great together—everything we already are, only I'd get to hold your hand. I'd get to kiss you. I'd get to tell you how beautiful you are every day."

For a moment, I didn't know which way things would go. Then Lo, the woman I'd pined for since the day we drove out of the San Corazón desert dust, pushed into me. Her lips were on mine, lightly, softly, sweetly. I closed my eyes, enjoying the taste of her for the first time, the balm leaving a strawberry lemon dream on my skin. I cupped her jaw in one hand. In the other, I smoothed the hair on her head. Time stopped. The air around us disappeared. The dainty twirl of the earth was dwarfed by the electric spin of my buzzing heart.

It was a five-second slice of perfection that felt like forever, and then it was over as mysteriously at it had begun. She stepped back and pulled her bottom lip into her mouth thoughtfully. Perhaps she'd surprised us both when she kissed me.

Behind us, a giant mascot stepped out onto the patio and everyone looked up from their tapas to greet him with a cheer. Under normal circumstances, an unexpected visit from a felt-covered hero might have given me equal pause. Lo was the only one who didn't look surprised. She picked up her purse and I grabbed the lilies before we made our way out the back gate.

We walked to her car, a charged energy between us. It was a nervous, brilliant, wild static. It was the last chance for me to write the ending I dreamed of. Beneath the dim light, I offered her my heart. "Lo, do you feel the same way about me?"

Sometimes the sound of a heart breaking is loud, like the waves of an ocean, like an explosion, like a scream. Sometimes, it's muted like a tide pulled back, like the dousing of a fuse, like a suffocation beneath a million quiet petals that cover you with the scent of lilies. I could no longer hear the world around me.

Lo breathed in, a long, shaky draw of sobering air. "I can't talk about this right now," she replied. "I'll call you tomorrow, ok?"

She didn't call. She left the next morning and took every bit of my soul with her. She visited only a handful of times since that night and we talked on our birthday and at Christmas. She told me we would always be friends. If that was all I could have, I would take it. The next day, as her flight was landing in Chef's LA, I was in a shop in Nob Hill getting the tattoo on my hand to remember the silence that broke me.

Just after Lo left for her new life, I moved to Denver for a job, hoping to find my own. I met Ellie when I started working at her father's law firm where she was next in line for a partnership. She was beautiful and smart and we flirted for weeks before the annual Valentine's Day chili cook-off the firm hosted for charity.

I'd never been good in the kitchen—that was always Lo's thing—so I brought a few boxes of mazapán as my measly contribution. When I set them down at the end of a long row of fancy, full Crock-Pots, Ellie picked one off the top.

She bit through the crumbly sugar and it broke apart in her hand. "I always preferred pulparindo to mazapán," she said, "but my grandma used to crumble these on top of apple pie."

Mazapán and pie . . . My eyes got hazy with a memory—some weird fever dream I must have had and forgotten. "I've always thought they'd be great in an empanada."

In the ensuing months, Ellie and I had struck a sort of deal. Her father wasn't keen on promoting her to partner, citing her twenty-something antics, the culmination of which involved the Cancun police and an A-list Hollywood couple she wouldn't reveal. It required the intervention of a US senator, and Ellie was effectively banned from any and all Sandals Resort properties in perpetuity. I didn't ask the details and, according to the settlement, she couldn't disclose them to anyone anyway.

I got along well with her father, and Ellie thought a relationship with me would show him how much she'd changed and settled down—no more need for congressional interventions. It didn't take us long to fall into a semi-real version of the relationship we'd curated for everyone else. In the shadows of what we professed to be, we'd become something of a safety net. A conversation at dinner. A friend with benefits.

I made it a point never to veer into a conversation about "us." It was too messy, and a deal was a deal. Nevertheless, it was getting increasingly difficult to pretend.

Chapter 5: Lourdes

THE TWO THINGS I WAS best at were cooking and running. I couldn't sauté my way out of my feelings for Jules so when he told me how he felt, I ran. I had my whole life ahead of me. I wanted LA. I wanted restaurants with my name on the door. I wanted to make beautiful food and serve it to happy people. I didn't want an orange alien to officiate my wedding—not even if it was to the most incredible man in the world.

Chef had been an easy choice. Our relationship was fun without the promise or foreboding of any future. It was casual intimacy at its finest and, like most relationships built on abs and adventure, it ran its course within a year. We'd both started our own businesses and the challenge of finding time to spend together was wearing on us.

"I got a job in Hawaii filming some cooking show," he said one night over dinner. "You should come. Six weeks on the beach will give us the time we need to reconnect."

I had work, I had life. Six weeks on the beach would have been nice but it would have meant a recommitment to a relationship I wasn't sure of. Chef was handsome and smart, but he never once came to see me run a race. He couldn't remember how I liked my coffee, and he didn't ask why I always had fresh lilies on the counter.

"It's a busy time," I replied, and set my fork down beside my plate.

He tilted a head of thick black hair to the side. He'd known about Jules since I moved to LA. He'd heard me talk about all the stories we shared as though they were merely the whispers of old memories that hadn't yet gathered into a storm. He saw the way my eyes got hazy after Jules called me on our birthday. It was hard to miss a best friend, wasn't it?

"Lourdes." Chef's voice was calm and clear. "You know how some dishes look beautiful on the table? Gorgeous food plated and drizzled and served?" I nodded. "Sometimes," he sighed with more than a hint of finality, "it's not as good as that one thing you just love, right? That grilled cheese you crave on a snowy day just because it makes you feel like home?" He lifted his chin and sat back in the chair across from me, over our china, wine, and braised pork. "It's always been Jules, hasn't it?"

There were no hard feelings between me and Chef, and we still remained friends. Yet, I felt a restlessness I couldn't quite figure out. Running hadn't worked, so I did the other thing I was good at—I cooked. My restaurant was doing well, but I'd grown bored with the everyday business of buying and selling and marketing. I missed the feeling of my hands in dough and the fire of a cooktop close enough I might get burned.

In LA the food truck scene was electric. I bought a nice rig and made it my own. I developed a great menu with all-new recipes and called it Dulce, after the truck that carried me and Jules out of San Corazón and into real life. The name was nostalgic. It was catchy and easy. It was perfect except for the fact that there was actually nothing sweet on the menu, a flaw I hadn't considered until after I'd signed off on the paperwork.

"Just make something up," Soraya had offered. "You can melt sugar fifty different ways and every way tastes great."

Easy enough. I just couldn't come up with something I loved—at least not in LA.

I could have gone anywhere, but the business incentives were incredible in Denver. Nice summers, a change of seasons each year, not too far from Mama if I needed to get to her, but not so close she'd expect me to visit every weekend. Maybe it was the taxes, the weather, and the location, but I'd be lying if I said it wasn't mostly Jules.

I knew about Ellie. Jules mentioned her the last time we spoke. I didn't think of moving to Denver as a romantic opportunity. He seemed happy despite his mother telling mine that he'd lost five pounds because Ellie didn't know how to cook. I just missed my best friend.

When I told Jules I was moving to Denver, I could hear the excitement in his voice. It was light and charged, but it ran just under a layer of caution I hated that I'd caused. We'd never talked about that night on the patio. We'd never talked about the kiss in the parking lot. We'd never talked about us. Being in the same place would dredge it all up again, but if I dug down deep enough, the truth was that I wanted that.

Chapter 6: Julian

LO DIDN'T HAVE TO ASK me to help her move into her new place. I told her I'd be there with two friends on a Saturday and we made quick work of everything in the moving trucks while she was downtown at the Christkindlmarket with Dulce.

I biked with Eduardo and Ben often and sometimes we spent days together on long weekend rides, talking about all the things that mattered between conversations about all the things that didn't. When they got to Lo's house, they already knew all about her.

Ed was only five-foot-one, but had decided carrying the heaviest item in the truck was the way he wanted to be remembered. When he set it down, it hit the tile with a thunk and yanked his body almost all the way to the floor.

"Try to have some respect, Ed." I gave him a stern look. "That's an expensive sous vide."

He tossed his gloves on the ground and rubbed his hands warm. "I thought her name was Lo."

"No." I closed the box and slid it across the floor into the kitchen. "Not Sue, S-U-E. Sous. Vide. It's a thermal circulator." I opened the cardboard and showed him the stainless-steel box. "Professional grade.

It preserves the nutrients and prevents overcooking of things like fish and poultry."

In the foyer, Ben, much taller with thick arms and a beard, jutted his chin at me. "Look at Emeril over here," he teased, ribbing me good-naturedly. "He must have picked up a lot being obsessed with a chef all his life." Eduardo's quick eyes shot him a look, and he shrugged. "What?" Ben held his arms out and gestured at me with a meaty palm. "One of us had to say it. It's not like he doesn't know."

I took a step back. "Know what?"

Eduardo crossed his arms and gave me the same concerned look one might give a friendly ghost who doesn't know they're dead. "That you're in love with this girl?"

Of course I was but apparently, I had a terrible poker face. This did not bode well for my contractual law career. "I'm not in love with her," I dismissed. It was a bold-faced lie and blood rose like lava into my cheeks. "We're friends. She dates cooks."

"Cooks?" Ben repeated. "Wasn't he the star judge on that reality food show?" He tapped a finger to his chin, trying to remember. "What was it called?"

"*Hot Chefs in Paradise*," I snapped, my eyes narrowed. "And most of that was shot in a studio, anyway."

"Hot chefs, huh?" Eduardo's mouth twisted to one side with a sympathetic surrender. "Well, given that bologna on wheat is your best dish, your only chance to is to convince her you're hot. You're not really *my* type, but you do have a certain vibe." He pointed at the combination of my five-o'clock shadow, the tattoos on my forearms, and the pastel polo shirt that collectively made me into a question mark. "Girls like not knowing if you're going to rob them or show them how to file an amicus brief. It keeps them guessing."

The polo shirts had been a gift from Ellie, or more accurately, Ellie's assistant. When Ellie realized he'd purchased the short-sleeve version, the polos got relegated to use only during times of manual labor like when I changed the oil in her car.

"No one wants an attorney with tatted sleeves of who knows what," she'd said, flipping her long, smooth hair with disdain. Ellie was laying across my chest, her hand in mine. The clouds filtering the morning sun through the window suddenly felt like steel wool in the air.

I lifted my head and readjusted my pillow so I could see her more clearly. "These aren't just doodles," I told her. "These are my memories, and my extensive repeat client list begs to differ."

She held my gaze, equally willful. "Memories of what?"

She'd never asked me about my tattoos before. "Trips, accomplishments, family, friends."

Her eyes narrowed and she lifted her body from mine. She slipped her hand out from under my palm leaving my drawn ink exposed. "And the lily?" she asked, gesturing with a look at the dangerous artifact on display between us. It was in her sight, but she didn't dare touch it. "Is that family or friend? Or is it something else, Julian?"

I didn't answer. The conversation was exactly what I'd tried to avoid. Ellie had tried to ask me about Lo a few times before—over dinner, in the car, and once when she saw my eyes get hazy as we watched a minor league baseball game on TV. I knew she wanted us to be more than we were, but I was too weak to admit to anyone that the only woman I loved was Lo.

She shook her head, a few wisps of hair gliding over her bare shoulders. "I know what we agreed to," she said, "but your contractual law degree doesn't mean shit if you can't tell when someone is trying to renegotiate."

I'd kept Ellie guessing in the worst way, and I almost wished it was as easy as an amicus brief. In another woman's living room, I readjusted on my feet, ashamed I'd let her get hurt by whatever game we said we would play. It wasn't her fault that she wasn't Lo. Eduardo and Ben watched cautiously, afraid to overcook the moment.

"Well," my voice crept out from under the magnitude of my reveal, "who doesn't love a man of mystery." I sat down at the bottom of the staircase.

Eduardo sat beside me and clasped his hands between his knees. "Look, all we're saying is that we've known you for two years and the only time you mention Ellie is when you complain that she makes you carpool to work instead of riding your bike."

I glanced up at Ben. He nodded a head of chestnut hair in solemn agreement.

"Now," Eduardo went on, "ask me anything about Lo. Her favorite coffee is a latte with caramel syrup and her hair has these golden strands that only show in the afternoon sun."

Ben joined in, reminiscing about a time he never had. "Remember when her shoe flew off the Tilt-A-Whirl and hit that old man in the head?"

We were freshmen, it was the State Fair, and the corndog he'd been eating shot out of his mouth like a projectile missile.

"You think I'm in love with Lo?" I asked.

Eduardo tilted his head. "I guess only you know for sure what's in your heart, but I know more about sous vide than I did when I walked in here, and that matters."

That had been three months ago. Now, it was Valentine's Day and downtown Denver was sparkling with ads for couples' dinners and horse-drawn carriage rides. All I could think about was Lo.

Ellie was out of town for a client meeting. When she got back home, I needed to tell her we were over.

Chapter 7: Lourdes

WEEKS AGO, JULES RECOMMENDED DULCE to his firm's administrative team to cater the sides for their Valentine's Day chili cook-off. I sat in the truck on the street in front of his building, worried I'd made a huge mistake.

Valentine's Day was always a mixed bag for me. If I was in a good relationship, it was great. If it was on the rocks, things were tense. If I was single and feeling okay about it, I treated myself to a new pair of heels. If I was single and sad, I called Soraya.

"What do I do?" I asked her, my arms draped over the steering wheel.

She wasted no time repeating what she'd told me many times before. "You have to tell him how you feel."

"But he's happy, Raya, I can't mess that up for him, right?"

"He had no problem telling you he loved you the day before you left for Chef. Maybe he's not as happy as he seems." She sighed. "Look, I wouldn't go to his house and hold a boom box in the rain or anything, but if you're interested, I know some *chingonas* just north of Española who would be happy to engage in some light brujería on your heart's behalf. Fifty dollars for a few chants and they guarantee no harm will come to any chickens involved." The offer was a joke, yet I was sure it was also completely legitimate. "I'd do it myself but I'm on overnights at the hospital this week." Soraya was a nurse, saving humans by night, and apparently saving chickens in her off time.

I mustered a small laugh. "I don't know if I trust witchcraft hobbyists for a job like this. You light one wrong candle and my eyelashes fall out."

"We're students of the craft, Lo. A modest amount of misdirected energy is to be expected. And I said '*light brujería*.' The most that could go wrong is you get a bad haircut."

I had a lot of questions for Soraya, but they could wait. All the witchcraft in the world couldn't help me, anyway. I glanced up at the gray, overcast sky. It was cold and humid, sure signs, everyone said, of a coming snowstorm. It was a perfect addition to a day I was already sure couldn't get worse. "I'll think about it."

"Great," she said. "My break's at nine. I'll call you and we can discuss wig contingencies."

I sighed. "I can't. I have a job tonight. A private cooking lesson for some couple. She called this morning last minute and wanted to surprise him. Isn't love . . . beautiful?"

My sarcasm transcended state lines. "Your Valentine's Day sounds worse than mine and I put IVs in people." I held my head in my hands. "Lo," she started. "Do you remember that night of your farewell dinner?

"Yeah."

"I had a whole thing planned. Orange alien and everything. Do you know why? When I called Julian to invite him to the dinner, I asked him point blank, whether he was going to let you get away."

I looked up at Jules's building, knowing he was somewhere inside, living a whole life he'd made without me. "And?"

"He said he'd never give up. I would have never gotten that mascot involved if I thought there was any chance the two of you didn't belong together. He gave up an off-the-clock gig at a bachelorette party to be there that night. It's not my thing, but who am I to judge?"

I was used to seeing Jules in a T-shirt and jeans, but in his element, standing in front of the office window overlooking the city in the last of the day's wintry sun, he looked almost like a different person. His suit fit him perfectly, tailored to his firm body, and the formality of it was unbelievably sexy. He wasn't cute Jules, my forever friend. He was hot, professional Julian, a lawyer I wanted to keep on retainer for naughty things. I bit my lip and squeezed the handle of my spatula in my palm.

"This is my friend, Lo," Jules introduced me to his firm's communications director who was overseeing the cook-off.

"It's lovely to meet you," she said with a friendly grin. Her short, brown bob bounced at her chin as she spoke and I noticed her taking stock of my hair in return. I had pulled most of it back into a bun, but I felt a lock wiggle free and settle at my cheek. "Jules's description of you is spot-on. Gold highlights," she mused. "I'd kill for my stylist to do that so well."

Apparently, my hair had a reputation, and it was better for everyone if we didn't talk about it. Jules dropped his chin to his chest with a shy smirk. "Lo owns a restaurant in LA and a very successful truck out there. She's a recent transplant, but she's already made the *Post*'s short list for trucks in the metro area. We're lucky to get her today."

Everyone needed a cheerleader like Jules. "I appreciate the opportunity to work with you," I said. "I'm glad Jules made this happen."

"Jules," she repeated slyly. "That's adorable."

He and I had known each other so long, I'd forgotten he had a real name. "Sorry." I blinked. "We're old friends. I guess I should call him Mr. Barrera here."

"Whatever you call him, it won't be Champion." She pointed to the long table where the lawyers lined up their entries. "See the mazapán there at the end?" she teased. "That's his contribution to the potluck. Maybe you can coach him to an actual entry next year." She dipped her chin with a nod. "Please let me know if you need anything, Ms. Gutierrez."

She walked away and I turned immediately to Jules. "Mr. Barrera . . ." I drew out my voice like an interrogation, motioning to the mazapán. "Have I taught you nothing?"

His eyes crinkled beneath the impossibly long lashes I'd been jealous of since the eighth grade. "You know me. I just can't cook." He paused, a fond gaze running over my face. "Ms. Gutierrez."

I rolled my eyes. "Please don't call me that. That sounds weird coming from you. I actually wasn't aware that we were grown-ups until I saw you in that suit."

He wore it with confidence. Dark-gray cotton. Soft, buttoned vest. I shivered.

"You like this?" he asked, noting my response. "If I'd have known that's all it took, I'd have shown up on your doorstep in three pieces a long time ago."

I felt my face get warm and my breath hitch. "Jules," I started, but before I could get the words out, he pulled a full bottom lip into his mouth and held it with loaded suspense.

"I'm sorry, Lo. It's just that . . ." He paused and reached out to hook the stray lock of hair behind my ear. In his touch was a tenderness wrapped in electricity. "Your hair really does look beautiful."

He'd caught himself. Whatever he was going to say had been arrested in the air between us. Too many people were around for any kind of real confession, and declaring one's love at a chili cook-off rarely ended well. Drama was par for the course in love triangles, and to that end, behind Jules, a brilliant lawyer in sharp high heels was heading in our direction. My heart shuddered. It could only be Ellie.

"The famous Lourdes," she drawled. Jules swallowed his breath as she laced a lithe arm around the back of his waist. "It's nice to meet you."

It was awkward, and Jules furrowed his brows, confused. "I thought you were in Dallas until Friday."

Seeing the two of them together made me nauseated. In a room full of his people, she belonged, completing the picture with a pinstriped skirt and a pending partnership. All I had was an apron and fifty dollars in my Venmo account teed up to be sent to Soraya. The tension in my body was so wound up that the spatula in my palm was digging into my skin.

"We finished early but I didn't tell you," Ellie replied. "I thought it would be a fun surprise for Valentine's Day." Her eyes drifted between me and Jules. The tension between the three of us was so thick I could slice it up and serve it julienned. The silence was overwhelming and the thick scent of chili in the air made me feel like I was drowning. Such an end would be ironic. "Single Food Truck Chef Suffocated by Love and Chili. Story at 11."

"Lourdes," she said turning back to me thoughtfully. "I wasn't going to say anything, but I'm terrible at keeping secrets." She leaned in as though we were confidantes. "Don't tell my clients that." I smiled weakly. "I was the one that booked you for tonight."

My eyes widened and I stopped breathing without meaning to. Outside, the first flakes of the storm fell. Invisible nunchucks battered my heart in my chest. Somewhere a chicken ran for its life. "The private lesson?" I asked. "It's for you? For the two of you?"

Jules was equally caught off-guard. "Ellie, I don't know if that's a good idea." He looked out through the penthouse window where we were almost in the clouds. "I mean, the weather's supposed to be terrible. I'd hate for Lo to get stuck out so late."

Bad weather was my only hope of escape, but the snow had barely begun and it was a relatively flimsy excuse. I was crumbling like mazapán but I couldn't show either of them how much I hurt. In marathon running, we called this the wall—the point at which you think you can't go any further. Yet, I had no choice. I could never break what made him happy.

"No. It's okay," I lied with a smile that I hoped hid my heartbreak. "I have snow tires. Cooking with you two will be really fun."

Ellie watched me, studying the lift of my brow, the pull of my lip into my cheek and the flush of my skin. It was everything she'd been trained to do to find a liar's tell. After a moment, she dropped her gaze. "I have to cancel. Unfortunately"—she rolled her eyes—"my clients in Boulder need quick counsel this afternoon." She nodded in my direction and patted Jules's back. "That's how it goes sometimes, huh?"

Chapter 8: Julian

WHEN ELLIE TOLD ME WHAT she'd planned, there was nothing I could say. We were in our office, in the light of day, surrounded by our colleagues who, for all purposes, considered us a couple—and she did it in front of Lo.

Ellie knew I was hiding something and she'd put me on the stand to call my bluff in true litigator fashion. The evidence was clear, and I stood speechless as she walked in one direction and Lo walked in the other. The Dulce crew cleaned up and Lo left before I got a chance to talk to her. Ellie went to Boulder.

I sat in my office looking out over the city. I thought about hot chefs and aliens and pulparindo. I thought about Lo's hair and lattes with caramel syrup. I thought about how whatever happened at Sandals resorts stayed there, but how I would never forget how a state fair Tilt-A-Whirl made me feel weightless, happy, and free. My hand was against the glass, the lily ink bright and clear beneath the overheads. I called Ellie and told her the truth.

"Julian," she'd said with her typical diplomacy, "I knew how you felt the day I asked you about the lily on your hand." She sighed, resigned. "I never lose a negotiation, but this wasn't a fair fight. How do you argue against love?"

She was bowing out to let me move on with Lo as gracefully as anyone could and I was grateful.

"Can I drive out to Boulder to pick you up?" I asked. Thick snowflakes were coming down more rapidly now and I worried about Ellie driving on the icy highway. "By the time you're done with your meeting, the roads might be slick."

"No," she replied, simply. "I don't have clients in Boulder. Happy Valentine's Day, Jules."

Chapter 9: Lourdes

STEAK EMPANADAS HAD BECOME MY specialty. I made them for Jules when he got home from the hospital after his bike crash. He'd requested that I make them stuffed with mazapán, but he'd been so out of it that either would have tasted the same to him anyway. When we talked about it that day, he told me that every one of us needed a safe place to melt. Whether it was with Ellie or someone else, Jules deserved that more than anyone.

I'd been working on a recipe for mazapán empanadas for a few weeks but could never quite get it right. Making them would be a messy challenge, but it was one I wanted to complete. The next day, I would drop them by his house, and then I would just let him go.

The snow was falling. It was the heavy, thick kind that melted on your skin. I often played Latin jazz when I cooked and the sax and timbale filled my kitchen with the kind of energy I needed for a new beginning. I grabbed a box of mazapán and laid out a row of candy on the counter.

Valentine's night in a snowstorm should have been the quietest night of the year. Instead, the knock on the front door startled me. Through the peephole, I saw Jules waiting on the porch, the dim light of the moon outlining his perfect face. He was the last person I expected, but the only one I wanted to see.

I pulled the handle and swung the heavy oak open. In his hand, he carried a bouquet of fresh lilies.

Chapter 10: Julian

THERE WERE NO WORDS TO describe how much I needed Lo. We'd shared a kiss two years before, on the night she broke my heart. Here we were, in another city, and so much had happened in between. The only way to measure those years was in lost time.

Standing in the doorway, she was beautiful. Her long, dark hair was loose around her shoulders; her almond eyes sparkling with candid surprise. "What are you doing here?" she asked.

There was no need for greetings and chit-chat. "There's no more me and Ellie," I said evenly. If I was going to tell Lo how I felt, I needed to do it with a clean slate. "We talked this afternoon. It was just time for us to move on."

Her chest dipped and the bow of her lip quivered. "Move on to what?"

I took a step into her foyer. The house was warm and it felt like home. "To move on to us, Lo." I slid my arms around her, and she fit into the place right next to my chest I hadn't realized had been empty.

She folded into me and I consumed her with an intensity I'd been holding back for years. I kicked the door shut behind me and kissed her rose petal lips. She tasted of wine and cherry balm; her perfume rose up from the warmth in the crook of her neck and together they held me bound.

I laid the lilies on the counter while Lo's hands ran through my hair. Her touch made my skin light up and every part of me ached for more of her. A dozen wrapped mazapán candies fell off the counter as we pushed against it, every one of them a beautiful, crumbly surrender.

It was a whirlwind, a hurricane of pent-up emotion. Like a calm in the storm, she halted me, her palms on either side of my face. "Two years ago," she said, "you asked me if I felt the same way about you. Yes, Jules. I did. I still do. I was afraid and I'm sorry I couldn't say it then."

I held her for a moment, my arms wrapped around her so tightly, there was no way she could get away again. "The only thing I want to do is make sure you feel like you never have to be afraid again."

Chapter 11: Lourdes

I DREW ONE HAND DOWN Jules's hard chest. His cotton T-shirt was damp with melted snow and his body shivered from both the cold and the heat. A single drop of water clung to a strand of hair that fell over his brow, suspended, just like the two of us. There was an equal tension in our kiss, and it held us for a moment on a precipice.

"Lo," he whispered, his breath hot on my earlobe, "this will change us forever. I need you to tell me you want this."

We were already changed forever. "I want this," I said. "I've wanted this for years. I want *you*."

His thumb was in the dip of my throat and he lifted it to run along my bottom lip. "You're so fucking beautiful. You're perfect. You're . . ." He paused, all the gravity in the world between us, "you're everything, Lo."

The seconds felt tangled, stretched, and folded. Jules pushed into me, pressing my body to the kitchen island. Against my back, the marble countertop fenced me in. In front of me, Jules's hips kept me firmly in place, though the last thing I wanted to do anymore was run.

With a tender urgency, his lips found mine. He cupped my jaw and his fingers wrapped around to the back of my neck. Our breath mingled, collectively faster and needier each time. The pressure and power of him dissolved me. I wanted every part of him.

Between my legs, I could feel how hard he was. I lifted my thigh to wrap around his and trailed my hands down to his chiseled hips. His stomach tightened and his taut, round ass flexed as I pulled him close, both of us eager to be everywhere at once. His shirt was off and his fingers dropped to my chest with delicate affection.

It was slow. He focused on the pop of each button, enjoying the reveal of my breasts, inch by inch. His slight touch on my skin made my body jerk and the tip of his cock through his clothes rubbing my clit was the biggest tease I never wanted to end.

I reached down to his waist to unbuckle his pants, but he grabbed my wrist and lifted it to his lips. With a slight kiss, he took a step back. "Not yet. I've imagined this too many times not to do it right. I need to take care of you first."

His hands were on my hips and he gripped my flesh. With one quick heave, he lifted and carried me to bed.

Chapter 12: Julian

SEEING LO BENEATH ME MADE me hard as fuck. I took her shirt off and slid her pants down her smooth, fit legs. Her skin was like silk, except in the places my fingers roamed. There, it picked up in a line of goose bumps, a tell she couldn't hide even if she wanted to. I'd dreamed of making love to her. I had fantasized about lying beside her, feeling her melt into me with all the trust and admiration we had for one another and sliding inside her with the sole mission of showing her how beautiful I thought she was. Most of all, I had longed to wake up next to her, after knowing her the only way I hadn't already.

"Fuck," I moaned, my voice a gravelly drag between us. I drew my tongue down her neck and ran it just inside the lace of her bra. Behind her back, I unhooked it and her breasts spilled into my waiting hands. I kneaded her, feeling how swollen she was for me. Her nipples in my mouth hardened and I played with each one, teasing her by teasing myself. "Can I taste you, Lo?"

Her hands clutched the hair on the back of my head. "Yes," she whispered, "I want to feel every part of you on every part of me."

Biting my way down her body, was an exploration I didn't deserve. She writhed, a beautiful response to every kiss. How could I have been so stupid as to let her go the first time? She was the only thing I wanted. Her skin smelled the way sugar tasted; she tasted the way forever felt; she felt like a gift meant only for me. My senses overlapped. I was losing control.

I hooked my finger under the band of her panties. With a contraction of my hand, the thin cloth balled in my fist so tightly, it snapped. There was nothing left to keep us apart. "Lo," I growled, kissing the inside of her thigh, "tell me what you want me to do."

"Fuck me, Jules," she commanded, and I was more than happy to comply.

Chapter 13: Lourdes

I GLANCED DOWN AT JULES'S fist, the cotton of my panties like a ribbon from a gift unraveled. The veins in his hand pulsed, the tendons flexed, and the lace of the last thing between us swished over the inked lily that curled from his wrist to his knuckles.

The sight of my damp panties giving in to his strength shot an electric jolt straight from my clit through my chest. The stroke of his tongue was slow and worshipful. Every flick and brush felt as though he needed it even more than I did. It was gentle, yet needful; careful, yet completely willing. It was loving and respectful, yet it pulsed with desire. All of it was bringing me to the edge. My head fell back, my fingers grasped at his hair. I couldn't keep the small moans I'd held in my chest. They tumbled out, my breath unsteady.

Jules pushed my shaky thighs apart with a firm hand, asserting his position between my legs. "Let me finish you, baby." His voice was dark, teetering between request and demand.

I closed my eyes. A roll of his tongue softened into a suck, his full lips completely surrounded me, pulling with a gentle urgency, coaxing from somewhere inside me a deep desire to completely surrender. He slipped a finger inside me and rolled up to my g-spot. A second joined in, rubbing me, responding to the way I moved, finding a new path between us.

"Jules," I breathed, "oh, fuck, Jules."

A moment longer, his hand rolled. His fingers caressed a place so deep inside me, a place I'd held just for him. I was building while he grinded, the sight of me enough to make the thick muscles in his arms and chest flex. "Tell me you're mine, Lo," he commanded and the authority in his voice left no room for miscommunication.

"I'm yours," my voice squeaked through my constricted throat. "I need you, Jules. I love you."

To say it felt like a million universes exploding all around me, creating a new world, a new reality, a heaven in the middle of life and death. Jules's fingers gently charmed me, his mouth making love to my clit, vibrating as his thick, deep voice drank me with a delicious devotion.

"Come for me, baby," he whispered. "Melt into me, my love."

As the waves washed over me, he slowed the pace of his tongue until I relaxed around his fingers. He pulled them from my pussy, and with a last kiss of my clit, he parted his lips to drag his fingertips along the edge, hungry for every part of me.

"Goddamn, that was beautiful." he whispered. "I want to make you come like that every fucking day."

Jules pulled his body up to hover over me, his lips on mine. I tasted myself on his skin. He smelled like gray cotton and leather and love. He was safe and soft. He was Jules.

Chapter 14: Julian

TO FEEL LO SHAKE WHILE I made her come was a brand new high. To hear her tell me that she loved me while she gave in made me sure the only thing I wanted to do in life was make her feel as blissful as she did then every moment of every day.

Her trust turned me on. Her love made me feel like I'd come home. I was converted to her divinity, a dangerous fanatic that would do anything for more. More of her words. More of her body. The taste of her pussy was my drug. My cock swelled and between her legs, I was no longer able to pretend that I wanted to be anywhere else but buried inside her.

I gathered her wrists in one hand and pushed them above her head. Both sets of fingers laced through mine and I held her arms taut, pinning her beneath me. My lips slid across hers softly. In my hand, my shaft ached, the skin stretched tighter than it had ever been.

She was wet and I slid into her, closing my eyes as she relaxed around my tip. She moaned, giving in to our mutual desire. "Your body's so beautiful, Lo," I said. "It feels like I belong inside you."

Another moan as I pushed into her further and found a delicate rhythm I could sustain. She felt like heaven and I wanted to enjoy every second, every slide, every breath we shared together.

Her hands ran along my back. "Fuck me harder, Jules. I want to feel you deep. Show me how much you've wanted me."

I couldn't. I would fucking destroy her. My voice was a sandpaper ribbon, even in my own ears. "Such a tease, Lo. You sure you want to take my cock that hard?"

She tilted her hips up to take more of me. "Do you feel how wet you've made me?" she breathed. "That's not a tease, Jules. That's what you do to me." Her words made me bolder. Lo telling me what she wanted was the hottest thing I'd ever heard.

I pulled out and pushed back in. A little faster, harder. Her body rolled into mine, a perfect reciprocation of my lust. I buried my face in her neck. Releasing her wrists, I dragged my hand away, stopping it behind her head and closing my fingers in her hair.

"You feel so fucking good, baby." My jaw was pushed out, my teeth bared. I was, at once, completely satiated and utterly mad with desire. The tip of my cock pulsed, lost in her sea.

Lo whimpered as I disappeared into her, swallowed by our mutual desire. The sound of it was making me crazy.

Chapter 15: Lourdes

HEARING JULES ON THE VERGE of losing control was my poison. I closed my eyes as he fucked me harder, and I bit my lip to keep from betraying the length of him. His body over mine felt like a blanket. A heavy, protective, blanket that was rubbing my clit close to a second orgasm.

His hand was on my throat, his thumb in the dip. I leaned back, opening my neck even further. With a slight pressure, he squeezed. My heart raced. Inside, my pussy shivered, and I came again, pulsing around the shaft of Jules's cock.

His lips settled under my ear. His breath quickened and I drew my legs tight around him. I wanted to hold every part of him while he shook. I wanted to make him feel like the only place he'd ever want to be was inside me.

His hips again connected with mine and he bit my neck softly while his cock delivered us both to the other side of everything we'd known until then.

We collapsed into each other with breathless satisfaction. Outside, the snow fell in solid flakes from the sky. It collected on the lawn like powdered sugar and along the corners of the sidewalk where it softened back into slushy clumps. Jules laid his head on my chest and I twirled a lock of his wavy hair around my finger. We'd come into this as friends and now, in a Valentine's dream, we, too, had melted into something new.

Chapter 16: Julian

I'D WAITED FOR LO FOR ten years. Maybe longer if you considered that we met on our first day on the earth, twenty-eight years before in the San Corazón hospital. She had been worth it and I intended to spend the rest of my life making sure she knew it. I held her as she slept that night, but I couldn't close my eyes. In the moonlight, the golden strands in her hair were somehow more beautiful than they were in the sun.

Chapter 17: Lourdes

JULES AND I HAD FOUND a new beginning. We laughed together, we slept together, and he read me amicus briefs while I cooked in the kitchen. Every once in a while, we danced past the sous vide equipment to Latin jazz. We watched the winter turn to spring and the foxtail lilies sprout in the backyard garden.

In LA, I'd struggled to find something sweet for Dulce's menu, but Jules had been right all along. On a Saturday morning, with no particular fanfare, I handed him a mazapán empanada, warm from the oven, gooey with melted sugar in its soft dough belly. Sometimes recipes take a while to perfect, but finally, we had something sweet.

What started out as his medicated, sweet-tooth dream had become the truck's most popular item. Our LA and Denver rigs did so well that we added another in Austin with a fourth back in Albuquerque. It was meaningful to us both that we'd come full circle and on a warm, Albuquerque spring day, we opened Dulce, Por Fin.

Over the Sandia Mountains, the yellow-gold sun lit up the open sky where there was enough room in the world for all the hope the desert could kick up. As I directed the staff, Jules pulled me aside.

"The original Dulce would be proud." He kissed me softly. "You know," he started, his dark eyes sparkling with an intimate warmth, "the first time I knew I loved you was the day we left San Corazón. We drove out in that truck. You were so excited, so ready for everything, so in love with the future." This future; our lives, perfectly whole on our own, yet somehow better together. "Thank you for letting me be a part of it."

Our friends had come to celebrate and sat scattered across the prickly lawn at Balloon Fiesta Park. I served Soraya the truck's first official empanada.

"This is so cute, you two." She gestured between us, a paper plate resting atop the long fingers of her manicured hand. "And *this*," she said, closing her eyes as she chewed the sugary pie. "I know you're not a pastry chef, Lo, but you goddamned nailed this."

"See?" I replied, recalling Soraya's tried-and-true matchmaking method that had proved entirely unnecessary. "We didn't even need an alien."

She grinned, mischievously, and licked the caramel drizzle from her lip. Off in the distance, across the park, I saw something orange.

Soraya raised her brows. "Need? Maybe not. But it never hurts to throw one in for good measure."

About the Author

Tamaya Cruz grew up in New Mexico and still calls the Rocky Mountains home. She writes sweet and spicy romances deep enough to fill your heart, and sparkling with friendship, humor, and the complexity of life. You can find Tamaya's work, including rockstar romance, *A Circle in Seoul,* and small-town adventure romance, *This Bowl of Stars,* on Amazon and KU.

You can find Tamaya on:
Instagram, Facebook, TikTok & BlueSky @tamayacruzbooks

Visit her website at:
linktr.ee/tamayacruzbooks

VALENTINI'S DAY

Valentini's Day

Annabel den Dekker

NIALL PACED BACK AND FORTH in his dorm room, occasionally eyeing the picnic basket he had packed for his date with Sam. He'd never celebrated Valentine's Day before. It wasn't that he disliked the holiday; there just hadn't been anyone who made him think it was worth the fuss. But now, with Sam back in his life, everything felt different.

If anyone deserved a day of celebration, it was Sam, and Valentine's Day seemed like a good excuse. Besides, it would give him the perfect opportunity to finally make their relationship official. To not only be best friends but boyfriends too. Unfortunately, this meant he had to actually ask Sam, and for some reason, that made him anxious.

Niall wiped his sweaty hands on his jeans. Sam was about to arrive any minute now. Over the years, Niall had made plenty of mistakes, yet on New Year's Eve his childhood best friend had agreed to go on a date with him. Now, two months later, they were going strong, despite their banter. Still, a part of Niall was anxious that Sam would turn him down.

Niall stopped pacing when a knock sounded at the door. He didn't have a roommate and rarely received visitors, so there was only one person it could be. He opened the door to reveal an amused-looking Sam, dressed in sweats and a thick winter jacket, with warm gloves and his beanie with a bobble on top. Niall used to think the beanie was ridiculous, but now he couldn't remember why. It looked so good on Sam—though, to be fair, everything did.

"I dressed extra warm, just like you told me to in your text this morning. But please tell me we're not going for a run." Sam chuckled. "I know I told you I'm okay with joining you daily, despite my hate for running, but not on Valentine's Day."

Niall faked his best cynical expression, his brow creasing into a skeptical frown. "Oh, is that today?"

"Very funny," Sam said dryly, leaning against the doorframe, a grin tugging at his lips. "There's no way you forgot. I've been bugging you about it for weeks."

Smirking, Niall grabbed the collar of Sam's jacket and pulled him closer, leaning in for a long, tender kiss. "No, we're not going for a run," Niall said after a while, his voice somewhat hoarse. "We *are* headed outside, though. It's your day, so I've made plans to celebrate it properly."

Sam's eyebrows drew together. "My day? Don't you mean *our* day?"

"Nope, I mean your day. Valentini's Day."

Sam stared at him for a moment, his expression deadpan.

"Like, your name? Sam Valentini?" Niall tried, giving a little shrug. "So . . . Valentini's Day?"

Sam snorted. "No, I got that part. It's just that it's the worst joke I've ever heard." A lopsided grin tugged at the corner of his mouth. "I can't believe I didn't think of it myself." Sam's gaze shifted past Niall, landing on the picnic basket. His eyes lit with a spark of excitement. "Oh my God, are we finally having a picnic?"

Niall couldn't help but grin. Sam had been hinting at wanting to go on a picnic ever since Niall had first asked him out. He placed his hand on Sam's shoulder and lightly squeezed. "Yes, so you can stop complaining that I only take you to fancy restaurants, like the spoiled brat you are."

Sam cocked an eyebrow. "I don't think it works that way, Niall. I'd be spoiled if you took me for a picnic and I told you I'd rather go to a restaurant."

Ignoring him, Niall grabbed the picnic basket and a thick woolen blanket from beside the door. "I thought we could go to the park where we usually run."

"What? We're having the picnic outside? But it's freezing!" Sam protested, gesturing toward the window. It had been a snowy winter, starting with a white December that hadn't fully faded. Aside from a few brief days when the snow melted, winter had held on strong, leaving the campus blanketed in white.

"It'll be fine," Niall insisted, though doubt crept into his mind. In his excitement to make their date perfect, he hadn't considered just how cold it was or how poorly Sam usually handled it. But when he saw the excitement in Sam's eyes, showing him that despite his complaint he loved the idea of having their first picnic together, Niall pushed aside his worries. He pulled on his winter clothes and opened the door wider, gesturing for Sam to follow.

❦

The snow crunched softly beneath their boots as they made their way to the park, the campus eerily quiet. Most students had stayed inside where it was warm. Niall wondered if maybe they should have done the same.

Despite his doubts, he couldn't help but feel a sense of satisfaction when they arrived. The park was beautiful, untouched by any footprints. Snow covered the open fields, glistening under the sunlight like millions of tiny diamonds. The trees were coated in frost, their branches heavy with snow.

Niall turned to Sam, who was gazing at it all with awe. "This is amazing. It's almost like we're in Pinegrove Ridge."

To his surprise, Sam's words made Niall long to be there, back home in their small town. Maybe they could go there together soon and visit their families.

They found a cozy spot beneath one of the trees. Niall spread out the blanket, the fabric sinking slightly into the snow. Sam eyed it with raised eyebrows but crouched down beside him anyway, shivering.

"I can't believe you thought it was a good idea to sit out here in the snow when we could be warm inside. To borrow your own words: it's absolutely ridiculous," Sam complained, sitting cross-legged and adjusting his scarf. "A picnic is still a picnic when you have it indoors."

"Ridiculous? I'd call it *romantic*," Niall retorted, emphasizing the word Sam usually used to describe such moments. He pulled a thermos of hot cocoa from the basket and handed it to Sam. He took it gratefully, warming his hands on the vacuum flask as he raised it to his lips.

Sam's eyes sparkled as he looked at Niall over the rim of the thermos. "Okay, fine, it's very close to perfect." He cuddled up against Niall, leaning into his chest. "What's in the basket? Besides hot cocoa."

"Mostly sandwiches, and some of your favorite snacks. I also made a vegan whipped cream pie," Niall said, a hint of pride in his voice. "But I left it in my dorm so it wouldn't get ruined. We'll eat it when we get back."

Sam blinked, looking up at him. "You made a pie? For me?"

"Well, yeah," Niall admitted with a bashful smile. "I wanted to make our date perfect for you."

A fond grin spread across Sam's face. "That's so sweet."

Niall wrapped an arm around Sam's shoulder, holding him a little closer. He could tell Sam was cold, his body shivering, so he hoped it would warm him up.

"I'm sure your pie's a masterpiece," Sam said with a teasing smirk. "I mean, it must be if it's anything like the stick figure drawing you made for me last Christmas."

"Oh, yes, for sure. I could win awards with it if I wanted to."

"Then it's too bad you don't want to," Sam joked, chuckling softly as he buried himself even further into Niall's embrace. His teeth were chattering now.

"You okay?" Niall asked, concerned. This had been the moment he'd wanted to ask Sam to be his boyfriend, but he told himself it wasn't the right time with Sam feeling this uncomfortable. He convinced himself that it had nothing to do with the anxiety fluttering in his stomach, the irrational fear that Sam might turn him down.

Sam tried to brush it off with a weak smile. "I'm fine. Just a little cold."

"Are you sure? You're shaking." Niall pulled him even closer, practically cradling him now, but it didn't seem to be enough. "We can go back."

"It's okay. We haven't even eaten yet. We can stick it out a little longer," Sam muttered. "I don't want to ruin our date."

Niall shook his head, his brow creasing into a frown. "You're not ruining anything unless you die out here of hypothermia."

Sam let out a shaky laugh.

"Come on, let's get back to the dorm," Niall urged as he stood up and helped Sam to his feet. "We'll eat there. And we've still got my pie waiting for us."

Sam nodded, still shivering but smiling. "I can't wait to see it."

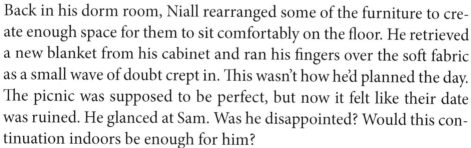

Back in his dorm room, Niall rearranged some of the furniture to create enough space for them to sit comfortably on the floor. He retrieved a new blanket from his cabinet and ran his fingers over the soft fabric as a small wave of doubt crept in. This wasn't how he'd planned the day. The picnic was supposed to be perfect, but now it felt like their date was ruined. He glanced at Sam. Was he disappointed? Would this continuation indoors be enough for him?

Niall spread the blanket out on the floor just as he had done in the park, determined to keep the cozy, intimate vibe of their picnic going.

Sam immediately took his place on the blanket. Still shivering, he pulled his knees to his chest. His teeth weren't chattering anymore, but Niall could still see the tension in his body. Without a word, Niall crouched beside him and slipped his arms around Sam's waist, pulling him close. He hugged him tightly, rubbing his hands along his back to warm him up.

"Better?" he murmured as his fingers gently brushed through Sam's hair.

Sam sighed, relaxing into the embrace, leaning against Niall's chest. "Much better," he whispered, his voice soft and content.

Niall exhaled. The day might not be going as planned, but Sam seemed happy. That was what mattered most.

They stayed wrapped up in each other for a few minutes, the warmth slowly returning to Sam's body.

After a while, Niall reached into the basket and pulled out the sandwiches he had packed. He handed one to Sam, who stretched out on the blanket, his legs lightly brushing against Niall's.

"I'm very curious about that pie you mentioned," Sam said after they finished their sandwiches. His eyes glinted with amusement. "You've been hyping it up."

Niall chuckled and got up to fetch the pie from his mini fridge. He carefully took it out, revealing the perfectly swirled whipped cream topping.

Sam's eyes widened. "It looks delicious," he said with a hint of surprise. "I mean, no offense, but I wasn't expecting it to look that good."

"What's that supposed to mean?" Niall placed the pie on the ground behind them, making sure it was safe from being knocked over. "I'm great at baking!"

"You were good at those Christmas cookies," Sam agreed and reached toward the pie, his finger poised to swipe some of the whipped cream.

Niall slapped his hand away. "Not yet. We'll save it for dessert," he said firmly.

"Really?" Sam asked, his voice teasing as he climbed onto Niall's lap, facing him and wrapping his arms around his neck. "I was thinking about another kind of dessert, honestly."

Niall laughed softly as Sam's fingers brushed against his cheek. His touch lingered as their faces drew closer. Their lips met, slowly at first. The soft touches soon gave way to deeper, more urgent kisses.

Sam's hands slipped beneath Niall's shirt, his fingers grazing his skin, sending shivers down his spine. Eager to return the pleasure, Niall slid his own under Sam's sweater. As his fingers roamed over his chest, Sam moaned into his mouth, wordlessly begging for more.

Niall tugged at the hem of Sam's sweater, hesitating. "Maybe we shouldn't get naked. I don't want you to get cold again."

Sam chuckled, his eyes gleaming with amusement as he leaned close to Niall's ear, his breath warm against his skin. "Trust me," he whispered, "I'm far from cold right now."

Instead of waiting for Niall to do it, Sam pulled his sweater off himself, revealing the lean muscle underneath. Niall's breath caught for a moment, his hands sliding over Sam's bare sides, feeling the warmth that radiated from him.

They kissed again, deeper this time, their movements more deliberate as they tugged at the rest of their clothes. When they were finally naked, Niall's hands traveled up Sam's back and gently pushed on his shoulders to guide him onto the blanket. His hand slid behind Sam's head, cradling it on their way down, their lips still locked.

"What do you want?" Niall whispered against Sam's mouth.

"The usual," Sam breathed, his voice heavy with desire.

Niall leaned back slightly, his eyes flicking toward his cabinet before refocusing on Sam, who stared up at him with a wild, passion-filled gaze. "A little rough and a little tender?" Niall asked.

"Yes," Sam answered, his voice barely a whisper. He scrunched his brow when Niall got up. "What are you doing?"

Niall opened a drawer and retrieved lube and a condom. "Just grabbing some essentials."

"Essentials?" Sam snorted. "You're such a dork. Just call them what they are."

With a smirk, Niall returned to his spot on top of Sam before popping open the bottle cap and smearing lube over his fingers. He pressed several kisses along Sam's neck, trailing lower to his chest and stopping at his stomach. His lips lingered there, brushing teasingly against the sensitive skin, drawing soft breaths from Sam. Carefully, he slipped one finger inside Sam. He took his time stretching him, letting the tension build, allowing them both to feel every second, every inch of closeness.

When he had three fingers moving comfortably back and forth, he pulled out. Niall's gaze flicked up to meet Sam's eyes, his heart fluttering in his chest when he saw the need in them. "Ready?"

"Yeah," Sam answered in a husky voice.

Niall ripped open the condom and put it on. He positioned himself, his fingers dancing over Sam's body, mapping out familiar paths. Then, he slowly pushed inside. As he did, his fingers tenderly traced Sam's jawline, his eyes searching his face, checking for comfort, for pleasure, for reassurance that everything felt just as it should.

Sam's eyes fluttered shut as he tilted his head back and pressed his body closer against Niall's. "I love all this slow stuff, I honestly do, but I think I'll go for 'a lot rough' this time after all," he murmured, his voice edging toward a moan.

"That's not very romantic, though, is it?" Niall teased. "And on Valentine's Day."

"You said it was Valentini's Day," Sam answered impatiently, peeking through his lashes. "And this is what Valentini wants. Besides, I think rough sex can be very romantic, too."

With a grin, Niall picked up the pace, his thrusts growing rougher, just like Sam wanted.

Sam's breath quickened, each gasp and moan urging Niall on. "Yes, just like that," he encouraged, his voice filled with need.

As Niall drove deeper, Sam trembled beneath him, each movement pushing them closer and closer to the edge, their bodies moving in a perfect rhythm. Niall's gaze never left Sam's face, watching the way pleasure unfurled across his expression, his lips parting as his eyes fluttered shut, lost in the sensations coursing through him.

When Niall delivered a particularly powerful thrust, Sam's voice broke into a loud, breathy moan. The sound sent delightful shivers down Niall's spine. Sam tightened around him as he came, the sensation desperately pulling Niall toward the edge, until he could no longer hold back.

Niall's release rushed through him like a tidal wave, crashing over him in a rush of euphoria. He collapsed on top of Sam, both of them panting and clinging to each other as they rode out the aftershocks, their lips intermittently finding each other.

They lay there for a few minutes, their breathing slowly returning to normal as they snuggled into each other. Sam lazily stretched out his arm. He froze, his eyes widening in horror. "Oh my God. I'm so sorry!"

Niall's heart skipped a beat. "What? What did you do?"

Sam revealed his hand. It was covered in whipped cream pie. "I ruined your cake," he said, his eyes wide with guilt.

Niall propped himself up on one elbow, glancing at Sam's hand, then at the pie—which was indeed a mess. He stared at it for a moment, then broke into a mischievous grin. Without warning, Niall scooped up a handful of the pie and smeared it across Sam's face, letting it trail down his chest.

Sam's mouth dropped open in shock. "Oh my God, you did not just do that!"

Niall smirked, leaning in closer. "What? It was ruined, anyway."

Sam grabbed a fistful of pie and flung it at Niall. Instead of retaliating, Niall flicked his tongue over a bit of whipped cream near Sam's collarbone. He leaned in, pressing a sticky kiss to Sam's lips.

Sam laughed breathlessly before running his finger over Niall's chest, scooping up a bit of cream and putting it into his mouth. He nodded approvingly, his eyes sparkling with joy. "Mmm, it's delicious," he teased, grinning as he licked his finger clean.

Niall playfully raised an eyebrow. "I told you I'm great at baking."

After cleaning themselves up, Sam sat down on Niall's bed, looking up at him. "I think that was the messiest Valentine's Day ever."

Niall chuckled. "Maybe, but it's not over yet. I actually got you something."

Sam raised his brow. "A gift?"

Niall crossed the room before opening his drawer to pull out a neatly wrapped present. With a shy smile, he handed it to Sam.

Sam's face lit up as he unwrapped his gift. He gently peeled away the paper to reveal a special edition of *Boyfriend Material*. He'd told Niall it was one of his favorite novels—it was both funny and relatable, with amazing character development and a lovable couple. It also helped that Sam was a huge fan of the enemies-to-lovers and fake dating tropes. "This is perfect," he whispered. "Thank you, Niall."

"I thought maybe I could read to you again," Niall said softly as he joined Sam on the bed.

"I'd love that!" Sam snuggled up into Niall's arms, both of them wrapped under a warm blanket.

Niall opened the book and began reading aloud. After the first chapter, he paused, glancing down at Sam. He was resting his head on Niall's chest, looking completely content. Niall leaned down and pressed a gentle kiss to his forehead. "Samu?" he murmured. His heart raced again, knowing it was now or never.

Sam tilted his head up, meeting Niall's gaze, his smile soft and tender. "Yes?"

Niall hesitated, his heart pounding against his rib cage. "I was thinking . . ." he started. He swallowed hard, annoyed at himself for being so nervous again. "We've been . . . well, we're sort of . . ."

Sam stared expectantly at him. "Yes?"

Niall took a deep breath. "I've been trying to ask you something, but for some reason, it's scary."

"Oh?" Sam encouraged, tilting his head. "What is it? You can just ask me. I might laugh at you, but like, I won't leave you or anything."

A nervous laugh escaped Niall. "I would hope not. I—" He sighed again, mustering his courage. "Do you want to be my boyfriend?"

Sam's brows shot up in surprise. "Is that—seriously?" He took Niall's face in his hands and pressed a kiss to his lips. "Yes, you idiot! Of course, I'll be your boyfriend!"

Niall felt a wave of relief wash over him. He kissed Sam back, deep and tenderly.

Sam grinned when they pulled away. "This is officially the best Valentini's Day ever."

"I couldn't agree more," Niall chuckled before pulling him in for another kiss.

About the Author

Annabel den Dekker (she/her) is a queer author from the Nether-lands. When she's not writing, she can be found strolling through nature, daydreaming about her favorite characters, or conjuring up new stories. She's also an avid admirer of books, music, and TV series and delights in sharing them with others.

After years of creating numerous short stories, novels, and fanfic-tion, she self-published her debut novel, *Ailene*. *Purpose* and *Just Like Christmas* followed only a year later. Now she is eager to add many more books to her repertoire.

You can find Annabel on:
Instagram @bellsbooksandwritings

Visit her website at:
annabeldendekker.com

MINE TO KEEP

Mine to Keep

Ann Marie Croft

Sarah

"WORKING LATE, MISS OLIVER?"

My head snapped up at the deep baritone on the other side of the office. I'd been so focused on my work I hadn't heard anyone come in.

"Joe. I mean, Mr. Thatcher. I'm sorry."

I watched as Joe Thatcher, billionaire bad boy and my boss, crossed the room to his desk where I was sitting. In his chair. Without his permission. Frantic to correct my mistake, I jumped out of the chair, tripping over my feet. Instead of landing on the floor, my body made impact with his. All six foot five of him. His arms wrapped around my waist, catching me, and I would have been brain dead not to notice the muscles in his arms. By the tailored suits he wore that showed off his best assets, he obviously took care of his body. But actually *feeling* said assets against *my* body? *Holy shit.* I might have fantasized about my boss on several occasions in the privacy of my bedroom, but I wasn't prepared for how good his body would feel against mine. Nerve endings fired and I couldn't form a thought, never mind a single word.

"Are you okay?" Joe looked down at me in concern. His jaw tightened as he searched my face for an answer, his blazing blue eyes holding me captive.

I needed to move, but my body was rendered useless.

"Sarah?"

The chime of a cell phone brought me back to reality. I cleared my throat, taking a step back toward the desk, and looked up at Joe, not knowing what to expect.

"Are you all right?"

"Y-Yes, I'm fine," I said, trying to find my voice. "I'm sorry, I didn't mean to—"

"Get caught in my chair?" he asked with a grin. I bit my bottom lip as he moved toward me and leaned in close, so close I could smell the fresh scent of his soap.

"Maybe I should . . . punish you, Miss Oliver." His voice was low and seductive, and dear God, I wasn't sure if I was going to survive this. *Survive him.*

His seductive glances ignited a fire within me, reminding me of how long it had been since I had any real action other than my battery-operated boyfriend. *Come on, Sarah, get a grip!* I shouldn't find him attractive, shouldn't fantasize about him being in my bed, not after what went down four months ago. My cheeks burned, and I shook my head to regain my senses. Why I always let him get inside my head was beyond me.

"Maybe if you had given me my own office, I wouldn't have to sit in your chair," I retorted, my voice weaker than desired. I crossed my arms, hoping to display some semblance of strength.

His low chuckle was enough to throw me off balance, and he reveled in it. He'd had me in his sights since the merger with no indication of backing down. *Damn him.* The merger wasn't even supposed to happen. At least, that was what I was told. Instead, the company I worked for sold out in the middle of the night to our competitor: Joe Thatcher. I went from managing an entire department to nothing, losing my employees in the process. I fought for my staff to stay employed with the company, to which the execs offered a deal: My staff remained employed if I took a new position as assistant to the CEO. Joe's assistant. I was given a timeline of two years. I had to stay in the position for two damn years in order to seal the deal.

Ignoring Joe wasn't an option, though I tried at first. My emotions and boredom in my new position got the better of me, and before I knew it, we were engaging in playful banter and light touches. A brush of the hand here, a gentle nudge of the shoulder there. But our innocent flirting had recently turned into something more. Something . . . lustful.

Joe reached around me, grabbing the stack of documents I had been working on.

"What are these?" he asked, plopping the papers down next to me.

"The contracts from this week. They're ready for you to sign."

He stared at me a long moment before speaking again. "I can't figure you out, Sarah . . ." As I opened my mouth to respond, he continued his thought. "But I'd like to."

"What are you talking about?" I rolled my eyes and leaned against the desk, my arms still crossed.

"You're here working late when all your colleagues have gone home. Some of them even left early to prepare for the holiday tomorrow."

My laugh echoed through the office, coming out louder than I'd meant for it to. "Wow. You're kidding me, right?"

"Oh, come on. People love Valentine's Day." Joe grinned.

"It's a stretch calling it a holiday."

"You don't celebrate?" he asked, raising a brow.

I picked up the contracts I'd prepared earlier and thumbed through them, trying to avoid the conversation. I hated Valentine's Day and did my best to avoid it each year. It was a racket that fed on people's insecurities and encouraged a false notion of love. Not wanting to egg Joe on any further, I kept my answer simple.

"No."

I plucked a pen out of the cup on his desk and held it out, willing him to focus on the contracts and not on this ridiculous conversation.

He ignored the pen and instead moved around me to sit on the edge of the desk.

"Why don't you celebrate Valentine's Day, Sarah?"

I gritted my teeth and turned to face him. "It doesn't matter. Can we please get these contracts signed so we can move forward with the clients?"

"Not until you answer my question."

"Why is it so important to you? It's just another day."

"Because most women I know love to be wined, dined, and supplied with jewelry, especially on Valentine's Day. It's been the talk of the office all week. You're the exception, and I'm intrigued. Plus, I'd like to have a conversation with you that doesn't involve work. Surely there's no harm in getting to know each other better."

"Look, Joe, you're a nice guy, but I can't have this conversation with you," I said, rubbing my forehead.

"Someone hurt you," he replied in a low voice, his tone changing. When I looked up, he was clenching his jaw, his hands balled into fists on his lap. A small gasp escaped my lips as I looked down at my feet, not wanting to meet his gaze. This was getting too personal, and if I was being honest with myself, I was afraid of letting him in.

He let out a sigh and shoved the contracts out of the way before patting the desk beside him. I focused on his hand and contemplated whether sitting beside him was a good idea. Despite feeling vulnerable, I craved comfort from him. I hadn't wanted to be close with another man, or anyone in particular, since my breakup. Getting close meant inevitably getting hurt, but being around Joe felt . . . different. Better, perhaps. So, against my better judgment, I took a seat next to him. Pen still in hand, I fidgeted with the cap as we sat in silence.

"So, while your friends are out enjoying their Valentine's Day dinner, what do you do?" Joe asked, his tone returning to normal.

I groaned, and he chuckled as he nudged my shoulder.

"Fine, if it will make you happy, I will detail my super exciting Valentine's Day night for you." I glared at him, only to be met with those blue eyes and his sexy grin. *Lord help me.* "I usually order takeout and get a nice bottle of wine, watch a movie, that sort of thing. Oh, and I make my famous pumpkin cheesecake for dessert. That's a must."

"Pumpkin cheesecake?" Joe wrinkled his face. "Why the hell pumpkin cheesecake?"

"Because it's the furthest thing from Valentine's Day I can think of," I said, trying to hide the tears forming in my eyes. I blinked them back, but he noticed. Of course he did. He always noticed.

In a silent gesture, Joe grabbed the contracts and held out his hand. I placed the pen in his palm, gently and slowly gliding my fingers over his. His skin was warm, and I wanted more than anything to feel his hands on me. He watched me, lust darkening his eyes. He signed the contracts one by one, the scratch of pen against paper the only sound in the room. When he was done, he placed them on the desk and got up to stand in front of me.

"Have dinner with me at my place tomorrow night, Sarah."

"What? No. Thanks for the offer, but no."

"Come on. I'm told I make a great Italian pasta, and you can make your pumpkin cheesecake."

"I don't think that's a good idea, Joe."

He stepped toward me, closing the distance between us. "It's just dinner between friends."

But I knew it was so much more than that. He was breaking down my barriers. The wall I had put up to protect myself was in serious danger of collapsing under his influence.

"It's against the rules," I replied, my voice barely above a whisper.

Joe inched closer, placing his hands on either side of me. His neatly groomed beard tickled my skin as he bent close, his voice low and husky in my ear.

"My company. My rules."

I pressed my thighs together in a silent plea to my body to stop reacting. He was so close, and I wanted nothing more than to pull him into a kiss, to wrap my thighs around him.

"But," I whimpered, unable to form a cohesive sentence.

He chuckled lowly as he lifted his gaze to meet mine. "Some rules were meant to be broken."

Joe

FUCK ME. IT WAS A miracle I didn't bend Sarah over my desk and fuck her right there. Thoughts of flipping up her skirt and baring her ass to me made my cock twitch the entire drive home. I'd wanted her since the moment I laid eyes on her during the merger. When I told her I wanted to know her better, I wasn't lying. I was tired of meaningless sex with brainless women. It had been fun during my twenties, but I was bored with just having fun. I wanted a woman I could have a future with.

Sarah was fucking intoxicating. Her body, her scent, her intelligence. I couldn't get enough. She kept herself at a distance from everyone, and I wanted to find out why. A woman like her shouldn't hide. She should be worshipped, and I was determined to do just that.

I know the merger hurt her. It was never meant to be personal, just a business deal. The company she worked for was drowning and needed a lifeline. I was that lifeline, but as with any merger, the restructuring process was tough. Positions were reevaluated or cut altogether. Through it all, Sarah fought to keep her staff employed, sacrificing herself in the process. Her loyalty knew no bounds, winning out over greed, and I found myself genuinely impressed.

I wanted her to know I wasn't the enemy. Throughout the past few months, I did everything in my power to prove myself worthy of her trust. I just hoped it was enough. I was ready for more than the flirtatious moments we shared. I wanted her—all of her.

The next day at work, the sexual tension between us was off the charts. I was afraid I'd scared her away the previous night, but surprisingly our connection only seemed to embolden her actions. Everything from the way her hand lingered on my shoulder in the hall to the short skirt she was wearing was enough to make me hard. Sitting through meetings all morning having to hide my massive erection was torture, and I was glad for the reprieve that came with the afternoon. Eager to get our evening started early, I shut down my office, then looked for Sarah.

"Ready to head out?" I asked, finding her hunched over a book in the break room. She looked up at me over her green-rimmed glasses, her amber eyes taking me in.

She glanced at the clock and then back at me. "It's only three o'clock."

"It's Friday and Valentine's Day. I thought we could get started a little early."

She frowned, and I was worried she'd changed her mind about tonight. Closing her book, she stood and put her snack in the fridge. My worries quickly disappeared when she spoke again.

"Actually, I need to go home first. I'd like to change, and I do need to grab my cheesecake."

"I can send my driver to pick you up. Say about five?"

"That's not necessary. I can drive . . ."

I stepped closer to her, cupping her cheek in my hand. She didn't finish her sentence, closing her eyes instead. "Let me pamper you, Sarah. This night is all about you."

Her eyes flew open at my admission, a question lingering in her gaze. A question she didn't ask.

"My driver will pick you up at five." I gave her cheek a stroke with my thumb before heading home to prepare for the evening. An evening she'd always remember.

Sarah

BY THE TIME I ARRIVED home, my nerves had almost completely un-raveled. My heart thudded in my chest with equal parts anticipation and nervousness. I hadn't been on a date in two years and worried I would make a fool of myself. But for now, all I could do was shower and get ready while waiting for my ride to arrive.

When the car pulled up outside and honked, I took a deep breath and gathered my things. *You deserve this*, I told myself one last time, checking the mirror for any last-minute touch-ups. I shouldn't have been shocked to see the limo sitting outside. After all, this was Joe we were talking about. But I about dropped my cheesecake when Joe stepped out of the limo. He looked sinful in his three-piece suit and sexy smile.

"Joe?"

"Hi, Sarah."

"I thought you were just sending a driver?" I asked with a laugh.

"Yeah, well, that isn't very romantic, is it?"

I couldn't help but smile. He was too charming for his own good, and mine, for that matter.

"These are for you," he said, pulling an enormous bouquet of red roses out of the limo. He handed me the roses while taking my purse and cheesecake before turning to safely secure them inside the car.

"Oh, Joe, they're beautiful. Thank you."

"Shall we?"

Joe helped me into the limo before settling in himself. He opened a bottle of champagne and poured two glasses.

"I've never ridden in a limo before." I smiled at Joe as he handed me a glass.

"I wasn't lying when I said I wanted to pamper you."

His intense stare made heat creep into my cheeks . . . and lower. I wanted him, as hard as it was to admit. And he was making it hard to stay away. I kept succumbing to his gravitational pull and knew I wouldn't be able to keep my distance forever.

We arrived at Joe's building and rode the private elevator to his penthouse. Everything about the building was magnificent. Our reflection shone off the pristine elevator walls, and I took in the sight of us standing together for the first time. Joe was confident, comfortable within the extravagance, and I felt lost, lacking the assuredness to share his space. With luxury surrounding me, insignificance seeped in, twisting my stomach. What if this night didn't go well? What if I didn't meet up to whatever expectations he might have?

The elevator opened into the entry of the penthouse, and I paused a moment, taking in the artwork on the walls.

"This way." Joe motioned for me to follow him, and we made our way to his kitchen to unload my things. I pulled the cheesecake out of the bag and placed it in the fridge. When I turned around, Joe was holding the can of whipped cream topping and raised a brow.

"It's for the cheesecake." I rolled my eyes and held out my hand.

"Hmm. You can never have too much whipped cream," he said with a wink, handing me the can. I turned to the fridge before he could see my cheeks blush again. I hated that he made me blush. It felt silly, like I was a naïve girl who knew nothing about sex or innuendo. I wasn't naïve, and I didn't want him to think that of me.

"I'm going to start dinner." He was behind me, his voice in my ear. He was so close the heat of his body radiated against mine. I bit down on my bottom lip to keep the whimper from escaping. He put his hands on my shoulders, running them down my arms. I cleared my throat and turned around, causing him to take a step back.

"Um. Could I use your bathroom?" I needed to take a breath and regain my senses.

"Of course. Through the living room and into the hall. It's the first door on the right."

I bolted, not stopping until I found the bathroom. I leaned against the closed door and let out the breath I was holding, the whoosh blowing the strands of hair that had fallen in my face. I wanted to let go, needed to let go, and I needed it to be with Joe. But how could I protect my heart if I gave it to another? It had taken months to heal after the breakup, and maybe I was still healing. I longed to be happy again, to love again, to feel the touch of a man again. I stood in front of the mirror and studied my reflection. The woman staring back at me deserved a chance. I owed her that much. Taking another deep breath, I opened the bathroom door, the scent of garlic and tomatoes permeating the air. I inhaled, indulging in the delicious aroma.

I walked back into the kitchen and took in the sight of Joe standing in front of the stove. He'd ditched his suit jacket, and his sleeves were rolled up over his elbows. God, even cooking he was sexy.

"That's brave," I said, walking toward him.

He looked at me, tilting his head.

"Cooking red pasta sauce in a white shirt with no apron," I finished.

He laughed and stepped toward the island, offering me a glass of wine. It was a moscato, my favorite. Taking a seat at the island, I watched as he continued to prep food for our meal. He had thought of everything: salad, the main pasta dish, garlic bread, wine. And all I'd brought was pumpkin cheesecake and whipped cream?

"Is there anything I can do to help?"

"You can sit there and enjoy your wine. This night is about you, Sarah."

I smiled and took another sip, trying to think of something to keep the conversation going.

"I forgot to tell you. I sent out the contracts today. We should be good to go for meetings next week."

Joe put down the spoon he was using and dipped his finger into the sauce. He walked toward me before lifting my chin with one hand and holding the sauce-covered finger in front of my mouth.

"Open."

His voice was seductive and commanding, and I was more than happy to oblige. I opened my mouth for him and took his finger inside, sucking every last drop of sauce from it. His eyes never left mine, and I could feel the wetness between my legs.

He took a step back and smiled. "We aren't talking about work tonight."

Returning to the stove, he placed the food in the oven before cleaning up some of the dishes. I couldn't get the feeling of his finger in my mouth out of my head and crossed my legs tight as if that would stop my arousal. I was so turned on and wondered if he was too.

"How was the sauce?" he asked, causing me to almost choke on my wine.

"It was good," I squeaked out.

He chuckled and grabbed his glass of wine, showing me to the living room. Dusk had appeared on the horizon, illuminating the view from the large living room windows with the city lights. Traffic and people looked so tiny from this height, and I couldn't imagine a more beautiful place to have a Valentine's Day dinner.

"You like the view?" he asked.

"Yes, it's so beautiful. I've never seen the city like this before."

"That's why I love it. In a weird way, it makes me feel less alone in the world. Knowing other people are out there no matter the time of day or night."

"You? Feel alone? I find that hard to believe," I replied.

"We all have our demons."

We stared at each other, a silent acknowledgment that we both had past trauma, but not knowing what to say.

Joe motioned toward the couch, and we took a seat, a cushion separating us. We talked about where we were from and our lives growing up. He discussed his mother abandoning him at a young age, leaving his father to raise him. A father who wasn't always around. I told him about my family and how close we were and how holiday get-togethers were always a big deal.

"Is that why you feel alone, Joe? Because of your parents?"

He stared at his wine glass, his hesitation unnatural to me. I'd never seen him vulnerable. It made my heart hurt for him.

"I suppose that's part of it. I partied hard in my early twenties. It helped me forget, but now that I'm in my thirties, I want more. I want stability. I want someone I can share the rest of my life with."

He looked over at me and laughed. Apparently I didn't hide my shock very well.

"Shocker, I know," he continued. "The media has me portrayed in a certain light. A lot of it isn't true for me anymore. I hope you understand that."

"So, the one-night stands . . ."

"Haven't happened in well over a decade," he quickly replied.

I leaned forward and placed my empty wine glass on the coffee table. I'd learned so much about him in such a short amount of time that my head was almost dizzy.

"What about you, Sarah? What is haunting you?"

Before I could even contemplate how to answer him, I was saved by the oven timer. He observed me a moment before getting up to remove the food from the oven. I followed, insisting I help set the table, but he wouldn't allow it. He poured me a fresh glass of wine, and I watched as he prepared the table for the food. The dinner looked amazing, and I was glad I'd agreed to come. As we sat down to eat, we engaged in light chitchat before he brought the conversation around to our earlier discussion.

"You didn't answer my question earlier."

"Hmm?" I looked up, putting a forkful of pasta into my mouth.

He continued to watch me, and I knew he wasn't going to give up. Maybe it was better to just get it out and over with. I hadn't talked about it out loud in over a year and was afraid of what emotions might take over if I did.

"This is a safe space, Sarah. I promise you that."

My heart skipped a beat, and I knew he was right. I found myself wanting to tell him everything: the good, the ugly, the dirty. *Fuck it.* What was the worst that could happen?

"You asked why I didn't celebrate Valentine's Day. It was never my thing. You needed a date for Valentine's Day, and I didn't have many dates when I was younger. Then I met *him.*"

"Who's *him*?"

"The man I thought was my forever. Steven. He was romantic, he took me on dates, and yes, we celebrated Valentine's Day. All was good in my little world. Then, two years ago, it all came crashing down." I stopped my story to drink more liquid courage before continuing.

"I decided to surprise him that Valentine's Day. I got off work early and changed into his favorite dress before heading to his place. I had a key, so I let myself in." I let out a little laugh that bordered on a sob.

"Oh no. Oh, Sarah," Joe got up from his seat across from me and sat next to me as I continued my story.

"I found him fucking another woman in his bedroom. Not just any woman, but my friend." I laughed as tears started streaming down my face.

"He tried to apologize, but I got out of there as fast as I could. I couldn't bear it. The betrayal from both of them. It was bad enough that *he* cheated on me, but I couldn't even go to my friend for comfort." I couldn't help the sobs that escaped my body. I had tried so long to bottle up my emotions from that day, and now they were overflowing. Joe pulled me close, and I let him hold me. It felt so good to be comforted.

"Fucking asshole," Joe murmured as he gently kissed my temple. "I'm so sorry that happened to you."

I looked up to Joe's mouth so close to mine. He leaned in, and I closed my eyes, ready for him to take what he wanted. To give me what

I needed. When his lips didn't touch mine, I opened my eyes. He studied me, and I finally sat up, wiping the tears from my face. I'd never bared so much of my soul to anyone before, but Joe made it easy.

"On that note, I think dessert is much needed. What do you think?"

Joe nodded, and we made our way into the kitchen. I removed the cheesecake and whipped cream from the fridge, placing them on the island. I took my time cutting the cheesecake as Joe cleaned up the table from dinner. We worked in silence, and I hoped I hadn't scared him away with my baggage.

"Joe, I'm sorry I got upset. That's not how I meant for this night to go. I . . ."

He approached me, a hungry look in his eye, and backed me up against the island. My breaths became heavy, and in that moment, all I wanted was him.

Joe

I WANTED TO HUNT DOWN the bastard who hurt Sarah and teach him a lesson. It was no wonder she hated Valentine's Day, and it explained why she was so closed off.

I loved having her at my place. I loved taking care of her and getting to know her. The fact that she'd confided such a personal wound made my heart feel something it hadn't in a long time. She listened without judgment when I told her about my past and how it shaped my adulthood.

I couldn't hold back anymore. I needed her, right there, right now, no matter the consequences. I backed her up against the island, my eyes roaming over her body. Her red velvet dress was begging to be ripped off her, the skirt of it skimming just above her knees.

"Take your panties off," I commanded, needing to feel her bare skin on mine. She stilled against the counter, gripping the edge as she looked up at me.

"Or I'll do it for you," I warned her.

She didn't move. Her eyes widened, but she didn't make a sound. My cock throbbed at her defiance before I reached under her skirt and ripped the panties off her. I stared at her, watching her chest rise and fall with her now heavy breathing. She leaned up, and I took the cue, crashing my mouth against hers. Holding her face with one hand and her hip with the other, I pulled her as close to me as I could, our breaths erratic as we kissed. I moved my lips to her neck, tasting and nibbling down to her throat and back.

"This needs to come off," I murmured, reaching behind her to pull down the zipper of her dress. She didn't hesitate, helping me tug the sleeves down her shoulders and arms until the dress pooled at her feet. Her black lace bra was next as I deftly unclasped it and threw it across the kitchen.

"You're so fucking beautiful," I told her. She put her arms together in front of her chest, crimson creeping into her cheeks. I gently pulled her arms apart, resting them at her sides.

"You don't need to hide your body from me. You are fucking gorgeous." My hands roamed her body before I took her breasts into my hands, massaging and teasing her nipples. She let out a gasp, and I kissed her again, sucking on her bottom lip.

I picked her up, and she let out a squeal as I hoisted her onto the island. She wrapped her legs around me, and I reached for the can of whipped cream.

"Joe, what are you doing?" she asked with a nervous laugh.

I didn't speak as I gave the can a good shake before popping the cap off with my thumb. I winked before spraying some into my mouth.

"Joe . . ."

But before she could protest any further, I sprayed the whipped cream on both of her breasts. She giggled until I started licking the cream off. Focusing on her nipples, I licked and sucked, flicking my tongue across the taut skin until she moaned with pleasure.

"Joe." My name was breathy on her lips as she sank her fingers into my hair.

"Lie back," I instructed, and she obeyed quickly. Christ, her obedience was making my cock even harder, and I wasn't sure how long I was going to make it before I exploded.

Lying on the island, Sarah was completely exposed to me. As I placed her feet on the edge of the island, I had a perfect view of her glistening pussy. I leaned forward and sprayed whipped cream from her chest down to just above her pussy. I took my time lapping up the cream, nibbling and sucking her skin along the way. Once I had cleaned every inch of the cream from her body, I nestled myself between her thighs, draping her legs over my shoulders.

"Joe . . ." Her voice came out as a whimper as she tilted her head up to look at me. I placed gentle kisses along the inside of her thighs, my eyes never leaving hers.

"It's okay, sweetheart. Lie back and enjoy." As she did, I continued my exploration of her thighs, moving ever closer to her pussy. I could smell her arousal and couldn't wait any longer. With one long lick, I dragged my tongue through her center and landed on her clit. Her body hitched as she let out a strangled moan.

"Are you okay, sweetheart?" I asked, not wanting to hurt or upset her in any way. I wanted her to enjoy this.

Without speaking, she grabbed my hair, pulling my face back to her center. I chuckled and began again, slowly stroking her with my tongue. Satisfied that she was relaxing into the sensation, I began working her clit. I moved my tongue in fast circles before sucking on her, reveling in her wetness. Her breathing became erratic as she let out soft moans and grabbed at my arms.

"Fuck me with your tongue."

My heart stopped, and I looked up. Had I really heard that?

Sarah leaned up to look at me before begging breathlessly, "*Please.*"

Craving the deeper connection myself, I left her clit and inserted my tongue inside her. I watched as her eyes rolled back into her head and smiled to myself. God, I fucking loved getting a woman off. And being able to get Sarah off? That was a dream come true. I continued fucking her with my tongue, her moans growing louder. Her body started to tremble, and I knew she must be close. I continued to lap her up, focusing on her clit once again. She grabbed my hair tighter, bucking with her growing pleasure. A few seconds later she cried out my name, and damn, it sounded like heaven.

"Oh yeah, baby," I murmured against her skin. I tried to keep going, but she pleaded with me to stop.

"It's . . . too . . . sensitive," she whispered.

I stopped and helped her up into a sitting position, pulling her close to me. She was still coming down from the high of her orgasm as she wrapped her arms around my neck. I kissed her forehead and her cheeks before placing my lips on hers.

"You okay, sweetheart?"

She peered up at me, a satiated look in her eyes. "That was . . . incredible."

I smiled at her response. She sounded surprised, and I wondered how long it had been since a man had fully satisfied her. I imagined her ex hadn't done the job properly, which made my blood boil thinking about what he'd done to her. As I lifted her, her legs wrapped around my waist, and I struggled to resist the urge to press her against the wall and claim her. I wanted to do this right. I wanted to do it for her. This night was all about her pleasure, not mine.

Sarah

INCREDIBLE. I'D JUST HAD AN earth-shattering orgasm on Joe's kitchen island, his tongue pleasuring the most intimate part of me, and the only way I could think to describe it was incredible. It was so much more than that, but my mind couldn't find the words. I didn't imagine at the start of the evening that this was where the night would take us, but surprisingly, I was glad it did. I'd been holding on to so much hurt and pain that I hadn't allowed myself to experience any kind of joy or pleasure. Isolating myself had been my only escape, but tonight proved I still craved human interaction. A man's touch. Joe's touch. He'd broken through the last piece of wall I had built, and I was left completely at his mercy. I didn't want to be anywhere else.

Joe carried me to his bedroom as I trailed kisses along his neck. He placed me on the bed, and I sat up on my knees, grabbing at him as he started to back away. I unbuttoned his shirt, kissing every inch of exposed skin until I reached his waist, his sounds of pleasure spurring me on. He removed his shirt and bent down, grabbing my face in a passionate kiss.

Fumbling with his belt buckle, I unclasped it and undid his pants, pushing them to the floor. His erection was solid under his boxer briefs as I pulled them down, his dick bobbing out from the restraint of the fabric. I took him in my hand, admiring his impressive length. Pre-cum had leaked from his tip, and looking up at him, I slowly licked it off. He let out a hiss and wrapped a hand in my hair, pulling my face back to look at him. I wanted nothing more than to please him, but as I tried to take his dick into my mouth, he stopped me. Tugging me toward him, he crashed his lips against mine before I pulled away.

"Did I do something wrong?" I asked him, worried that I'd crossed a line.

"Christ, no." Joe looked at me, his eyes hooded. "I would love nothing more than to have my cock in that sweet mouth of yours."

My pussy clenched at his words. With the high of my orgasm over, I craved something more. I wanted him inside me, needed him inside me.

"But tonight is about your pleasure. I want to make you come over and over until you are thoroughly satisfied," he continued. "And then, I want to fuck you until all thoughts of him are erased from your mind."

I yanked him to me, kissing him with frantic need. I sucked his lower lip as his fingers stroked my nipples, sending a shock wave to my core. He picked me up and shifted me further up the bed.

"On your knees," he commanded.

I obeyed, and he moved behind me, gently pushing me forward until my forearms rested on the bed. I felt exposed with my ass in the air, but I trusted him. He left a trail of kisses on my lower back and ass cheeks before settling over me. He moved his arm between my legs, and from behind, he started circling my clit with his finger. I gasped, pleasure shooting through me like wildfire. He moved his finger down until he reached my opening, slowly inserting it inside. A loud groan escaped me, and I covered my mouth, embarrassed at the noise I had made.

"Don't be afraid to voice your pleasure, sweetheart," Joe murmured in my ear, his free hand stroking my arm. "I want you to. It helps me know what you like or don't like."

He removed his finger before plunging it back into me. Over and over he continued to fuck me with his finger, and I couldn't help the grunts and moans that escaped my lips. It felt so good to have something other than a vibrator inside of me. Something real and warm.

His erection dug into my thigh, and I spoke his name, desperate to find my release again. Removing his fingers, he pulled me against him. With his chest to my back, I could feel him breathe, his body tense. He wrapped a hand around my throat, his grip gentle yet firm.

"Joe," I breathed.

"Say my name again." His tongue trailed along my jawbone, and I couldn't find the words to speak.

"My name. Say it," he growled.

"Joe," I whimpered.

"Good girl."

He plunged his finger back into my pussy, hooking it to capture a spot I'd never felt before. He continued working me for a few more moments, his thumb joining to rub my clit. Stars formed in my eyes, and before long, the sweet, satisfying heat of my orgasm ripped through me. Desperate for him, I turned my head, and he leaned forward to kiss me, our breaths erratic.

In one swift movement, Joe picked me up and placed me on my back. He continued to kiss me as he reached into his bedside drawer, pulling out a condom. He leaned back and rolled it on, his eyes roaming my body. Leaning forward, he gripped my hip with one hand while the other stroked my hair. His dick rested against my entrance, and I bucked my hips, needing to feel him, all of him. He entered me slowly, giving me time to adjust to his size.

"Fuck," he groaned. "You're so fucking tight. You feel so good."

I reached up, wrapping my hands around his neck, and pulled him in for a kiss. He removed himself from me, the sensation causing an empty void. I didn't want him to stop, but before I could protest, he spoke.

"I want you to be mine, Sarah," Joe said, his eyes searching mine.

"I'm yours."

As soon as the words left my mouth, he plunged into me, his cock filling me entirely. Tears stung my eyes at the welcomed pain, pain that quickly subsided into pleasure. Our bodies moved in perfect rhythm, our moans echoing around the bedroom. I clung to him as if he were my lifeline, the only thing keeping me from floating away. His grunts became more forceful, and I knew he was nearing his climax. He reached down and started circling my clit, the sensation almost too much.

"Come with me, Sarah," he said through heavy breaths. That was all it took. I shattered against him as his groans filled the room, his own orgasm ripping through him. He pulled me against him, and we kissed, our moans getting lost in each other's mouths. We clung to each other for what felt like an eternity before Joe got up to remove the condom. He came back to bed, pulling me close to him, and I rested my head on his chest. We were quiet, the silence a stark contrast to the noises we were making just moments ago. I absently played with his dark chest hair, wishing we could stay in this moment forever.

"Did you enjoy yourself?" Joe asked, breaking the silence.

I let out a small laugh. "Yes, very much. You?"

"Oh, God, yes." He kissed my forehead before settling back into silence. My heart hammered in my chest as anxiety started racing through me. What if this was it? I didn't want this to be over. I didn't want just one night with him.

"What are you thinking about, sweetheart?" Joe asked. He always knew when something was bothering me. Even now, he could sense it.

"Nothing." I didn't want to sound needy or emotional after what we just did. Joe leaned up on his elbow and reached for my chin, pulling my face up to look at him.

"What's wrong, Sarah?"

I had nothing to lose by telling him the truth, and I knew I would feel better if I didn't keep it bottled up.

"What do we do now?"

"What do you mean?" Joe took an errant strand of hair and tucked it behind my ear. His touch was gentle, loving, and I wasn't sure I could bear to lose him.

"Where does this leave us? Do we just go back to work on Monday like nothing happened? I'm not a one-night-stand kind of girl, Joe. I shouldn't have let it go this far." I sat up, wiping tears from my eyes. How would I be able to face him at work after what we just did? At the end of the day, he was still my boss.

"Hey, Sarah, wait a minute. Come here," he said as he scooted closer to me. He wrapped his arms around me and placed gentle kisses on my temple. "This isn't a one-night stand, Sarah. I want to be with you and not for just one night, one week, one month. I want you for good, if you'll have me."

I looked at him in disbelief. My mind couldn't comprehend what he was saying. He wanted me? And not just for a fling?

"What are you saying, Joe?"

"Isn't it obvious, Sarah? I meant what I said before. I want you to be mine. Not just for Valentine's Day. I want you to be mine to keep." He sat up and pulled a box out of his dresser drawer and placed it in my hand. I hesitated a moment, peering up at him.

"Open it."

Joe smiled, and I knew I would do anything to see him smile like that. I opened the box, nervous as to what I was going to find inside. Sitting in the black velvet was a single key attached to a heart keychain. I looked up at Joe in confusion, his gaze intense on mine. Picking up the key, I studied it before looking back at him, not sure how I should respond.

"It's a key to your own office," Joe explained. "I want us to run the company together. Co-partners, if you will. In business and in life."

I covered my mouth with my hand to keep the sob from bursting through my lips. Closing my eyes, I reminisced about our evening together, from our ability to be open with each other to the amazing sex. I wanted to always feel like this. Feel like I mattered. Feel like I was loved. It might have taken years, but I finally found that person in Joe.

"Please say yes?" He looked at me with those devastatingly beautiful blue eyes.

"Yes!" I squealed, and wrapped my arms around his neck, straddling him while we kissed.

"Wait, Miss Oliver. I almost forgot." Laying me on my back, Joe whispered in my ear, "I still owe you a punishment for taking over my desk."

I giggled and reached around him to grab his ass. "I'm ready, Mr. Thatcher."

As he kissed me, I knew that I'd found my happily ever after. He was my future and I was his. His to keep.

About the Author

Ann Marie Croft lives in the Wichita, Kansas, area with her husband and their spunky Boston Terrier. A longtime writer of romance, she's never had the courage to share her work until now. "Mine to Keep" is her publishing debut, and Ann Marie couldn't be more thrilled to share her writing with the world.

In her spare time, she loves to crochet, cross stitch, and read all the spicy books she can.

You can find Ann Marie on:

Instagram @annmariecroft_author
Facebook @annmariecroftauthor

CUPID'S CROOKED ARROW

Cupid's Crooked Arrow

Nichole Steel

Chapter 1: Jagger

FUCK ME . . . MY HEAD IS throbbing with the worst headache I have had all month. I rub my temples before stacking this month's invoices into a neat pile on my desk. The club's books can wait another day. I need to get this headache under control.

Moving from my oak desk, I swing the big office door open. "Ryan!" I yell down the hall, and in thirty seconds flat, my tall, blonde, and overeager assistant stands in front of me.

"Yes, Mr. Carter?" She smiles and clasps her hands in front of her. The motion pushes her tits together, and I know it's done on purpose. Like I said, she is always overeager.

"I've got a migraine," I mutter. Ryan has been with me long enough to know what is being asked of her without me spelling it out.

"Of course, sir." She nods and drops to her knees. No one comes to the basement unless I summon them, so there is no need to worry about someone seeing.

She fumbles with my belt buckle, and my cock hardens with anticipation. Finally, she gets the damn thing undone, and my cock springs free.

She stares up at me before wetting her lips and takes me into her mouth until I hit the back of her throat.

"Fuuuckk," I groan, and lace my hands into her hair. She has never been anything special to me. Just someone to help me manage my schedule and occasionally dump my load into when my headaches get out of hand. A good orgasm is the only thing that gets rid of them.

Taking control, I fuck her face at a punishing pace as the poor thing chokes on my cock. Tears stream down her cheeks, but I'm too damn close to give her any sort of reprieve. My balls pull up, and I spill my load down her slender throat.

God, that feels good, and almost instantly my headache starts dissipating. Once I release her, she stands, breathless as some of my cum drips down the side of her lip.

"Thank you, Ryan." Nodding to her, I tuck myself back into my jeans. She shifts uncomfortably like she has something to say, but this is far from the first time she has sucked me off. "What?" I bark.

"Well, sir, I was thinking, with today being Valentine's Day, that maybe we could go out this evening?"

Jesus, she is a ballsy woman to be asking me out.

"No. This is nothing more than business. You knew this when you took the job and agreed to help with my headaches on the side. If you feel like you need more, then it may be time I find someone else to help bring me relief," I bite out, and straighten my suit coat.

"I know the boundaries and love assisting you in all areas, sir. I apologize for asking," she says, looking at my feet.

"As you should. Now, please get Nathan on the phone and tell him to get his ass down here with my shit."

She only nods and scurries away to her desk, and I head up to the main floor.

We won't open for a few more hours, but my club, Dancing Brandy's, will be filled soon enough. If Nathan fails to get me my liquor order as promised, he can call himself a dead man.

Chapter 2: Zoey

"PLEASE TELL ME THIS IS not the hot-ass date you have planned to-night?" my best friend and roommate, Nyla, asks from the doorway of my bedroom.

I'm sitting on my bed in my favorite pink pajama pants and tank top, with a glass of white wine on the nightstand, clutching my favorite book to my chest.

"What? This is a hot date." I shrug at her. "My book boyfriend and my vibrator will treat me just fine this evening."

"Nope, this is a cry for help. When was the last time you got railed by a real-life man?"

"Um . . . can I plead the fifth on that?"

Truth is, it's been months. Six months ago, I broke up with my boy-friend of two years and haven't been with anyone since. Not from lack of desire, but men can suck, and at least with Buzz in the drawer I am guaranteed an orgasm.

"Okay. That's it. We are going out tonight. We'll go to Dancing Brandy's, and then you will go home with someone who isn't me."

"Ugh, Nyla," I protest, but she comes over to me and yanks me to my feet.

"No. You're not arguing this. It's high time you get out in the world and get laid by something that isn't battery powered."

"Fine," I concede, because Nyla is insufferable when she sets her mind to something, and if I hadn't agreed, she would have brought somebody back for me. She's fucking nuts, but God knows I love her for it.

"Yay!" she squeals, and starts ushering me out of my room and into hers. "I have a new dress that will be perfect on you!"

A little while later, I stand in front of Nyla's full-length mirror, cursing myself for not fighting her harder. The dress she had me put on is cherry red and covered in glitter, but that's not the worst part. It's strapless, stops mid-thigh, and is so tight it's like it's been painted onto my skin.

"Oh my—" Nyla looks me over with a grin the size of Texas. "Zo, you look gorgeous!"

I shift uncomfortably. "Really?"

I never wear clothes like this or go out to clubs. My ex was an extreme introvert, and I got used to never going out. Now, I thoroughly enjoy living vicariously through my books.

"Girl, you look so damn good you would tempt cupid himself."

We both laugh at that.

"Thank you. You look great too."

"Yeah, yeah, we both know you look better," she teases, modeling her black leather leggings and hot-pink bra top before picking up the wine glass from her dresser.

I wish I had Nyla's confidence. She doesn't give a damn what anyone thinks and lives her life the way that makes her happy.

She claps her hands. "Okay, now let's fix your hair and get some makeup on you."

I just roll my eyes and walk to her bathroom. I am committed to this now. May as well let her doll me up how she wants.

Chapter 3: Nathan

JAGGER IS UPSET ABOUT MY screwup—that much is certain—but that fucker has been wound too tight since the day he was born. He likes to act like the club is his, but we opened it together about five years ago and have been friends since we were little kids living next door to each other.

Driving down the main strip, I pass way too many signs advertising candies, flowers, and stuffed bears. Please someone tell me who on God's green earth needs a five-foot teddy bear. Valentine's Day has always been a load of crap that the hallmark industry created to make more money. I know there is real history to it, but cupid's arrow is not all it's cracked up to be.

My phone lights up in the center console, and I don't even need to look at it to know it's Jagger.

"Emergency liquor runner reporting for duty. How can I help you?"

"There would be no emergency liquor runs if you remembered to place the order on time, fucker!"

Great, he is extra bristly tonight.

"Calm the hell down. I'm three blocks away, okay?"

"Whatever, just get here. We open in less than an hour." With that, he ends the call.

I am no idiot; I know tonight is a big night for us. Valentine's Day always brings out the couples looking to lavish their dates, and the singles looking for their special someone.

I pull up to the club where our bouncers and security team are waiting for me out back to help unload. Jagger must have everyone on edge this evening, but the boys and I make quick work of it while Jagger hounds the waitstaff and bartenders about God knows what.

"All right, security, we all know how tonight is going to go, and I don't need to tell you how to do your jobs. Jagger and I will be here for a while, but as always, Ryan will be here until close. Any questions?" I'm met by shaking heads, not that I expected any different. These men have all worked for us for several years now. "We open in twenty, so get to your posts." Without another word, they all disperse to where they need to be.

Jagger strides out of the back storage room and heads straight for me. He looks as menacing as ever, but that is part of what I like about him. "Did you brief security?" His eyes scan over the men.

"I did. You know, I actually know how to do my job."

"Knock your shit off, Nate. I don't have the patience for it," he barks at me, but we both know I enjoy his bite, so it's not much of a threat.

"Nah, my shit is what keeps things interesting." I stuff my hands into my pockets and turn to face him. "So, I plan to have fun tonight. Are you going to join me or just grimace all evening?"

"Fuck off. The big boys have work to do," he snarls at me as he storms off.

Yeah, he answered that exactly how I thought he would, but I'll find a pretty pussy all for myself tonight and he can sit at home like the stick-in-the-mud he is.

Chapter 4: Zoey

THE CLUB IS BOUNCING WITH the bass of the obnoxious techno music when we arrive, and to my surprise, it's already packed with people. You would think with it being the holiday of love, there would be more people wooing their significant other.

Dancing Brandy's is the hottest club in Atlanta, and I see why. There are two floors. The bar, the dance floor with neon lights, and the DJ stage are on the first floor. The second floor appears to be VIP, because private booths overlook the balcony, with servers walking around and a security guy blocking the stairs, and everyone up there is dressed to the nines.

"What do you want to drink?" Nyla asks me over the music.

"Water is fine." I pat uncomfortably at my dress, feeling more than ever like I am revealing too much skin.

"Umm, no, I'll get you a vodka cranberry," she states, and then whisks off to the bar.

With every passing minute, I regret more and more not fighting her harder. I'm not built for this. I met my ex in a coffee shop and now she expects me to meet someone here and go home with them.

Someone smacks my ass, causing me to yelp in surprise as a man steps in front of me. To say this guy is nothing special is an understatement. He is tall, with spiky blond hair, and wearing a plain black T-shirt with skinny jeans.

"Look at you. Aren't you just a sweet little cherry ripe for the picking?"

Gross. I roll my eyes at him. "Excuse me! You don't get to touch me whenever you please."

"What, you dress like that and expect men to keep their hands to themselves? Yeah right." He scoffs and steps into my space, reaching down and touching my bare thigh.

"Ugh! Go get fucked, asshat!" I yell, and shove him back from me.

He smacks into a man who towers over him and is built like a truck. He growls and grabs the dude's shirt collar. "You think it's fun to touch women when they clearly don't want you to?" His voice is dangerously threatening.

"No, I—"

"I should beat you to a bloody pulp for this, but I'm sure your time will come soon enough." He shoves him in the direction of the door and runs a hand through his shaggy black hair. "Now, get the hell out of my club!" he orders, and the guy runs away like a scared little puppy.

He turns his attention to me now, his chocolate-brown eyes raking over me almost like he is measuring me up. This guy screams danger, but an electric current surges between us and draws me to him.

"Are you okay?" he asks while fixing his tailored suit jacket, but my mouth is frozen. My brain can't form what to say.

He clears his throat and raises his eyebrows, clearly annoyed by my lack of response.

"Yes. Um . . . Thank you. I'm Zoey, by the way."

The corner of his mouth pulls up into an almost smile. "Jagger." He takes a step closer to me and puts his hands into his pockets. "Are you here with anyone, Zoey?"

"Yes, my friend Nyla is getting drinks at the bar."

He nods, and his eyebrows furrow like he is contemplating something. "What does your friend look like?"

I don't really understand why that matters to him, but it's not like it's a secret.

"She is short with brown hair and wearing black pants with a pink bra top. Why?"

"I need to tell my security who to look for and bring up to my booth. I would like you to join me."

My stomach somersaults at his statement. *My club. My booth.* Holy hell, this whole place is his. His very presence alone is commanding, but when he walked up, I never would have imagined he was the owner. Now he is asking me to his booth! He could have anyone in this room, but somehow, I caught his eye. I should refuse. Every fiber of my being is screaming I should walk away, but I can't.

"I would like that," I sputter out like the inexperienced idiot I am, but that almost smile returns, and I can't help but gush a little on the inside when I see it.

Chapter 5: Jagger

I SAW HER THE MOMENT she entered downstairs. She was like a damn homing beacon with that short sparkly red dress on. Her strawberry-blonde hair was long and loose over her shoulders, and her lips were as cherry red as her dress.

I don't play with women; they get too attached and are easily hurt. So, I watched her with no intent to do anything past that, but then her friend left her. She looked unsure what to do with herself as she gaped at the dance floor and nervously brushed at her dress. It was cute and so innocent. Usually, the girls who come in here are whores looking to shack up with powerful men. She was clearly a fish out of water.

Then that fuckboy touched her. I can't explain what happened, but something red hot lit up inside me, and I found myself next to them in a minute. She held her own with him, and that made her even more intriguing. How does something so innocent and delicate have the tongue of a sword?

When I return to my booth, Nathan is there. He stands and smiles as soon as he spots the guest I have brought. I assume this is his so-called "playboy charm." She stands next to me and shifts uncomfortably like she doesn't know what to do with herself. Hell, I barely know what to do with her. The last time I brought a woman up here was almost a year ago, and that ended in disaster. If I want pussy, I just bring them to my office. There is a reason I have a solid oak desk, and looking at her, that is probably where I should have taken her. It's unfair for me to think she can handle both of us.

"Hey there, I'm Nathan. And you are?" He holds out his hand, and she takes it, sitting down next to him. I take a spot across from them to watch how this plays out, but I'm still close enough to touch her if I want to. It's our unspoken rule that women brought to the booth are meant to be shared, though I rarely partake these days. I haven't been interested in the women Nathan's brought up here recently, so he just brings them back to the apartment we share for himself to enjoy.

"I'm Zoey. Are you part of his security?" Her eyes dart between us, trying to figure out why he is here.

Nathan bites his lower lip, suppressing a chuckle. "Straight to the point. I like it." He pauses to take a sip from his whiskey glass. "No, I'm not part of the security. I'm part owner of this club, and Jagger's best friend."

She toys with her dress and bites her bottom lip. The sight has my dick starting to throb, and a vision of her on her knees before me fills my mind. I have to will it away while Nate flashes me a look of approval, which I don't fucking need.

"Are you having fun this evening?" he asks her.

"Yeah, I guess. This isn't my normal scene." She looks around the room as she answers, as if she is looking for something, and I assume it's her friend.

My head of security approaches my booth, holding a short cocktail and a napkin. "Sorry to interrupt. I found the woman you described, and she gave me this for you."

He hands the beverage and the napkin with scribbling on it to Zoey, and her eyes widen. My gut twists in concern. The fuck . . . I don't get concerned, but for some odd reason, I don't like the face she makes.

"Everything okay?" I ask.

"Yeah, just a slight hiccup. Nyla decided to go home for the evening." She is trying to sound casual, but she doesn't like the fact she got left here alone. It's written all over her face.

"Oh, well, we will make sure you're taken care of this evening. You have my word."

At that she takes a long drink from her glass. I feel the need to bring some peace to the anxiety radiating off her. She is sweet and innocent, and God does that make me want to defile her even more.

Leaning in close to her ear, I don't miss how her breathing hitches. "Even if it means just giving you a ride home."

Chapter 6: Zoey

I MAY ACTUALLY KILL HER. Too bad I wasn't built for prison life. She left me here with these men and went home. I look at the note she wrote on the napkin the bouncer gave me.

Damn, girl, you work fast! How did you manage to score so big?! I'm heading home, so have fun with the owner! Get some, please, for both our sakes! –Nyla

PS: If he is a total creep, there is a gift card for an Uber in your app. XX

She was slightly off, though; I am not sitting here with one owner but two, and I'm pretty sure both are flirting with me.

Nathan is just as good-looking as Jagger, but rather than dark and alluring, he has a playboy look to him. His messy brown hair and a studded earring in each ear definitely sold me on that vibe, and with his looks, he should wear that title like a crown.

"So, Zoey. Tell me about yourself," Nathan says casually, shifting so one arm is on the back of the booth and the other rests on the table in front of us. The change of position shows off just how much muscle lies beneath that suit jacket. Hell, if he flexed, he might pop a seam.

"Well, I'm nothing special. What do you want to know?"

"I highly doubt you're nothing special," Jagger grumbles next to me, and I feel my cheeks flush pink. "How about what you like to do for fun, because obviously you're not a regular here."

"How would you know?" I ask, slightly defensive. "It's not like you can keep track of everyone who comes here every day."

"Trust me, Little Red. I would have noticed you." His voice is gravelly, and his dreamy light-hazel eyes bore into mine with a natural smirk playing across his lips. Instinctively I squeeze my thighs a little tighter together. I'm learning why my instincts screamed danger before. It's because he is dangerously sexy and has a way with words that has my sex throbbing.

Clearing my throat, I shove away the hungry beast inside. "I'm a baker and a bookworm," I blurt out like an idiot, and Nathan chuckles.

"A book worm, huh? What do you like to read?" he asks, leaning closer to me.

"Romance, mostly. Occasionally, I love a good suspense novel as well." This is simple and easy to answer. I could talk about books all night.

"Romance . . . like the sweet stuff or of the spicy variety?" He raises an eyebrow at me, and fuck, this was easy until he asked that.

"I like the sweet stuff . . . but I've always preferred spice." I cast my eyes downward as my cheeks heat to a thousand degrees.

Jesus, Zo. Find some damn confidence. You are holding the interest of two powerful and sexy men!

I shift in my seat, sitting a little straighter, willing the confidence into my bones. "What about you? What do you like outside of owning this club?"

Nathan is the one to answer me. "I'm a sports guy. I play soccer regularly and like to watch pretty much anything. Grumpy over there is a workaholic and has no hobbies besides the gym and the shooting range."

I turn and lock eyes with Jagger, who cocks a half-smile, confirming what Nathan said. "I also enjoy cooking. That's why I cook for us almost every night, asshole."

With that, Nathan stands from his seat, turning to me. "I say we leave him alone for a few and hit the dance floor. What do you say?" He extends his hand to me, and Jagger nods his approval, though I'm not sure if it's for Nathan or me.

I take his hand and rise from my seat. With his hand resting on my waist, we walk from the booth to the stairs. Anticipation and butterflies swirl in my abdomen. This is not how I saw my night going. As I reach the bottom of the stairs, my eyes wander up to the balcony. There sits Jagger with his eyes directly on me, and my skin prickles with electricity, knowing his gaze will be on me the whole time.

Chapter 7: Nathan

WHEN JAGGER BROUGHT HER TO our booth rather than his office, my interest was instantly piqued. She had to be something special to hold his eye. She is all coy and innocent, which is a refreshing change from the normally power-hungry club rats we get in here. They are good for a quick lay and not much else.

Already my mind has wandered to all the ways Jagger and I could defile her, but that is where the dance floor comes into play. I want to see if she will open up; if she will trust me, because the only way she will make it through an evening with Jagger is by leaning in instead of running away. Dancing with me is a test, and she doesn't even know it.

Getting to the dance floor, she looks around nervously, but I take hold of her hips and pull her flush against my body. "If you don't like it, just say so and we'll go back to VIP, okay?"

She nods and begins swaying her hips to the beat of the music. This shy thing lets go and rocks into me as she runs her hands over my shoulders and into my hair.

I'm not sure what happened, but it's like she lets go and is now living in the moment with me. My cock throbs, and if this was our apartment, I would have her naked in two seconds. I spin her so her back is to my front, and she throws her head back against my shoulder. As I run my hands down her sides, her breathing shudders.

I press my rock-hard appendage to her backside. "You feel what you're doing to me, Red? I'm aching for you." If I thought she would shy away, I'm pleasantly surprised when she presses into me harder. "Are you wet for me under that dress of yours?"

Her voice is husky with need as she says, "So fucking wet." She rocks harder into me.

Holy shit . . . If this goes on much longer, we won't make it back to the apartment, because I'll fuck her on Jagger's desk myself.

"What do you say we get out of this club and go somewhere I can take care of you properly?"

"Yes . . ." She sounds so fucking needy. "But what about Jagger?"

"I'll text him and he can choose to meet us at the car or not."

"You mean he will join us, too, if he wants?" Concern laces her voice, and her body stiffens.

"If you want this to be just you and me, say the word. No one will make you do anything you don't want to," I say soothingly into her ear, and she relaxes once again into my arms.

"No, invite him to join. It's just I've never been with two people at the same time before."

This is no shock, but open communication is so important with intimate situations. Her admission is just another reason she is a good fit for us to bring back to the apartment.

Leading her from the dance floor, I pull out my phone to message Jagger.

Nate: She's ready and interested. Meet us at the car if you care to join this evening.

Jagger: I saw. Meet you in five and keep your cock out of her until I get there.

Chapter 8: Zoey

WHAT THE HELL DID I just get myself into? I've only ever slept with two men my entire adult life, and now I'm on my way to an apartment to sleep with two at the same time. On the dance floor, I felt confident, sexy, and like I could handle anything these men threw at me. Now, with every passing second that confidence is being replaced with uncontrollable nerves.

Nathan is driving while I ride as the passenger princess. Jagger is in the back seat, playing on his phone, and they both seem oblivious to how nervous I'm becoming.

He pulls the car into a large parking garage, and I shift in my seat, knowing the time to show up for these men is coming quickly. If Nyla were here, she wouldn't have an ounce of hesitation and would rock their damn worlds. But me, about the only thing I am confident in is that I can suck a man off with expert-level skill.

After Nathan parks the car, Jagger climbs from the back seat and opens my door for me.

"Thank you." I smile at him and move toward Nathan, who is standing at the hood of the car. I follow him to the elevator, and he gestures for me to walk in first.

"After you, Red."

I walk in, and the realization of how unsafe this is smacks into me. These guys could be serial killers! I hardly know them, but I find myself blindly following this unparalleled desire. I guess guys aren't the only ones with half their brain located between their legs.

With all of us piled in and the elevator climbing the building higher and higher, I pull out my phone and drop a location pin for Nyla. At least if anything happens to me, she will know where my body can be found.

"You guys aren't serial killers, are you?" I ask, letting my anxiety win.

Jagger chuckles, and his eyes lock on to mine. "No, but if that's a turn on for you, I'm open to role play," he teases, and my cheeks heat.

Once we reach the penthouse, the elevator opens to a kitchen. The gray tile floors, light-blue walls, and long marble countertops topped with every appliance you could wish for look like they came straight out of a magazine. A beautiful island with a bar top and stools sits in the middle, and on the back wall is a gas range and two ovens.

"Oh my God! This is your kitchen?" I squeal, a little bit too excited. The baker in me is screaming to use it.

"I told you; I like to cook. This room is my happy place." Jagger sounds proud of my adoration as he steps in front of me. Nathan comes up behind me, placing his hands on my hips. This is it. This is why they brought me here and why I wanted to come. Still, I tense at their touch.

"So, are you going to take me to the bedroom now?" My voice is shaky, and Jagger tucks a strand of hair behind my ear.

"No," he says sternly, taking me by surprise. "Nothing will happen this evening unless you're comfortable and want it. Zoey, you are in control."

His words help release the pressure I've been feeling. I may be slightly nervous, but I still want this. I want to touch the flames that have the potential to burn me, and the closer they get, the more confident I feel in knowing they won't.

"Well, if we are not going to the bedroom yet, maybe we can utilize this beautiful kitchen? You make some snacks, and I make dessert?"

Jagger's lips tilt up into an almost smile.

"Well, I'm always down for food!" Nathan cheers, and I can't contain my laughter. Jagger rolls his eyes at his outburst.

Nathan goes to the bar and sits down while Jagger moves to the fridge and starts pulling out stuff.

"The kitchen is yours. Just do me a favor and bake something with frosting." Jagger has a dangerous glint in his eyes, and my curiosity spikes.

"Why do you need something with frosting?" I ask, and he turns, wrapping his arms around me, twisting me so my back is pulled into his firm chest.

My body feels electric under his touch, and heat sears at the apex of my thighs. Fuck, this man is a walking orgasm with his dark and quiet personality.

Leaning close to my ear, he says, "I want some sweet cream, Little Red. Now be a good girl and do as you're told."

I melt into a puddle at his words. I've never been called a "good girl" before, and I have never been with a man like Jagger, which is why I feel like a woman possessed.

"Yes, daddy," I whimper, and his hold tightens as a growl escapes him. Then he releases me, steps back, and smacks my ass, causing me to yelp.

"Get to work and show me your baking skills now before I fuck you over this counter."

Doing as I'm told, I go to pull out the ingredients from the pantry next to the fridge, but only enough to make a small batch of cupcakes. Jagger appears to be making some sort of chip dip, but I am fumbling with the batter, because I can't take my eyes off him.

"Do you have a cupcake pan? And Nathan, will you preheat the oven to three seventy please?"

"Yeah, no problem, and the pans are over there in front of Jagger in the bottom cupboard."

I move over to where Jagger is working, motioning toward the cupboard in front of him. He doesn't pause or shift. "Excuse me." I sound so meek. Feminist Zoey would be disgusted with herself, so I guess it's a good thing I have no interest in being a strong, independent woman around these men.

"I'm not moving, Zoey. So, if you want that pan, you better figure out how to take it." He raises his eyebrows at me in challenge.

Challenge accepted. Aware he might end up with a show of my lace panties in this short dress, I drop to my knees at his side without breaking eye contact. Then I lean forward, crawl in front of him, and open the cupboard. His eyes sear into me, but God does this feel so powerful. Grabbing the pan I need, I force his legs open and crawl between them. He lets out an umph, but I press on. When I am almost all the way through, I raise my eyes to Nathan, who stares at me with a hungry gaze.

"If I knew you were going to do that, Red, I would have made the oven wait." His voice is deep and husky. Fuck me, this beast inside me wants to be devoured. He palms himself, and it's all the confirmation I need to know he wants me too.

Standing, I move over to the mixing bowl and add the batter to the cupcake pan, refusing to look over my shoulder at the men I am sure are watching. I want to say fuck the baking and snacks and tell them I can be their snack. Fuck, I am starting to sound like one of the characters from my books. I'm no longer a woman living vicariously through my books; I'm the new damn novel.

With the cupcakes in the oven, I decide to make whipped vanilla frosting. Something sweet, easy, and creamy, just like Jagger asked for. At some point Jagger stops cooking and leans on the bar, watching me just like Nathan is. Their collective stares make me feel sexy, and damn do I love it.

The timer for the cupcakes sounds, and Nathan is quick to pull them out, setting them on the stovetop. Jagger moves from around the bar at the same time to stand in front of me. He places his hands on the counter, one on either side of me, effectively trapping me.

"Is my frosting done?"

"Y-Yes." My breaths are shaky with him this close to me, but not because of nerves this time. No, this is anticipation as butterflies fill my belly.

He seemingly moves in slow motion as he swipes a finger through the frosting bowl and sucks it clean. Holy shit . . .

Need for this man burns my insides, and I desperately pinch my thighs together, needing to be touched. My body responds to him like a magnet to metal. I can't help but be sucked in.

Nathan walks up next to him. "Why don't you let her try her own creation?"

Jagger doesn't hesitate. He swipes another finger through the frosting and holds it in front of me. I wet my lips and take his finger into my mouth, sucking off the sweet vanilla cream, and both men groan in unison. He pulls me from the counter and presses me into Nathan, whose hands run up my bare thigh to my abdomen. His touch sends goosebumps over my skin. I feel like a live wire.

"Now, Red. If you don't like what is happening or want us to stop, just say so."

A soft moan is all that comes out of my mouth as Jagger's hands start hiking up my dress.

He freezes. "Zoey, we need words. We need to know you understand."

"Yes, I understand," I say, breathless from my need.

"Good girl," Jagger says with a devilish smirk, and the next thing I know, I am thrown over his shoulder and being carried out of the kitchen with Nathan walking close behind us, undoing his tie.

Chapter 9: Zoey

JAGGER TOSSES ME ONTO A large king-size bed, and a shirtless Nathan climbs over me, slow and teasing. I could feel his thick muscles through his clothes, but my imagination seriously underestimated just how attractive he really is. Both shoulders and biceps are covered in tattoos, and his ripped abs go with his sculpted arms.

When he finally is directly above me, he kisses me softly. His tongue invades my mouth, but I am too worked up to go slow. I nip his bottom lip, and he growls. His kiss becomes firm and demanding as he presses himself into me. I run my hands over his firm back, loving the feeling of his skin.

"You going to tease her all night, Nate?" Jagger asks with a rough, husky tone.

Nathan sits up and, without warning, grabs my dress and rips it open, exposing my lace bra and panties.

"My God . . ." I say in shock, but this is sexy as hell.

"I know I'm like Cupid himself, but there is no need to pray. I'm no Roman god."

Before his words can register through my lust-filled haze, he claims my mouth once more, pulling me up, removing my bra, and pushing me back down.

Jagger comes to the side of the bed and starts painting my tits with the frosting, and the coolness on my searing-hot skin makes this so much more erotic.

"Please . . ." I whine, desperate for them.

"I love to hear you beg for us. Nate, give her some relief and suck her tits," Jagger commands, and fuck does it have me soaking my panties.

Nathan teasingly licks the frosting from my left tit, then pulls my pebbled nipple into his mouth. I mewl and arch into him, needing more, so much fucking more.

He climbs off me, only to be replaced with Jagger pulling my panties down and forcing my legs apart with his own.

"Let me look at you, baby girl," he orders.

I do as I'm told, spreading my legs wide to show him every inch of me. He stares at me with hooded eyes, and I should feel shy, but I find myself reveling in his desire.

"You're fucking soaked for us already, aren't you?"

"Yes . . ." I move my hand to touch myself, desperate for relief, but Nathan catches it.

"No, only we touch you." His words only make me more desperate for them. "What do you think, Jagger? Is she going to taste sweeter than that frosting?"

"Let's find out."

Nathan runs frosting from the inside of my knee up to my hip, and Jagger follows the line with his tongue.

He stops just above my center and looks up at me. "I'm going to eat this sweet treat now, baby girl," Jagger says, and instantly runs his tongue up my center and starts circling my clit.

Moaning loudly, I lace my fingers in his hair as his tongue devours me. "Ah, don't stop. That feels so good." I throw my head back and feel myself building.

Nathan removes his pants and begins fisting his large cock as he watches, but I'm here for both of them to enjoy.

"Let me . . ." I moan, and he steps closer, swiping some frosting over his tip. I wet my lips and take him into my mouth, swirling my tongue over the sweet vanilla flavor. He groans and starts pumping into my mouth as Jagger thrusts two fingers into me with the same rhythm.

Nathan laces his fingers into my hair, and I moan around his dick. Both of them are worshiping my body right now, and I've never felt more alive.

My climax builds higher until my thighs start to quiver, and Nathan removes himself. "I want to hear you come, Red. Say his fucking name."

His words send me over the edge. "JAAGGER . . ." I mewl, and he continues to work me, dragging out my pleasure as long as possible.

"Such a good girl for me," Jagger growls, standing from the bed, allowing Nathan to take his place.

He stares down at my aching and needy pussy, then dips his head low, tasting my sensitive center. "You are so much sweeter than that frosting." He runs a finger through me and places it in front of me. "Taste yourself."

Their filthy talk fuels me, and I lean up, sucking his finger into my mouth and licking it clean.

"Fuck, Red. You're going to have me busting in two seconds if you keep this up."

Jagger is naked now and stands next to my face. His cock is large like Nathan's, but curved, and I know that thing will feel wicked inside me.

"Nate is going to fuck you now, baby girl, and I'm going to fuck that beautiful mouth of yours."

"Yes . . ." is the only word I can form with the need to feel them overshadowing any apprehension.

"That's my good girl."

His praise fuels the fire that is already burning inside. Nathan climbs over me, kissing and nipping at my skin the whole way up until he hovers over me.

"Are you clean and on birth control, Red? Jagger and I got tested last week and are clean, but I've got condoms in the drawer if you're uncomfortable getting fucked bare."

"I have an IUD and I'm clean. Please, Nathan, just fuck me."

I've never skipped the condom before, even with my ex, but with these two, I can't stand the idea of that barrier. They have proven I'm the priority tonight, so I know I can trust their word of being clean.

In one powerful thrust, he fills me completely. I arch into him, and he kisses me, claiming my mouth as he claims my needy pussy, pumping me up with a punishing rhythm, and God, it feels so fucking good.

I claw at his back, and he groans before I turn my face to Jagger. He takes his cue and presses himself to my lips, prompting me to open for him. He fucks my face while Nathan fucks my pussy, and I am already building to another glorious peak.

"Are you going to come for us again, baby girl?" I moan around his cock. It twitches in my mouth, but I want his cum somewhere else.

Pulling off him, I say, "Come on me. I want to wear you, daddy."

"Fuuuckkkkk," he groans as I take him back into my mouth. Nathan's cock starts twitching inside me, and he slams into me harder. I know he is close.

Jagger pulls from my mouth, and Nathan lifts higher off me. Ropes of Jagger's spunk cover my tits as he grunts, and I've never felt sexier.

"Fuck!" Nathan bellows as he fills me up. Then my orgasm racks through me with such ferocity I damn near black out from pleasure.

"You look so beautiful covered in me," Jagger says, leaning down to kiss me, and Nathan flops onto the bed next to me.

"That was so fucking good, Red. You and that damn pussy could be the death of me."

The post-fuck bliss is heavy, and my limbs feel like Jell-O. Jagger joins us on the bed, and we all lie there, trying to recover. When the high starts to pass, I sit up and begin climbing from the bed.

"I think I need a shower before the night ends, and boys . . . it's an open invitation." If I get to experience this only once, then I am damn sure going to take advantage. "And if you're interested, I think I would like Jagger's cock to fill up my pussy this time, but you got to catch me first."

Those boys move from the bed faster than a racehorse, and I run away like a prize to be caught, searching for the bathroom. Nathan is the one to catch me and smacks me hard on the ass, causing me to yelp, and heat floods my core.

This night is far from over, and I am damn ready for it.

Chapter 10: Jagger

ZOEY PASSED OUT BETWEEN NATE and me after the shower, and we all slept in my bed together all night. The girl is a fucking queen. I never would have guessed how good she was going to be in bed with the two of us when I first brought her up to the booth. Hell, she was better than any other woman I've brought here.

I'm pretty sure last night was just a way for her to have fun on a holiday it sucks to be single on, but I want to do that with her a hundred times more. Any other time I fuck a woman, it scratches an itch and I'm happy for them to leave. Not her. No, she has me craving her more than ever.

Moving from the bed, I throw on my pants and go to the kitchen to take the frosting bowl back and to clean up. Cleaning and working have always helped me clear my mind, which is why I do it so much. I've never craved a woman like this, and it scares me a little because she is a drug I'll probably never have again.

Grabbing three cups of coffee, I head back to my room. She looks so innocent curled up to Nate's side in my bed, like we didn't just defile her.

After setting the coffee mugs on the nightstand, I rub her back soothingly and she stirs awake, looking at me with a tired and satisfied smile. It makes my chest clench, and my cock throbs a little. *Now is not the time, little fucker.* She may be flattered by my hard-on, but I don't want to fuck her. Not yet, at least.

"How are you feeling?" I ask, searching for any indication that we were too rough on her.

"Sore, but in a good way." She sits up, and Nate wakes up as well.

"Are we going again?" He rolls over to face us, morning wood standing tall and proud. Jesus. The only time I want to see his cock is when it's entering a woman in some way.

"No, fucker. You mind covering your shit? I don't want to see your dick while enjoying my morning coffee."

"There's coffee?" Zoey asks, and I grab a mug to hand to her. She moans at the first sip, and the sound goes straight to my dick. Once again, I have to will it to stand down.

Nate climbs off the bed, grabbing his boxers and sliding them on. "I don't see why you wouldn't like seeing my dick first thing in the morning. In my opinion it's a pretty glorious sight," he teases, and of course he would think his dick is beautiful. Only fucking Nate.

"I concur." Zoey looks at him with hooded eyes, and this is seriously lining up for another round.

I change the subject. "So, Zoey, what are your plans today?"

Nate pins me with his eyes. Apparently I'm not the only one who wants to keep her around.

"Nothing, really, but I can get out of here. I hope it was okay I stayed? I don't really have a ton of experience with hookups." She starts moving from the bed, but I stop her. Cupping her cheek, I pull her gaze to meet mine.

"What if this wasn't just a hookup? Little Red, I don't think I want to let you go. I would like to see where this can go for us."

Nate climbs back onto the bed right next to her. "We could take you out on dates and share you in the evening. This doesn't have to be a one-night thing. I want to keep you, Red." He kisses her shoulder, and her eyes flutter at his touch.

"I don't want to let you go, either. Call me yours." She whimpers as she presses her body into Nathan's.

"Ours," he says.

"Only ours now, Little Red." And I claim her mouth with a searing-hot kiss. What the fuck did this little temptress do to me?

About the Author

Nichole Steel is a spicy romance author who lives in West Michigan close to Grand Rapids. She loves to write morally gray men who are obsessed with their women, and all of her stories have some darker tendencies to them. Outside of her creative space, she enjoys connecting with people and the world around her.

You can find Nichole on:
Instagram @nicholesteel.author

Visit her website at:
bio.site/NicholeSteel

FALLING

Falling

MK Edgley

"SO, THOSE ARE ALL THE themed spa specials." Serena swiped the screen of the tablet in her hand, moving it to her next checklist. "Let's go over the Valentine's drink specials."

Several of her employees groaned. She looked up from the tablet to see the dozen of them standing in a circle on the pool deck. Most were rolling their eyes or had sour expressions.

Serena sighed. "I know, I know. But come on, we don't want the golf course attendants to beat our department again, do we? I'll never hear the end of it from their manager if we lose to them *again*."

One of her employees, Hasan, raised his hand. "Yeah, but how am I supposed to ask if someone wants a 'French Kiss' or a 'Hanky Panky' with a straight face?"

"That's never stopped you before." A few people snickered. "And while we are at it, no one is to suggest getting a couple's massage with one of the guests."

Hasan spread his hands out in front of him. "Hey, that was one time!"

"Whatever. That's not—" Her phone buzzed in her pocket.

Serena's heart leapt but the feeling was almost immediately replaced with her heart hammering against her ribs. She pulled out her phone, and disappointment punched her in the gut when she saw it was just someone texting they would be late for the morning shift.

"You okay, boss?" Serena looked up to Hasan tilting his head.

She shoved the phone back into her pocket. "Fine. Uh, that is everything then. Let's get back to work. We open in less than an hour and I see only a few delightful towel animals on those chairs."

The group of employees scattered as she turned away from them. Serena then walked across the pool deck toward the pumphouse. Once inside the small shed, she flipped the switch so the filters could run, then checked that off her list of opening shift tasks on the tablet. When she exited, the manmade waterfall on one end of the pool sprang to life, creating that quintessential fountain sound.

She watched as the current agitated the previously calm water. Bubbles erupted where the stream hit the surface, sending ripples cascading outward. Serena felt something similar happening in her stomach. She thought it ironic that something so beautiful could bring such ruin. With a sigh, she walked back toward the towel station so she could take inventory.

When the pool at Tranquil Grove Resort and Spa was open for the day, Serena managed everything from the bar. As she made drinks, she blocked out the sounds of the screaming children from the pool and the giggling, happy couples that walked by. She couldn't tune out the hum of her nervous system though. Something rang in her ears like she had tinnitus. Her body operated on autopilot as her hands went through the motions, stopping to occasionally wipe sweat from her brow.

Around noon, Hasan walked up to the bar, putting down his tray. A wide smile peaked out from behind his squared off facial hair. "Miss Tate would like you to bring her the usual."

Serena stopped wiping down the bar, gritting her teeth. "And let me guess, she said it had to be me?"

"Yup." Hasan leaned on the bar with one elbow, looked out toward the pool deck, and then ran his free hand through his coif of black hair. A too-tight polo shirt hugged the young man's biceps as he looked out at the pool deck. "Did we ever decide how old she is?"

Serena's jaw twitched but she finished wiping down the bar, then took a sip of her water. "She's thirty-five."

"Huh, she does not look like she's in her thirties." Hasan turned back to face her. "Course, you don't either."

Serena scoffed. Shaking her head, she found a plastic glass and turned toward the back bar counter that held the drink machines. "Whatever."

"Listen, boss, her bikini today . . . it's . . . there are no words."

She paused, hand on the lever for the daiquiri dispenser. She closed her eyes for a brief second and sighed. "I'm sure."

Once the glass was full, she put the drink on the tray, the sides already sweating. Hasan had turned back to the pool deck while she worked. "I might have a go at the Fuentes nanny. I mean, these cougars are great and all, but they can get too attached, you know?"

"What *I* know is that you don't get paid to scam on women." The now deafening ring in her ears made it hard to keep her hands steady as she sliced a strawberry. Serena managed, putting the fruit on the rim. She topped it off with a curly straw and a tiny umbrella.

"Well, it's been a while since you've wanted to go clubbing with us, it's a lot harder to score without you being our wing—"

She cut him off. "Okay, go pretend you work here."

Hasan snapped back around, his hands up while he grimaced. "Sorry." Before walking off he added, "That bikini, I swear, you're just gonna drool everywhere."

Just then, her phone buzzed in her pocket again. She tasted bile in her throat as her hand reached for it. Finally, the screen read "Amber," though it just made her nausea worse. When Serena unlocked her phone, a rather busty photo greeted her. Two triangles of blue fabric barely covered the points marking the summits of two already voluptuous mountains. Thin strings led upward, disappearing behind her shoulders. The woman didn't show her entire face, just a devilish smile. Serena felt something stir in her abdomen, at least this time it was below her stomach.

Hasan was right—it was quite the bikini.

She briefly checked her hair in the mirror. Her shaved sides were filled with beads of sweat and the dark spikes on top she had so carefully created with hair wax had all drooped. She shrugged but then looked around. *One more time*, she thought to herself.

Serena turned back to the mirror, setting her face into a neutral expression. "So, we've been doing this a few months and I was wondering . . . ugh. No, that's not how I want to say it. Okay, I think you're really great but I kinda need . . ." Serena put her head in her hands for a second and groaned. The ringing in her ears returned. *Best it's gonna get.*

With a sigh, she picked up the daquiri to cross the pool deck. As she walked, she dodged screaming children while the lifeguard whistle blew almost constantly. The happy couples all around made her stomach feel even worse.

When she reached the grouping of private cabanas, she went straight for the last one. The beaded curtain was parted, so she stood just inside the entrance to announce herself.

Serena coughed. "Good afternoon, Miss Tate. I've got your drink here."

It was one thing to see the photo and another to see the woman in the flesh. Serena's heart beat faster, and she did salivate, though she would never admit as much to Hasan. A sheer, floral beach cover-up enveloped Amber's shoulders, but it was open, revealing the blue bikini that had caused such a stir.

The secluded, shaded area was just big enough for two lounge chairs and a side table between them. Amber read a magazine in one of the chairs. A laptop lay abandoned at her well-manicured feet while a large, beach tote rested on the ground next to her. She looked the very embodiment of relaxation.

"On the table." Amber didn't bother to look up.

Serena did as she was told, placing the drink on a coaster on the faux-wicker side table. As soon as the drink was down, a hand reached up, yanking her by the shirt collar, almost causing her to fall as she was pulled downward.

"Whoa." The empty tray clattered to the ground as Serena put her hands out to brace herself on the edge of the lounge chair. The next second, her mouth was too busy to speak.

With those plump lips on her own, tongues swirling together, her mind went blank. So wrapped up in the pleasure of kissing Amber that the feeling in her stomach dissipated for a moment. Instead, the feeling in Serena's crotch intensified.

Amber pulled away first, still holding Serena by the collar, their faces close together. "Mmm. How do you make that hideous uniform look so fucking good?" She ran her free hand through Serena's sweaty hair.

Unable to speak, Serena blinked rapidly. Amber smirked as she went in for more, kissing down Serena's neck. Serena held back a moan and then stopped her. "Hey, come on, I'm still on the clock."

"I just needed a little taste." Amber's tone feigned innocence as she batted her eyelashes.

Serena chuckled, then stood back up. "You get lipstick on me?"

Amber tilted her head a little to look at Serena's exposed neck, her loose, light brown bun fell to one side. "No and none on your shirt either. Thanks for the drink."

"Yeah, yeah." Serena took a deep breath. *Come on, like you practiced*, but her stomach felt like she was one of those people going over Niagara Falls in a barrel. She certainly had the urge to scream. "Hey, listen, I was thinking . . . that is, I wanted to, uh . . ."

Then Amber's phone rang. Serena sighed as Amber scrambled to find it in her bag, her pastoral expression replaced by a frown and furrowed brows.

"I'm so sorry. I have to take this. Ugh! I was just trying to take a break from work for two seconds!" Without waiting for a response, Amber picked up the phone. "Give me a sec," she said into the mouthpiece before reaching into her bag and pulling out a room key. She placed it into Serena's back pocket, groping her ass as she did so. Amber mouthed, "I'll see you tonight," with a seductive smile. She returned to her phone call. "Okay, I know what they said, but they are idiots. This is what they need to do . . ."

Serena had no choice but to leave.

After her shift, she changed out of her uniform in her office. She tried to eat dinner in the employee cafeteria, but her stomach hurt too much. She managed a few bites of salad before giving up and walking up the back stairwell to the tenth-floor suites.

Her stomach plummeted several times as she walked down the empty hallway. She felt as though each footstep plunged her underwater. She surfaced briefly while the current moved her ever forward toward the next precipice, rendering her helpless to avoid the gut-wrenching drop of each cascade. The lavender aromatherapy diffusers in the hallway had no effect on her. The artwork that lined the hall seemed to mock her. The serene-looking pond made her audibly grunt.

In front of the room door, she went to unlock it, but hesitated, key-card inches from the lock. She bounced on the balls of her feet, arm frozen in midair. She could just call. Or text her to meet somewhere else. She could do that and keep a level head for their discussion. She *should* do that.

She didn't.

The door lock beeped, and the luxury hotel suite came into view. Except, it was hard to see. The only light was the soft flickering of LED candles everywhere. The coffee table in the sitting area shimmered, light bouncing off the screen of the laptop that was perched haphazardly on the table's edge. The round table in the breakfast nook glowed, illuminating the papers strewn about its surface.

Despite the low light, something stood out against the beige carpet, so she looked down at her feet. A trail of rose petals led to the bedroom. Through the open door, she could make out the shape of a room service cart next to the bed.

But then Amber walked into the room. A fluffy, white cotton robe clung to her, hiding her curvaceous hips and firm tits. She tossed her wavy, russet hair over her shoulder as she rounded the corner. Serena swore her hair moved in slow motion, like one of those shampoo commercials.

Serena had to shake her head to keep her focus. Still, she was curious. "What's all this?"

Amber spread out her arms, her delicious lips curved into a wide smile. "Happy Valentine's Day!"

Serena scrunched her eyebrows together. "That's not for another week."

"Yes, but I will be in Phoenix by then and Chicago the day after, so I won't be able to come here." Amber started walking toward her, as Serena hadn't moved from the doorway. Every second that passed though, she felt the pull grow stronger. Serena willed herself to stay put. To stay standing. To stay clothed.

"I . . . I see. So, we're . . . actually this is kinda what I want to talk to . . . you . . . about . . ."

Before the full sentence left her mouth, Amber dropped her robe. "We can talk later."

Amber had a perfect hourglass figure. Her toned body was now adorned with black, fishnet lingerie. Red straps clung to her shoulders, circled her thighs, and crisscrossed down her torso. The garment mostly hugged her sides, only the lacy edge covering her nipples. The two pieces of fabric connected down near her groin, making a lovely "V" shape. A strap with a silver clasp ran across her sternum. Amber looked like she walked off the page of an underwear catalog. She spun and shook her hips, giving Serena a view of the entire red and black lacy outfit. The straps wove around the whole thing, complete with a single strap running the length of her ass crack.

Serena stood there with her jaw on the floor. She knew Amber's promise to talk later was a little white lie, a slight fabrication to placate her so Amber could get what she wanted. It wasn't the first time it had happened, but Serena had sworn to herself she was done after the last time.

"Uh huh." The situation was as see-through as the mesh on parts of Amber's lingerie. She knew it, Amber knew it, and for all the pep talks she gave herself, the skimpy outfit rendered her powerless. Amber even more so. Serena had passed the event horizon that was Amber's gravity.

Serena pounced. Their lips crashed together, her hands on Amber's hips as Amber held her by the face. The feeling of the rough netting with Amber's smooth skin underneath was overwhelming. She slowly walked forward while they kissed, pushing Amber backwards toward the bed. As she did, Amber seized the hem of Serena's shirt and pulled it off.

She kissed down Serena's neck, sucking at the spot in the crook that drove her crazy. Serena let out a loud moan, then dug her hands into Amber's round ass, lifting her from the ground. Amber squealed and laughed as she clung on, hands around Serena's neck and legs around her waist. Amber nibbled at her earlobe, causing Serena to hold on tighter as she walked toward her destination.

Serena threw her on the bed. Amber's body bounced, her tits rebounding pleasantly a second after the rest of her. Serena climbed between her legs, thrusting their hips together.

Amber moaned but then propped up on her elbows. "Here, let's . . ."

"No." Serena pushed her back down by her sternum and looked at her for just a second. "That outfit . . . fuck!" She moaned as she leaned down to kiss and suck at Amber's neck.

Amber giggled but it turned into another moan. "All right but I get my way with you next."

"Yup."

They kissed more while Serena ran her hands down Amber's body, admiring the lingerie as much as possible. Serena's fingers traced down the sides to Amber's hips until she felt the smooth skin of her thighs, then she moved back up again. She pulled away from Amber's mouth, using one hand to support her weight and another to lightly pinch Amber's nipples through the fabric. Serena kissed her neck, receiving squeals and moans in equal measure. The scent of Amber's flowery shampoo filled Serena's nostrils as she lost herself in pleasuring the other woman. Amber hooked her legs around Serena's, and they slowly gyrated their hips in unison.

Undoing the front clasp of Amber's lingerie, Serena let the halves of the garment fall from Amber's shoulders onto the bed. Her breasts were the size of grapefruits but there was nothing sour about them. Kneading them, Serena smirked and flicked her nipples a few times. She leaned back down to kiss Amber again, deeply. Their tongues wriggled against each other while Serena rolled Amber's nipple between her fingers.

Moaning into Serena's mouth, Amber tried to put her hands on Serena too. She released Amber's tits to snatch her hands, pinning them above her head. With a grunt, Serena lifted herself up, so their groins no longer touched, and used her knees to keep Amber's thighs down. A dark chuckle rose from Serena's chest as Amber fussed. Leaning down, she took Amber's pink, perky nipple into her mouth, sucking it slightly before using her tongue to lick circles around it.

Amber moaned and bucked but Serena was stronger. Switching nipples while Amber wriggled underneath her was a challenge, but she managed. Amber's motions made Serena shift to keep her in place and Serena's foot hit something. Lifting her head, she pulled Amber's nipple with her before releasing it with a *pop*.

She looked over to see the food service cart again. "So, what's all that?"

"Huh?" Amber looked over too. "Oh! I thought we could have some fun with dessert."

"What do you . . . oh!" Serena used her free hand to pick up the can of whipped cream.

She sprayed the white foam on Amber's nipples. Going from one to the other, she licked the sweet stuff off the already delicious peaks. Amber's moaning turned into whines. Serena chuckled more but released Amber's hands.

Looking over at the cart again, she took stock of the contents. "Let's see, ice cream. Then there's some hot fudge. Couple of strawberries and a banana. Hm, we doin' a whole little sundae thing?"

"A *sexy* sundae." Amber nodded, her face serious.

Serena laughed as she took off her black sports bra and threw it across the room before doing the same with her blue basketball shorts and black boxer briefs.

"Is this expensive?" she asked, pointing at the remaining lingerie.

Amber scoffed. "Don't care."

"Mm. Good."

Reaching over to get a spoonful of vanilla ice cream, she proceeded to put some on each nipple. A shout erupted from Amber as soon as it touched her skin, but Serena let it sit there as she worked, taking some of the hot fudge and drizzling it on top. Amber squirmed while Serena licked it off. The combination of hot and cold was delightful on her tongue, and the nipple underneath was better than a cherry on top.

Serena licked down Amber's torso, nipping and biting as she went. When she got to the bottom half of the lingerie, a damp spot in the center already greeted her. Grasping the straps hiding the real treat, Serena gave them a powerful pull. They emitted a satisfying *snap* as they broke. Amber cried out in shock. With both hands, Serena ripped the remaining fabric between her and her prize.

A set of glistening lips met Serena, and she licked her own. "Mm. So beautiful."

Reaching out, Serena traced her fingers across the newly exposed skin. There was only a thin landing strip of light brown hair, the rest of Amber's vulva felt smooth to the touch.

But she wasn't there just to look. Serena built a sundae right on top of Amber's pubic bone, just above where Amber wanted her to lick. Ice cream first, then a drizzle of hot fudge. Next, a strawberry and a banana hunk. Finally, she sprayed just another dollop of whipped cream with a cherry on top. The food dripped everywhere but it wasn't the first set of sheets they had ruined together.

"Fuck." If the fire alarm had gone off then, she would have ignored it.

Lying on her stomach, Serena hooked her arms underneath Amber's knees, and dove in. Her licks alternated between fast, short ones and long, lazy ones. Each time Serena got closer to Amber's clit, her cries of pleasure grew louder. When Serena retreated, Amber whimpered. Still, every last bite was gone within minutes.

Serena lifted her head when she finished. "That was the perfect dessert."

"P-Please!" It was the first real word Amber had managed in a while.

"Mhm."

Serena spread open Amber's folds. Bending down to take a small, teasing lick, she moaned herself. "I was wrong. *This* is the perfect dessert."

"Ngh!" Amber's back arched.

Leaning back down, Serena sucked her clit into her mouth, just as she had done her nipples. She pumped the delicious bud in and out. When she used her tongue to circle around it, Amber grabbed the back of Serena's head. The iron grip on Serena's skull made her moan. The taste as she lapped at Amber's opening was far better than either of the white, sticky substances she had eaten a second ago.

Resituating, she pushed Amber's knees to the bed and sat up. Amber's whine turned into a moan once Serena took a finger and started playing with her opening. There was no sense in leaving her waiting. Serena watched two of her fingers get swallowed up, the pressure of Amber's muscles clenching around them immensely satisfying. More moans met her ears once she was all the way inside. Leaning back down again to use her tongue, Serena held her fingers still for a moment before she gently hooked them. Amber seized her head again, this time with both hands, and started grinding against her tongue.

Amber's mewls of ecstasy fueled Serena as she massaged the spongy top wall inside her. When Serena finally thrust in earnest, she made her fingers flat on the way in, and a slight curve when she pulled out. Amber's hips attempted to go faster but Serena reveled in the power she felt in making this domineering woman wait.

Amber's noises of elation turned into frustration. Smiling against Amber's clit, Serena went faster. A wet, smacking sound accompanied each thrust. All the while, she used the broad side of her tongue on Amber's clit, like she was eating ice cream again.

Launching her hips into the air, Amber went silent. She shook and writhed. The sharp pain on Serena's head increased as Amber pulled her hair harder. Sercna kept pounding, licking even faster. After a few seconds, Amber cried out again. Her legs snapped together, crushing either side of Serena's head.

Keeping her fingers still, Serena loved the feeling of Amber's insides throbbing around her. Amber clenched Serena's digits with the same force her thighs used to trap Serena's head. Once she relaxed, her legs fell to either side. Serena pulled out gently, licking her fingers clean, and then went to lay up next to Amber's face.

They were both breathing heavily but Amber wrapped her arms around Serena and then kissed her. The saliva just added to the juices dripping on Serena's chin. Amber pulled away first, still struggling for air.

Serena just chuckled again. "Mm. You are so sexy."

"Y-Yeah."

"I really don't think I've ever seen someone as beautiful as you."

Serena had said it before, but she realized after she said it that the tone she used was not sexy or sweet. It was truthful.

In her post orgasmic bliss, Amber looked dazed, but now she snapped to attention with a slight gasp. Her breathing sped up. Before Serena could figure out the expression on Amber's face, it changed. Amber made a half moan, half whine sound, and then surged forward to kiss her.

The next thing she knew, Amber rolled them over. She pushed Serena's shoulders to the mattress and straddled her. As she rubbed herself against Serena's abs, her wetness coated her stomach, matching her chin. Reaching her hand behind her back, Amber rubbed at her clit. Serena's eyes went back into her head as she moaned but she reached out to clutch Amber's hips at the same time.

"Fuck!" she cried out as Amber shoved a finger inside of her.

Her insides clamped down on the slender finger. Digging her fingers into Amber's hips, she feverishly moved her own hips against Amber's hand. Over and over Amber thrusted. Serena's motions became more erratic with each insertion. Her moans turned into grunts.

Just as she approached the precipice of blessed release, the weight lifted from her. Her stomach felt cold, her vulva equally so. Whining, she looked up.

"Don't you dare touch yourself." Amber stood across the room, bent over, digging through her suitcase.

The sight of her perfectly round ass was enough to distract Serena from her plight for a moment. A leather harness dangled from Amber's fingers the next second. As she stepped through it, she secured it to her body, the straps cutting into her backside. She retrieved a hot pink dildo from the suitcase as well. Amber put it through the ring of the harness and then rolled a condom on the dildo before walking back over to the bed.

Leaning up as if for a kiss, Amber pulled Serena's legs to the edge of the bed instead, so they dangled off the side. Serena plopped back down with a grunt, trying to focus on her breathing while she waited. Though she heard Amber rummaging around the room service cart, all she could see was the ceiling. When Amber's beautiful face finally appeared as she stood between Serena's legs, her hand reached up. A shooting pain hit Serena's nipple, causing her to jerk. Howling, Serena just laid there as Amber continued to rub ice around her nipple. A sadistic smirk was plastered on her face as the sensation switched to Serena's other nipple. Serena shifted but didn't pull away from the exquisite torture.

The next second, hot fudge drizzled onto Serena's nipples. The temperature change after the ice cube overwhelmed her. All her senses were on fire as she shouted and thrashed around. Amber licking it off made it even worse. Or better. Amber pushed Serena's shoulders down while her tongue licked the chocolate, biting at Serena's nipples too.

"Oh, silly me. I haven't had any ice cream yet." Amber briefly stepped away. Without warning, her pubic bone was freezing cold. Her buzzed hair offered little protection from the ice cream. She shouted but then hot fudge penetrated right through the ice cream. Jerking her body again, she was surprised she didn't fall off the bed.

"Payback sure is a bitch, huh?" Amber disappeared, but Serena felt her tongue licking up the dessert soon enough. The delightful agony of the mix in temperatures and Amber's repeated caresses with her hot tongue had Serena screaming like she really was plunging off a cliff.

After the food was gone, Amber let her tongue slip down to Serena's clit. Fingers probed at her opening next and just that first thrust was enough for her to fall over the edge. Her inner muscles contracted around Amber's fingers, or, at least, they tried to. Amber thrusted fast. Every cell in Serena's body screamed, even louder than her mouth. Once the final wave of the climax subsided, Amber didn't let up. Her tongue swirled around Serena's clit and then flicked it for a few seconds, then back to swirls, biting it once or twice.

Serena clawed at the sheets, and she was sure her throat would be sore the next day. Just as she got lost in the sensations, Amber stopped. Cool air hit her again but not for long. Amber's fingers felt around Serena's opening.

"Mm, you're so wet for me. I don't even think we need lube." Amber pulled up Serena's knees and looped her arms underneath them. Pressure increased at her center as Amber thrust the dildo unceremoniously inside of her.

Amber immediately set a grueling pace, just as she had done with her fingers. Whining and squealing, Serena wrapped her legs around Amber's waist while Amber thrust the neon member inside her. After a while, Amber smiled above her once more before everything stopped again.

Amber licked her lips and her eyes darkened. "Flip over."

She put a few pillows on the edge of the bed and then Serena laid across them, her ass in the air. A *crack* resounded at the same time Serena felt a sting across her ass cheek. She barely had time to yelp before her face was pushed into the mattress, and she felt Amber lining up.

Pounding into Serena from behind, Amber had a death grip on Serena's hips for a bit, before she pushed on the small of Serena's back, thrusting at a new angle. The sweat and juices dripping down their thighs made repeated slapping noises. The only pause of Amber's hips was when she turned on the vibrator. That was almost too much. If they got a noise complaint, Serena wouldn't be surprised.

One hand pulled her hair, and the other arm hooked around her torso as she was lifted from the bed. After releasing Serena's hair, Amber reached around and rubbed her clit. Serena felt short, up and down movements on the overstimulated bud in time with Amber's hips.

Amber's breath tickled Serena's neck, and she nibbled Serena's earlobe. "I'm real close. You got another, gorgeous? Mmm. Just relax, baby."

Amber went faster. That familiar pressure built in the pit of Serena's stomach, flowing down to her center. The buildup was excruciating as she plunged down the river, reaching the edge of the cliff of what promised to be the largest cataract yet. The tension finally snapped, far more satisfying than when Serena broke the straps of Amber's lingerie earlier. Moving her hips erratically, Amber screamed too as they fell together, both figuratively over the waterfall and literally onto the bed.

The next thing Serena knew, they were lying next to each other, heads on the pillows, and Amber held her, stroking her back. Amber kissed her forehead and cheeks while Serena tried desperately to catch her breath.

Too tired to care about anything, Serena nuzzled closer to Amber, giving her a brief kiss on the mouth before passing out.

***

When Serena woke, she trudged lazily over to the mini fridge for a bottle of water. She drank most of it in one gulp, then turned back to face the bed. Amber lay there, snoozing away. Serena was restless, the tumult in her gut akin to whitewater rapids. She was determined not to drown in the temptations this woman offered.

With a heavy sigh, Serena went to find her clothes. She dressed, then sat to put on her shoes. When she was halfway through tying her sneakers, she saw movement in the bed.

Amber sat up, hair tousled, squinting. Even like that, she was stunning. "What are you doing?"

"Leaving." Serena tried to tie the other shoe but fumbled as her hands shook.

"I see that. But why?"

Serena scoffed. "I'll leave you some cash for a water I drank."

She stood then and made for the door, but footsteps sounded behind her. Amber seized her arms, turning her around.

"Are you . . . are you upset with me?" Amber tilted her head.

She scoffed again and rolled her eyes. "Do you even care?"

Amber's head snapped backward. "What's that supposed to mean?"

Serena shook her head, looking downward. "Forget it. Just . . . forget the whole thing."

She tried to turn and leave again but Amber ran ahead of her and barred the door, still buck naked. "Please. You said earlier you wanted to talk, right?"

Serena kept looking at the ground. "That was earlier." She shrugged.

"What happened?" Amber's voice was soft. Sympathetic.

Serena was beyond words though. Only a grunt came out when she tried.

Amber sighed. "Come on."

Serena felt a warm hand in hers. She hated how good it felt. Amber pulled Serena to the bed. All of her ire left as she went limp, letting Amber lead her. She sat on the bed, nausea back in full force. Amber walked away but then sat down, a white cotton robe rubbing against Serena's arm. She stared at the ground and tried to recapture some of her resolve from earlier.

Amber pulled her in for an embrace and spoke first. "I thought we had a nice time."

"That's . . . that's the problem." Serena held back tears, but her voice betrayed her with a crack.

"I don't understand."

Serena pulled away. She could not do this while Amber breathed on her neck, holding her so gently like that. With yet another heavy sigh, she closed her eyes and launched into her prepared speech.

"I can't do this anymore. I like you. A lot. I don't want to be your dirty little secret any longer. I've tried to bring it up and you've deflected each time. Or distracted me with your . . . everything. I can't think clearly around you. I get caught up in how good the sex is, how hot you are, but it's like a hangover each time you have to leave town. I feel awful and swear to myself I'm not doing it again. But then there you are, a few weeks later, making me bring you a daquiri, and slipping me your room key. I don't even know where you actually live."

It wasn't exactly how she rehearsed it, but she got the meaning across.

Serena was met with silence. For several long minutes there was nothing. Finally, she looked up. That face she adored so much looked like she had smelled something foul. Amber twiddled her thumbs in her lap and kept her eyes down, but still said nothing.

Serena sighed and stood. "I shoulda known." She walked away toward the door again, keeping her back to Amber.

"I haven't said anything."

Serena stopped walking, but she still faced away. "Exactly. I just put my heart on the line, and you have nothing to say. So, I'm going to go lick my wounds and look for another job. Have a nice life." Serena resumed her walking.

But Amber blocked Serena's way to the door again. "You just sprung this on me."

Serena looked up. Amber's full, plump lips were curved into a frown. Her perfectly sculpted eyebrows furrowed. The water Serena drank threatened to surface but she pushed forward. "Yeah, well, do you like me or not?"

Amber scoffed. "That's not the issue. Of course I like you."

"No, you like *fucking* me." Serena jabbed her finger in the air.

Amber looked taken aback, blinking rapidly. "Yeah, but I like you too."

"You have a funny way of showing it."

Serena tried to push past but Amber grabbed her by the shoulders. "Please, just, I need a minute."

Serena pulled away. "A minute for what? To tell me all the ways it's hilarious that a pathetic simpleton like me fell for some rich businesswoman like you? A minute to really twist that knife? No thanks."

Amber's already furrowed brows touched now. "Hey, I never said any of that!"

Serena spread her arms, gesturing forcefully with her hands. "How would I know? I'm not part of your life. You fly around these different cities all the time. Hell, you could have a girl in every state."

Amber looked like she had been struck across the face. "That's not . . . that's not fair either. We have never asked about—"

"Because you shut me down when I try to talk about these things! How many other people are you sleeping with, then?" Serena couldn't help her volume. Something had snapped inside of her, demanding an outlet.

They stood there staring at each other. Amber pursed her lips and moved her jaw a bit, then her face settled in a grimace. "Do you really want the answer to that?"

Serena sighed, her shoulders deflating. "Probably not." She managed to lower her voice, at least.

Amber reached a tentative hand out, placing it gently on Serena's bicep. "I do care about you. Please, believe that."

Serena looked down again but let the hand stay there. "How? Because you get us a cart of desserts? Left a trail of rose petals? Come on, this is all from the 'Emotionally-Unavailable-Cis-Hetero-Men-Who-Will-Never-Grow-Up Playbook.' Big gestures to avoid having to talk about feelings. I'm not some clueless bimbo."

"I never said you were. Will you please sit back down and give me a second to think?"

Serena sighed again. She opted for the table, leaning back and crossing her arms. Amber followed suit, propping her elbows up and rubbing her temples. The LED candles were still on, flickering ethereally.

It was several long minutes before Amber spoke. "I'm from here. My parents still live here. When I'm in town on business, I usually see them for a meal. I lived in Orlando for a bit—flying from there was easier—but I rent the place out now and just . . . do this." Amber held out her hands. There was a slight quaver in her tone. Serena said nothing.

Amber closed her eyes and sighed. She crossed her arms too, like she was hugging herself. "Even when I thought someone was worth it, they couldn't handle my commitment to my job. I'm on the road all the time. I can't even enjoy my days off. So, yeah, sitting on a lounge chair poolside, ordering you around while I have to have my laptop open and be glued to my phone is one of the ways I get some actual down time. And then, we come up here, fuck our brains out, and I get to just . . . forget about everything else for a little while. Spend time with you in this bliss-filled bubble. So, why would I want to have this conversation? Knowing that it means losing . . ." Amber's voice cracked. She hugged herself again, looking away, but she didn't continue.

Serena sat back in her chair, letting her hands fall to her sides. They were talking, which was an improvement, she reasoned. "I'm confused. You said that you're not turning me down. Then you just said you avoided this conversation knowing it meant losing the sex. I've been sitting here, trying to hear what you have to say but all you've had so far are excuses. I wanna take you places. I wanna get dressed up and go for a drink. I wanna laugh at the tourists wearing sandals on South Beach. I wanna meet your friends. Or snuggle on the couch watching a movie. Make you dinner. Buy you stupid little presents just to make you smile. If you don't know what you want, I'm not gonna sit here and try to convince you."

Amber rubbed her own arms, shifting in her seat. "It's not about what either of us wants. I'm trying to discuss reality. Your version of things sounds nice. It's been years since I've done all that and there are reasons why. I'm not a good girlfriend for anyone. You've made this entire thing about you and whether *you're* good enough, not actually considering my life at all. If things were as simple as how much affection people had toward each other, I'd still be with my high school girlfriend. But other things get in the way."

"Maybe I did make it about me, but I cannot keep getting hurt. I thought you might feel a fraction of what I do. Even just enough to get to know each other outside of the bedroom more. I don't think it's a stretch to think at least some of your trepidation has to do with me."

Amber looked up. "You . . . I don't wanna make you feel bad or anything, but you just don't have a clue how I feel about you. The other people . . . they are . . . they *don't* mean anything. Not a single other person has . . . you just used the word *trepidation*, for fuck's sake!" Her eyes were glossy, tears threatening to spill over.

Serena shook her head. "I don't understand."

Amber rubbed her eyes with her palms. "Okay, look, I'm staying in the robe, no nakedness, but we were at it until late and I can see the sun rising. I'm making coffee so my brain can work properly. Then we can talk more."

Serena just huffed as Amber went to the coffee maker in the kitchenette. A few minutes later, Amber set a mug in front of Serena before sitting back across from her with her own. They stared at each other from across the table while the coffee cooled. It wasn't like she could drink it anyway, as her stomach was still in knots. Amber's expression alternated between indigestion and close to tears.

Amber finally looked away, both hands hugging her coffee cup. "My schedule is grueling. No one understands it. Most people I've dated don't even know what a business intelligence analyst does but all of them *have* done something like this before. 'Me or the job.'" She sighed and looked back at Serena. "Which, honestly, I think is bullshit. Why should I give up what I love to do? If I *were* in a serious relationship with someone, I would hope that I could talk it out with them, and we could come up with a solution together that works for everyone. But people give me ultimatums, deciding for me the only possible outcomes, having had a discussion inside their mind with me instead of the *actual* me. And then I'm the bad guy. So, I stopped dating. And every time I shut down this conversation with you, it's because I'm trying to protect you from getting hurt. That is all . . . all that . . . w-will happen if w-we . . ."

Amber cried, face in her hands, and, despite her anger, Serena stood, stooping to hug her. Amber clung on, crying into her shoulder, and Serena gently rubbed her back. After several long minutes, her breathing slowed.

"I wasn't saying 'me or the job.' I want to have the conversation with you. It didn't seem like you were interested each time I tried, so I was trying to set the boundaries I needed. I didn't mean to upset you like . . . like this."

Amber sniffled. "You didn't know." Her words were muffled since she said them into Serena's shoulder.

"Still." Serena kept caressing her back.

Amber pulled away to look up at her but held fast to Serena's hand. "I didn't mean to make you feel like this either. I've been trying to show you how I feel about you in my own way. So, what you see as shallow moves, are really . . ."

"You showing affection. I'm sorry. But I don't know what you do for other people or how you are normally. Which is kinda my point too. I don't know much about you aside from how to make you come."

Amber laughed. "I mean, that is pretty important."

Serena laughed too. "Do you wanna go sit on the couch?"

Amber nodded. Serena helped her stand. They walked to the couch, hand in hand, and this time they sat on the same one together, cuddling immediately.

This felt different than the usual post-coital cuddling, but maybe Serena imagined the change in atmosphere.

Amber cupped Serena's cheek after a while, stroking it with her thumb. "Are you still mad?"

"A little. But I'm not really sure where to go from here. I'm glad we're talking but I cannot continue on as we have been. Something has to change for me."

"Okay."

Serena pursed her lips. "What does that mean?"

"It means that we will not continue what we were doing."

The bottom dropped out of Serena's stomach. She moved away, holding back tears. "All right. I-I guess I should g-go, then. I've got s-stuff to c-catch up on at home and I-I . . ."

But Amber cut her off with a kiss. And maybe she imagined it again, but she felt a change there too. Serena wrapped an arm around Amber's back as Amber clutched Serena's bicep.

Amber pulled away, leaving Serena slightly dizzy. "Hush."

Serena tried to listen. Their faces were still close together and Amber's moving lips were so tantalizing.

"I do like you. I have no problem ending it with the other people if that's what you want. As long as you're not banging anyone else either."

Serena's heart leapt. She took Amber's hand, stroking her thumb. "I'm not. And yeah, that would be nice."

"So, that's settled. Exclusive."

"Great." Serena's mouth curved into a smile. She couldn't stop staring at Amber's lips.

Amber returned her smile but then her face fell. "And you're sure that you wanna try this? With . . . with me? Even with my crazy schedule and everything else?"

Amber looked like she was going to cry again. Serena leaned in for another kiss. "Yeah. I'm sure," she whispered against Amber's luscious lips.

Amber nodded. When the kiss deepened, Serena put a hand on her cheek, feeling dampness on her skin. "What's wrong?"

"I . . . this has been a . . . a l-lot."

"I'm sorry. We don't have to talk anymore. Let's go back to sleep, yeah?"

Amber nodded but she let the tears fall now. Serena held her, letting her sob until her breathing evened out, and then picked up the beautiful, sleeping woman. The sun lit up the sheets as she laid Amber down, so she closed the curtains. She got into the bed herself, glad it was her day off. Holding Amber close, she drifted off immediately too.

When they woke later, they just stayed there cuddling and kissing each other. The pit of dread in her stomach was finally gone. No longer did Serena feel the stab of longing, the worry of how she would feel when they parted. She was able to fully enjoy Amber's presence. Amber seemed more relaxed too.

"Wanna shower?" Amber smiled, stroking Serena's hair.

"Mm. Thought you'd never ask." Serena leaned in to kiss her.

They both stood and walked toward the bathroom. Serena stripped and Amber hung her robe on a hook. The river rock shower floor felt good on her feet but the warm water on her muscles felt better. Serena got her hair wet, then they switched places. Before she could get the shampoo, Amber pulled her in for a hug and cried again.

"What's wrong?" Serena rubbed circles on her back.

"I'm s-sorry. That I m-made you f-feel . . . I'm sorry."

"It's all right. Well, I mean, it wasn't, but we talked. That was what I wanted, more than anything."

Amber nodded against her chest and pulled away, the streams from the rainfall showerhead hitting the back half of her hair. She turned, clutching the shampoo to hand it to Serena.

Once they were both massaging shampoo into their scalps, Serena asked, "Can I take you to dinner tonight?"

Amber stopped her motions. She walked forward again, grabbed Serena by the ass, and then pulled her in close. Her smile was still just as mischievous as before. "That means less time to spend together this afternoon. If we're going out, I need to go shopping. I only have business attire and workout clothes with me."

"And lingerie." Serena leaned in.

"You ruined those." Amber leaned in too.

It was another thing that felt different. The shower wasn't just a thinly veiled excuse for sex. They kissed and touched plenty, but it stayed sweet.

Serena pulled up to the front of the resort. One of the valets was already crossing behind her car.

Stepping out of her SUV, Serena turned to face the valet in the same motion. "Hey, I'm just picking someone up. No need for . . . Hasan?"

"Oh, hey, boss." He grinned when recognition hit him. They clasped hands and pulled each other close enough to give quick pats on the back.

"What are you doing?" She gestured up and down, pointing to his black slacks and red vest.

"They were shorthanded tonight, so my buddy Clyde asked if I wanted some extra cash. I mean, with the holiday coming up and all, I gotta be able to show the ladies a good time." Hasan put his hands in his pockets and shrugged.

"Gotcha, well, good for you." Serena turned to walk around to the other side of the car.

"Who are you picking up, then?" Hasan followed her.

"I . . . uh . . . well . . ." Serena stood next to the passenger door.

Hasan gasped. "Your face is red. You've got a date, don't you? Who is it? Is it that woman from accounting or . . . ?"

"It is none of your business." She pointed a finger at him then moved her hands to smooth out her purple button-down shirt.

He opened his mouth, but the front doors opened. Serena looked over to see Amber walking outside. She tossed her hair over her shoulder, and it did that slow motion thing again. Serena couldn't breathe for just a second. Amber wore a black halter dress with a high neckline. Even without her cleavage on display, she was radiant. Honestly, Serena couldn't decide if she looked hotter in the lingerie or the dress. She was certain Amber could wear a burlap sack and still be sexy.

When she saw Serena, she smiled and waved. "Hey."

"H-Hi. You look . . . wow." Serena stood there, mesmerized.

"I was thinking that about you."

They leaned in for a kiss. Serena would never tire of those lips on hers. When they parted, they still embraced. Over Amber's shoulder, Serena locked eyes with Hasan. She grinned smugly at him while his mouth hung open. He backed away, picking up his phone as he did so.

Serena chuckled to herself before she turned to open the car door for Amber.

They sat next to each other in their private booth that overlooked the Intracoastal Waterway. Serena wrapped her arm around Amber's back while she sipped the last of her wine. The water's surface was relatively calm, muddled by only a few wrinkles that danced and shimmered in the setting sun. She took a deep breath, letting the calm of the water wash over her.

Amber leaned into Serena's side. "This is nice."

"Mmm. Yeah." But Serena felt her phone buzz in her pocket. "Ugh."

"What is it?" Amber traced light circles on her sternum with her finger.

"Just another coworker." Serena wondered vaguely how many people Hasan had texted as she put her phone away without responding. Even if Serena and Amber had fallen and popped their bliss-filled bubble, the rest of the world could wait while they were out.

Amber placed her palm fully on her chest now, using it to push herself up. She moved so they were face to face. "When the waiter comes back, what do you think about ordering dessert?" Amber licked her lips and then leaned close to Serena's ear. "To go?"

Her breath tickled Serena's neck. All she could do was nod. When it came to Amber, Serena would never turn down dessert.

About the Author

MK Edgley always has something to say. She took her love of storytelling and channeled it into a passion for writing sapphic romance. MK's works center on women loving women and other queer identities. From modern-day witch tales to simple meet-cutes, her stories showcase the magic of love and the things that unite us as humans. Originally from the suburbs of Portland, Oregon, MK now resides in Seattle, Washington, with her wife, cat, and dog.

You can find MK on:
Instagram @mkedgleyauthor

Visit her website at:
www.mkedgley.com

THE
COMPULSORY
DATE

The Compulsory Date

Rowen Burrows

Prologue: Gracie

THE DOOR CHIMED AS GRACIE walked into the restaurant she now worked for. It was one of those that served a little bit of everything, and she breathed in the divine smell of roasted chicken.

Smiling, she walked to the host stand. She couldn't wait to get started; she had heard nothing but good things about this place. At this hour, the restaurant was closed, so there were no diners waiting.

"Hi, my name is Gracie. Fiona is expecting me," she told the staff member at the host stand. The woman twirled strands of black and blue hair around her finger as she read the reservation list. "I am the new waitress."

The woman looked up and smiled brightly at her. "Oh, hey! Yeah, the boss said we had a newbie starting today. Welcome to the team. My name is Caitlyn. I am always happy to help, so give me a shout if you need anything."

That was sweet, and Gracie would most definitely need it. She had worked in retail before, but this was her first waitressing job, so she had a lot to learn.

"Thank you. I am sure I will take you up on that. It's lovely to meet you."

"It's great to meet you, too. I love it here, and I hope you do, too. Fiona is an amazing boss." Caitlyn pointed behind them. "Just head on through that corridor there. Fiona's office is the white door. Knock and she will call you in."

"Okay, thanks!"

Gracie was about to follow those directions, when someone loud barged through the front door. He was whistling and singing. His clothes were disheveled, like he had gone for a run.

"Here comes trouble," Caitlyn muttered with a smile.

The man beamed at her as he pulled his long blond hair back into a bun. Then, he straightened his waistcoat and wiped a smudge of dirt off his shoe.

His gaze met Gracie's, and it was like being hit with spotlights. She froze. His crooked smile almost blinded her. "Ah, is this the new waitress my mother told me was starting today?"

He was most definitely attractive. He shook her hand, and it was warm. She had to remember to let go. Judging by his smile, Caitlyn was correct. He was definitely trouble.

"Connor, this is Gracie. Gracie, this is the man you avoid like the plague," Caitlyn said with a sarcastic smile. He gave an exaggerated smile back. "He's a menace and the boss's son."

"That's a bit mean, Caitie." He sidled closer to Gracie. "Did she tell you she is the sarcastic one of the team? Take nothing she says seriously."

Caitlyn snorted. "Oh, so if I tell her you are one of our bartenders and make an excellent cocktail, she should ignore that?"

Connor rolled his eyes. "Anything negative you can ignore. Anything positive you can believe."

He smelled like whiskey and sandalwood. Gracie *loved* whiskey. It was a good scent for him.

"Connor Hall!" Fiona appeared from the corridor.

The older woman looked immaculate in her gray business suit. Seeing her new boss, Gracie checked her uniform to make sure she was presentable. Nothing was out of place, thank goodness.

The owner of the restaurant did not look impressed as she raised an eyebrow at her son. "You're late."

"Hello, Mother." He pouted, but it changed into a grin before he kissed Fiona's cheek. "I am only five minutes late. That's a record for me!"

Fiona rolled her eyes.

His green eyes met Gracie's once more. "Duty calls. See you around, Gracie. I am sure we will get on *very* well." He winked at her and disappeared down the corridor.

Fiona approached her with a smile. She offered her hand, which Gracie took and shook. "Gracie, lovely to see you. I see you have met my son, Connor, and Caitlyn, our hostess for this evening. I do hope they haven't put you off. Are you ready to sign some paperwork and start training?"

Gracie put thoughts of the cocky bartender from her mind. "Most definitely."

Chapter 1: Connor

CONNOR BURST INTO HIS MOTHER'S office, so excited with his latest idea. His uniform was a mess, but that wasn't important right now. He could fix that in a minute. He took a moment to breathe after his run, his hand on his side to relieve the developing stitch.

His mother ignored him and continued with whatever she was doing at her desk. Gracie, who was leaning over her shoulder to read the same thing, accompanied her. The expression in her blue eyes as she looked up told him how unimpressed she was.

"You're late," she stated. "*Again*."

Connor shrugged as he took a seat opposite them. "Am I late or are you really fucking early, as per usual, so it just feels like I am late?"

Gracie rolled her eyes at him.

His mother looked up. "You're late." She put the pen down. "And mind your language. You *are* at work."

He winced, momentarily scolded. "Sorry." Then he cheered up again, remembering why he was there. He slapped his new idea down on the desk.

"What is *that*?" Gracie asked.

She looked absolutely horrified by the little white plastic bow. It came with small pink targets and pink arrows with the suckers on the end.

"I have a great idea. You'll love it, Mother," he declared. Gracie would absolutely hate it. "It's Valentine's Day in a few days. We have a lot of bookings for couples. What if we had our own restaurant cupid? We can place these little targets on each table. The cupid could pick a really lovey-dovey couple and shoot the target on their table. That couple then gets a discount or free drinks. Something special to add to their special date!"

His mother looked impressed. "I like it. We will need a risk assessment, of course, since arrows are involved. As long as the person fires right next to the table so there is no chance to miss, I see no problem."

"No problem?" Gracie squeaked. Her eyes hadn't left the bow.

Connor snorted. "What is the worst that could happen?"

"Someone could get *shot*!" she sputtered.

He slapped one of the arrows onto his own arm. "I doubt it will hurt anyone. Besides, I have considered that risk. *You* will be the one using it, as you are the least likely to shoot someone."

Gracie went so, so pale. He tried to hide his glee, but he wasn't sure he was succeeding.

Revenge is sweet.

She always said no to his new ideas, wanting to keep it nice and simple for the diners and staff. His mother normally backed her up. Connor kept trying, however, because he didn't want the restaurant to get boring. He wanted to make it exciting! Today, he may finally be getting his way.

"What if I do shoot someone?" she asked.

"Then it will be funny as hell as you stress about it."

"Connor . . ." his mother warned. She looked at her. "Change can be good, and this idea might be fun. It will really add to our diners' experience. We can make it work."

Gracie straightened, obviously unhappy, but she wasn't going to argue. She smoothed her hands down her pink dress. As always, there wasn't a wrinkle in sight. They made a right pair together since he was nothing but wrinkles.

How did mud get on his collar?

"Yes, Fiona," she responded.

"Wonderful. Now, I think we are done here if you want to make sure the restaurant floor is ready?"

Gracie nodded, looking relieved to leave. "Yes, of course."

She walked straight past the bow, pointedly ignoring him.

"Did you not want to take it with you to practice?" he taunted.

She didn't storm out, but the door closed louder than it needed to. He'd gotten to her.

One point to Connor!

His mother gave him such a withering look. "Be careful, Connor. I have warned you about your behavior before. I hope I don't have to warn you again."

He groaned as he leaned back in his chair and stared at the ceiling. Yes, she had warned him not to upset Gracie. Many times. But it was so damn easy, and she regularly got him back. His mother had warned her just as much.

"Fine. But do we get to use my bow idea?"

"Yes. Now get going, you need to check the bar."

Walking out, he saluted her and took the bow with him. Excited by his win, he had a spring in his step as he headed over to the bar to start his checks.

Movement in the corner of his eye distracted him.

Gracie was busy tying up her long brown curls into a ponytail, revealing that luscious neck of hers. A neck he would love to nibble on. Once done, she checked the menus. As floor manager, she liked to ensure the menus were clean and in good condition each shift. No doubt she would inspect them again in twenty minutes just to be sure. She liked to be thorough.

Connor had learned the hard way *not* to mess with her menus. He'd deliberately spilled tomato sauce on them once, and she'd responded by putting tomato sauce in his coat pocket. The one he kept his house keys in.

One hundred percent worth it.

She walked past the bar, smiling at his team and greeting them as she completely ignored Connor. His team snickered, knowing he'd done something to piss her off.

She glared at the evil bow, drawing Graham's attention to it. Sensing her anger, he was smart enough to wait until she was out of earshot to ask about it. "What's with the bow?"

"Oh, we are going to have targets on tables over the next few days. Gracie is going to choose the best couples, then fire the bow. That couple will then get something like free drinks to add to their date."

"That's such a cool idea!" Graham grinned, picking up the bow. "I wonder what the range is on this thing?"

"No idea." Connor took it from him. "Unfortunately, we won't get to test it. The idea is that she will be right next to it."

Gracie had returned to the host stand, this time with a glass of water. She was trying not to look at the two men with the bow, but she was visibly nervous as she ignored them.

He had promised his mother not to provoke her. This time, that promise lasted less than five minutes.

While they discussed his idea, he loaded the bow to feel the weight of it and guess the range. Only, in his enthusiasm, he let go. It sailed across the room, hitting Gracie's glass. Water went everywhere, including on her.

"Shit," Graham whispered. The smart man ducked behind the bar.

Connor wasn't fast enough, and she turned to face him. Good thing the restaurant wasn't open, as she was fucking furious.

She took a deep breath, but it didn't help control her anger. "I bloody swear, Connor!"

He raised his hands in surrender. "That was a complete accident!"

"Oh, really? What did you think was going to happen while you messed about with it?" Gracie snarled. She stormed up to him, waving the damn arrow around.

She really was something else. He lived for these moments, for her eyes on him. "You're so pretty when you're mad."

"Fucking idiot," Graham muttered under the bar. He crawled away, out of the war zone and toward safety.

Connor's eyes widened. Had he really just said that out loud?

Gracie hesitated, and her breath caught. She was still mad, but the comment had thrown her. Was that pleasure he saw in her eyes? Did she like the compliment?

The hesitation didn't last long, and the anger returned. "I will shove this somewhere the sun doesn't shine."

"Oh." He pouted. "How cliché. I was hoping for a bit more originality."

She raised an eyebrow. She'd learned that from his mother. "Oh, I was going to suggest down your throat. Your mouth is so big you'd deep throat it no problem."

Caitlyn, who'd walked into the bar area, minding her own business, spat out her drink in surprise. Connor was sure it came out of her nose, too.

"Gracie!" Caitlyn laughed. "I did *not* expect that from you!"

"What can I say? He brings out the worst in me," Gracie mumbled.

"I did say to avoid him," Caitlyn reminded her.

"That you did." Now that she had shouted, she calmed down a bit. She returned to her station to clear it up.

Connor snorted. "I can't be that bad. You come back. If you hated me, you'd have left by now. I am surprised you still put up with me for how much I push you."

Gracie paled. "Is that you telling me to go somewhere else?"

He frowned. He really should have worded that better, especially since he was the boss's son. "Hell no. I'd be bored and I would miss you."

No. He couldn't stand the idea of her leaving. The thought of her gone left him cold and empty. He lived for their moments, even if all they did was argue. How sad that it was the highlight of his day.

Gracie stormed off. Ah, shit. He should have handled that better after pissing her off.

Caitlyn glared at Connor. "Give her a break. She doesn't like Valentine's Day, so she is stressed enough as it is."

He put the bow down before he was tempted to play with it again. "What's not to love about Valentine's Day?"

He loved it. He may be single, but he enjoyed watching couples go on their dates. It just seemed magical with all the love in the air.

Caitlyn rolled her eyes. "There are single people. Some don't believe in it. Some have lost their love. Add in the fact that she has to deal with you. Yeah, I can see why she hates it."

Connor was going to respond, but he never got a chance.

"CONNOR VINCENT HALL!"

"Oh, shit." That was his whole name. He was in a lot of trouble. No doubt she had seen an angry Gracie. He should have apologized.

His mother stormed in and took the bow off the bar counter. "My office. Now!" He followed his mother back to her office. The door shut. "Sit!"

He did as he was told as she went to sit opposite him. She looked so done. "Gracie knew this was a bad idea! I should have listened to her."

"It's a great idea," he whined.

"Stop winding her up." His mother glared at him.

"It was an accident!" Connor argued. "Besides, it's just a little bit of fun."

"For you, yes. For Gracie, it isn't."

Gracie came in. She looked so vulnerable. She was still carrying the arrow and had found a cloth. Her dress looked a bit drier.

"Take a seat, Gracie."

She nodded and did as she was told.

His mother took a deep breath. "You two need to make up. As entertaining as your arguments can be, it's toxic for the pair of you. It isn't good for the workplace or the team. You are going on a date."

Gracie looked absolutely horrified. "What?"

His mother smiled. It wasn't a nice smile. "I have asked you so many times to stop aggravating each other. I changed your shifts to minimize your time together. That didn't work. So, guess what? Now you'll have to deal with forced exposure to each other. Maybe, just *maybe*, spending time with each other, just the two of you, will give you a chance to get it out of your system."

Or we will kill each other.

"You two have so much potential together. When you're friendly, you are an amazing team. But you deal with each other only at work. Go on a date. Just one. Get to know each other personally, outside of work and these pressures. You may finally start getting along."

Neither of them argued. Yet. Gracie looked like she was gearing up for it.

"You need to respect how the other works, so this is what is going to happen. Connor, you're going to organize the date. You will do it properly and make sure Gracie will enjoy it. You need to understand the importance of organization and planning.

"Gracie, you're going to let him. You need to understand that you can't control everything. Other people have ideas. Sometimes it's good to let others take over, to switch off, enjoy, and have some fun."

Gracie tried to argue.

"No arguing. You two need to figure it out. I am done tiptoeing around the issue. Your attitudes affect the team, and customers can sense it. Find common ground. Now, get back to work."

Gracie tried another tactic. She raised her hand. His mother sighed and nodded.

"What if I say no to this?"

"I can't have staff who cause problems. If you do this and show you're willing to change, then I can work with that. You have to give me *something* to work with," his mother responded. "That goes for both of you. If you don't, then I am sorry, but I have to consider the needs of my business and my team."

Gracie paled.

"I love you, Connor. You're my son. I love having you here. Gracie, you are hardworking and amazing at what you do. I don't want to lose either of you, but you are pushing it. Give it a go. *Please.* If it doesn't work, it doesn't work. I will think of something else, but at least we can say we tried this."

His mother looked so worn out. With that happy announcement, she got up and walked out.

Fabulous. He had to organize a date with a woman who wanted to shove an arrow down his throat. An arrow she was still clinging to, and by the look on her face, she was still thinking about it.

He smiled at her. Then promptly ran off before she came after him.

Connor had some thinking to do. His mother was deadly serious this time, and that was scary.

He knew his mother liked Gracie. Was this her way of setting them up and acting as their personal cupid? Her idea had some merit and could be a lot of fun. There were worse punishments than going on a date with a fiery, beautiful woman. He just had to make sure he did it right. His future was at stake.

So was Gracie's.

He gulped. For some reason, that thought terrified him more.

Chapter 2: Gracie

"LUCY?" GRACIE WATCHED HER COLLEAGUE return from her break with tears in her eyes. "What happened?"

Lucy slumped and wiped her eyes. "My mum called. Grandma is in the hospital. She fell. She will be fine, but it was just a bit of a shock."

Gracie felt for her, completely understanding her worry, and rubbed Lucy's shoulder in comfort. "Go and check on her."

Lucy shook her head. "I can't go. You won't find cover this late!"

Gracie shrugged. "That is a me problem, not a you problem. You need to check on her. Go and see her."

Fiona came over and frowned. "What's wrong?"

"Lucy's grandma had a fall and is currently in the hospital. I am telling her to head off so she can check on her."

Fiona nodded. "Yes, I completely agree. Family comes first. Send her our love and keep us updated. I can call around and see if we can find cover. If not, I am sure Gracie and I can do it between us. Now, off with you." After giving Lucy a quick hug, Fiona disappeared.

Gracie smiled. "See? Sorted."

Lucy sniffed and gave her a tight hug. "Thank you! You're the best."

It was a busy night and would now get busier since they were down a team member, but that was simply the way it was sometimes. She loved waiting tables, and she rarely got to do it now since she was promoted to floor manager a few months ago, so it was no hassle. She loved the pace of the job. The challenge. Talking to customers.

It was exhausting, though. After hours of rushing around on her feet, it was finally time for her break. She sat down at the table, enjoying the rest.

Caitlyn appeared with a big smile on her face. "Sooooo . . . are we ready for the Compulsory Date tomorrow?"

Gracie groaned at the reminder. "I don't know," she answered honestly. She sighed as she slumped, her head in her hands.

It terrified her to give Connor that power. She had no control over anything. But she had upset Fiona, and if this got her back in her good graces, then so be it. She was doing her part by pretending it wasn't happening, so she didn't feel overwhelmed and demand answers. She wasn't allowed to get involved in the planning at all. She had to hope Connor was doing his part and would make it enjoyable instead of doing something to humiliate her or wind her up.

But she was also looking forward to it. She *liked* Connor. She enjoyed going to work just so she could see him, even if he did make her mad.

She craved seeing him. Sad, really. She just didn't have the guts to tell him. They argued so much she didn't think it was worth it, but now she would finally know what going on a date with him would be like. All she knew so far was that it was tomorrow, which was Valentine's Day.

Gracie couldn't stand Valentine's Day. The very idea made her cold as she thought back to a previous Valentine's Day that had not gone well. She couldn't cope with another disastrous one. She knew he liked the holiday, however. Whether he picked this day because there would be loads of people, meaning arguments would be harder to have, or to get it over and done with, she had no idea. It didn't matter. He had picked a date and asked if she was free, and she had to show willingness. So tomorrow it was!

It didn't mean she was happy about it, though.

Caitlyn leaned on the counter. "It will be fine. Connor may be a pain in the ass, but he will look after you. Just switch off and enjoy it. You never know, something may come of it."

Gracie raised an eyebrow. "And what do *you* think will come of it?"

"You know . . . kissing, hand-holding . . . sex." She shrugged.

Gracie's jaw dropped. "No!" Not that she would complain if it did happen. . . . She just didn't want to set her hopes too high.

Then she thought back on his comment. The one after he fired the bow, telling her she looked pretty when she was mad. It had thrown her off. Her heart had paused, enjoying those words. Did he really think that, or had he said it to slow her down?

Caitlyn waggled her eyebrows. "We've all seen how you two look at each other. You want to either kill each other or rip each other's clothes off."

Gracie sputtered. "No . . . that's not . . . no!"

The idea that everyone had seen how she looked at him horrified her. Had Connor seen how she looked at him?

Caitlyn rolled her eyes. "You like him. I know you do. He likes you, too. I have seen him get upset with people who touch you inappropriately. He gets very loud and threatens to throw them out. *Very* upset."

Did he? He got upset if any of the staff were harassed. A few times, drunk people had touched her, and Connor had always come to her rescue, tucking her behind him to keep her safe. It was sweet.

"I mean it, Gracie. He's a lot meaner if it's *you* upset. He likes you, even if he uses strange ways to get your attention. So go on this date and see what he has up his sleeve. Maybe you can finally decide for yourself whether to ask him out."

"Am I that obvious?" She would make sure she controlled her eyes a bit more if that were the case.

"Oh, definitely. I've seen how you look at him in waistcoats." Her friend winked. "Your eyes glaze over, and you stare. You *like*."

Gracie covered her face and groaned. She thought she was sly. "He *does* look good in waistcoats."

"Who looks good in waistcoats?" Connor asked as he came through the door. Clearly, he was on break, too.

Gracie's head shot up out of her hands in surprise, and she blushed bright red, panicking about how much he had heard. Good thing her work bestie had her back.

"Graham," Caitlyn lied without missing a beat.

He narrowed his eyes. Was he jealous? "Seems I have competition, and I need to up my game."

"You do that, Connor," Caitlyn said sweetly, and patted his arm. "You do that. Oh, and FYI, you upset Gracie tomorrow, I'll break your legs."

These two were like siblings. They bickered and threatened each other, but they were great friends.

"Mean!" He guffawed. "I'll tell my mother that this is workplace bullying!"

Caitlyn laughed. "No doubt she will pin you down while I do it."

He snorted, then shook his head in defeat. "No doubt. Therefore, I promise I will not hurt Gracie. I will do my best to make sure she enjoys the date."

He looked so genuine. It made Gracie's heart stutter.

Caitlyn pointed at her eyes, then to him. "I better get back to work. See you later, Gracie."

"Bye, Caitlyn."

Caitlyn left the room, leaving an embarrassed Gracie alone with an intrigued Connor.

Fantastic.

"So, Graham, huh?" he asked.

She nodded. "Uh-huh."

He scowled as he crossed his arms over his chest, leaning back against the counter so he could stare at her. Oh, he *was* jealous. Gracie likey.

His face softened. "I noticed Lucy went home and you were waiting her tables. Is she okay?"

"I hope so. She had family matters to take care of."

"No hope of cover?" he asked.

She shook her head. Fiona had confirmed no one was available. "Nope, so your mother and I will be covering her tables for the rest of the night."

"You were lucky it was a waitress you had to cover." He smirked. "You would have no idea what to do behind the bar if you had to cover one of us."

His smile told her he was trying to make her smile, not provoke her right now.

Gracie chuckled. "I can't do what you do. I am in awe of how you remember how to make all those drinks. Saying that, if you needed cover, at least two of our waitstaff on each shift are trained behind the bar. They would cover, and I would cover them." She smiled softly. "I know my organization drives you mad, but there is a reason I do what I do, Connor. Why I train them the way I do or create schedules the way I do. It's called resilience. We can keep the team going, even with low numbers. These things pop up, and our team needs to know we will support them when they need it."

Did he actually look like he respected her? It made her shiver in delight.

"Maybe I will have to train you behind the bar." He grinned. "It'll take forever, as you would have to double-check everything, but if any-one will get it the first time, it'll be you."

"I will take that as a compliment." She looked at him. Perhaps this was her chance to get out of their predicament. As much as she wanted to go on a date with him, she didn't want to go with anyone who didn't want to actually be with her. "We are currently getting along." She gently nudged him. "Maybe we don't need that date after all. This proves we *can* be nice to each other."

"Us being nice for five minutes doesn't count." He winked at her. "No doubt I will do something to piss you off by the end of the night." He moved closer. "So are we still on for tomorrow? *Graham* isn't interfering with that?"

Gracie shook her head. "No, we are still on for the Compulsory Date tomorrow."

He flinched. "You sound like you're dreading it."

"It's on Valentine's Day. Does it have to be *that* day?" Her palms were sweaty just thinking about it.

He rubbed a hand down his face. "The idea is to get to know each other. I wanted to share that day with you because I love it. It means something to me. The longer we delay it, the longer we upset my mother. I just thought tomorrow would be a good day to do it. If it makes you uncomfortable, however, you could always wear a Santa hat."

She chuckled, then sighed. "You can't honestly tell me you're looking forward to going on a date with me?"

Connor's smile was devilish. "Would you believe me if I said that I am, actually?"

She frowned, not expecting that answer. "Really?"

He nodded. "There are worse things in life than going on a date as a punishment, especially when the woman is you. I mean that."

Her heart stuttered again. Lowering her head, she blurted, "I am looking forward to it, too. Terrified, but looking forward to it."

Worried about his reaction, she raised her eyes just enough to see his face. He was positively beaming as he sat beside her.

"Look, I thought you might be worrying, which is why I wanted to talk to you. I won't tell you everything, but I will tell you enough so you have something to work with. Wear something warm and casual. Oh, and it's dog friendly, too."

"Dog friendly?" she asked.

"I thought you would feel more comfortable if you could take Noodle."

Noodle was Gracie's white toy poodle. Connor's consideration of him and her feelings meant a lot. "Thank you."

"Now, I have to ask. What is your favorite dessert?"

That was an easy one. "Whipped cream. I love it."

"Okay, but what do you put it on?"

Sensing a chance to tease him, she took it. That was what she had to learn to do, right? Have some fun. "Who says I put it on food?"

His eyes widened.

Break finished, she got up to leave.

Connor stammered, "Oh, no! You can't walk away after that! What do you do with it?"

She winked at him. "I am sure you can use your imagination. I can't tell you much, per your mother's rules." She handed over the bow. "But as I can't leave you upset with me, here. Go shoot the bow."

He had kindly told her something so she could worry less. The least she could do was let him use the bow once, which he had been dying to do. See, they were learning to work together!

"The couple at the back is adorable. The woman in the blue dress with pink hearts. I was thinking two free cocktails."

He grinned in delight as he took the bow. "You are distracting me, but I will allow it, as I really want to use the bow. Until tomorrow, then, date."

She shook her head and laughed. "Until tomorrow."

He rushed out, and she followed him to watch his joy as he ran to the table. Fiona happened to come out of her office, noticed, and walked past with a smug smile.

Chapter 3: Connor

"WHO SAYS I PUT IT on food?"

Connor had been obsessing over that one question all night and most of the morning as he got ready for their date. Now he was imagining her licking it off his body. Hell, he was thinking about licking it off hers. Whipped cream had never appealed to him until her comment and the possibilities it held.

He was picking up Gracie in an hour, so he had to concentrate or he would be late. Hearing her call their date the Compulsory Date had hurt him. He understood, as it wasn't by their design, but he had genuinely thought she was dreading it. He was actually excited and wanted to make sure he did a good job, and not just to appease his mother.

Connor had surprised himself with how much effort he had put in. He now had a healthy respect for Gracie and how hard she worked. Planning today had been a lot of fun for him, and he wanted her to like it. He wanted to make it work with her. At work and personally. Today, he would find out what taking her on a date would be like and whether they would get along. It had made him so giddy to hear she was looking forward to it.

He had a funny feeling she and Caitlyn had lied about Graham, as he had checked. Graham didn't wear waistcoats. The only one on the team who did was Connor.

Did Gracie like *him* in waistcoats? He was wearing a black one today just in case. He was also wearing a button-down shirt with the top buttons undone and jeans. Smart, sexy, and casual.

He groaned as he thought about Gracie again. And whipped cream. He imagined her naked on his bed. Whipped cream tipping her breasts and between her legs. He would clean her off nice . . . and slowly.

Today, he *would* find out what she meant!

Happy with his outfit, he went about doing final preparations. He kept checking his watch, making sure he was on schedule. It was so weird having a schedule, but this was the one day in his life he didn't want to be late.

With the car packed, he headed over to her home. Parking outside, he checked his mirror to make sure he still looked okay. He had never been so nervous in his life. Or so excited.

He left his coat in the car. He didn't need it now, and he wanted to see her reaction to his waistcoat.

Before he even got out of the car, he could hear barking. He laughed as he looked at the window. The little white poodle was there, wagging his tail and barking at him even more as he came down the small path. A pair of hands snuck through the curtains, grabbed the dog, and sucked it back in. It didn't stop the barking.

He was one hundred percent sure she knew he was here, but he knocked to be polite. A few seconds later, Gracie opened the door with a big smile on her face. She looked amazing in jeans and a turtleneck jumper. Her hair was up in a ponytail.

She took notice of his waistcoat, and her eyes darkened. Oh yeah, she liked *him* in waistcoats.

"Hi, you're early." Her voice was breathy. She moved her eyes up to meet his.

"I am. Simply proving that it is possible for the right reason."

She blushed. "Come on in. I just need to grab my shoes and coat. You can meet Noodle."

"Perfect."

He stepped in and closed the door. The ball of white fluff was contained behind a baby gate in the living room. He was up on his back legs, bouncing at the gate as his tail continued to wag.

"He's friendly, just very bouncy. You can let him out if you want, but I didn't know if you liked excited dogs."

"Love them." He didn't have his own, but he did love dogs.

"Be gentle and calm, Noodle."

She opened the gate, and he knew the poodle had ignored everything his mum had just said. He was bouncing all around Connor's feet, trying to lick his fingers. Connor spent the few minutes Gracie was getting ready playing with the dog so they could get used to each other. It ended up with Noodle on his lap for head scratches. The dog looked ever so happy.

With her coat on, Gracie appeared in the living room with a small orange coat and a leash.

"Do *not* tell me Noodle has his own coat." Connor choked back a laugh. He'd never seen one before.

"Of course he does. He hates the cold."

The dog ran over, excited to see the leash and coat. He had to admit, the dog looked cute in his own outfit.

"Come on, you two. I have only a few hours to make it count, so let's make the most of it."

They were both working this evening, so he had to get them back in enough time to get ready for work.

They followed him out, and the dog went happily into his travel crate that Gracie had placed in his car. She had also brought a towel and a blanket for Noodle since the weather forecast called for rain.

With everyone finally in the car, they made their way to their destination. Gracie's leg was twitching nervously, and she read all the road signs for a hint. She was behaving, though, and asked no questions.

Eventually, they stopped.

Gracie frowned. "We are at the canal."

It was a frown, not a look of disappointment, which was a relief to him.

He nodded. "I love Valentine's Day. I think it's great seeing all the couples together. I know you are not keen on it, however. I didn't want to pressure you into a public date or into an environment you were uncomfortable in. I thought we could go for a picnic date. It's quieter here, so we can talk without having to shout or worry about being overheard. We can take our time instead of being rushed so the table can be given to someone else. Plus, we could bring Noodle. As you are at work later, I didn't want you to feel you had to be without him even longer."

She gripped his hand. "Thank you. It means a lot."

He savored her touch, relieved he had impressed her.

"I didn't want to do anything overly complicated," he continued to explain. "If we went to another restaurant, no doubt we would have judged or looked for ideas we liked, which means we would have gotten distracted from our original purpose. If we went to my mother's restaurant, we would have been watched."

That made her laugh.

"I wanted to start with something small and simple. Here, we can be ourselves. And if we end up arguing, no one is here to hear it." He said it as a joke. He didn't think they would be arguing today.

She laughed even more before she raised an eyebrow. "Start?"

He shrugged. "Who knows? Maybe you'll find out you like me after all."

Please like me.

Her smile was lovely. "Indeed, who knows."

That gave him hope.

"Come on, then." He stepped out. It was cool, but at least it wasn't raining yet. It looked like it might soon.

They had a lovely walk along the canal. Noodle had to sniff every blade of grass, even when it started to drizzle, but it gave them a chance to talk. He made her laugh a lot.

When they found a great sheltered spot to watch the birds and the boats, they set up their picnic. He had even packed something for Noodle so he didn't feel left out. Not knowing what he liked or could eat, he picked up a few different dog treats. His thoughtfulness toward her beloved companion made her smile even more. Noodle was the most important thing to her, and so he should be.

For the humans, he had made sandwiches and had packed a variety of fruits, vegetables, hams, and cheeses. Judging by her excitement, it looked like he had done well.

After the food was eaten, they sat silently together. A peaceful, comfortable silence as they watched a boat covered in pink balloons go by.

He observed Gracie when the boat sailed past. "Why don't you like Valentine's Day?"

She dropped her gaze to her lap. Her sadness was the first negative emotion she had shown today. "A few years ago, my boyfriend at the time booked us a table to eat at a fancy restaurant. It turned out he had done it to break up with me. He had used the expensive restaurant as an apology for cheating on me. He hoped being in a busy environment meant I wouldn't get too angry."

"What an absolute fucking dick." Connor wanted to punch the fucker for dimming her shine.

Gracie shrugged as she held back tears.

And that would explain why she was so nervous of it being today. She was scared Connor was going to do something. Hopefully, he had turned Valentine's Day into something positive.

He lifted her chin. "Hey, I'm sorry he did that. I am not sorry he broke up with you, though. If he hadn't, I wouldn't be here with you today."

Her face softened as she looked in his eyes, seeing how genuine he was being. "I have really enjoyed today. It's been the best Valentine's Day I have ever had."

Didn't that boost his ego.

"I am glad to hear it. This has been my favorite one, too."

Their lips were so close together now. He hadn't noticed he had leaned in. After her admission, it didn't feel like the right time for that. She was vulnerable, and he would not take advantage of her.

Wanting to make her smile at him again and take her mind off the dick, he went hunting in the picnic basket and pulled out a can of whipped cream and various desserts.

"And it is not over yet! I wasn't sure what puddings you liked, so I got a mixture."

She grinned. "I notice you brought whipped cream." Her eyes lit up as he handed it over. She shook the can excitedly.

"Are you going to tell me what you do with it now?" he asked.

Her smile turned seductive as her eyes hooded. "What do you think I do with it?"

He gulped. *I think of me as your dessert.* "I didn't think anything."

"Liar."

He narrowed his eyes at her. "Why don't you show me?"

She chuckled. "You asked for it, but you will be so disappointed." She shook the can again, opened it, and poured it directly into her mouth. "See, no food."

His jaw dropped. "Are you *serious*?"

She looked innocently at him. "I thought you didn't think about it?"

He scowled at her.

"Here. Try it." She held out the can, ready to squeeze it into his mouth. She was on her knees, leaning toward him.

Noodle paid no attention, as he was fast asleep.

Connor obliged. Why not? She squeezed, and his mouth filled with the cream. He swallowed it nice and slowly, keeping eye contact with her. Her pupils dilated.

"You have a bit on your chin," she told him.

He rubbed his face but didn't find it.

"No, here." She leaned closer so her thumb could swipe it.

She held it up to show him she had gotten it. Without thinking, he sucked her thumb into his mouth, licking it clean. She gasped, and her eyes widened.

"What if I told you I did think about it? I was thinking about licking it off your naked body. I was thinking about you licking it off *mine*."

Her grin was so naughty.

Chapter 4: Gracie

THEY HAD BARELY SPOKEN ON the way back to the car. The tension was simmering. A good tension. Sexual tension they both wanted to see to the end; they just needed privacy first.

Connor had admitted to wanting her. He had admitted that he wanted to lick whipped cream from her body, and he wanted her to do the same to him. She had taken his hand and led the way.

One lick of her finger and she was done for. She ached between her legs, desperately needing *him*.

The drive back had been just as silent. Connor's hand had rested on her knee as much as it could, slowly rubbing circles. He was reminding her of what he wanted. If she stopped him, he would stop. So, she let him carry on.

Back at her house, Noodle was very quick to run to his bed, happy after a long walk.

That left the two humans staring at each other in the doorway. Connor was waiting at the front door for her final decision. She swallowed. This was a man ready to claim. Who knew all it took was some whipped cream?

She tried to find her voice. "Are you coming in, Connor?"

His eyelids lowered. His head dipped, too, barely leaving a gap between their lips. "Are you asking me?"

She nodded. "Yes."

"Then I will be right back." He turned around and headed to the car, grabbing the can from the picnic basket.

She trembled, looking forward to what was to come. Both Connor and Gracie, and very, very soon.

He stepped back into the house. "Last chance."

As an answer, Gracie lunged at him, desperate for his touch. Her arms wrapped around his neck while her legs circled his waist. One of his arms embraced her, keeping her steady. His free hand grabbed her ass and squeezed.

He kicked the door shut. Once it was closed, his mouth descended on her own. Claiming her. His lips were demanding as they moved against hers. His tongue slid past her lips, tasting her and mating with hers.

He pulled apart just far enough so he could pant one word. "Bed?"

"Top of the stairs. First door on the right."

His mouth dropped to hers again. His teeth gently pulled her bottom lip, nibbling as he carried her. He didn't miss a step as he devoured her on the way up.

After kicking open the bedroom door, he threw her onto the bed. . They were both panting as they stared at each other. The ache between her legs was now thrumming.

She needed him. She needed him now. With her arms held out to him, she silently asked him to join her.

His smile was wicked as he gently put the can down on the bedside table. "Hmm. I fancy something sweet. I think I'll have you for dessert."

He fell on her and began kissing down her neck. After each item of clothing he took off, he kissed the revealed skin. Each kiss left her a panting mess beneath him. Her hands clung to his shoulders for dear life.

He raised an eyebrow at her when he paused, looking down at what he had left her in—a matching blue lingerie set.

"Something you want to tell me, Gracie?"

He cupped a breast, squeezing it. It felt so damn good. He then kissed between her breasts. She moaned.

"I was hoping we would argue," she admitted. "Every time we argue we get so close to this. But this time, we wouldn't have work in the way."

He swore and continued to kiss her. Now he was starting to stroke her. His left hand had dipped under the waistband of her panties. His fingertips grazed the spot between her legs, making her jolt.

"Disappointed we didn't argue?" He pulled back. "I suppose we could. I could get up and leave . . ."

"Don't you dare!" she snapped, making him laugh as she pulled him back down.

"There. We've argued. Now, let me enjoy." He peeled her bra and panties away, leaving her bare beneath his gaze.

"*Fuck.*" His mouth claimed her breast, teasing her nipple with his tongue.

Gracie wrapped her fingers in his hair, keeping him exactly where she wanted him. She pouted when he pulled away. When he peeled off his coat, revealing his waistcoat, she stopped pouting, biting her lip instead. She loved seeing him in a waistcoat.

And he knew it.

He leaned down to whisper in her ear, "Now, are we sure it's *Graham* you like in a waistcoat?"

She lowered her eyelids. "Jealous?"

"*Very.*" His kiss was savage. "But it's me in this bed with you. It'll be me you think about. It will be me who's going to fill you. I will buy a whole damn wardrobe full of waistcoats if I have to, but you will think of only *me.*"

She purred beneath him. "Only you."

"Damn. Fucking. Straight. Now spread those legs. I need to feast. I am ready for dessert now."

She watched him finish undressing, enjoying every inch of tanned skin that came into view. His cock was erect, so he fisted it and pumped it a few times, making sure she saw.

Having taunted her enough, he shoved her knees further apart and scooted down the bed until his mouth was level with her thighs. He grabbed the can on his way.

Without delay, he poured a healthy dose between her legs. She moaned at the sudden sensation and tried to close her legs.

"Not a fucking chance." Connor's hands kept her wide open.

He went down and his tongue came out. He *licked*. His whole face was buried between her legs, getting covered in the cream. It was messy and so damn good.

"Connor!"

"Hmm?" He looked up, slowly licking clean what he could reach. "More?"

She couldn't speak, so she nodded.

He poured another dose, this one much bigger. He also covered her breasts. "For seconds."

His mouth got back to work, licking and sucking. Her hips tried to buck, but he pinned her down. His tongue penetrated her, moving in and out just like she wanted his cock to do to her. He moved one hand so his fingers could join in. Two fingers pushed inside, going in deep. She felt full, but not full enough.

His mouth alternated between claiming her with his tongue and sucking on her clit. With his fingers constantly moving, it didn't take long for her body to clench around him. She cried out from the orgasm. He kept licking her until she was a sated heap on the duvet, lapping up every bit of cream.

"You're fucking delicious, and I want more." He climbed up her body. His tongue glided over her skin as he went.

When he reached her breasts, he lapped them gently. His cock was nestled between her legs, so he started to rock.

"I could slide into you right now," he told her. "But I won't. Not yet. I need to taste more. I need you to taste *me*."

He kissed her, and she could taste her own essence mixed in with the sweetness of the cream. She licked her lips.

"You have a bit on your face," she told him.

"Then perhaps you need to clean me up," he suggested.

She obliged, holding his cheeks as she drew her tongue across his face, claiming every last drop.

"Have you ever tried chocolate sauce and marshmallows?" she asked. "It's *divine*."

Connor actually whimpered. "You're going to drive me insane, woman. So let's make that mouth and tongue busy."

He stood up at the end of the bed and grabbed her ankles to pull her to the edge. With her feet planted on the floor, he knelt over her, spreading the cream over his cock. Her mouth watered.

She tried to roll him over, but he shook his head. "Oh, no. You can stay right where you are. I want you under me."

He lowered himself, placing his cock between her lips, and pushed down. Elbows resting on the mattress, he moved his hips up and down, pumping into her mouth. Cream filled her mouth every time he moved. She licked and sucked. She loved the sweet and salty taste as his essence mixed with the dessert. Her fingers gripped his ass so she could hold on and get a better angle.

"What was your comment the other day about deep throating?" he asked, panting.

She chuckled around his cock, vibrating her throat. Loving each of his curses, she relaxed a little bit more, letting his cock hit the back of her throat.

"Oh, fuck me! Gracie!"

His hips moved faster, losing their rhythm. His forehead pushed into the mattress as he grunted.

Suddenly, he pulled out, leaving Gracie feeling empty.

"You're going to make me come, and I am not ready yet."

He looked like a god as he knelt over her, his hair falling over his face.

He smiled. "I made a mess of you. Let me help you clean up." He kissed her, his tongue sneaking out to catch the cream around her lips. "Perfect. Now on your knees. Hold the headboard."

She did what she was told, shaking her ass at him.

He spanked it. "Hold still or I can't fuck you. We don't want that, now do we?"

He used his knees to spread her wider. He cursed and grabbed his jeans, retrieving a condom from his wallet. Once covered, he got back in position, pushing between her shoulders to lower her upper body to the mattress. Her ass went higher into the air.

"You better hold on tight, baby, because here I *come*."

He pushed into her, making her gasp at the sudden invasion. One of his hands gripped her waist, keeping her close to him. The other fisted her hair to pull up her face so he could kiss her.

"Right here is where I belong. Say it, Gracie."

"Right . . . here . . ." she panted out.

Connor pounded into her body, taking her as hard and deep as he could. Her body craved him and rushed toward a release. Every time he thrusted, her body bounced. It was a rough mating. A claiming. And she loved it.

Her body tensed around his, and she cried out. He shouted out her name as he followed right behind her.

He chuckled as he leaned down to whisper, "Guess what, Gracie? We've clicked. And now you're fucking *mine*."

Epilogue: Connor

One Year Later

TOO LATE TO TURN BACK now! Connor aimed and fired. The plastic arrow hit the whiteboard. It stayed stuck, thank goodness! He needed her to see it.

Gracie saw it and glared at him. "Connor!"

"You should be used to this by now." He grinned. "Just remember you love me. Out of all the humans you could have picked, you picked me to be your human."

She pulled a face at him that warned him she was regretting her decision at that moment, then pulled the arrow off the wall. That was when she noticed something attached to it. Her eyes widened. "Connor?"

He approached her. The whole team working that day now watched as he took the arrow and got down on one knee.

The restaurant was quiet, as they were closed, so there were no diners to interrupt this moment.

Gracie's jaw dropped. She couldn't take her eyes off him.

"Now that I have your attention." He untied the ring and took her hand. "The legend goes that if someone is hit with Cupid's arrow, they fall in love."

"I wasn't hit with it. And neither were you." She seemed to be in shock.

"Well, I wasn't going to fire it *at* you." He laughed, taking it from her and slapping it against his arm. "There, I have been hit with it."

She rolled her eyes at him.

"Gracie Watts, I love you with every fiber of my being. One year ago, we went on our Compulsory Date. It was the best punishment I have ever had to endure."

She smiled. The team chuckled.

"You told me it was the best Valentine's Day you had ever had. I accepted that as a personal challenge to make each one better than the last. I am asking you this Valentine's Day to accept me as I am. To take me as your husband and love me forever, so I can love you forever. Will you marry me?"

Waiting for her answer, he had never felt so terrified in his life as silence filled the room.

Tears formed in her eyes. "Yes. YES!" She jumped up and down. "I love you so much!"

Connor quickly slid the ring on her finger and got up so he could catch her mid-jump. He wrapped one arm around her waist. The other held her cheek so he could kiss her gently.

The room cheered as they kissed.

His mother had the best reaction. Her jaw had dropped, and then she had excitedly shaken Caitlyn and Lucy, who both looked terrified at their boss.

While they cheered, he took the opportunity to whisper in her ear, "I was hoping you would say yes. I think I'll have you for dessert again. This time I bought strawberry sauce and sprinkles."

She shivered in delight. "Oh, that sounds delicious." Her smile turned devious as she grabbed the arrow still stuck to his arm. "But just because we are getting married does not mean I will not deep throat you with this if you shoot near me again."

He grinned wickedly. "As long as you stay with me, I can cope with that."

He kissed her senseless as the room continued to celebrate. His mother interrupted so she could hug them both, kissing Gracie's cheek and welcoming her to the family. She already loved Gracie, and now she could love her as her daughter. Of course she did it with a smug smile on her face.

He watched his wife-to-be and his mother admire the ring while the team congratulated him.

Life was better than good. He'd never have guessed last Valentine's Day that this would be where he was now. He didn't have a single regret, and he'd spend his life making sure Gracie didn't either.

About the Author

Born and raised in Warwickshire, UK, Rowen Burrows lives with her husband and miniature poodles and has a background in museums, customer service, and retail.

Her main focus is paranormal romance, but she has recently delved into contemporary romance, as well. She is currently working on three series: The Wing Mate series, The Legends series, and Sweet Christmas standalones.

Rowen started her writing journey at a young age, but in 2023, at the age of thirty, she decided to push herself and share her stories with the world.

You can find Rowen on:
Instagram and Facebook @rowenburrowsauthor

CUPCAKES &
COMPLICATIONS

Cupcakes & Complications

Carrie Bassen

ERIC MOVES CLOSER TO ME as he lifts his hand and rubs powdered sugar from my cheek. Not taking his impossibly dark eyes from mine, he brings his fingers to his lips, licking the white powder off. Before I can think better of it, my mouth is against his as I press my body into him. He grips me just as tightly as I'm holding on to him, with his hands touching the strip of exposed skin between the waistband of my leggings and my shirt. From my position on the counter, I can feel the length of him against me even through his jeans. When I shift ever so slightly to push myself closer, he makes a noise that is almost a growl before moving his lips off my own.

"Where?"

Anywhere would be my reply, but probably the bedroom is best, so I point toward the door to the left of the living room. With my legs still wrapped around him, he picks me up and we make it to the bedroom in record time. He practically throws us onto the bed and begins kissing my neck. When his mouth finds an especially sensitive spot under my ear, I let out a breath and feel my body temperature rise.

He must take my noise as encouragement, because his hand makes its way inside my leggings and two of his fingers slide into me, finding me achingly wet. How many times have I watched his hands as he ran them through his hair or ate dinner, even having some not-so-platonic thoughts? And not once did I accurately imagine his skill.

When I feel like I can't take it anymore, I push his hands off me, which he allows me to do, and begin taking off my clothes. He follows my lead until we are both naked. I have a moment to appreciate Eric naked before I pull him back to me and guide him inside of me.

"Cat, you are so fucking beautiful."

His compliment comes out as a whisper against my ear, and then we don't talk anymore.

If I had to describe my relationship with Eric, I'd say it's complicated. Although, complicated doesn't really explain it accurately. My best friend, Mollie, and I started a baking company when we graduated from college. Our business does okay, especially between the months of October and February with all the holidays. Even though we have been in business for almost three years, dating hasn't been on our minds. We are entrepreneurs conquering the world one cupcake at a time. There hasn't been time to date. Until Mollie met Eric.

Although they aren't dating, she desperately wants to, and she's been very vocal about this for the past two months. If I'd been the one to open the shop that day, it would have been me who saw him first, and I wouldn't be in this mess. But I had to deliver a tray of cookies to a school for a Christmas party. By the time I returned, she was giddy with excitement, telling me all about this guy who came in to get prices for an anniversary cake for his parents. *He's so cute. He's so handsome. He's so smart. He's amazing.* How she could tell all this from a ten-minute conversation is beyond my understanding. When she told me she asked him to coffee the next day, she was proud of herself. And even after that coffee, when she told me he was a gentleman and they mostly just discussed the cake and other things he might want to order for his parents' anniversary party, she had a determined expression of someone who would get her way. She would be Eric's girlfriend one day. Maybe even in time to attend that anniversary party.

While being single was by choice for me, Mollie had gotten her heart broken in college and just hadn't shown any interest in men again. She was finally moving on, and I was happy for her, honestly. But then I met Eric when he came to place his order.

I didn't even know it was him for a while, or maybe I didn't want to know. A man ordering an anniversary cake for his parents isn't so common, so I should have known immediately. But I didn't. Not while he picked out a design, leaning a bit closer to me than necessary to look through our catalogue. Not while I typed his contact information in my computer as he said I could call him anytime if I had questions about the order, or if I didn't have questions.

I didn't know it was Eric until he told me his name to type into the computer, which was the exact moment Mollie came in from the kitchen. He was nice to her. Perfectly polite. And it was so obvious that she wanted more from him and he just . . . didn't. But that was enough for me to stay away. While she flirted and he kept glancing at me, I finished my work on the computer and excused myself, not looking back. I'm a good friend. I let her deliver the anniversary cake I baked and decorated for his parents. I listened when she told me about the house and how adorable he looked in a dark-green sweater. I wrote him off as a guy I would not ever be with. Then I ran into him at the grocery store near the shop when I needed vanilla extract.

❤━━━━━━━━━❤

"Fancy seeing you here."

Hearing a deep voice that inexplicably curls my toes, I glance up from my crouched position in the baking aisle. Eric stands next to me, holding a shopping basket and looking down at me with a smile. Even though the answering smile lifts my cheeks before I can stop it, I quickly turn my head back to the various bottles staring accusingly at me, as if they, too, know my thoughts aren't platonic with this person.

"Hey." This is the only response I can think of that seems appropriate, since my best friend is three doors down and I've decided to stay away from the man towering above me.

Eric's breath ruffles my hair as he leans next to me, probably to see why I'm so engrossed in a bottle of vanilla extract.

"Help settle this debate I was having. Do you actually need vanilla when baking?"

Keeping my eyes forward, I ask, "Do you often find yourself debating the necessity of flavorings and spices?"

"On a daily basis."

"Really?" I mean it as a sarcastic comment, but instead it comes out sounding like a genuine question.

"Sarcasm not really your strong suit, huh?"

"Much like your baking knowledge."

"I won't lie. I am not a baker, made obvious by my shopping habits."

Looking in his basket, I see a bag of prepackaged sugar cookies. Don't say anything. Just get the vanilla and leave. As I stand, my mouth moves without my permission. "Huh."

He straightens also and crosses his arms. "What?"

"Nothing." I start walking, deciding not to get the noodles and sauce I was going to purchase for dinner.

Eric keeps pace with me as I make my way down the aisle. "I can feel the judgment radiating off you. Out with it."

Stopping near the chocolate chips, I turn to him. "Prepackaged cookies are oversweetened and full of crap. And dry. And prepackaged sugar cookies? It's the most boring cookie."

"Wow. I've never seen someone so passionate about my cookie choices."

A laugh escapes me as I take in his stance, legs spread slightly and arms raised in a gesture of surrender. His eyes light up at the sound, like I've just given him a compliment he wasn't expecting.

"So, what kind of cookies should I be buying?"

I give him my most deadpan glare, and it takes him only a moment to understand.

"You win. From now on, all my cookie purchases will be done at your store. Promise."

We look at each other for probably an entire sixty seconds until he broadly smiles at me, and it is the most natural thing in the world to smile too.

The next thing I knew, we were at dinner. Then the next night we went to the movies. Suddenly I am spending most of my free time with the man my best friend, who is practically my sister, hasn't stopped talking about. She even found out where he worked as a commercial architect right down the road. She was so excited to discover he helped design our building when he first started working there.

Once she knew where he worked, she managed to run into him a couple times, which sounds a little stalkerish, but anyone who knows Mollie knows she's just a sweet person. Sometimes a little too enthusiastic but sweet just the same.

And it wasn't intentional, me hooking up with Eric. It wasn't planned. I was testing out new recipes at home, trying to figure out something new we could offer for Valentine's Day, when he called, asking if I wanted to meet him for dinner. When I told him what I was doing, he wanted to come over and help. And get free cake. So I laughed and told him my address. Once the words left my mouth, I realized what a mistake it was for him to come over, where we'd be alone, which I'd been careful not to do. Even when we hung out, I'd meet him at the location to avoid riding in a car alone with him. And some small part of me always thought that was safer. No temptations. Friends eat dinner together. Friends go to the movies. Hell, me and Mollie do both those things all the time and we are certainly not dating.

The morning after our hookup, as I walk into the shop, I realize there is no getting around it. I crossed a line, probably a while ago when we first started spending time together, but definitely after last night. Do I tell Mollie? What good would that do? Do I break it off with Eric? We aren't anything official, so it's possible he won't even want to see me again. That causes an ache in my chest that I ignore. Mollie comes in just a few minutes after me, her hair still in curlers.

"I know, I know. I'm headed to the bathroom right now to fix my hair."

While it's common for her to come in not completely finished getting ready, she doesn't usually go to the trouble of curling her hair. I notice her makeup has been carefully applied as well.

Even though I fear I already know, I can't stop myself from asking, "What's the occasion?"

"I'm going to go see Eric."

"Oh yeah?"

Since he failed to mention that to me last night, I silently wonder if this is an unexpected visit. It's not like we spend much time talking about Mollie, but he knows how she feels about him, and he's tried to let her down gently.

"Guess who called me last night?"

Trying to adjust to her abrupt change in topic, I ask, "Who?"

"Nick."

"What?"

"Yeah! I tried to call you, but you didn't answer!"

Since I don't think telling her I was having sex with the guy she's been trying to date for two months would go over well, I just ask her what Nick wanted.

"He wants us to make desserts for this Valentine's Day party he's throwing. He even invited us."

If anyone ever thought it was odd for a grown man to throw a Valentine's Day party, then they just didn't know Nick. The man has a well-paying job and the most social personality I've ever seen. He could start a conversation with anyone. When he and Mollie were dating in college, I saw him talking to a guy at Home Depot about which brand of paint was best. The next weekend, that guy was playing video games on Nick's couch. Of course, that social personality is probably why he wasn't ready to settle down three years ago. They had dated all throughout college. But in the end, she had given him her virginity and he hadn't found her worth spending his life with.

"Did you tell him to fuck off?"

A small bubble of laughter escapes from her lips as she begins taking her curlers out right at the counter.

"No, but I had an idea. I was thinking of asking Eric to go with me to the party. As my date. To make Nick jealous."

She must see some sort of involuntary disapproval on my face, because she puts both hands up in front of her as she says, "Hear me out! I know Eric said he wasn't ready for a relationship. But this is a win-win either way. Nick sees me with Eric and realizes he made a huge mistake dumping me and that it's too late. And possibly Eric sees how much fun I am and decides maybe he is ready to date. Even if that doesn't happen, won't it be amazing to see the look on Nick's face when I bring tall, dark, and handsome Eric with me? And maybe Eric has a friend he can bring so we can double!"

There's not much that sounds less appealing to me than going to my best friend's ex-boyfriend's house with her, the man she's been pining after who I happen to have had sex with, and one of his friends as my date for the evening.

"Does he have any idea how busy we're going to be next week? He certainly waited until the last minute to call you."

"We have time! I'll work nights."

I love Mollie. I do. But she sometimes doesn't think about everything. For instance, she doesn't decorate any of our desserts. They turn out terribly. So, more likely, I will be the one working late into the night next week on all our Valentine's Day orders. Baking the stuff doesn't take nearly as much time as icing it all does.

While I'm debating how much I don't want to do this, Mollie finishes her hair just as the chime above the door goes off, announcing a customer.

We both turn to the door to see Eric enter, holding a drink carrier with three cups of coffee. Our eyes meet briefly, and I can't help the small smile that creeps onto my face before I look away, instead focusing on the coffee.

"Speak of the devil! We were just talking about you."

In her excitement, Mollie sounds like she's a five-year-old on Christmas morning.

Eric looks again at me before focusing his attention on Mollie as he makes his way up to us, where I'm sitting at the computer and she's leaning against the counter beside me.

"Is that so?"

"Yeah! What's this?"

She looks at the coffee like he is about to get down on one knee and propose. The guilt that was already in my stomach grows until it's hard for me to look at her.

"Thought you guys might need the caffeine . . ."

Because I'd been up half the night naked in bed with him. One part of me is touched by this act of kindness; another part wonders if this looks suspicious to Mollie. And while I'm so grateful he thought to get one for her too, I have to wonder if this is getting her hopes up.

"Thank you so much. I was actually going to come by and talk to you today."

He takes a sip of his coffee as he responds, "Oh?"

"So, my ex-boyfriend invited us to this party he's having on Valentine's Day. And we were thinking it'd be cool if maybe you came as my date. It's not that I'm into him anymore or anything, but just to show him what he missed out on and that it's too late to get me back."

She takes a deep breath and continues, talking even faster. "Okay, that sounds dumber when I say it out loud all at once."

I'm careful to keep my eyes on my coffee as I bring it to my lips and take a sip. The warmth of it helps the chill of the shop. Even though we have heat, we usually keep it turned very low when we are closed, so it takes a while in the morning to heat back up. I also notice he remembered what type of coffee I like, but I push that thought away to focus on their conversation.

"Not so dumb. What do you think of the idea, Cat?"

Looking at Eric, I appreciate that he's letting me have an opinion on this. What I want to tell him is no, he can't take my best friend out and pretend to be her boyfriend, because I want him to be my boyfriend. Of course, I don't say that.

"Mollie, why on earth would I want to go to Nick's party? He dumped you the night of our graduation with no reason except he wanted to 'spread his wings and fly.' I'd rather just turn down the business and let him find someone else to make a cake for his party."

"Not a cake. Cupcakes. And maybe cookies. We didn't really go over specifics. I told him to call us today. And I know he was a crappy boyfriend, but please do this for me! I'll be grateful for the rest of my life!"

It's not the words that finally make me agree; it's her pleading face. The bottom line is this will make her happy. Since I feel partially responsible for ruining her chances with Eric, even if she doesn't know about it, I have to do this for her.

Eric leaves shortly after agreeing to find me a date for the party, and I can't read his expression. Mollie is ecstatic as soon as the door shuts behind him.

"Thank you, thank you, thank you! You're the bestest friend a girl could have."

As if my guilt couldn't get any worse.

We are discussing one of my ideas about having miniature cream-filled chocolate cakes available just for Valentine's Day when one of our regulars comes in. Mrs. Meadows is a retired chef who's probably in her seventies. She's been one of our regular customers since the month after we opened.

"Hello, Mollie. Hello, Catherine. How are you girls doing today?"

"Doing good. How are you?" Mollie replies.

We both smile at the woman as I go to the back to pick up her monthly lemon pound cake.

When I return to the front, Mollie is already oversharing, but that's just a common thing for her, especially with Mrs. Meadows, who is only second in her kind disposition to Mollie.

"He's wonderful, but I don't know. He doesn't seem into me."

As I ring her up, Mrs. Meadows responds, "Well, how wonderful can he be if he isn't into you? And how about you, Catherine? Seeing anyone?"

Aware of the slight blush that tinges my cheeks, I hope Mollie doesn't notice as I finish sliding her credit card and keep my eyes on the machine in front of me.

"Not at the moment."

Not technically a lie, right?

Once Mrs. Meadows leaves, I'm relieved when Mollie continues our discussion on cream-filled cakes instead of bringing up a certain someone I'm not currently seeing.

I take my lunch at one, right after Mollie returns. This isn't an uncommon thing, but today I have another reason for not eating lunch with her.

When I finally find Eric, he's leaning over his desk in a small office in the back of his building. Rolled-up building plans and papers are scattered on a table by the door. His desk is neater, with a laptop and just a few papers and sticky notes lying about.

"Before you ask, Mollie was literally telling me about her plan when you walked in. I had nothing to do with it. And thank you for the coffee."

He looks up from his desk and smiles as he leans back in his chair.

"Glad to hear it. I was half-convinced I'd imagined last night. Hi there."

Moving around his desk, I set the bag of Chinese food down. "Hi."

I lean against his chair as I examine what he was working on. It appears to be a drawing of the interior of a building. A much fancier building than the one either of us work in.

"Did you draw this? It's beautiful."

He grins at me as he nods, and his cheeks turn a slight pink. "Thanks. What's this?"

Still examining the detailed drawing, I reply, "I brought you lunch."

"I have sex with you and get fed the next day? Should've done this a lot sooner."

Lightly shoving him, I glance back to make sure I shut his office door when I came in. There weren't a lot of people in his building, but a few noticed me come in.

Instead of opening the bag and eating, Eric stands up. With our height difference of about a foot, I have to look up quite a bit to meet his eyes.

"Thanks for lunch. Stay and eat with me?"

He lightly touches his lips to mine in a way I think is supposed to be just a quick kiss but turns into something deeper. A light knock sounds on the door just as his hands roam down to my ass. We separate, and I take a seat across from his desk while he returns to his chair.

"Come in."

A portly man with a bald head and a bushy mustache opens the door. He apologizes for interrupting but doesn't seem to realize just what he interrupted. He asks Eric some question about an email concerning an approaching deadline. I admit I tune out as I look around Eric's office, realizing at least some of the drawings of various buildings must have been drawn by him.

When his coworker leaves, shutting the door behind him, Eric takes out our food.

He must feel my eyes on him, because he asks, "What?"

"You're an artist."

Again, his face pinkens slightly and he doesn't make eye contact. "Not really."

Pointing at the pictures on his desk, I say, "These are really good."

"Thanks."

Since he seems embarrassed by the praise, which is both adorable and unpretentious, I change topics.

"Did you always want to be an architect?"

"After I got over my dreams of being a cowboy and a superhero. You?"

"No, I never wanted to be an architect."

Taking a bite of broccoli, he responds, "Funny."

I give him a slight bow in my chair before answering his question. "I used to want to be a teacher."

"What kind?"

"Elementary school. It's actually what my degree is in."

"What happened?"

"Senior year of college, we had to student teach, where we went and worked in a classroom every day for a semester. It was okay, helping teach the kids and working on lesson plans, but the teacher was always throwing parties for the class. I swear almost every Friday would be some celebration in her room. I started bringing snacks in for the parties too. Well, one time I was bored at my apartment and decided to try to bake something from scratch. And I loved it. Everything about it. Shopping for ingredients. Measuring. Mixing. Taste-testing, obviously. Every week after that, I experimented with different things. It was so much fun. By the time the semester ended, I could tell you all these different recipes but couldn't tell you any of the students' names. Decided that fact alone meant I was pursuing the wrong profession."

"Based on what I've tried from your bakery, you definitely made the right choice. But for what it's worth, I think you'd have been a great teacher."

"Thanks."

"I mean, you taught me a thing or two last night."

Deciding another change of subject is in order, I say, "So, thanks for going with Mollie to that party."

"It's not every day that the girl you're dating thanks you for taking another girl out on Valentine's Day. Although I would've said no if you weren't going with us. At least this way I get to spend Valentine's Day with you . . . in a weird way."

Hearing him call me the girl he's dating sends a happy shiver through me, but I just roll my eyes at him as I ask, "Have you figured out who you're going to set me up with?"

He chuckles. "Haven't gotten that far yet."

The night before Valentine's Day, I know I have made a mistake. Not the hooking up with Eric part, which I've done a total of three times now, but agreeing to Mollie's idea. It is seven o'clock and dark outside. It might be snowing, but it's hard to tell since I only get glimpses of the windows in the front of the shop as I move through the kitchen in the back. And I am a mess trying to decorate these cupcakes for the party tomorrow night. My apron has icing all over it, as do my hands, and I am pretty sure I've gotten it on my face too. Mollie left after baking everything, which really doesn't matter since she couldn't be any help to me anyway. It just would've been nice for her to keep me company.

As I'm adding more red icing to the piping bag, I hear a knock on the front door. Even if the lights are on, we've been closed for hours, so I ignore it until I hear it again a minute later. Sighing, I set down the bag and go out to the front to let whoever is there know we are closed, since the locked door and sign didn't tip them off.

When I get close, I realize it's Eric at the door. I move a little faster since it is snowing outside. Ushering him inside, I lock the door behind him as he pulls his knit hat off his head.

"Thought you were in here. What are you doing?"

"Running behind. Decorating cupcakes."

He grabs my waist and pulls me close.

"You're going to get icing all over your coat."

Shrugging, he kisses me quickly before replying, "Worth it. Need my help?"

"You can keep me company."

Taking one of his hands, I pull him after me into the kitchen. After one try, it's obvious all he'll be able to do is alleviate my loneliness. He's worse at this than Mollie is, which makes me laugh. Unoffended, he just sits on a counter away from the mess, eating one of the cookies that I broke earlier in the evening while I fix his attempt at icing a cupcake.

"You want a ride home tonight?"

Giving him a skeptical look before continuing, I ask, "How will I get to work tomorrow?"

"I can give you a ride to work. It's not far from me."

Since he works right down the street, I can't help the snort that escapes me.

"Your plan is to drop me off at my apartment, drive to your place to sleep, and come all the way back to pick me up in the morning?"

"Oh no. My plan is to stay the night at your apartment."

Keeping my attention on the cupcake in front of me, I say, "Huh. What about clothes? And a toothbrush?" Glancing at the slight stubble that has grown on his cheeks, I add, "And a razor?"

Eric rubs his hand against his chin before shrugging. "If you think I haven't kept an overnight bag in my car since the first time I went over to your apartment in case a situation like this presented itself, you would be sorely mistaken."

He gives me that half-smile of his that I have a hard time resisting, and I turn back to the cupcake I'm decorating. "Okay."

Thankfully, decorating goes by a lot faster having Eric to entertain me, and we make it to my apartment before nine. Since it's still not too late, we make popcorn and change into our pajamas to watch a movie, which means I wear a large T-shirt and no pants. He gives me a heated look but picks a movie, choosing an absurd film about genetically modified sea turtles living in Florida that kill everyone who ends up near their beach. We curl up onto the couch, and eventually I pay attention to the movie after getting used to his hand running up and down my bare leg.

I've decided Eric must have chosen this movie to just watch me laugh, because there are two obvious facts. This movie is ridiculous, and Eric hasn't taken his eyes off me the entire time. As I'm chuckling at a nest of sea turtles hatching and attacking an old lady tanning on the beach, I meet Eric's eyes.

"What?"

"You are so beautiful."

Before I can reply, his lips are on mine and my body responds instantly. As he grips my waist, I move to straddle him on the sofa.

Warmth gathers deep in my stomach as his hands slide under my shirt and move up to caress my breast. I pull his shirt over his head before running my fingers along his smooth skin as he slides mine over my head and looks at me.

Eric whispers, "Incredible."

Then his mouth is on me, moving from my neck to my nipple, nibbling and sucking all along the way. The only things between us are his pajama pants and my panties, which we easily remove. I kiss his neck as I hear the familiar rip of plastic and help roll the condom over Eric's erection, which is so rigid in my hand it must be painful to him. I lower myself onto his hardness and enjoy the moan that escapes his lips.

After a moment, we get a rhythm. I move on top of him, gaining speed, my hands wrapped in his thick hair. One of his hands grips my hip, and his mouth is always on some part of me. I tremble in his arms as he bites my ear and drags his teeth to my neck, kissing my skin as a moan escapes me.

"Damn, Cat. You feel so fucking good."

As I continue moving, Eric takes the hand not holding me to him and finds my clit, moving his fingers so that the pressure builds until I'm unraveling in his arms, taking him with me as I go.

Catching my breath, I am about to get off him, but he just stands, lifting me up with him, and carries me into the bedroom, where we curl under the covers. And somehow cuddling turns into kissing, kissing into touching, and we are doing it all over again.

The next morning, the smell of bacon wakes me up, which is not an unpleasant way to awaken. Pulling on my robe as I walk into the kitchen, I find Eric cooking at my stove in his boxers. There are definitely worse ways to wake up.

"Good morning, beautiful."

Making my way to the coffee maker, I pour myself a cup as I say, "I need to invite you to stay the night more often. What's all this?"

"Well, I seem to recall I invited myself over last night. And since I don't get to celebrate Valentine's Day with you properly tonight, I figured the least I could do is make you breakfast."

As he pulls the last strip of bacon from the pan, he nods toward the coffee table, where I see what looks like a jewelry box.

"There may be a small present for you over there. Nothing big."

Since presents are probably my favorite thing (who doesn't like presents?), I do a little happy dance to the table, where I open the box to find earrings. Two small odd-shaped studs, each made of half diamonds and half some red stone like rubies. It takes me a moment to realize what they are, and I laugh.

"You got me cupcake earrings!"

He smiles at me. "It took me longer than that to figure out what they were. I was convinced the jeweler was playing some prank on me."

Lifting myself onto my toes, I wrap my arms around his neck and hug him with all my strength. When I put on the earrings, I watch them sparkle in the mirror. After we eat the delicious breakfast and take the longest but best shower I've ever taken, I give him the present I picked up earlier this week. While I'm convinced it's not nearly as good as the earrings he got me, he seems to like the faux leather sketchbook I got him.

"Because you're an artist."

That adorable blush appears on his cheeks again as he replies, "Sure."

"You are! I saw the pictures in your office. Amazing. You should draw me sometime."

He watches me for a moment, seeming to decide if I'm being genuine. I absolutely am.

"I'll use my new sketchbook."

"I'll pose naked."

"You better."

Eric drops me off near my building with a kiss and a promise to see me later, and I make it into work before Mollie, which is a relief since I didn't have any explanation for why my car was parked in front of the building all night. She comes in while I am packaging up all our orders for pickup. Valentine's Day is one of our busiest days for foot traffic, since couples come by after lunch or men come in last minute for something sweet for dessert later.

Mollie helps me place labels on our individual cupcakes, not saying much this morning.

"Nervous to see Nick?"

She glances up as she presses down on a label. "No. Yes. I don't know. I'm thinking of canceling. Maybe you can drop off the stuff."

"Why?"

Shrugging, she picks up another label as she answers, "Lots of reasons. For one thing, he dumped me. Years ago. Why do I care what he thinks of me anymore?"

"Can't argue with that."

"And Eric. He's not into me. So why should I keep trying?"

There's not much I can say to that, but I let her think in silence as we finish the task at hand.

Since the lunch rush is busier than usual, neither of us leaves for a break, instead eating snacks between customers. By closing time, I'm tired, hungry, and hoping Mollie's decided to cancel our plans for the night. But since she doesn't mention that again, I drive to my apartment to pick up my clothes and head to her place to get ready, remembering to bring the cupcakes and cookies for the party.

Mollie's apartment is much smaller than mine, but it's in a nicer part of town, so I figure it's an even trade. She answers the door looking subdued, but while we get ready, her mood seems to pick up. We curl each other's hair and help with makeup. Since I focus on Mollie's goal of making Nick regret ever leaving her, I do my best to help her look as gorgeous as I can. We somehow find ourselves sharing stories of times Nick did something ridiculous.

She's applying blush on my cheeks as she laughs. "Remember when he got so drunk at that keg party that he thought the black trash bag was a dog? He kept calling for it to come here."

I laugh as I say, "And when it didn't move, he finally crawled under the fence to pet it."

"Even though he sucks, he was fun. Nice too. Until he broke up with me."

"You're right. He does suck."

After much debate, she decides to wear a pink tube top covered with sequins, paired with a short black skirt over black tights and black ankle boots. When I point out she might be cold, she just shrugs and says she has her jacket until she gets inside. And I have to admit, with that outfit and her curled long blonde hair, if I'd broken up with her, I'd be regretting it right now.

Mollie quickly deems my clothes to be unsatisfactory. After some arguing, I finally convince her my black pants are fine, and she doesn't fight me about my ankle boots since they are almost identical to the ones she's wearing. But there's no debate in her mind as she thrusts a shirt at me, saying the deep-red color goes great with my black hair. And she's not wrong. The shirt she gives me is a halter top made of a dark-red velvet. I'm happy it matches my earrings too, but it shows a bit more skin than I'd planned. My date for the evening is bound to like that. I wonder what Eric will think.

My answer comes soon enough when the doorbell rings. Mollie is putting on the last touches of her makeup in the bedroom, so I go to the door. Eric is wearing a burgundy button-up shirt and black pants under his gray coat. He even ran a brush through his hair, which isn't usual.

I smile at him. "You clean up well."

He looks like he wants to say more, but he returns my smile and says, "You too. I like your hair."

His hand moves up as if he's about to touch one of the curls hanging across my chest, but he clears his throat and moves to the side, introducing me to the man I didn't notice next to him.

"Cat, this is Michael."

Keeping the smile on my face, I shake the hand of my "date" for the evening. Not a bad looking man—just a few years older, with sandy-blond hair and kind eyes—but I'm happy Mollie comes out of the bedroom then. Examining her again, I'm struck by how gorgeous she is. Anyone would be lucky to have her. I glance over to Eric, curious to see his reaction, only to find his eyes on me. The way he's watching me makes my heart race and heat spread deep within me, so I turn my attention to Michael and see that at least he is appreciating Mollie's appearance.

The ride to Nick's isn't terrible. After loading our stuff in the trunk, Mollie and I sit in the back, which seems odd considering Mollie chose to sit next to me instead of in the front next to Eric. But I give her a grateful look for not making me sit in the back with Michael and try not to think about how one week ago Eric and I were naked in his back seat. Although, from the couple of times our eyes have met in the rearview mirror, I know it's on his mind as well.

Michael seems nice enough. He works with Eric, but he's not an architect, having more to do with the actual construction instead. He and Mollie do most of the talking, which is fine with me, and by the time we arrive at Nick's, I'm convinced they might be a good couple.

When we arrive, we park on a packed street and walk toward the sound of a loud bass. The house is easy to pick out, since even in the cold people are hanging out and smoking on the porch. We get inside and deliver our desserts to Nick, who might already be drunk. He hugs me a little too tightly and gives Mollie an appreciative whistle before hugging her with even more enthusiasm. After doing a pink Jell-O shot and getting a drink that looks like fruit punch but tastes strongly of vodka, I'm feeling the slight buzz in my head. I'm a pretty small person, so it doesn't take much. Mollie pulls me to the side once Nick's attention moves on to someone else.

"Nick doesn't seem as great as I remembered."

Watching him dance drunkenly to the music playing in the living room as he spills his drink on the already stained carpet, I can't say she's wrong.

After I nod my agreement, she asks, "What do you think of Michael?"

I swallow the last of my punch. "He's nice."

She has this intense look about her as she says, "Cute too."

"Sure."

"Maybe not your type."

"No, not really."

"Maybe Eric is more your type."

Her comment takes me by surprise, and from the look in her eyes, I can see she knows. I expect her to be angry or upset with me, but the only emotion I can see on her face is hurt.

"You could have told me. It's not like he was my boyfriend or anything."

There's a moment of silence between us before I ask, "When?"

She rolls her eyes. "Well, the thought occurred to me when he called you by your nickname that day he brought us coffee, since customers always call you Catherine."

That was a while ago, after the first time we hooked up.

"But I didn't really know until yesterday. I came back to the shop to keep you company. I felt bad you were working so late. When I pulled up, you were letting Eric in, which I thought was odd. But when he kissed you, it all made sense. Just please tell me you did not get it on in our kitchen. I'm sure that's against so many health codes."

Her comment makes me laugh, but I quickly stop and meet her eyes.

"I'm sorry. The longer I waited to tell you, the worse it got."

Mollie struggles to form a reply, possibly examining me to make sure I'm appropriately apologetic. She must like whatever she sees, because she responds, "You're my best friend. He's just a guy I had a crush on. It'll take more than that to make me hate you. Now I have a question for you. How much of a chance do you think I have with Michael?"

She leads me to Eric and Michael, who are drinking beers and discussing some football team. She releases my arm and touches Michael's shoulder.

"Wanna dance?"

How anyone could turn down this woman, I'll never know. Michael gives me a brief glance, since I am supposed to be his date for the night, but I just smile at him and nod.

Seeming happy enough at the turn of events, he takes her hand and follows her into the living room. Just before I lose sight of them, Mollie turns back and winks at me.

Eric looks at me with his eyebrows raised and a small smile on his lips.

"What's that about?"

Since there's only one reply I can think of, I stand on my toes and turn my face up to kiss him. With our height difference, there is no way I can reach him without his help. He doesn't hesitate to meet me halfway.

About the Author

Carrie Bassen writes romance stories filled with passion, chemistry, and irresistible connections. Her books are full of steamy, heartfelt moments that keep readers hooked. When she's not writing, Carrie enjoys hot tea, chocolate, and cozy nights in. Dive into her stories for your next unforgettable read.

You can find Carrie on:
Instagram @carrie_bassen

Visit her website at:
https://sites.google.com/view/carriebassen/home

THE TASTE OF SIN

The Taste of Sin

Caz Luan

I SWERVE OUT OF THE way just in time. I am sick of being ignored on the road but can't give up my bike. It is the only thing I have left of my old life. A life when I was still loved and had the freedom to go anywhere and be anything. Now, I am the manager of this prestigious restaurant in the middle of midtown Sandton. Though it makes sense to take the bike when traffic gets going, I barely make it in time for the night shift. And then, I almost get run down by something that resembles a delivery truck. Just what I need today of all days.

"What took you so long, Boss? We almost started without you." Mel, my second-in-command and my best friend, pulls me to the side. "Are you okay, Vi? You look a little rattled."

I slightly changed my name when I disappeared, but my mother gave me the name Aviana, and that is all I have left of her.

"Yeah, no. Just some asshole who cut me off on my way in. I swear, one of these days, my luck will run out."

"Or it is going to change. I saw that someone dropped off a little delivery for you. I put it on your desk and wanted you to look at it

243

before the staff meeting, but of course, you decided to come late." Mel gives me some side-eye.

I take off my gear while walking to my office and throw it on my chair before I slip into my heels, ready to work. They make me a little taller and give me a fraction more authority over the new lanky waiters. Taking a deep breath, I push everything else to the back of my mind and start my shift.

Eight hours later, I kick off my heels and lower myself into my rickety old chair, done with not only work but the whole day. I put my feet on my desk, which isn't as empty as always. My feet push up against a pretty little pink box with a flamboyant turquoise bow. I look around the office as if the giver of this gift is hiding in the dark corners or under the desk.

Mel pops her head into the office. "Did you find your little gift? I thought it was quite cute. I wanted to rip it open, but I saw the tag with all the instructions."

"What are you talking about?" I bite my lip and give my head a slight shake.

She playfully hits me against the shoulder and reaches for the foreign object that has now captured my full attention. She picks it up and places it in my lap.

"Go on, open it. I have been dying all night to see what is inside. I would have pestered you earlier if we weren't so slammed."

My hands are practically shaking. I haven't received a gift in about five years, and the excitement threatens to break my last hold on this insane day. Mel is oblivious to it all.

"Come on. The suspense is killing me, and I might think you are doing this to get back at me for that horrible Karen you had to sort out for me earlier."

The distraction is welcome.

I place my hand on her shoulder. "You know that is my job, right? Besides, I would do anything for you. You have been a wonderful friend to me."

"Well, if that is the case, then let's open this puppy up and see what goodies are hidden inside. But make sure to read the tag first."

I look down at the elegantly written tag.

"For the night manager. Only to be opened and consumed by Vi Valentino. I will be available to discuss this at the next delivery."

The next delivery? What is this guy on about? Is it a guy?

I wet my lips and lean in. "Mel, did you see who dropped this off?"

A relaxed smile crosses her face, and she tilts her head to the side.

"Why are you doing this to me? Won't it be easier to just tell me?" My foot starts tapping. "You could put me out of my misery, and I would owe you one."

She takes the box from me and puts it back on the table before hugging me tightly.

"You might not want to see it, Vi, but you deserve more than all this. And I feel this little pink box might just contain the adventure you need. That is why you must let go and give yourself a chance."

I know she is right, but I can't admit that even to myself. I gently push her away and blink rapidly to regain some control. Mel's hand is covering her mouth, and her hands reach for me but abandon the motion halfway.

"Stop analyzing me. You aren't a psychologist yet," I grumble.

"That is true, but it doesn't stop me from being your friend. And noticing that you need more in your life than this secret sadness that has a chokehold on you. Recognizing that you are hiding from life doesn't take a doctor to see."

I look away, clearly trying to avoid this situation. And my eyes fall on the box.

Mel backs up to the door and disappears without another word, noticing that I have already checked out of our conversation.

I cautiously move closer. It has been years, but you never know. The past has a way of finding and exploiting your weaknesses. Mel, however, is convinced this box contains something good. And I need something good. I have needed something good for so long that I have forgotten what it is supposed to feel like. I touch the dainty bow and feel the silky smoothness under my fingers. It reminds me of things long gone. I slowly remove the lid from the box and can't contain my high-pitched squeal. In the box neatly placed in the middle are four white petite fours with little pink flower decorations. They look too beautiful to eat, yet they are my favorite in the whole world. I pick up the one closest to me and admire it. The work is so delicate, and I feel that awkward, lost feeling flooding back.

I haven't touched decadence like this in so many years. It always reminded me of a time long gone. I walk to the kitchen, take out a plate, and put the most beautiful thing I have ever seen right in the middle. Do I dare believe that it is even possible? Could I ever be happy after all that I have lost? After everything that has happened, someone somewhere sent me a bite of happiness. I take a fork out of the cutlery tray, slide it seamlessly through the dessert, and put the bite in my mouth. The flavors of vanilla and raspberry explode on my tongue, and I can't contain the graphic moan that falls from my lips. It tastes even better than I remember, filling me with nostalgia for the bakery close to the clubhouse. Daddy would always stop there on his way home and pick up my favorite pastries. But I have never tasted anything as sinful as the masterpiece in front of me. This must be what desire smells like, what sinning feels like, and what giving into temptation tastes like. And even though I have no idea where this sinful delight came from, I am kneeling at the altar and ready to confess all my sins.

❤———————❤

I take the other petite fours home and stumble through the front door, vibrating in anticipation to taste them again. I go to bed feeling different, changed somehow. And if I were a stern believer that Wonderland was real, I might have said that I had fallen down the rabbit hole.

Fortunately for me, my confusion doesn't last long. My mysterious little rabbit hops into my life a few days later. I look up to see the same delivery truck as before pulling out of the loading bay at the restaurant. At least I missed the calamity that is his driving today. The driver intentionally stares at me in recognition, but I have no time to deliberate the possibility of being spotted by anyone from my past. The giver of my special gift has been my main focus every waking moment. I practically run into the kitchen where Mel smiles while holding a white box this time. Fuck! I must have missed him by seconds.

"Looks like all you need to make it to work on time is a little treat waiting for you."

I have eyes for only the box and don't even bother answering her. I start walking to my office, and I know she will follow.

Reverently, I place the box on my desk and remove my gear, intending to absent-mindedly drop it on the floor.

Mel picks up my helmet and places it on my chair. We are both silent for a few moments before she breaks.

"What are you waiting for? Divine intervention?"

If she only knew how much of a sinner I genuinely am. After going to bed last night, I had the filthiest dream of my life. I woke up early, moaning loudly, because the faceless pastry chef had started to lick the little pink flowers he had piped off my nipples. The hardening buds still tingle at the thought.

The tag hanging by the side says it's for my eyes only and includes a phone number.

"See, now you can call him. I think he is trying to get an in at the restaurant. Maybe we can even use him for the Valentine's dessert buffet. You seem to like his goodies."

Hell, yes, I like his goodies. Each bite filled me with a yearning for more. I have never been a prude, but Daddy always told me I was destined for better things, and he ensured I would get a man who deserved me. Once I left everything behind, I just couldn't face the fact that now I would never know what he meant. Since then, every man has failed compared to the promise he made me. Every man until now, and I haven't even seen this man yet.

"Are you going to open it, Vi?"

My hands shake as I reach for the lid and carefully pry it off. The contents take my breath away.

Mel leans over my shoulder and exclaims in delight, "It's beautiful. Is it real?"

Inside the box is a brightly colored bouquet of intricate buttercream roses. The rose scent wafts up and encloses me in the intoxicating smell of beauty and the unattainable. I am speechless while I stare at the wonder. Could something as precious as this creation be meant for me? This must have taken hours to make, and I already know it will taste heavenly. Mel shakes my shoulders, and I step back to not disturb the most beautiful flowers I have ever seen that look too real to be a cake.

"That is the most fantastic thing I have ever seen. You must get this guy to do the dessert buffet. Can you imagine what a killing we would make if we could bring true romance to every Valentine's date?" She takes a photo with her phone. "Hell, I am sure we can spin this as the perfect place to get engaged. I will call the rest of the crew to take a look. Be right back."

That brings me back to reality, and the word leaves my mouth with far more aggression than necessary.

"No!"

Mel pauses at the door and turns back.

"Why not, Vi? It is beautiful. And trust me, no one in this kitchen has ever created something as beautiful as that cake. Why not share it with everyone?"

Then, I realized the reason for my hesitation.

"The tag said for my eyes only, Mel. I already broke his trust in me by letting you see it. This was meant for only me. Besides, I can always call and ask him to make samples for the others to see. This is for me," I say in wonderment.

Mel slowly approaches and places her arm over my shoulders. "I am so happy for you. You deserve something as beautiful as that, and the man who made that surely thinks so, too."

This breaks the enchantment.

"Do you really think it is just a ploy to get me to place orders for the restaurant?"

She rolls her eyes and playfully pushes me away.

"How could you ask something like that? Of course it is for you. All he said this morning is that you must receive this package. It was imperative, Vi. Who talks like that? I will tell you who, a true gentleman. And you, my friend, have caught his eye, and if I am reading this situation correctly, it looks like he is wooing you. How lucky are you? And just before Valentine's Day? At least one of us won't be sulking at home alone. Again. Like always."

I snort and barely contain the incredulous disdain on my face. There is no way someone would go through all this trouble to woo me. Nobody really knows who I am. I have barely let Mel be a part of my life, and if I want to stay safe, that is how it should stay. But what if this man could change all that, and I could dare to have more? Hell, even one night would be more than I have now. I shake the remnants of my dream that force their way into my thoughts and focus on what I must do now. The shift has already started, and I need to get going. I rip the tag off the box lid and put it in my pocket before I close the cake with the lid.

"We need to get going. I will focus on this later. This is not the time to dwell in confusion over this guy's motivations."

I turn to leave, but her words bring me to a halt again.

"What you call motivations I call romance with the possibility of a blossoming love. Either way, you can't hide forever, Vi. At some stage, you will need to start living again."

If she only knew.

I have touched the tag in my pocket a thousand times throughout the day. Every time, my courage has failed me. Wouldn't it be better to stay trapped in the illusion than to call him and have it broken by the greed that might motivate his decision to contact me? I fear that I am just a pawn in his game, and if I am honest, I also fear that I might have fallen a little in love with the idea of being wooed. In the motorcycle club, nobody paid attention to me because they knew I was the president's daughter. And being a one-percenter club, it was difficult to cultivate any lasting relationships. I begged Daddy to change their ways. He always said the same thing. *You deserve more, my sweet, and someday you will have it all.*

The day I left, I cried so hard that I could barely drive, but I couldn't stop. I needed to get as far away as possible. It was by accident that I met Mel at the gas station. She was on her way to start a new job at the restaurant and dragged me along without delay. That is how we ended up having jobs and being best friends. She wanted us to be roommates, but I couldn't take that chance. What if someone found me and hurt her in the process of getting to me?

I rub the already scuffed edge of the tag representing a real chance at something. It might not be what my daddy had in mind, but it is more than I ever dared to believe.

When the dinner rush is over, I quickly escape to my office and lift the lid again. Is it too late to call?

I decide to instead send a text.

Thank you for the delicacies. They are too beautiful to eat.

The response is immediate.

I feel the same way about you. But know that it is not going to stop me.

What the fuck? That is not very professional, and yet I feel my blood racing as if preparing to be ravaged. I try to play it cool. It is the only way to discern his true motives.

Would you like to come see me sometime? Or would you be interested in collaborating? We could meet here at the restaurant.

I am definitely interested. See you at closing time.

That's not exactly what I had in mind. I was thinking more about meeting a complete stranger when the restaurant is full of other people. Not that he left me much of a choice. I become quieter as the night progresses and am a complete wreck by the time everyone else has left.

Only Mel remains, and I know that if I tell her I am meeting the mystery baker here after hours alone, she will insist on staying, and I don't want to inconvenience her. Besides, it was a long, difficult shift, even without me checking out halfway through.

"Are you sure you are fine locking up by yourself? You know I don't like leaving you like this."

I try unsuccessfully to hide the tremor in my voice.

"Of course, this is not the first time I have done this, you know. Just go. We will chat tomorrow."

She waves and closes the door behind her. All alone, I stare at the door and consider locking it. You never know how long I will have to wait for him to arrive. As I step closer, the door silently opens, and the figure that fills the void sets my nerves on fire. He is so quiet that I hardly have time to scream before he stands so close to me that I can't breathe without inhaling the smell of nutmeg and comfort that radiates from his body. It is mixed with something that reminds me of burnt honey and decadence. Silence and warmth envelop me, and a sense of safety floods my body. Safety, familiarity, and need.

"Nice to meet you. I am Vi. But I guess you know that already." I try to reach out my hand, but his body is so close that I only succeed in brushing against his rigid torso. He is solid and strong, and he hardly flinches at the action. The tiny smirk on his lips makes it seem like touching him is precisely what he wants. I take a step back, trying to break the spell he has put on me. He just steps closer again.

In a growly voice, while tucking a stray hair behind my ear, he answers, "I am Nicolas. My friends call me Nico, but you can call me anything you like as long as you are mine."

Am I in danger? He doesn't feel dangerous, but isn't this how these things always start?

"You are incredibly presumptuous, Nicolas. What makes you think I would ever agree to something like that? I barely know you."

I see something that could be hurt flicker across his golden-flecked hazel irises, and it knocks me back. Is he a stranger? He certainly doesn't feel like one. Then, an arrogant smirk forms on his face, and I know I am in danger. His words confirm what my heart already suspects.

"That might be true now, but if you are honest with yourself, you have already started falling for me. You can deny it all you want, but we were meant to be, and I don't care what I have to do to prove it to you, but I will have you and make you mine."

I need to say something, but I only think of how much I want that to be true. How much I wish I belonged to someone who could care for me and make me feel wanted, someone who could make me feel loved again. My brain must have left the building, because the words I whisper back are filled with yearning and are the most inappropriate thing I could have said.

"What would it mean to be yours?"

He places his hand against my cheek before simultaneously slipping it into my short black hair and stepping even closer. His grip becomes possessive, and his lips are so close that I no longer want to resist. He might be a stranger, but my body craves him, and when I press my lips to his, my hands start roaming the hard planes of his body, trying to find possession. A growl pulls his lips from mine, and we are both panting.

"You ate some of my honey-rose cake."

I know it wasn't a question, but I answer the only way I can. "I needed to taste it. It was calling to me."

He closes his eyes as if searching for restraint. I wish he would never find it.

"I can't wait to taste your honey. That is what that cake means, you know. Every creation is a craving my mind has conjured up of how you would flood my senses."

I never considered the possibility, and now I have to ask.

"What did the petite fours mean?"

"Oh, that one is easy."

He pushes me up against the stainless-steel table at my back, and I can feel him hardening. His body overpowers every possible sense of self-preservation I could have.

"The creamy buttercream and the smoothness of the icing repre-sent the velvety texture of your divine pussy when I push myself into your honey-soaked heaven. And the raspberry jam, I am a big guy, baby girl. And I could only hope."

I know I must stop, but I don't want to. "And what if I am not a virgin?"

He throws his head back and groans again, and the vibration that flows from his throat down to the point where our bodies touch mes-merizes me. When he looks deeply into my eyes, I can see the lust. And my body craves more.

"Then, baby girl, I will fuck you so hard that your body will turn into a deconstructed mess before I gently scoop all your parts back together and make you feel like the most desired meal in the world. And I will devour you until nothing is left but your eternal devotion."

My pussy is practically weeping, and this man has hardly touched me. He abruptly moves away, and the coldness that fills the void brings me back to reality.

"What do you want from me? And why me? I am a nobody," I say, breathless.

At least, that is what I have tried to be. It is easier to hide behind humanity's mundanity; at least here, I'm safe from my past.

"You know exactly who you are, far from being a nobody. Just know that you will always be safe with me, and there is no reason to hide yourself from me. And as to what I want from you . . ." He intensifies his gaze, and I feel the words etch into my soul. "I want everything."

My body convulses at the weight of his declaration, but I don't move when he turns and walks out just as silently as he came in.

We have been texting quite a lot the last few days. He has agreed to meet me at work today to discuss the Valentine's menu. We have talked about everything and nothing, and my days have turned into me de-liberating, yearning, and aching to be close to him. I have never been instantly attracted to anyone as much as I have Nico. Waiting to see him only allows me more time to agonize over the fact that I want him so much. I have been pacing the whole day, and people are starting to notice.

"Chill, boss. I am sure you will figure out this whole buffet situation. It isn't like they will fire you. You are the best manager we have ever had."

I can't recall the waiter's name now because my nerves are fried. But I nod and give him a pathetic smile to appease him. All I need to do is get through this meeting, and then I can decide my next step. I still can't believe I allowed him to kiss me like that. If anyone were to find out . . . what? I can't think of one valid reason right now to not give in and take what I crave. And if he was that good with his words, imagine what he could do with the lithe way he moves his body.

I am almost salivating when I see him enter the restaurant. The hostess is gesturing in my direction, but his eyes have already found me. He walks over and I turn to lead him to the kitchen. I have never noticed how dim the lights appear in this room, and I curse at myself for not considering it earlier. Nicolas has his back to me, which is good because I feel myself reaching out to touch him, and only his voice stops the motion.

"I came a little later because I will need to use your kitchen to whip up some stuff and would prefer that everyone finish their shift first. You don't mind being here after hours alone with me, right?" he says with raised eyebrows.

His smile mocks me, and I can only nod in agreement. He is playing with me and luring me to deny the influence he has on my body. But the question I have asked myself repeatedly in the hours that I have been waiting for him to appear is, if it was only my body craving his, why are my thoughts filled with how he makes me feel safe and wanted? Why am I yearning to step into his arms and forget about everything that was and might still be coming for me? I look at the bowls and containers he takes from his little Mary Poppins picnic basket and stare in awe as he unpacks it on the kitchen counter. Every object is meticulously packed, and although it seems to have no order, I know he knows exactly what he is doing.

He calls out to Mel when she runs past. "Mel, we are going to have an important discussion about the menu now, and we would prefer not to be disturbed." He gestures to the rest of the crew.

She salutes him, and he closes the door after everyone leaves while turning the lock.

"Are you afraid I will try to escape?"

"Of course not, baby girl. You are not afraid of me. But I do have plans with you, and if anyone were to see you in that position, I would have to poison them."

I smile at his arrogance.

"You know they say women prefer to use poison."

He smirks and doesn't waste any time stepping into my personal space.

"Obviously, they have never tried my food. Besides, you are so infatuated with me that even if you knew I poisoned the cake, you would still eat it."

He touches my face again, and I lean toward the warmth he provides. We both know I don't need to answer for him to see the truth.

"You didn't send me a gift today."

He smiles, and the pull of his eyebrow tells me how amused he is at my confidence. The last few days have reminded me how much I have missed being the old me. The woman who was confident in what she was and what she wanted in life. Although I don't have it all figured out, I am slowly realizing that I might be able to regain what I lost.

He reaches past me and picks up one of the brightly colored bowls. "Close your eyes."

I look at him sceptically, and he gives me the smile of a killer.

"Still don't trust me completely, do you? That is good. You always need to be careful, but not when I am around. You will always be safe with me. I promise you."

I reluctantly close my eyes, and his finger swipes at my bottom lip.

"Open for me and keep your eyes closed. I want you to experience the sensation."

My bottom lip opens, and his fingers gently push something into my mouth. When I close around it, the first taste that assaults me is the sour tang of pomegranate arils bursting in my mouth. The explosion causes juice to flood down my throat in a stream of lust. I chew slowly and open my mouth for more without opening my eyes. His fingers enter my mouth again, and I grab the opportunity with both lips. I lock them around his last digit to leave my mouth and moan while I suck.

"If you keep doing that, baby girl, I might need to put something else in your mouth. And that explosion will be a hell of a lot bigger. Trust me. I have been looking for you for a long time."

Something in his words sends an alert to my brain, but my head is drowning in lust and unable to make any sensible decisions right now. "How long have you been dabbling in food seduction?"

He chuckles. "Truthfully, my father had other plans for me. He wanted me to join the family business, but his best friend saw the potential in me and sent me away to culinary school as soon as I finished school. My dad disowned me, and I never bothered to make contact again. When the authorities came to see me, it was too late to make peace. He was already gone. And since I was almost graduating, I decided to focus on the promises I made a long time ago."

That is a lot of information, and I am so intrigued, but somehow, it feels wrong to pry more information out of him. If he wants to tell me more, it needs to come from him.

"I know firsthand how difficult it can be to leave your loved ones behind. I am sorry you had to go through that."

He looks at me strangely, and I feel completely exposed. I have said too much. I keep forgetting that I need to choose wisely who I trust. You never know who might be looking for me or to what extremes they will go to find me.

"Anyway, tell me more about this menu you have planned. It looks quite complicated if I look at the list of ingredients you have here."

We discuss his plans, and I am enraptured by his passion for changing the world with food. I giggle a little at his stories about difficult vendors and idiotic chefs. He is charismatic, and it is easy to see how one could fall for his charm. He sets up and hands me an apron.

"Did you think I would be the only one getting dirty?"

I can't help it. I really try, but my brain has joined the party, and he is a filthy fucker. Therefore, my answer could only be, "Don't I have too many layers of clothes to get dirty like that?"

The pensive look he gives me is filled with something resembling indecision, and I make a choice for him.

"Let me make you a deal. I will help with anything you need, but only if you do it with your shirt off."

"You know that is not sanitary or allowed in a commercial kitchen."

I huff out in fake frustration and fold my arms. "I am asking for a little eye candy while forced into hard labor. Is that too much to ask?"

He chuckles and uses one hand to pull off his shirt from the back. I can barely keep my eyes off the exposed skin. He is gorgeous—tanned with muscles bulging in all the right places.

"You know, I heard you were a good girl."

"Whoever told you that obviously didn't know me very well."

"I seriously doubt that. But I must say I am loving this side of you. Where has it been hiding?"

Did he just say *loving*? Not quite love, but close enough. My heart fills with the need to unburden myself to anyone just to feel like myself again if only for the few minutes I spend with Nico.

"Can I tell you something, but you promise to tell no one?"

He nods solemnly, and I wring my hands while taking the plunge.

"My dad was a good man and father, but he was a criminal. I begged him to go to the police or to turn his motorcycle club around. He didn't want to do that, and when I couldn't stand it anymore, I decided to run away. I needed to leave everyone and everything I loved behind, which almost broke me, but it needed to be done. I couldn't live with the uncertainty and the threat of danger anymore. I wanted a family someday and didn't want my children in constant danger."

He doesn't respond, apart from folding his arms over his chest and nodding for me to continue.

"Shortly after I left, someone sent me an anonymous threat saying they knew what I did and were coming for me. I, of course, had no idea what they were talking about, so I started digging. The police apparently got an anonymous tip or an informant, and a raid occurred at the clubhouse. Most of the club brothers were arrested and are still awaiting trial, or they were killed, like my daddy. Everyone believed I was the informant who orchestrated the club's downfall."

I suppress the sob, though tears still billow over my cheeks. Nico steps closer, but I lift my hand to stop him. If I am going to get it out, I need to do it now.

"I never told anyone about the club or their business. I would never do that to my brothers or my daddy. They were my only family after my mom passed away, and I loved them. But someone thought I would betray them, so I needed to go into hiding. And this was the best place I could find. No one looks twice at the shy little wallflower that blends into the background and only comes out at night to slave away at dealing with every hard-ass bitch who wants to complain about her chicken being too dry."

I inhale deeply to regain control, but it is in vain. Emotions tumble over each other to come out first, and the commotion refuses to be contained. Nico folds his arms around me and pulls me closer. Instantly, a sense of peace flows over me. I was last held the night before I left when my daddy hugged me. I don't know if he suspected something, but he never said anything. He held me close and told me that he loved me, and everything would work out how it was supposed to. He said he had made sure of it. I still don't know what he meant, but it gave me some comfort to know that he was planning for my future. Even if nothing could become of it.

Nico has been leaving little tasters everywhere I go. They are accompanied by notes that make it hard to focus on anything other than my tumultuous emotions bubbling close to the surface. We haven't talked about my revelation again, and after letting me go, he changed the topic. We had a blast preparing all the unique desserts he wanted to show me. I chose the most decadent ones, and while I was daydreaming about being in his arms again, or perhaps even more, there was just no time for that. My schedule has been completely booked between planning the roster and taking reservations. I come home exhausted and barely change before I pass out on the bed to start it all over the next day. That all comes to an end today, however. It is finally Valentine's Day, and we only have a few more hours left of this dreaded holiday. In about eight hours, I will be free and will have a very deserved few days off. Nicolas explained he would prepare most of the desserts and would do some final touches in our kitchen. I asked the chef to allocate some space for him, and now I am standing in front of the empty stainless-steel table in the kitchen, considering if I want to go through with my plan. We met only a few weeks ago, but he seems to occupy my every thought.

I even bought him a Valentine's gift and carefully wrapped it. It is an apron that says, "The cook is naked under this apron." I thought it was fitting for the banter we have been exchanging. But is it too serious to give him a gift? I hate second-guessing my decisions. I wasn't always like this, and since I met him, I feel more like myself every day. That is why I planned the second part of my gift. But that is my secret alone. My plan is all in the invitation I included in the gift bag. The only question left to ask is, do I leave the gift here out in the open where everyone can see? Or do I give it to him personally and feel like a fool when he tries to explain that he didn't buy me anything? The decision is taken out of my hands when his voice sounds behind me.

"I hope that is for me. I didn't work this hard to get your attention only to be ignored on Valentine's Day."

I smile lightly and pull my shoulders back before I turn around. I almost whisper my response because this is still my place of employment, after all. But I can't keep the sass from my tone.

"I hardly think you worked hard to get my attention. Besides, I told you how to keep me interested the first night we cooked together."

He chuckles and grabs me around the waist, pulling me closer, audience be damned.

"If I had known that was all that was needed, I would have walked around without a shirt everywhere."

I consider his answer, and something that has been niggling me at the back of my brain comes to the forefront.

"Have we met before, or do we know each other somehow?"

A look of panic flashes across his face, but he quickly shuts me down.

"Let's get back to the prepping. We have little time to make the romance happen, right?"

I let him go, but first, I need to ensure he got the envelope with his gift inside.

"Aren't you going to open your gift first? You never know what kind of surprise might be inside."

He starts unpacking the crates next to his feet on the floor.

"Oh, I promise I will get to it later. I don't want to interrupt the flow of the kitchen with my things cluttering the floor. Besides, it should be a spicy gift, and do you want me to open that in front of everyone?"

He has a point. I simply nod and turn to attend to my other duties. I might work tonight, but the boss will relieve me at 10:00 p.m. That is his way of saying thank you for all the extra hours I have been putting in lately. The hours fly by, and I am on my way home by 10:20. I planned a special Valentine's feast for Nicolas. And since I was craving a taste of my old self, I was bold enough to plan something completely different. I bought all the ingredients for a charcuterie board earlier today, and I plan to present all the goodies to Nico . . . on my naked body.

I take a shower and wash off all the grime and perfume. Afterward, I grab a colorful silk tablecloth and drape it over my bed. I remove my robe and lie down naked and unashamed before finding the most comfortable position and unpacking the food on my midriff. It isn't a lot, but it includes some cheese and crackers, dark chocolate, fruit, and nuts. But hopefully, he will want to eat something else for dessert. The strawberries keep rolling off every time I move, so I abandon them on the bedside table. The chocolate, broken into smaller blocks, starts melting on my skin, and I pray he makes it in time before they slip off. Luckily, my prayers are answered as soon as a knock sounds at the front door.

"Come in, it's open." Thank goodness I thought ahead; otherwise, this would have been awkward. "I am here in the bedroom. Just follow my voice."

I lit candles everywhere to hide any flaws that might impede my plan, and by the light in his eyes, it seems to have worked.

"I see you have opened your gift?" I say.

He stands with the invitation in his hand and a gobsmacked look on his face. I play my part perfectly and act utterly unaffected by the sparks in his eyes when he openly stares at my body.

"It is said that you really get to know a person when you share a meal, so I thought I could ask you some questions and get to know you better while you feast."

He still hasn't said a word. He rounds the bed and falls on his knees beside my head. When he finally speaks, it is a hoarse whisper as he stares at my puckering nipples.

"You did all this for me?"

I recognize the same uncertainty that has been eating at me, and I soften at the thought that this wonderful man could doubt himself. But haven't I done the same thing for years now? Haven't I feared that my anonymous threat was right and that it was my fault my dad was killed? That it was my fault so many people were hurt and that their lives changed irrevocably? Isn't that the real reason I have been hiding from a better life? That I believed I didn't deserve to be happy because I caused so much pain? I choke back the emotions and put on my bravest face.

"Of course I did this for you. Or are you expecting some friends? Because in that case, we might need to leave the door unlocked." My sass brings him out of his daze, and he slowly trails a finger between my breasts before he picks up a cube of cheese and pops it into his mouth.

"This is the best fucking dinner setting I have ever seen. Where do we start?"

I point to the comfortable chair I carried into the bedroom specifically for this reason. He gets comfortable, and his eyes return to my curves.

"I ask a question that you answer, and then you can indulge in something on my body." I watch his reaction. His hands reach out hesitantly, but his eyes show awe.

"This will only work if you tell the truth. I am sure I don't need to reiterate that I am in a fairly vulnerable position here. I don't want to waste my time on something that isn't real."

"Oh, this is very real. And I have been looking for you for a long time." He becomes quiet as if contemplating how much to say while grabbing a piece of cheese and shoving it into his mouth. All is quiet while we wait for him to swallow, and I recall the way his lips felt on mine.

"Have you ever seen somebody, and your body knew instantly that that person was meant to be with you?"

I nod slowly and barely whisper, "Only once."

My eyes convey what my lips struggle to say, and he nods in understanding. He takes a sip from one of the two glasses of red wine I placed on the bedside table.

"I felt like that when I saw you. You nearly caused me a heart attack when you appeared out of nowhere, and I almost clipped you on your bike. Figures the first time I attempt to make a good impression, I almost knock you over."

A silly giggle escapes, and I am thankful I didn't disturb all the food. I relax more in the bed and nudge toward the food. He hesitantly picks up a piece of fruit and starts chewing.

"Why did you decide to step over the line with me? Or do you immediately start seducing every girl you date . . . see . . . whatever?"

My struggle is clearly amusing to him. He pinches another piece of fruit and chews to hide his smirk.

"You're trying to trip me up, but there is only one girl for me, baby, and that is you. And no, I wanted to take my time with you, but you overwhelmed every instinct of self-preservation I ever had. I couldn't take the risk of you getting away. And now that I have you . . ."

He takes a piece of chocolate and trails it over my skin toward my hip, where he leaves it to lick the chocolate from his fingers.

"You know that is going to melt."

He lazily circles my nipple, and the ache bows my back off the bed, causing several items of food to fall around me. His words send sparks to my already-soaked pussy.

"I am counting on it. What other questions do you have? I can't wait to ravish you, baby girl."

His finger traces concentric circles that grow bigger and bigger until my breast rests in his hungry grasp. My heart beats violently, and my brain can hold on to only one thought.

"What happened to your father?"

His actions halt, and the fog of lust starts clearing.

"Baby girl, are you trying to kill my cock with your questions?"

I viciously shake my head, and his hands move along my side toward the chocolate he left on my hip. He picks it up and slides the melted piece through my slit while his eyes never leave my face. My inhale is abrupt but lust-filled, and anticipation crushes my chest. He gets up and walks to the end of the bed, his eyes perusing my body while burning with possession. He takes off his shirt and smiles openly at the moans coming from me when he starts unbuckling his belt and pushing his pants down.

"I've decided to eat dessert first, but I don't want you to ruin my dinner, baby girl. Therefore, you will keep still until I say you can move. Do you understand?"

I nod, but then something else dawns on me. I am not this kind of girl. There was a time when I would have obeyed, but not anymore. And not with Nicolas. If I have only one chance with this man, I am taking exactly what I want.

He lowers himself between my thighs, and the first lick is so slow it feels like he is draining my body's will to object. I sneak a look at the few items left on my stomach and decide on the best way to dispose of them. By Nico's third slow, deep lick, I am close to changing the plan and surrendering. But he starts devouring me like a starved man, and I want more. I take my forearm and swipe the food toward the side of the bed, letting it fall to the ground. The melted chocolate leaves a streak across my skin, and I savor the thought of Nico's sinful tongue licking me clean.

He growls at my disobedience, and it encourages me to open my thighs wider and pull his mouth closer with my fingers in his hair. All my nerve endings are on fire, and desire consumes me. Nico expertly drives me to the edge by sucking my clit hard, to only soothe it a moment later. Two of his fingers pump punishingly into me, reaching exactly where I need him to be. His other hand grips my thigh, and I know bruises are forming. I love knowing I will see his marks on me for days to come. I look down at his face covered in my juices, and my last resolve breaks. My screams fill the once-depressing space of my apartment, and something inside me snaps. The chains around my caged being fall to the ground of my guilty conscience, and I let go of all my inhibitions.

Nico crawls up my body, setting my skin alight with kisses from his soft, wet lips. He settles between my already sticky thighs and looks at me questioningly when the head of his cock rests at my opening. I give him no chance to rethink us and thrust my hips up to take him as deep as I can. We groan in unison, and my nails start to draw blood from his back.

"You feel so good. I don't know how I survived staying away from you for so long."

All I can do is murmur in agreement as he slowly pulls out. I want nothing else to distract me from the feeling of his cock sliding into my greedy slit. I feel so complete when he is entirely seated in me. He pauses, and his deep exhalation flutters over the fiery skin of my throat.

"Please move, Nico, I need it."

"What do you need, baby girl? Tell me, and I will give it to you."

I look into his eyes and see the same need reflected at me.

"I need to feel you surrender to me."

"What do you want me to surrender?"

My voice is barely a whisper, but he feels the word reverberate against his own lips.

"Everything."

His lips fuse to mine, and the need is palpable on my tongue. His arms slide under my body and pull me even closer to his. His hips set an impossible rhythm, and my body welcomes the pain and exhilaration. My frayed nerves combine to send streaks of immense sensation running ragged through my body. His sweat drips onto my shoulder, and his body convulses in preparation. He is so close but must be waiting for me. He doesn't have to wait long. A passionate groan tears out of my throat when I finally let myself be consumed by Nico. When my overwhelmed senses finally yield and my soul volunteers as a sacrifice, I feel myself slip into the comfortable peace of belonging to someone worthy.

⬩━━━━━━━━━━⬩

The next morning, I wake up alone and immediately feel the void. At least I am not greeted by an ant army, because Nico cleaned all the food from the floor. He left without so much as a note or a text, and I'm contemplating what to do over my first cup of coffee when a piece of paper slides underneath my front door. Finally, he came to his senses. I run to open the door and stop him from leaving, but no one is outside. I return and open the folded paper, only to drop it again. The words burn into memory as the wind mockingly plays with the falling paper.

I should have known. Now I will be coming for both of you.

I try calling Nico, but he does not answer. Not once. And when the understanding of him ghosting me finally takes root in my mind, I decide I have done all I can to warn him about the situation. I thought our night was extraordinary and the beginning of something. He obviously disagrees and didn't even bother to inform me of as much. Besides, I have other things that warrant my attention. My anonymous threat is back, and I can't hide in my apartment forever. I need to go back to work this afternoon, and then I could be a sitting duck. Daddy taught me how to use a gun, but without being able to use my own name, there was no way for me to get another gun.

There are so many opportunities for someone to hurt me that I don't know where to begin. I cautiously drive to work and try to keep from crashing while frantically observing my surroundings. What if I am with Mel, and he hurts her out of spite? Not only should I fear for myself, but now I am also placing my only friend in harm's way. My life is so fucked. How did I get here? Who would think that I would do something like that to the club? Who is vindictive enough to hold a grudge for five years?

Unfortunately, it doesn't take long to find the answer. I was busy in my office and did not realize it would be this empty when I came out. Everyone has left, and I anxiously try to hasten my pace while going through the motions. With my backpack in hand and my hand on the light switch, I hear the door open. It could be Nico because I barely heard the noise. Unfortunately, when I glance around the pantry shelf, I am met with the business end of a 9mm. And I am surprised to find Darren on the other end.

"Darren, what are you doing? And when did you get here?"

Darren was my daddy's best friend and his second-in-command. He snorts derisively and motions for me to move away from the switch.

"I should think my notes warned you enough, little girl. Or did you think anyone else had the balls to go after the president's spoiled brat? If only you had left things alone, you could have ridden into the sunset with that pathetic waste of space. But no! You had to fuck all of us over before you left. And for that, you need to pay. Because of you, there was nothing left to take over from your dad. Everything we worked for was destroyed because you wanted him to be something else than what he has always been."

My heart jumps out of my chest, and I start looking around for anything that could save me, anything that could give me an edge over the man I've treated like family for so many years. He has always had a mean streak, and as far as I know, the only person he treated with some respect was my dad. The rest of us knew what evil he hid beneath the surface—no one more than his own family. I try to placate him to buy myself some time.

"My dad always thought the world of you. Why are you doing this to his only family?"

"Because you forced me to go underground. You betrayed your family, and we lost everything because of you, you little bitch. And now it is time to pay."

"She didn't betray anyone."

We both look to the door to find Nicolas standing there with his hands balled into fists and his face wrapped in a look of hatred.

"She didn't betray anyone. I divulged every dirty little secret to the police, and Vinnie was so proud of me. He made me promise. So, if you want to punish anyone, it should be me, Dad."

My eyes widen and I press my hand against my temple to still the sudden throbbing.

"What are you doing here? After I dropped the first note, I saw you run with your tail between your legs."

"What! What first note?" I scream.

Darren belts out a disturbing, sinister laugh. "He didn't tell you? I saw you two together and left a note earlier that morning that said I would get you both. The moment he read it, he left you there to fend for yourself and went into hiding like the cowardly little shit he is. I can't believe you fell for his shit. I should have gotten rid of him ages ago."

"Yes, you would have liked that, but unfortunately, Vinnie saw potential in me."

The gun is pointed steadily at me again, and I curse myself silently. The best thing I can do is fade into the background. That is my only chance to escape. But can I really leave Nicolas to fend for himself? He is just as unarmed as I am, and even though he treated me like a piece of shit that was easy to discard, I am not like that. Besides, I still have too many unanswered questions.

"Didn't he tell you, princess? He and Vincent were thick as thieves. Vinnie even paid for his tuition. I told him he was just wasting his money. This one will never amount to anything. He was a traitor from the start and came from useless spawn. He is just as weak as his mother."

Nico flinches this time, but it doesn't stop him from hitting back.

"If I was so useless, why did I succeed in taking down the only thing you ever loved besides yourself—the club?"

"You are lying to try to save the little princess, but I promise you that will never work. I am not leaving here without tying up all loose ends."

If I am going to die today, I am going to do it on my own terms and certainly with the knowledge of what really transpired all those years ago.

"What did you promise my father and why?"

My question is directed at Nicolas, who steps closer, even under the threat of the gun swinging between us.

"Your father wanted to make the club legit. But my dad kept stirring the pot and promised the brothers a larger cut if they voted your dad out and made him president. Now, he is here pretending to be loyal, but he is just a rat trying to save himself from a sinking ship. Your father gave me all the information I needed to take the club down, and as soon as I was of age, I took everything I had to the police. But it was too late. Someone caught wind of some questionable transactions my father arranged, and the raid was executed. Because your father knew nothing, he was also taken by surprise and perished. I am so sorry for that. They would never have believed a kid."

Tears flood my eyes, but I stand tall and try to absorb the pain that radiates through my body.

"That doesn't answer the question of what he gave you in return."

His answer is simple and yet so alarming at the same time.

"You."

Darren lets out another obnoxious chuckle, and I seriously wish we could have discussed this before and without an audience.

"So, the old man sold you his daughter in return for ratting out and betraying all his brothers and his family. Damn, she must have some golden pussy lips down there. Maybe I should take a look."

Nicolas steps in front of me and cuts me off from his father's predatory stare.

"Come on, Son, this is hardly the time to grow some balls. Besides, will you stand up to your own flesh and blood?"

Nicolas sneers, and I hear the disdain and blatant hatred in the words he spits in his father's direction.

"You are fucking nothing to me. She is my whole world. And she is the reason I worked all those years to become the best pâtissier on this side of the country. I did it to save her from scum like you. That is what her father wanted; he entrusted me with her care and heart. Whether she wants to admit it or not, she is mine and I am hers. And nothing you could ever do will come between us."

I see the second Darren decides he has had enough of this situation. His face is sinister, and his eyes become dead globes of emptiness.

"In that case, I see it fitting that you die together. You are of no use to me, anyway."

I step closer to Nicolas, and his hand pulls me closer to his back. The gun is trained on his chest, and I see no way of getting out of this. But if he goes down, then so will I. I will not hide and fade away from loneliness. This is where I belong. Close to Nicolas, having his back. That is what Daddy wanted for me. He has kept his promise to me all these years, and I didn't even know. When this man appeared on the scene, I could hardly be expected to remember that he was Darren's son who was sent away. But now I understand why he felt so familiar. He was meant to find me. His heart was promised to me. And no matter what happens, we will be together.

"I wouldn't do that if I were you," Nico says.

Darren snorts. "Where is all this bravado coming from? Do you honestly think I am scared of the little boy who cried for days when his mother died? You have never been strong. Don't pretend now."

Nico's voice is confident and even a little bit arrogant. "You don't have to be strong when you are smart. And that is something you never were, dearest dad. Or did you honestly think I would venture in here alone when I could get you sent to jail to rot your miserable life away?"

The back door swings open and crashes against the wall. The room fills with officers with guns already raised and pointed at Darren. They knock him to the ground and cuff his hands behind his back. All the while, Nico keeps me behind his back and only turns to me when he is confident the danger is contained.

"Are you okay?"

"Why did you leave me? I thought you didn't want me anymore."

His smile is contagious, and although my body is still shaking, I smile back.

"Never. I've tried to lure him away from you the last few days, but he decided you were the better prize. And it took some time to arrange all this."

"I am sure it did, but it doesn't excuse you for lying to me."

"I never lied to you. I told you; you were mine, and I was yours, and nothing has changed."

"I meant about you knowing my father. I told you everything about the club, and you hardly reacted."

His face pales in shame. "It was another promise I had to make to your father. He didn't want you to think he was meddling in your life, and he was also scared you would only be with me because you felt guilty."

I gently push him away to think about the position I was put in. Daddy was right. I would have taken any man who said my father sent him, because I felt so guilty after abandoning him. That guilt is only soothed by the knowledge that he was trying to change everything for the better. He wanted a better life for us, and he kept his promises. All of them.

"Aviana, what are you thinking?"

I smile broadly, happy that the time of Vi is now over forever and I can return to the person I was before. I can be the woman who was unafraid to take what she wanted and to love in abundance.

"I like the way my name sounds on your lips, and my dad was right. I could be happy because you are the perfect man for me."

"Is it because you have a sweet tooth and I know how to bake?"

I laugh at his silly attempt to calm me down. But my sass is always close to the surface, so I answer honestly and whisper in his ear, "No, silly. It is because you have a sweet tooth, and I have all the honey you will ever need."

About the Author

Caz Luan is an enthusiastic romance author from the Free State, South Africa. She has an honors degree in English from Northwest University. After years of lecturing English, she decided to dip her toes into self-publishing with her first romance novel, *Sweet Torture*. Two of her short stories will be published in upcoming anthologies. All this is even more impressive considering English is her second language. When she is not pestering her husband for ice cream, she reads, bakes, and enjoys life.

You can find Caz on:
Instagram @cazluanauthor

Visit her website at:
cazluan.com

ALPHA IN HER OWN RIGHT

Alpha in Her Own Right

Rowan Delacroix

TANESHA DASHED THROUGH THE BAR with plates of wings, tacos, and chili cheese fries on one arm and two pitchers of ale clutched in her other hand. She swerved past guests and ducked under swinging glasses of whiskey as more people poured in. Tanesha liked busy nights like this at her father's bar; they went by faster. Before long, she'd be back at her comfy cabin in her fuzzy slippers after a nice bath spritzed with some Florida water.

Thinking of home carried her the rest of the way to her next table. When she finished serving the customers, she seized a moment to wipe the sweat from her brow. Her eyes wandered over to her brother and his wife—the sole couple in the middle of the dance floor, bathed in the glow of twinkling fairy lights and heart-shaped candles. He gazed deeply into his mate's eyes as they swayed. Her elegant wedding dress glided over the wooden floorboards laden with red and pink rose petals. Tanesha had once been the center of such admiration when she was married. She thought briefly of the alpha she used to love, the man who had gifted her status and respect. Now she was here, serving drinks and cleaning dishes—an outsider.

Pasting on a smile, she shoved her hands in the pockets of the apron covering her brown cotton dress. She spotted her father clapping when the music slowed down. Others joined and clapped too, whistling and cheering on the newlyweds. Her hands clenched in her pockets when her father glanced her way. His jaw tightened before he turned his attention back to her brother—back to the pride of the family. Tanesha's eyes fell to the floor, and her toes curled in her padded kitchen shoes. Despite her father's disdain, she faced the hopeless frustration festering in her stomach. When was he going to forgive her for choosing what she thought was right? She turned toward the tables and thrust herself in the flow of work, shoving plates in front of customers and plopping down beverages like a ghost fulfilling its haunt.

Her brother tapped a glass half-filled with red wine to gather the room's attention. Just as he parted his lips to speak, the doors to the bar burst open. A hot tall black woman entered. She raised her chin, her eyes glinting with specs of mischief. The thunk of her brown cowboy boots disrupted the tense air as she set her black leather jacket against her back, revealing strong, toned muscles.

Tanesha's mouth fell open. Her skin tingled, and a fluttery feeling intruded upon her stomach. Her gaze gravitated toward the diamond pear laced with a golden chain around the woman's neck. It conjured up memories of grass stains, muddy hands, races, and wrestling. She was back. Her nostrils flared as a growl crawled up her throat.

No longer a rebellious pup, she smelled like a powerful woman—she smelled like a thunderstorm. A warmth crept up her cheeks. A group of women trailed behind the woman she recognized as Rayna. She took a seat at the bar. Everyone was whispering; some watched every move she made.

The bartender smashed a glass near where she sat. "You have some nerve showing your face 'round 'ere."

Rayna set her elbows on the table and met his glare with a smirk. "I have some nerve asking for a drink in a bar?"

Tanesha's father barged through the crowd, puffed out his chest, and bared his teeth. "You know you're not welcome here."

Tanesha scurried over to her. "Rayna, what are you doing?"

Rayna turned to her and winked. One of her pack members growled back at her father and started to rise, but Rayna placed a hand on the woman's shoulder. She stood and opened her arms, facing the angry crowd as if she were a musician on stage. "It's Valentine's Day, so I thought I would gift myself a drink, but lemme pay my respects." She snatched a glass of wine from a nearby table and lifted it into the air as wolves from the crowd, some transformed, some not, circled her. "Cheers! Cheers to a line of bullshit!" She gulped down the wine. Then, she ducked as a wolf lunged for her. The glass splintered against the wall, shards scattering on the tables. A hush broke over the room. Then, chaos exploded. The crowd ripped strung-up paper hearts from the ceiling as fist and claw performed a violent dance of scratch and bite.

With a sour taste tingling at the back of her tongue, Tanesha tried to find a spot to get out of the way. She didn't want to fight. Her heart weighed heavily with the thick tension in the air as she found her place amid ripped paper hearts and satin tablecloths. Her own heart was split between the love she harbored for her family and her best friend.

Another emotion joined her internal brawl. Rayna's dark curls thrashed in the mix. Her sharp brown eyes calculated every possible scenario as she fought. She had always worn defiance like a second skin—always fighting. In the remaining light of the heart-shaped candles and fairy lights, however, Rayna was such a magnetic force that Tanesha could not keep her eyes off her. A longing to reach out to her and the frustration at Rayna's current shenanigans left a cacophonous thrum in her pulse.

A banner with the married couple's names spooled onto the floor, and she lamented at how much of this she was going to have to clean. Before she could get a sigh out, someone grabbed her wrist and whisked her away. She relaxed when she saw it was Rayna. As Tanesha trailed behind and watched her tight curls in the wind, she felt like a little girl again, running with her best friend from her latest shenanigans—just like old times. Some things never changed. They ran and ran and ran, and Tanesha followed behind like always. But things were different. They were grown now. She snapped out of her daze and snatched her wrist free. Rayna laughed.

Tanesha crossed her arms and turned away from the black moon in the sky toward the bar that was now out of sight. "This isn't funny! Look at the mess you've made! Guess who's going to have to clean it, and my father will be so angry!"

Rayna wrapped her arms around her neck and hugged her from behind. She whispered into her ear—her thunderstorm scent electrifying her skin. "I've missed you too, T."

Tanesha almost relaxed. Instead, she shook out of her embrace. "Right." She met Rayna's eyes; her gaze pulled her in. She unnecessarily cleared her throat. "Why are you here?"

Rayna stepped close to her, a tower of muscle and beauty. "So you didn't miss me?"

Tanesha stepped back and balled up her hands. "Why should I?" She turned away from her, trembling as she thought about that day she learned her best friend had run away from their village without any explanation. It was more heartbreaking than divorcing her ex-husband and having her family's scorn. Not many had dared to divorce a high-status alpha before, but she'd done what she'd thought was right—much to her father's obvious dismay. "I thought I'd never see you again."

Rayna gazed at her, and the cocky smile dropped from her face like a drop of rain. In that moment, it felt right to stand there with Rayna. The weight of her family's expectations could not touch her here. Through all the destruction and chaos, Tanesha felt oddly relieved.

Her nose jerked into the air, disrupting the tense moment that had blanketed them. They were being pursued. She rolled her eyes. "Let's go to my place. I have a protection spell near my cabin. We'll be safe there."

Rayna nodded. Tanesha transformed into her wolf form and led her childhood friend to her cabin. Once they approached the hill overlooking her home, Rayna slowed.

Tanesha paused and glanced at her.

"I see you like your privacy."

"Yes."

"Race ya!"

"Wait, there's—" A flash of blue and gray bolted ahead. Tanesha rolled her eyes but still obliged. She surged forward, trying to catch up, trying not to be left behind again. Soon as she caught up to Rayna, she pounced on her, and they tumbled on the ground until Tanesha was on top, gazing down at a laughing wolf. They slipped out of their wolf forms. "I have to disarm the spell, stupid."

Rayna grinned, and Tanesha frowned. She hated that she liked seeing her lopsided grin, bright with the mix of mischief and confidence that Tanesha had always envied and admired. She jumped to her feet.

Her stomach fluttered against her will. She tucked her hair behind her ears, as if to bat away the flutters, brushing away all her usual frustrations with Rayna. A warmth filled her cheeks, hidden in the darkness of the night and her sable skin. She couldn't allow herself to feel what she could hardly name, not when Rayna had made her position known, especially not when she stood on the opposing side of her pack, her family. Except, she had never felt more at peace and content than when she was standing there admiring the shape of her friend's jaw and the curve of her cheekbones.

Rayna smirked. "Admit it, I won."

Tanesha ignored her, and they entered her home. She breathed in the incense she left in her dragon-shaped holder. The frankincense and myrrh curled around her. She was used to this smell grounding her and alleviating her of stress and worry. Right now, however, her mind was restless, wondering why it felt so right to have Rayna here.

"Since when did you get into witchcraft?" Rayna asked.

"A lot happens when you run away without saying goodbye."

"Hey!" Rayna grabbed her by the arm and spun her around, a growl escaping her throat. "I did what I had to. That day was hard for me, alright?" Her rainstorm scent swelled over her like dew over grass. Her brown eyes, speckled with a wild kind of yellow, warmed her cheeks, and she hated that she felt more at home with her here.

Tanesha narrowed her eyes. "You left me behind."

Rayna's shoulders lowered and her face softened. "T, I'm sorry." She released her and paced the cabin, rubbing her neck. "You'll be happy to know I did everything I promised. I started my own pack free from the traditions forced on us. I've created a place where we can make our own traditions—where we can be free. I came back just to tell you—well, that, and how could I not ruin that stupid mating tradition? You should be proud of me."

Tanesha pulled out a bottle of mezcal and poured a couple glasses. "Way to make this about you." She set the glasses on the kitchen counter with as much restraint as she could summon.

Rayna backed away. If she were in her wolf form, her ears would be flat against her head. "You're right; I am making this about me. I didn't come here to make you upset. I'll go." She turned toward the door.

Without thinking about it, Tanesha wrapped her arms around her friend's middle and hugged her from behind. "I thought I'd never see you again."

Rayna set a hand on her arms, holding her there. As they embraced, Tanesha's heart beat fast. This was new. Different—everything was so different. Rayna's heartbeat matched hers, and they both breathed as if they had been running for a long time. Was it exhaustion or relief that bound them? Tanesha couldn't tell. Maybe it was time for both of them to stop running.

Rayna's rain scent baptized her, the newness of this situation setting on her skin. Tanesha tightened her arms around Rayna, and she listened to the steady thrum of her breathing. Their embrace warmed her cheeks, and the warmth shined a light on Tanesha's realization that all that really mattered was this moment.

"I'm sorry I left you behind, but I made sure that I won't have to run. From anybody ever again."

Tanesha wanted to be angry, but the apology and sincerity in her eyes melted away all traces of anger, leaving behind the shining fragments of their friendship. She simply smirked. "Tonight didn't count?"

"Nah, I planned to do that."

Tanesha rolled her eyes. "So you planned to get me alone?" She let go of her friend and covered her mouth. Why did she say it like that?

Rayna didn't turn around, and she said in a voice that hid a shy tremble. "Yeah."

Pleased knowing this alpha showed a little nervousness, Tanesha cleared her throat and picked up the glasses of mezcal before giving one to her friend. "You don't need me to be proud of you. I should've always suspected you would go off and do your own thing." She sighed and took a sip of her drink, savoring the smoky, spiced vanilla that connected deeply with her feral being. "So, what's the plan?"

Rayna sipped her drink, her gaze intensely on Tanesha. "Dunno."

"Okay, are you hungry? Do you want me to fix you something?"

"No."

Tanesha frowned. "Well, what do you want?"

Before she could blink, Rayna flashed over to her so that her nose was inches away. Her scent washed over her. "Gods, T, take a hint."

Stepping back, Tanesha whispered, "Ray?"

Her sharp eyes peered over her. She wove Tanesha's hair through her fingers. "You look and smell so different from when we were kids, don't you think?"

Tanesha blushed. "I don't know, Ray."

Rayna backed away with her hands up. "I won't do anything without your consent."

"I-I don't want this to ruin our friendship." She glanced at the ground. "What if things change after we—" She shook her head and backed against the wall next to her bed.

"It doesn't have to. I won't do anything you don't want me to do." After a long silence, Rayna said, "I didn't mean to make this awkward."

"But the problem is, there are so many things I want you to do to me." Her voice came out in a whisper, trembling. The air between them thickened with tension; neither of them moved, frozen in the moment. Tanesha stepped forward, and Rayna's hand rose, brushing away a stray curl. The gentle glide of her fingertips made tingles along her skin.

Her cheeks were on fire. Then, the instinct smoldering deep within her psyche ignited. Her boyish grin that always surfaced whenever they escaped from trouble as children reappeared on her face. The fire of the hearth gave light to the muscles, eyes, and jawline that belonged to an alpha. She caressed Rayna's cheek, and a sliver of shyness flickered in her eyes. She kissed the alpha. Jolts of electricity pulsed through her body. Her blood rushed. Desire awoke from its long slumber and thundered between her legs.

As she held Tanesha's cheek, Rayna's lips strolled down her jaw. In response, Tanesha threaded her fingers through the alpha's hair as she gasped at feeling the nip of her teeth on her neck.

Slipping her hands under Rayna's top, Tanesha reached under her bra to rub her erect and eager nipples. Rayna moaned and let her jacket fall to the floor. Tanesha—the timid girl who had always followed in her best friend's shadow—pulled away and led her to her bed. She wrapped her arms around Rayna's neck, and they both fell backward. The alpha climbed over her, peered into her eyes, and kissed her so deeply Tanesha released a moan.

Rayna dipped down to her stomach and took off Tanesha's dress. She kissed her bare stomach until she reached her breasts, beginning with a gentle suckle of her nipple before releasing her hold and stroking it back and forth with her tongue. Then, she brushed her nipple in circles like an inspired artist pouring passion out on an easel. Tanesha's hands found home in between her wild curls. Rayna attended to the other nipple, taking it into her mouth and sucking. The light feeling of teeth jolted the underrunning current electrifying her body. Tanesha moaned. She would have never thought silly and rebellious Ray would turn out to be such an attentive lover, but then again, she never imagined they would end up like this.

Once Tanesha's nipples were erect, Rayna lowered her mouth, leaving a trail of kisses. After sliding off her panties with her teeth, sending shivers across Tanesha's skin, Rayna lifted her legs and kissed her thighs until she reached near the center. "Your smell is so intoxicating," Rayna whispered against her skin. She sucked on the inner sides of her thighs before finally cradling her legs and stroking just below her clit. She started off with wide, deep strokes before making circles near her clit. Tanesha arched her back and clawed her bed. Rayna grabbed her ass.

Tanesha slid from under the alpha and guided her on her back. "I want to ride your face," she said, a surge of confidence blooming in her voice.

Rayna smiled and leered up and down at her. It felt good to be the center of this alpha's desires. "Well, when you lookin' like that, how can I say no?"

Tanesha smirked and climbed on top of her, setting her pussy on Rayna's mouth. Rayna grabbed her ass again to guide her as she rode her face. Tanesha felt the tip of her claws dig into her skin, and then the alpha smacked her ass. It made her go faster and harder. She moaned so loud it almost turned into a howl. Then, she burst, and Rayna drank all her cum.

She wanted more of Rayna. She slipped off and nestled in a spot by her side. Their hearts thumped in rhythm. She took Rayna's nipple into her mouth, giving it the same attention she was given. Then she stroked the other between her fingers before sliding a finger into her pussy, savoring the wetness dripping onto her skin. Tanesha summoned a cocky grin of her own as she gazed upon Rayna's face coming undone with rapture. "You feel so good," Tanesha confessed before licking her finger. Then, she bowed her head between Rayna's cleft, worshipping her with her tongue and stroking attentively against her clit. Rayna blessed her with cries of satisfaction as she carefully threaded her claws between her hair.

"It feels good to have you inside me," Rayna said between moans.

Tanesha's body throbbed with pleasure at the realization that she was fucking a powerful, badass alpha. Here, she forgot all her shame and loneliness over being divorced, over losing rank in her family, over surviving off the pity of her father. She wasn't the waitress of her father's bar or the ex-wife of a prominent alpha or the disgraced daughter. She was just T, and T was making this beautiful alpha orgasm out of her mind. Her pussy clenched around her finger, sending waves of thrill down her spine. She slid in another finger and then another; she was so wet. And the way Rayna gasped out her name made her smile as she continued to lavishly eat her pussy until her thighs clenched.

Afterward, Tanesha rested in the crux of Rayna's arm. Rayna grasped her hand and took the finger Tanesha used to penetrate her. She wrapped her tongue around it and licked the cum off each finger while maintaining eye contact. Tanesha moaned as Rayna sucked on her fingers, kissed the palm of her hand, and moved down her arm. Rayna walked her fingers down to her pussy and eased inside with a finger. When she slid in the second finger, she thrusted harder and harder. She lifted Tanesha's leg and set it on her shoulder and thrust so deeply until she hit her cervix in just the right spot. Tanesha felt like there was a storm between her legs, and when she came, she bit her tongue so as to not howl and draw attention to her cabin—to her safe haven, even if it was hidden with protection magic.

In between heavy breaths, Tanesha rolled her body against Rayna's fingers still in her pussy. Smirking, Rayna gently turned her around and filled her from behind, two fingers deep into her sloppy wet pussy. Tanesha drooled on her sheets, and Rayna slapped her ass again. When she came, she fell against her pillow, Rayna hopping beside her with a knowing smile. They knew they both wouldn't be done for a while. Their wolf stamina kicked in, and they fucked until dawn brightened the sky outside her window. It was the best sleepless night she'd ever had.

Rayna fell asleep with one arm wrapped around Tanesha as she stroked her arm with her thumb. Her gaze drifted over to the calendar on her bedroom wall, and she mused about how they became lovers on Valentine's Day—a day she hadn't cared to acknowledge until now.

As she lay there, the memory of them lying in that meadow when they were kids played in her head. Rayna was asleep just like this, only they weren't embracing. She remembered watching her sleeping face and smiling at the starry night sky. Was it then that she realized she was in love with her best friend? Was she in love with her now? How much of Rayna was the same and how much was different? She decided she didn't have to have all the answers right now. Instead, she closed her eyes and fell asleep.

About the Author

Rowan Delacroix (they/she) is a full-time romance author, originally from Houston, Texas. They have a bachelor's degree with a major in English and a minor in psychology. They wrote research in the field areas of mythology and nutritional psychology. After their start in the technology sector, they embarked on a career in professional writing, social media marketing, and sales. When they are not writing, they are visiting museums and reading historical romance.

You can find Rowan on:
Instagram @rowandelacroix

Visit their website at:
romanticrevenant.blogspot.com

TIRAMISU

Tiramisu

Amy Hepp

OLIVIA NEEDED TO GO BACK to high school and learn how to flirt. She finished her morning ocean swim and walked parallel to the shore, pretending not to ogle the surfer out of the corner of her eye. The dark-haired man waved and smiled at her across the water.

"Want a turn with the board?" the guy shouted over the din of the surf.

Olivia shook her swim cap–covered head. "Don't know how."

"You're a strong swimmer. I'll teach you."

Her nausea flared as it always did when she met new people. She turned her back to a wave and inhaled the salty air in an effort to settle her stomach. When the tanned stranger flashed her another warm smile, she calmed. Ten minutes wouldn't kill her. "Well, all right."

The dark-haired man taught her how to belly board first, then balance on the board. He demonstrated how and when to stand on the surfboard. Though he made catching the wave look easy, she fell off and into the water again and again. He didn't laugh and urged her to keep trying. She caught her first wave a half hour later, and they hauled their tired bodies onto the beach.

They stripped out of their wet suits and plopped onto the sand. A breeze blew over her skin, and she shivered in the bright February sun on Florida's Atlantic coast. Her surfing teacher pulled a beach towel out of his bag and dried his legs before sitting on it.

"It's chilly this morning." Olivia wrapped her own towel around her shoulders and whipped off her swim cap to free her blond hair. She rubbed her body dry and stole a look at the man. Water dripped from his chin, and his shoulders rose and fell with heavy breaths.

She couldn't remember the last time she hung out with a guy. A year ago? Two? She'd spent the last two years in Sandee Pointe, Florida, working as a chef in a small Italian bistro on the main drag of the quiet beach town. She poured all her energy into her first professional job and spent every dime of her paychecks, after food and rent, paying off her culinary school loans. Money was always tight at the end of the month, and she didn't go out much. The bar scene wasn't for her, and online dating sites gave her the creeps.

He turned toward her and brushed a strand of hair off her face. "It'll warm up soon."

His soft touch sent a bolt of energy through her veins, and she shivered again. "Um, you're a good teacher." Olivia bent her head so he couldn't see her red face after her inane comment. Her friends knew how to flirt. What was her problem? Ugh. She never knew what to say to men.

He bumped her shoulder. "Hey, thanks."

She turned toward him, and their eyes locked. His amber eyes sparkled like champagne bubbles. The guy blinked, and a drop of water dripped from his long, wet eyelashes. Olivia's hormones surged, and she leaned closer to him. He cradled her neck and closed the distance between them. She placed her lips against his. The warm, soft touch sent liquid heat through her limbs, and her heart smashed against her chest. Their lips sealed together, and his mouth molded to hers like a custom-made dress. The salty kisses sent tingles down her spine. They shifted on the sand, and he groaned when she teased his lips with her tongue. The kiss deepened.

Alone on the beach with only the seagulls as their witnesses, they kissed until their chests heaved. He pulled her earlobe and nipped a spot on her neck before returning to her lips. Olivia angled her head for a deeper kiss and trailed a hand over his square jaw before lying back on the sand and urging him closer to her. She welcomed the heavy weight of his body on hers.

Their bathing suits didn't leave much to the imagination, and she pushed against him. A surge of electricity skittered to her toes. She ran her hands along his muscled back and down to his slim hips.

Their sand-encrusted feet tangled, and she winced from the scratch. The moment of pain snapped her out of her trance.

"Ow! Shit," said Olivia. The guy lifted off her, and she scooted away from him. "I'm so sorry. I never do this. Sorry." She grabbed her towel and wet suit and ran from the beach.

The short sprint home left her breathless. Or was it the kiss? She burst into her oceanfront studio apartment and stripped off her bathing suit. Soapy bubbles sluiced over her breasts and trailed down her thighs in the hot shower. Her breathing returned to normal, but her humiliation flared. What had possessed her to kiss a stranger in broad daylight on the beach? She angled her face to the hot spray and worked to calm her nerves. The guy didn't know her name or where she lived. Chances were, she'd never see him again.

Olivia grabbed the shampoo and squirted a dollop of the lavender-scented hair product into her palm as her brain niggled. But did she want to see the guy again? She massaged the shampoo into her hair and smiled. Maybe. He encouraged her when she attempted to surf and waited for her to make the first move on the beach. She rinsed her hair and remembered how the hard planes of his body contrasted with his soft lips. Maybe she'd see him at the beach tomorrow, and if she did, she'd suggest they meet for coffee. Besides, it was Valentine's Day weekend. Perfect timing for a first date. She shut off the shower. She had a plan.

Olivia pushed into the back door of Coppola's Italian Bistro fifteen minutes before her shift began. Loud rock music blared from the kitchen. She frowned. Who was in her kitchen? She stopped short in the entryway. A slim man with black hair chopped tomatoes at the stainless-steel island and swung his hips to the music. His knife danced across the counter, and perfectly diced tomatoes lay in its wake.

Olivia cleared her throat. "Um, excuse me?" She didn't have the energy to meet another new person today. She wanted the small kitchen all to herself for the busy Valentine's weekend.

The man either didn't hear her or ignored her. He zipped through another tomato.

She walked toward him and tapped him on the shoulder. He jumped, and the knife skittered across the surface. Tomatoes splashed onto the floor.

"Aagh!" yelled the man. He stepped back from the mess and turned toward her. His eyes widened and his nose flared.

The surfer from the beach met her stare. His initial scowl morphed into confusion, and he pulled his phone out of his pocket to kill the music.

Olivia's cheeks heated. "What're *you* doing in my kitchen?"

Before he could answer her, the kitchen door swung open, and her boss, Mama Coppola, waddled in to join them.

"Olivia." Mama Coppola clapped her hands together. "My son will help for Valentine's weekend." She pinched the surfer dude on the cheek. "Such a good boy."

Mama Coppola's heavy accent and broken English tripped her up on occasion, but she understood her today. She recoiled. Her son? The man she kissed on the beach was her boss's son?

She found her voice. "I don't think we need any help, Mama Coppola. I can manage six tables."

Her boss smiled and tilted her head. "I need his help this weekend."

Olivia walked over to the desk in the corner of the kitchen and plucked her apron off the wall. "I promise you, I'll manage."

Mama Coppola shook her finger. "No *discussione*, dear. Staff meeting."

Antonio cleaned the tomato mess and washed his knife. Mama Coppola retreated to the front of the house, and Olivia skittered out of the kitchen before the guy said anything to her. She slid into a booth beside the host and gave the teen a smile. The two servers scrolled their phones, and the busboy hadn't shown yet. Mama Coppola passed around the menu for the weekend. Olivia didn't even look at it. The offerings never changed.

"How about a special lava cake for Valentine's Day?" she asked. "The diners might love a fun change from tiramisu."

Mama Coppola shook her head. "No. We make tiramisu. My best recipe from the old country."

Olivia sighed. She prepared a tiramisu daily to serve the following day. The decadent dessert chilled overnight for optimal flavor. Although she loved the sweet treat, she longed to prepare different desserts. A larger resort on the beach might allow her flexibility with the menu, but she'd have to work in a huge environment with sous chefs and a revolving door of servers.

During culinary school, she interned at big restaurants and left most nights with either a splitting headache or an upset stomach. The thought of returning to a noisy, chaotic environment made her skin crawl and her heart pound. Olivia loved to cook and preferred to work in a small kitchen without any drama. She followed Mama Coppola's recipes for traditional Italian fare, and although she didn't make a ton of money, it worked for her.

Mama Coppola reminded the host to change the flowers in the bud vases before the first reservation and dismissed the staff.

Olivia returned to the kitchen and glanced at Mama Coppola's son dicing peppers while she tied her apron. Was he a surfer or a chef?

Both? She pulled a saucepot out from under the stainless-steel island and placed it on the stove. She then coated the bottom of the pot with a drizzle of olive oil and opened her knives to slice an onion.

The surfer guy cleared his throat and interrupted her thoughts. "Um, Mama asked me to dice peppers and tomatoes, but if you have something else you'd like me to do, let me know. I'm your sous chef for the weekend."

Olivia kept her head bent and didn't look at him. "Peppers and to-matoes work. I'm Olivia."

"Antonio."

She stopped chopping. "Listen, I'm sorry about this morning. Can we forget it? I don't know what came over me. I'm always a little crazy around Valentine's Day. I'd appreciate it if my boss didn't know."

Antonio's lips curled into a smile. "I don't usually share my sexca-pades with my mama."

Olivia's cheeks flared again. "Got it. Thanks for the help."

They chopped and sautéed for an hour before speaking again.

"How about I start on the tiramisu?" he said.

Silence.

"Olivia?"

"Sorry, what?"

"I asked you if I should begin the tiramisu."

Her head snapped up from layering pans of lasagna. "Oh. Sorry. Yeah. I mean . . . yes, thank you. Why don't you brew the espresso, and I'll make the custard?"

Olivia shoved the giant pans of lasagna into the oven and turned her attention to the signature dessert. The bean grinder whirred under Antonio's hands while she gathered mascarpone cheese, sugar, and separated eggs for the custard. The rich aroma of espresso filled the kitchen.

With all the ingredients for the tiramisu ready to assemble, they stood beside each other at the island to layer the decadent dessert to-gether. He dipped the ladyfingers into the brewed espresso and layered them in the pan. Olivia spooned the custard over the ladyfingers, and their hips bumped while they worked. She finished off the dessert with a dusting of cocoa.

Two ladyfingers remained on the tray. Antonio took one and dipped it into the espresso and along the side of the custard bowl. He bit half of the treat and offered the rest to her. She wrapped her lips around the soft pastry and caught the tip of his finger between her teeth. He groaned. Olivia's chest fluttered, and she carried the tiramisu to the walk-in fridge.

Grateful for the chill of the fridge, she stored the dessert and checked on the completed one to be served tonight. She retreated to the kitchen to begin the Alfredo sauce and asked Antonio to form the meatballs. They stirred and chopped through the evening in between plating the meals with precision. The servers were on point, and the night went off without a hitch.

Antonio's arm muscles flexed as he washed the dishes. He caught her staring and smiled. She busied herself with the dishwasher.

"You're a great chef," he said.

Olivia stammered. "Thanks. Your mama hired me right after graduation from culinary school. I didn't have any experience." She wiped her hands on a towel. "She's kind."

He furrowed his brow. "You're the first chef to stick around longer than six months. She refuses to change the menu or expand the seating."

"I'm comfortable in a small kitchen." She leaned against the island. "I like to control the pace and flow. Your skills aren't too shabby. Are you a chef?"

Antonio smiled, flashing his white teeth. "My parents raised me in this kitchen. Mama gave me no choice except to learn how to slice and dice. But no, I'm not a chef."

Olivia hung her apron and packed her bag. They stood toe to toe in the kitchen. Her heart picked up, and she cleared her throat. "It's late. Thanks for the help tonight." She grabbed her bag and hustled out into the dark night.

The alarm blared the following morning, and Olivia yawned after a long night of dreaming about Antonio. She couldn't get the guy out of her mind. He'd patiently taught her to surf and didn't question her direction in the kitchen. He loved his mama and spoke his mind. When she remembered making the tiramisu with him, her hormones raged.

Sunshine streamed in her window, and she pulled on her wet suit over her bathing suit and made her way to the ocean. As she approached the shore, her face broke out into a smile. Antonio paddled his board near the pier. She waved and headed south to put distance between them for her workout. A half hour later, she ran out of the surf and onto the beach. She stripped out of her wetsuit and sat on her towel to watch him.

He caught wave after wave. The foam in the ocean swallowed him at times, but he always got right back on the board. When he finished, he jogged out of the surf and unzipped his wetsuit.

"Hey, Olivia."

She lay back on her elbows. "Your board floats over the waves when you surf. You make it look so easy,"

Antonio grinned. "I do all right. It's a perfect day."

"Hmm."

He set down his board and lay beside her. Her heart smashed against her chest, and all her lady bits woke up. He pulled her in like a magnet.

"Don't you love it when there isn't a cloud in the sky?"

Olivia didn't date a lot of men, but she'd never met a man who commented on the color of the sky. The men she dated droned on and on about their cars and golf scores. She didn't know if he possessed some sort of kryptonite hormone or what, but as soon as he turned toward her, she scooted closer to him. His golden eyes pierced her gaze, and their lips came together in a perfect union. When his hand brushed her hip bone, blood rushed from her brain to her core, and she moaned.

He nudged her onto her back, the new angle allowing him to deepen the kiss with his tongue, and he shared his salty taste.

Antonio ended the kiss too soon. "I'm eating lunch with Mama, but I'd love to cook dinner for you after our shift. How about we eat in the restaurant?"

She couldn't remember the last time someone cooked her dinner. "Sounds great." Olivia fused with his chilly lips one last time.

Antonio gathered his board and jogged off the beach. She stayed on the sand and let the crash of the waves calm her body and mind. Her physical attraction to him scared and exhilarated her at the same time. She craved details about him. Why wasn't he a chef? What did he do for a living? Where did he live? Did he live close to Sandee Pointe?

Her phone chimed. A message from Mama Coppola to the whole staff filled her screen.

I be late to the restaurant today. Antonio will help.

Her heart skipped a beat. Maybe they'd make the tiramisu together again.

Upon her arrival at the bistro, she found Antonio in gray slacks and a black shirt fending off a server caressing his bicep with a manicured nail. She couldn't tell from the look on his face if he wanted the woman. He caught Olivia's gaze and shook his head. She raised one eyebrow.

The woman pouted and stormed out of the kitchen when he removed the server's hand and told her no thank you. He looked at Olivia. "Sorry 'bout that."

"No need to apologize. Can't say I blame her."

They sliced and diced with the same routine as the day before. Once the lasagna hit the oven, her nipples pebbled under her shirt. Today, Antonio didn't even wait until they layered the dessert to tempt her. He dragged a finger along the edge of the custard bowl and offered her a taste. She opened her mouth and sucked the tip of his finger.

Creamy goodness hit her taste buds. She gathered a dollop of custard on her own finger, offering it to him, and he drew it into his mouth and sucked until her sex pulsed. He released her finger and brought her tight against his body.

"Not sure how I'll survive until the end of the night." he whispered into her ear.

Olivia cleared her throat. "We need to layer the dessert."

He kissed her cheek, and she somehow managed to finish the dessert and carry it to the walk-in fridge without dropping it. She leaned against a shelf and placed a hand on her forehead in the cool room.

The Saturday night crowd mirrored Friday night, and the restaurant ran at full capacity. Olivia listened to Antonio's stories while they worked in the kitchen. He told her how he'd come into the restaurant after school and steal garlic bread straight from the hot trays. She smirked when he described how he dillydallied with his homework to put off washing the dishes. His parents dragged him to Italy the summer he turned twelve, and he missed the playoffs for his baseball team.

The bistro closed, and she and Antonio washed the dishes. He insisted on blasting classic rock when the restaurant emptied. To her surprise, she sang along and swung her hips to the music.

"Go grab a bottle of your favorite white wine. I'll start on dinner," he said.

Olivia chose a dry Riesling and set a table in the dining room. She kept the overhead lights off and lit a candle in the middle of a table for two near the window. When she returned to the kitchen, Antonio sautéed garlic and onions in a pan of butter. He added white wine and squeezed a fresh lemon into the hot pan. The garlic and onions sizzled as he doused fresh pasta into a pot of boiling water. Olivia observed with a practiced eye and smiled when he added the shrimp at the perfect time. Antonio drained the pasta and added it to the sauce. He flipped the contents of the skillet to mix it all together and finished the dish with fresh herbs and a pat of butter. Olivia brought over two plates, and Antonio divided the food between them.

Once settled in the dining room, he lifted his glass. "A well-deserved meal after a long day."

They sipped their wine, and Olivia twirled the pasta around her fork and speared a shrimp. The buttery lemon jolted her taste buds. She swallowed and pointed her fork at him. "You should be a chef."

Antonio chuckled. "Nah. My skills aren't refined; I know how to make a few dishes."

They ate in silence for a few minutes. Olivia sipped her wine and set her glass on the table. "It's nice to eat with someone. I usually grab a plate of food and eat at the island before closing the kitchen."

"I eat by myself most days."

"Do you live alone?"

He swiped a shrimp through the sauce and nodded. "I'm not married and don't have a girlfriend. What about you?" asked Antonio.

"Same. Sandee Pointe's a pretty small town. There's not a huge single scene, but even if there was, I wouldn't be into it." She shared a story about a disastrous date with a guy she met at a bar. They drank and laughed until all foot traffic stopped outside the restaurant window. When Antonio brought out a plate of tiramisu from the kitchen, Olivia shivered from head to toe.

"One piece left," he said. "We can share it."

He speared a bite of the dessert and held the fork to her mouth. She wrapped her lips around the tines, and he slowly pulled the utensil out of her mouth and ate a bite himself. He repeated the action until she whimpered. Antonio shoved the empty plate to the side and grasped her hands across the table. They met in the middle for a tender kiss. The sweetness of the dessert lingered on their lips. He pulled her around the table, and she straddled his lap and looped her arms around his neck. The light and airy kisses evolved into an intense union. Olivia ground against his hardness to quell the ache between her legs.

In between kisses, Antonio worked the tiny buttons of her shirt and opened it wide. He drew his thumb across her black silk bra and grazed her swollen nipple. Heat shot through her chest, and she gasped from the spark. He left her lips to place featherlight kisses on her collarbone, increasing her pulse. The desire to be closer to him surged and she flicked open the front clasp of her bra.

He sucked a nipple into his mouth, and Olivia leaned her head back to give him full access. When he released her nipple and blew on the damp flesh, she cried out and the noise bounced off the walls of the empty restaurant. She squirmed on his lap and uttered, "More." Antonio cradled her breasts as if they were porcelain teacups and trailed his lips along her cleavage.

A passing car flooded the restaurant with light, and the lusty haze between them shattered. Olivia yelped and held her shirt closed. "I forgot about the window."

He panted. "Me, too."

She giggled. "I can't believe we were strangers yesterday, and now look at us." She clasped her bra. "Don't worry, we have all the time in the world to get to know one another."

Antonio winced, and his face fell. "I leave next week."

"Leave?"

"I live in California. I own a surf shop there."

Her fingers fumbled with the tiny buttons of her blouse. "Oh. Um . . . Sure. Okay."

California? Ugh. She knew he was too perfect. She stood and gathered the dirty dishes from the table.

Antonio took the plates out of her hands and set them back on the table. "I'll do the dishes." He wrapped his arms around her. "I'd love to spend Valentine's Day with you tomorrow. Meet me at the beach in the morning?"

Olivia bit her lower lip. Meet him at the beach and enjoy the silly holiday or wallow at home before work? "Sure."

He swept her away with another soul-drenching kiss. Her head spun, and when he finished the kiss, she placed a hand on his chest to steady herself. She whispered, "Bye," and pushed out the front door into the dark night.

Valentine's Day dawned cool but sunny in Sandee Pointe. Olivia ate a quick breakfast and hustled to the beach. Antonio stood by the shore and pointed to the sand. Hand-drawn hearts surrounded a huge Happy Valentine's Day etched in sand. She chuckled on her way to the shoreline.

Her heart pulled in a weird direction when she thought about him, but she tamped down the feelings. Her short-term fling would end next week when he headed back to California. Olivia snapped on her swim cap and dove into the waves while Antonio readied his board. Once again, he gave clear direction, and she caught wave after wave in the rough surf. He cheered her on and shouted encouragement through the morning.

They pulled themselves out of the water and lay on the beach. Antonio kissed her lips, and the familiar sensation quickened her pulse. She lost herself in his kisses until two kids ran past them toward the water.

"Hope we didn't scar them for life," he said.

"Nah. I'm sure they didn't even notice us."

Antonio smiled and checked his watch. "I need to get home. I promised Mama I'd help her with the books this afternoon."

"Yep. I'll see you at the bistro."

"We're still on for dinner?"

"You bet. My turn to cook . . . at my place."

He hummed and treated her to a toe-curling kiss. Olivia grinned like a fool and soaked up the sun for another hour.

Later in the afternoon, she entered the back door of the bistro, and the familiar scent of the old restaurant washed over her. She began the meal preparations in the clean and quiet kitchen until Antonio appeared with a scowl.

"Trouble with Mama?" she asked him.

He shook his head and tied an apron behind his back. Then he washed his hands, and by the time he turned back from the sink, a smile replaced his scowl. "Tomatoes and peppers?"

She laughed. "Sure."

Antonio diced the vegetables with speed while she raced through the lasagna. When the oven door snapped closed, he grinned at her and ground the beans for the espresso. The whir of the coffee bean grinder flooded her panties, and she swallowed hard. She placed the dessert ingredients on the island and measured the sugar. After separating the eggs with practiced skill, she beat them with the sugar. He came behind her and kissed her neck as she folded in the mascarpone with smooth strokes. Olivia added the vanilla and rum to the creamy mixture, and they layered the dessert together before she sifted the cocoa on top. Antonio held the door to the walk-in, and she set the tiramisu on a shelf. When she turned around, he pushed her against the closed door. Their lips collided, and her purrs echoed throughout the small space. He held her hip and urged her closer. Her body molded against his, and she thrust against him.

Olivia pulled away first. "I'm sure we've broken a million health code violations."

He chuckled. "Worth it."

She tapped his chest with her finger. "I'm not losing my job over you." She straightened her apron and returned to the kitchen to cook for the night. Antonio supported her efforts in the kitchen and somehow turned every part of her normal routine into foreplay. He brushed her hip at the sink or whispered into her ear when she stirred a sauce. By the time the orders came in, her sex throbbed.

Mama Coppola bustled into the kitchen and shook her finger at Antonio. "Don't flirt with my staff."

"Yes, Mama."

Olivia blushed a fierce red and stuck her head in the oven to check the manicotti.

Mama Coppola pinched his cheeks. "Don't be trouble."

"Never."

When the last customer walked out the door, Olivia leaned against the stainless-steel island. Antonio gripped her waist and kissed her. "Go home. I'll clean up here."

She grinned and removed her apron. "Bring a bottle of red and what's left of the tiramisu."

❤━━━━━━━━━━━━━❤

The warm February night wrapped around Olivia as she walked home. Darkness settled over the beach town, and the waves broke in the distance. She pushed Antonio's impending departure from her mind and vowed to relish Valentine's Day. Her friends talked about hookups and flings. Now it was her turn. Antonio felt different than a fling, but what did she know?

She entered her studio apartment and tossed her bag beside the chair. The bathroom mirror reflected her sparkling eyes and perpetual smile. She washed her face and released her hair from its tight bun. Blond waves cascaded over her shoulders. A trace of mascara brought out her brown eyes, and she swiped her lips with gloss. She changed into a sundress over her favorite white lace bra and matching V-string panty.

The tiny apartment didn't leave much to the imagination, but she kept it clean and neat. Her desire to live on the beach outweighed her need for extra rooms. She fluffed her pillows, straightened the bedspread, and turned on the soft bedside lamp.

Across the room, she organized the meal ingredients in the kitchenette and streamed acoustic love songs on her phone. A quiet knock at her door sounded as she peeled a potato. She opened the door to Antonio grinning with a bottle of wine and a take-home box of tiramisu. His damp hair curled at the ends, and he smelled of soap. He set the wine bottle on the two-person dinette table and popped the tiramisu into the fridge as she returned to the potatoes.

"I love your adorable apartment."

"Thanks. It's small, but I wanted to hear the ocean every day."

He threaded an arm around her waist and used his other hand to move her hair off one shoulder. When he kissed her on the neck, sparks singed down her arm, and she tilted her head for more. Antonio nipped her jaw and rubbed his hand across her stomach. Her nipples hardened like rocks against her lace bra and ached for his touch.

He shifted closer to her and pulled an earlobe into his mouth. Liquid heat surged to her core, and wetness flooded between her legs. "Your skin is so soft." Antonio murmured.

Unable to form words, she leaned her head back on his shoulder and let the potato and peeler drop into the sink. She gripped the edge of the counter and whimpered as his right hand cupped her breast. Heavy breaths filled the room as her breasts swelled under his touch and her legs melted. She twisted around in his arms, and their mouths collided.

Antonio's soft lips sent vibrations to her toes, and when she opened her mouth for him, their tongues joined in the dance. Olivia curled her fingers behind his neck and twisted the ends of his hair. He slipped a finger under her dress strap and let it slide off her shoulder before he broke their kiss and met her gaze. His eyes dilated, and he let the other strap drop. With the top of her breasts exposed, he placed tender kisses on her hot flesh, slowly lowering her zipper until the dress puddled to the floor. His gaze raked across her body.

"You're beautiful," he whispered.

"I'm not hungry for food right now," said Olivia.

Antonio shoved the lamb chops into the fridge, and she hit the overhead light. Her bedside lamp illuminated the small space with soft light. They crossed over to her bed, and she lay down as he tossed a package of condoms on the bedside table and stripped off his clothes. She held out her hand, and he joined her. After another soul-drenching kiss, he pulled away from her mouth and kissed his way to her breasts. His lips teased a swollen nipple through the lace, and she gasped.

"More," she said in a hoarse voice.

Antonio unclasped her bra, and Olivia offered him her other nipple to satiate her desire, but it only increased her arousal. When his tongue flicked the nub, she squeezed her thighs together. He kissed down her stomach, toying with her curls once he nuzzled her mound.

Her hips arched off the bed, and he freed her of the V-string. In the heat of the moment, her shyness vanished. She spread her legs wide, inviting him to taste her.

Antonio kissed the inside of her thighs and indulged in her nectar. She ran her fingers through his hair and mewled when the smooth slide of his tongue learned every nuance of her sex. Time evaporated, and she reveled in the sensations until his repeated ministrations sent her body headlong into a desperate climax that shook her soul like never before. After her muscles relaxed, he kissed his way back up her body. His hard cock rested against her hip, and he smiled at her.

"You're delicious." His lips glistened with her taste.

"Kiss me," she said.

Antonio shared her taste, and the erotic gesture spurred on another jolt of arousal, and she snatched a condom off the bedside table. When they joined, Olivia uttered a husky sigh. He filled her and they held still, reading each other's expressions.

She trailed a finger along his flushed cheek. "Incredible."

"You're my match."

He never took his eyes off her when he began to rock. She met his movements with thrusts of her own and dug her nails into his ass as he brought her to the edge once again.

"Faster," she panted.

The increased pace caused Antonio to swell inside of her. Their bodies moved as one until she squeezed her eyes shut and cried out as she came. After another thrust, he shouted his release. A thin sheen of sweat covered both of them, but they stayed connected. He placed light kisses on her cheeks, nose, and shoulders.

He rolled them to their sides. They murmured to each other, and he brushed her hair off her face. A shiver coursed through Olivia when Antonio left the bed and disappeared into the bathroom. Olivia pulled down the duvet and snuggled under the sheets. When he returned to bed and settled onto the pillows, he lay on his back and closed his eyes. She shifted to lay her head on his chest and was lulled to sleep by the gentle pulse of his heart.

Hours later, a clap of thunder woke Olivia. Antonio snored, and she marveled at the man who turned her life upside down in a matter of days. His lovemaking skills catapulted her to a place she didn't even know existed. She ran a finger over his chest muscles and across his abs and gripped his cock. Her lips followed the path of her hand, and his musky scent triggered new flutters in her chest. She tossed her hair to one side and drew him into her mouth.

Antonio stirred and moaned with his eyes closed. After a while, he hardened again. Desperate for him, she sheathed his cock with a condom and swung a leg over his thighs. He opened his eyes and gripped her hips when she sank onto him. The moonlight cast a silver glow across their bodies while she rode him to completion.

In the wee hours of the morning, Antonio brought the box of tiramisu to bed, and they shared the large piece. She pulled her lips from the fork and swallowed the last bite of the sweet treat. "I will never make or eat tiramisu again without thinking of you." She set the empty dish on the nightstand before spooning into Antonio and dozing off again.

A heavy rain pelted Olivia's sliding glass door the following morning. Antonio looked at the time on his phone and growled. "I need to get home."

She draped a leg over his. "Don't go."

He held her tight to his body. "I fly home the day after tomorrow. Dinner tonight?"

"Sure. We never ate the lamb chops. I'll start over on the potatoes, though. I think they're still in the sink." She wrinkled her nose. "The bistro is closed today. I'll make the tiramisu here."

"No. Wait for me. Let's make it together."

"It chills for hours."

"I think we know how to fill the time."

Olivia lazed around in bed on her day off and replayed her night with Antonio. Her body thrummed. Why did he live so far away? How would a relationship work on different coasts? She drank coffee and listened to the rain pound the sliding glass door. She cleaned the non-dinner from the previous night and changed the sheets on her bed. The rain lightened after lunch, and she walked to the restaurant to borrow the sifter to dust the cocoa for the tiramisu. Her personal kitchen lacked special tools, and Mama Coppola allowed her to use the bistro's.

A quiet Main Street was devoid of tourists on the drizzly day. Olivia used her key to unlock the back kitchen door. She pushed into the dark space and went straight to the drawer where the sifter lived. Voices sounded in the dining room, and Antonio's voice raised in an angry tone. She stepped toward the door. His voice boomed through the empty restaurant.

"Mama, you can't sustain the business. You've been in trouble for months. After this month's payroll, you're out of money. You need to close the bistro and sell the space."

Mama Coppola sniffed. "I want to cook food from the old country."

Antonio's voice softened. "I know, Mama. I know. You can still cook for your friends, but you can't run the business."

"My staff."

"Tell them tomorrow."

Olivia doubled over as all the air left her lungs. Close? Sweat beaded on her upper lip, and her heart pounded. Without thinking, she shoved open the kitchen doors to the dining room and strode toward Antonio and her weepy boss.

"We're closing?"

"Olivia, dear." Mama Coppola wiped her face. "*Sì*. I need to close bistro. I'm sorry."

"I need this job, Mama Coppola."

"I know. I know. I'm so sorry."

Olivia gritted her teeth and faced Antonio. "Is this why you came to town? To talk your mother into closing her restaurant and ruining my life? Did you think getting me to sleep with you would soften the blow?"

Mama Coppola sucked in a breath.

Antonio stood and held her hand. "Olivia, no. Listen, I'll be over later, and we can talk about it."

Olivia stepped back from him and pulled her hand away. "Don't you dare come to my house tonight." She tossed the sifter onto the table and slammed out the door into the rain. She made it halfway down the street before the tears fell.

When she reached her apartment, she curled into a ball on her bed, and sobs wracked her body. Why did he do this to her? They had a magical connection, but he slept with her when he knew about Coppola's closing. He knew she'd lose her job. A shuddering sigh escaped her body. At least he lived in California—she never wanted to see him again.

Mama Coppola brought all the employees into the bistro the following morning and informed them of the closing. She promised one last paycheck and references. Olivia couldn't even look at her boss and left the bistro without saying a word.

Every hotel and resort along the beach supported restaurants, but the mere thought of cooking in a large restaurant turned her stomach. Her competitive culinary skills weren't the problem. She struggled working among a sea of people. She controlled the pace and flow at Coppola's. But the fancy resorts did pay better and offered decent benefits. Maybe if she got ahead of her debt and saved money, she'd be able to breathe at the end of the month.

She drafted a short list of resorts and restaurants to send her CV. She reviewed her bank account and estimated she could spend two months job searching before resorting to hourly work to pay the rent.

The job search allowed Olivia to focus on something other than Antonio for a few hours, but when she crawled into bed, fresh tears pricked her eyes.

The sun reappeared the next day, and she swam through the ocean like a machine. The churning waves absorbed her pain, and by the time she finished, her arms hung by her side like Jello. She jogged out of the water and onto the sand. Antonio stood beside her towel in jeans and a button-down shirt. A duffle bag hung from his shoulder. She avoided his gaze.

"Can we talk?" he asked.

Olivia whipped off her swim cap and goggles. "I think I've heard enough."

"I'm so sorry. You weren't supposed to find out until Mama told the staff. I know it's awkward, but there's something special between us."

"Are you serious?" she spat. "You swooped into town with an agenda to close your mama's business and destroy my life."

"I didn't have any idea you worked as my mama's chef when I taught you how to surf."

"Yet, when you learned who I was, you knew I'd lose my job. And you never said a word. You lied to me." She grabbed her towel and stomped across the beach. It took every ounce of her willpower not to turn around and glimpse Antonio one last time.

After two weeks and four disastrous interviews, Olivia asked Mama Coppola out for coffee. The older woman plopped into a chair across from her in the local café. Dark circles framed her eyes.

Olivia narrowed her gaze. "Are you all right?"

Mama Coppola wiped a bead of perspiration from her brow. "I'm fine. Tired."

"You look exhausted."

Mama Coppola shrugged. "The leukemia in early stages."

Her words hung in the air. Olivia leaned back in her chair. "Leukemia?" She whispered.

Mama Coppola nodded. "No medication yet."

"That's why Antonio wanted you to close the bistro."

"And I made mess of the books. I cooked. My husband did the money. But he died. Antonio taught me, but I never . . ." Mama Coppola's plump fingers grabbed Olivia's hands. "I'm sorry. I know you loved my restaurant, and I loved your cooking."

"I didn't know about your illness. Why didn't you tell me?"

Mama Coppola waved her hand in Olivia's face. "Old lady problems."

"Stop. Please let me know how I can help you."

"I'm okay. I tell you when I need help. How's job hunt?"

Olivia pulled her hands away. "Not good. I didn't make it beyond the first round of interviews at four different resorts. I was late to one because I threw up in the bushes by the front door. I don't think I can work in the big kitchens."

Their server placed two lattes and plates of tiramisu in front of them. Olivia's body heated. She hadn't eaten tiramisu since Antonio left.

Mama Coppola's eyes twinkled, and she pulled a business card out of her ginormous purse. She slid it across the table to her. Surfboards of every color covered one side. Olivia flipped it over and traced a finger across Antonio's name on the back. Her eyes welled with tears. Mama Coppola patted her hand and said, "My Antonio is smitten. Lots of small restaurants in his town." Mama Coppola winked at her.

Olivia flushed and hid her face behind her coffee cup. "Well, we had fun for a couple of days, but he's gone back to California. Besides, he knew about the bistro closing and didn't tell me."

"*Copa mia.* I beg him not to say. I tell the staff."

"I'm sorry I eavesdropped."

"It's all right, dear. Don't blame Antonio."

Olivia ate a bite of tiramisu, and all the memories flooded back. She slipped the business card into her purse and chatted with her old boss for the rest of the afternoon.

The late February sunshine warmed them on the sidewalk outside the café. She hugged Mama Coppola goodbye.

Mama Coppola pinched her cheek. "Call my Antonio."

"Maybe. Thanks."

Palm trees swayed in the small town twenty miles north of Santa Barbara a week after her coffee date with Mama Coppola. Olivia parallel parked the rental on a side street and locked the car. The warm wind blew against her cheek as she walked through town. She pulled the business card out of her pocket and rubbed the smooth paper between her thumb and forefinger.

Antonio's business was three blocks west along the oceanfront. She squared her shoulders and turned the corner. An eclectic array of restaurants, bistros, and cafés dotted the downtown streets among antique shops and clothing boutiques. People rode bikes, and foot traffic dominated the town. A small Greek restaurant tucked into the corner of a building displayed a help wanted sign in the window. She snapped a photo of the address.

On the next block, her mind wandered. What if Antonio didn't want to see her? What if he found another woman? She couldn't get their instant bond out of her head, and she had to know if it was real. The rhythmic sound of the ocean soothed her nerves.

Colorful boards lined the wall outside the shop, and the open door led her inside a small but tidy space. A mixture of sunscreen and salt filled the air, and beach music piped through hidden speakers. Antonio's smooth baritone voice sounded over the din of the store.

"The warm ocean temperature and mild tides are perfect for surfing today," he remarked to an employee standing beside him.

Olivia walked to the counter. "Sounds great. I'd love a lesson."

"Olivia." he whispered. He scrambled around the counter and brought her into his arms for a fierce hug. "What're you doing here?"

She returned the hug and relaxed for the first time in three weeks. "Like I said, I'd love a lesson."

"You flew two thousand miles for a surfing lesson?"

"I'd fly around the world to see you again. Your mama and I talked."

Antonio shook his head. "You were right. I should've told you about the bistro, but Mama asked me not to. I didn't know what to do."

"I know." She looked around the small store. "Is there someplace we can talk?"

He held up a finger. He retreated behind the counter and talked to the employee before patting the guy on the shoulder. "Thanks, man." He disappeared into an office and emerged ten seconds later. "Let's go."

Grabbing her hand, Antonio led her to the beach, and they slipped off their sandals as soon as they hit the warm sand. Once they walked down to the surf, the cool water splashed their ankles with a regular cadence.

"I'm so glad you're here," he said.

"I couldn't stop thinking about us."

"Me neither. I'm so sorry. I wanted to give you some space before I called you."

"Your mama explained everything. I didn't know she was sick."

"Yeah. I'll bring her out here at some point. She's all right for now. She loves Florida and has a million friends there, but I still worry about her."

"She's an amazing woman."

"Have you found a job yet?"

Olivia shook her head and smiled. "Maybe I'll look for a job around here."

Antonio stopped and pulled her close to him. Their eyes locked as their bodies melded together. A rocket of heat blasted through her after his kiss. He pressed his forehead against hers and panted. "Let's go to dinner. I know a great place on the beach with a waterfront view and delicious tiramisu."

Olivia licked her lips. "Perfect."

About the Author

Amy Hepp writes love stories from her screened-in porch among the birds and blue skies of Raleigh, North Carolina. She has published two novellas with the Fifth Avenue Press of Ann Arbor, Michigan. *Northern Woods* (2022) and *Ripple Effects* (2024) are contemporary romance novellas set in the Boundary Waters of northern Minnesota.

When she's not writing, she enjoys running, working jigsaw puzzles, gardening, and visiting her three young adult children scattered across North America.

You can find Amy on:
Instagram @amyheppstories

Visit her website at:
https://amyheppstories.wixsite.com/my-site

SWEETS FOR MY EARL

Sweets for My Earl

Christina Diane

Norfolk, England
February 1819

GRACE, THE COUNTESS OF SIDMOUTH, stared at her sleeping husband with all the love and adoration she felt for him in their almost two years of marriage. Arthur, the Earl of Sidmouth, was the kind of man who worked alongside his tenants, rubbed her back and waited on her hand and foot when she had been sick from pregnancy, and stayed up all night rocking their son when James struggled to sleep at night. All of which were tasks considered unfashionable and beneath most men of their society, but not Arthur.

He blinked his eyes open and grinned at her. "How long have you been awake, sweetheart?"

"Not long," she replied, tracing her finger along the ridges on his hard stomach.

"And just what are you smiling about?"

"I'm just looking at my handsome husband."

Handsome was a bit of an understatement. Given the work he frequently did outdoors when his tenants required a helping hand, he had a chiseled, taut form. A bit of his chestnut hair fell across his forehead as his green eyes sparkled with nothing but love and a hint of mischief. He was utterly irresistible, which had been proven time and time again on the number of occasions they'd scandalized their servants with the compromising positions they frequently found themselves in.

Her wicked husband put his hand on hers and slid it lower. "Are you just intending to look, or shall there also be touching?"

She was wanton when it came to Arthur and shifted so that she straddled him, his cock protruding between them. As she reached over him to the bedside table, he took the opportunity with her chest so near to his face to cup her breast and suck one of her budded nipples into his mouth.

Grace arched her back, releasing a series of low moans as she continued to reach for Arthur's spectacles. She sat up, and he shifted his hands to grip her hips.

In a careful movement, she placed her husband's spectacles to rest on his nose and ears. "There," she whispered, "now you can see me."

While she wished to enable Arthur to see what she intended to do to him, it was equally a self-serving gesture. He was far too attractive in his own right, but add the spectacles and she'd turn feral. The spectacles also weren't considered high fashion among the members of their society, but that was their loss.

The way his emerald eyes, hooded with desire, looked at her through the gold rims had her so wet and needy for him. Grace shifted higher on her knees and then speared herself with her husband's cock in a single fluid motion.

"God, yes," he ground out, biting into his bottom lip.

She braced herself with her hands on his hard chest and leaned closer to look into his eyes.

"Does my earl like this?" she teased, rocking her hips with intentional slowness.

He pushed his head up to meet her mouth and kissed her, then smiled against her lips. "You tease, my little minx, but I know what you wish for me to do."

Grace pressed her lips to his again before pulling back and smirking at him. "Well, are you just intending to talk, or shall there also be doing?"

Arthur gripped her hips and thrust himself up while helping her to ride him. He had been correct in what she wanted, always in tune with her every need.

No matter how many times they had coupled, of which she had lost count, the passion and intensity never diminished between them.

She released her long blonde hair from its plait, knowing it would drive her husband to the brink of madness when her curls fell around her. The way he turned primal and moved her hips to ride him in an unbridled frenzy was her reward for knowing him so well.

A few moments later, she was crying out and moaning from the way the pleasure overtook her entire body when he brought her over the brink of her orgasm. He held her tight against him when he groaned and filled her with the warmth of his release.

Leaning down, she kissed her husband as they both fought to catch their breath. "I love you," she whispered against his lips.

"And I love you," he replied, running his fingers through her hair.

They remained that way for several minutes, him still inside her while she lay on top of him, feeling his heart beat against her chest.

"Are you still helping repair that door today?" she asked, knowing they'd have to get out of bed soon.

"Indeed. I should get dressed."

She feigned a pout, not because she truly wanted him to leave, as she would much prefer to spend the day abed with her husband, but on that given day she needed him away from their home.

Grace climbed off of him and scooted to the side of the bed until she could place her feet on the floor. After grabbing her dressing robe, she wrapped it around her shoulders and departed to the adjoining chamber that she only used as her dressing room.

Once she was dressed, she returned to their shared chamber and found Arthur waiting for her.

"Are you departing soon?" she asked.

He eyed her curiously. "What exactly do you have planned for today?"

"Nothing much," she replied. It was a bit of a white lie, depending on how one looked at it. "Marina is going to visit this morning." Marina was Arthur's sister and only sibling. It was convenient that Marina and her husband Evan, Viscount Ockham, lived in the next estate over. Their lands bordered each other.

It would mean that Grace and Arthur's son, James, and any other children they might have, would grow up to be quite close to their cousins.

"What is she up to?" Arthur asked in an accusatory tone. He adored his older sister, but the pair could bicker and fight worse than anyone Grace had ever seen, and she had grown up with an older brother and two older sisters.

Grace waved him off. "She's just visiting. Probably to catch me up on the latest news she's heard from friends." A point that likely wasn't untrue.

Arthur grabbed her hand and brought it to his lips. "Let us visit James and then I shall break my fast with you before I depart."

"That sounds lovely." And it would work out well if he departed before Marina arrived.

James had been awake when they visited, each taking their turn to hold him. He would be one in a couple months, and time seemed to fly far too quickly.

Afterward they broke their fast, with Arthur reading the paper and discussing current events with Grace while they ate.

Finally, he kissed her goodbye, then gave her another curious glance before departing.

A quarter hour later, Marina came strolling into the drawing room where Grace waited. Marina had grown up in the home, so they never stood on formality or found it necessary for their butler to introduce her when she arrived.

"Am I too early?" Marina asked, crossing the room with a basket in her hands. The women bussed each other's cheeks.

"Your timing is perfect. We should have a few hours."

A noise came from the basket. Something that sounded like a low mewl.

"What do you have in there?" Grace asked, staring at the cover of the basket.

"I wanted to show you this gift," Marina said excitedly. She opened the basket and pulled out the cutest, fluffiest little kitten Grace had ever seen. "Isn't she the sweetest?"

"Oh, she's darling," Grace said, reaching for the kitten. She nuzzled her to her cheek and the kitten instantly settled against her. Cradling the kitten in her arms, Grace stroked and patted down her back. Her fur was longer and solid white. "She looks just like this cat I had growing up, Snowball."

Grace had loved her cat, and still got teary-eyed every year on the anniversary of Snowball's passing. She thought Arthur would think she was a ninny when she told him, but he just hugged her and listened while she spoke of Snowball.

"She used to sleep in my bed and followed me all over the house."

Marina grinned at her. "This one is such a sweet kitten. I just love her."

Grace continued petting the kitten as she purred in her arms. "What did you name her?"

"She doesn't have a name yet." Marina eyed the kitten, and her expression turned thoughtful.

"Well, I am certain you will come up with something adorable for this sweet girl."

As much as Grace didn't want to, she handed the sleeping kitten back to Marina to settle into the basket. They wouldn't have long before Arthur returned.

"Are you ready?" Marina asked.

"Indeed."

Marina left the basket in the care of one of the maids, and then Grace followed her to the kitchen. Marina knew the home's cook well and possessed far greater skill in the kitchen than Grace did. And when Grace had come up with her idea to surprise Arthur, and outdo his Valentine's gift, Marina agreed to help.

"Do you think he has any idea what you've been up to?"

"He's suspicious. That's why I needed him out of the house. I can't trust that he won't come looking for me when he's home."

Marina grinned. "Do you think that vexing brother of mine is going to do something outlandish for Valentine's Day this year?"

Grace rolled her eyes at Marina. Most would probably agree that Marina was far more vexing than Arthur, but she supposed her loyalty would always lie with her husband.

"I don't know," Grace replied. "He may have forgotten. I have intentionally not mentioned the date drawing near in hopes that I will outmatch his gift this year. His poetry reading by candlelight last year, which he wrote himself, I might add, beat out the note I wrote him."

"Well, you are certainly going through a lot of effort," Marina said, grinning at her. "I am quite certain he will appreciate the gesture."

Grace knew that Arthur loved sweets, and she set out to learn to make a pie for him all on her own. The trouble was that she didn't seem to have a knack for baking. She had been grateful that Marina agreed to help her practice the recipe.

Gently bred women in their society would rarely dirty their hands with baking and cooking. If she could pull off such a feat, it would be the best Valentine's gift for her romantic husband.

But she had a feeling that even Cook believed her to be a lost cause. Her crusts never set up right, the filling was lacking sugar the first time, and she overbaked it the last two attempts.

Valentine's Day was tomorrow, so it was her last practice session to get it right before she baked him the final product after he went to sleep that evening.

After a few hours, Marina and Cook helped her to prepare a pie with a simple recipe that was tasty when it came out of the oven. She was mostly confident that she could repeat all the steps that night. Cook had even shown her how to work the stove.

Satisfied with the lesson for the day, she knew she must freshen up and return to the drawing room before Arthur returned home. She and Marina each did so and then took a seat together on the settee, just a few minutes before Arthur appeared.

"Goodness, Brother," Maria chastised. "Couldn't you have bathed first?"

Grace took in the sight of her husband. His hair was windswept, his cheeks flushed, and his spectacles slightly foggy from returning from the cold. The work he had been doing had made his clothing dirty. It wasn't the typical look of an aristocratic earl, but Grace took no issue with the state of her husband's appearance. The opposite, in fact.

"Always a pleasure to see you, Sister," he replied, but his tone didn't quite match his words. "You do recall that this is no longer your home? Or has Evan sent you back here?"

Grace shook her head and giggled. Marina and Evan were quite the love match, just as she and Arthur were.

"The opposite, in fact," another voice said from behind Arthur. "I came to retrieve my beautiful wife." Evan appeared and didn't seem taken aback at all when he noticed Arthur's appearance. The pair had become best friends after Evan and Marina married. Evan handled the estate management for Arthur while he attended university. Arthur and Marina's father had passed away when Arthur was eight-and-ten, but her husband had still wanted to earn a proper university education.

"You can't be away from me for a few hours, my love?" Marina asked.

Evan strolled over to her and placed a quick kiss on her temple. "No, but it's not that. Little Arthur seems to have caught a cold, and he's asking for you."

"Is he all right?" Arthur asked, the worry evident in his brow.

"I think so. Nanny is with him now, and Cook sent up soup just before I departed," Evan replied, then shifted his focus to Marina. "I thought you'd wish to return."

"Indeed," Marina said, tamping down her own worry, then bussed cheeks with Grace before standing to take her leave. "I am sure we shall see you both soon. Hopefully, my brother will smell far better." Marina smirked at him and then also bussed his cheek.

"Give Arthur our best," Arthur replied, seemingly ignoring his sister's barb. "Send word on how he fares."

Marina and Evan started toward the door. "Oh, my basket," Marina exclaimed. Arthur flashed her an amused grin as if he would make some kind of jest, while Grace reached for the bell pull and requested the footman who appeared to fetch the basket.

"I'm going to go wash up," Arthur said. "I shall return shortly."

Marina smirked, but to her credit, she didn't resume their banter. A few moments later, a maid delivered Marina her basket. She opened it and smiled when she looked inside, and then covered the basket again. Evan carefully took it from her, and they both said their goodbyes to Grace and departed.

Once they knew little Arthur was well, they'd go over and visit him. And Grace would get to see Marina's cute kitten again. Hopefully, the sweet girl would have a name by then.

Late that evening, Grace quietly crept from the bedchamber and made her way to the kitchen. Her hair was in a loose plait down her back, but she might have had an easier time baking if she had taken the time to pin it up. She had donned a serviceable day dress that she could put on without assistance from her maid, since she had to dress quietly in the dark to keep from waking Arthur.

He had stirred for a moment when she climbed from the bed, but soon his breathing became even again, returning to a comfortable sleep. By the time she snuck out, he didn't stir at all.

Cook had left everything she needed out and ready so that she could make quick work of mixing the ingredients. A servant had heated the stove for her, which was another thing she could likely thank Cook for coordinating on her behalf. It would certainly make things much easier, and she could focus on the task at hand.

Grace made the crust for her pie and then pressed it into the pan, just as she had done with Cook and Marina earlier that day. She prepared the filling and then filled the pie before placing a crust cover over the top. Smiling at her finished creation, she slid the pie pan into the warm oven.

She glanced around the scene she had created. Flour was all over the table, and it covered the front of her dress.

"What in the devil are you doing?" Arthur asked from the doorway, confusion marring his handsome features. He had donned his banyan and, of course, his spectacles.

"I . . . uh . . ." She froze, unsure how to respond, caught creating her perfect Valentine's Day surprise.

He took a few steps closer. "I woke up, and you were gone. When you weren't in the nursery . . . Do you have any idea what terrifying thoughts raced through my head?"

Probably similar ones she would have if her husband was missing from their chamber in the middle of the night. "I've been right here," she said softly, closing the distance between them and wrapping her arms around her husband's waist.

"What were you doing?" he asked again, looking around her at the mess.

"It was supposed to be a surprise," she started. "For Valentine's Day. But I suppose it's ruined now." Her shoulders fell, and a small frown formed on her face.

He brushed a bit of what she assumed was flour off her nose, then hooked his finger under her chin to raise it. "Well, I'm indeed quite surprised, and it's after midnight, sweetheart, making today Valentine's Day. So your surprise wasn't ruined."

The corners of her lips curled into a playful grin. "I suppose you are right. I still won't tell you what I made just yet. But I am going to best you this year by giving you the greatest Valentine's Day gift."

"Ah," he said, smirking at her. "I know a formidable competitor when I see one."

He picked her up and set her on one of the tables, shoving the few items on the table to the side in a quick sweep of his arm.

Arthur lifted her skirts so her thighs were bare and exposed to him. "You should know that my favorite sweet treat is here." He ran his fingers along the seam of her opening and pressed his lips against hers, their tongues quickly finding each other. She needed his kiss just as much as the first time he had kissed her, more so even.

He gripped her bottom and scooted her to the edge of the table and then knelt to the floor, pushing her thighs open wider. Placing his hand on either side of her slit, he spread her open, then ran his tongue from the bottom all the way to the sensitive pearl at her opening.

Grace whimpered when he pulled back.

"There is nothing sweeter than the taste of my wife on my tongue."

She leaned back onto one hand to support herself and gripped his head with the other, encouraging him to put his mouth where she wanted him. He obliged, licking and sucking her nub, making her back arch and her hips move against his face.

"That's it, good girl," he said against her core. "Come on my face and then I'll make you come again on my cock."

With her fingers digging into his hair, she held his head in place while she undulated against him to the pace she wanted to set. All the while he licked and sucked, groaning between her thighs in response to her every moan.

No longer able to hold back, she released a series of unintelligible words when her orgasm overtook her entire body and she slowed her movements so that she could revel in each delicious second of her climax.

Arthur dipped his tongue inside of her. "Mmm." He rose to stand between her legs. "Always the perfect confection. And so ready for my cock."

He leaned forward and kissed her again with the erotic taste of herself on his lips. She sucked his tongue into her mouth, massaging it with her own tongue, rewarding him for the wicked things he did. Or perhaps, driving him to distraction, knowing what it would do to him.

He untied his banyan without breaking the kiss, then pressed his bulge against her, covered by his breeches. Grace reached between them and unbuttoned his fall front, stroking his cock once it sprang between them. After a couple years of marriage, she knew every inch of his body and how he liked to be touched. And more importantly, what would bring out the feral side of him she adored so much.

Arthur moaned into their kiss as she stroked, and she ran the tip of his cock down her seam to cover the head with the wetness from her body.

"Grace," he groaned. "I need you."

"I'm already yours," she whispered, as she placed the head of his cock at her ready opening.

Arthur thrust forward, entering her fully from the single movement, making Grace's head fall back from the intense rush of pleasure.

"I hope you don't expect me to go slow, sweetheart," he groaned, nipping at her neck and earlobe.

Her entire body was on fire for him and she most certainly didn't wish for him to go slow. "Take me, Arthur. Make me come."

He released a growl and placed his hand on her waist, pushing her to lie back on the table. Arthur pinned her in place with a hand against her stomach and his other hand gripping her hip. Grace wrapped her legs around him, not making any attempt to stifle her moans with each powerful thrust.

"I know my wife enjoys that," he ground out, increasing his speed. "Come for me, and milk the seed from my cock like my good girl."

She whimpered from his words and how his thrusts became frenzied as he pounded into her, the power of his movements rocking the table.

Grace tightened her legs around him when her climax began, crying out his name and perhaps a few obscenities. Her core clenched hard around him through the wave of pleasure that lasted for several seconds and took her breath away.

Arthur moved inside of her twice more before making a last thrust and spending deep inside of her. As she fought to catch her breath, she hoped that perhaps their frenzied lovemaking in the kitchen, where any servant might come upon them, would result in a sibling for James. That would be the ultimate Valentine's Day gift.

Her husband pulled her to sit up and placed a tender kiss on her brow. He was naughty and wicked in their coupling, yet sweet and tender in how he loved her. The perfect combination, she found. "Perhaps we should actually get some sleep," he whispered, nuzzling her neck.

"I have to finish your gift." Grace was still trying to catch her breath. "Go on up, and I'll be there shortly."

"Don't take too long." Arthur lifted her from the table and gave her a light tap on the bottom after helping her right her skirts. Then he tucked himself back into his breeches and tied his banyan closed again.

She grinned at him, knowing that he would be fast asleep the moment his head hit the pillow after their exertions. "Shouldn't be much longer."

Arthur cupped her cheeks and pressed his lips to hers, then pulled back and stared into her eyes. His gaze still had the power to melt her. "I only hope my gift for you shall compare." He winked at her and then strolled from the kitchen without looking back.

His expression confirmed he had something planned after all, and as much as she wanted to give him the most thoughtful gift, she also couldn't wait to see what he had come up with.

Grace went to the oven and checked the pie, deciding that it was ready to be removed from the oven to cool overnight. She set the pie in a safe place, knowing that Cook would ensure it remained untouched. She did her best to tidy up the mess she made in the candlelit room, hoping that Cook didn't curse her when she saw the state of the kitchen in the morning.

As she exited the kitchen, she thought she heard a mewling and listened for a few moments. A gust of wind flew and shook the windows, so she shrugged and continued out of the room.

Once she finally returned to their bedchamber, Arthur's breathing was even and deep. She giggled at her mental victory of being right.

Quickly removing her dress and washing herself as best she could at the wash basin, she then slid into bed with her husband.

She scooted up beside him, and he wrapped his arms around her, seemingly not even waking up. Laying her head on his chest, she quickly drifted off to sleep.

❤━━━━━━━━━━━━━━❤

The next morning, she woke to find that she was alone in their chamber with her husband nowhere to be found. She rang for her maid to help her dress for the day and then quickly found Arthur rocking James in the nursery.

"Happy Valentine's Day, sweetheart."

"Why didn't you wake me?" she asked, crossing the room to kiss his brow and then smile down at their sleeping babe.

"You were sound asleep." Arthur smirked at her. "Likely from your late-night activities in the kitchen."

She wasn't certain if he meant her baking or their lovemaking, but either was likely accurate. She gently took James from her husband's arms and snuggled the babe.

"Have you broken your fast?" Grace asked him.

Arthur shook his head. "I was waiting for you."

Grace kissed James's cheek and then gently laid him back in his crib. Arthur had moved behind her and looked at their son over her shoulder.

She took his arm, and they strolled to the breakfast room. When they arrived, Grace's jaw dropped at the elaborate spread that had been laid out for them. There was all manner of savory options and sweet treats, chilled champagne, and themed decorations for the holiday. The pie she made had been placed on a tiered display in the center of the offerings on the sideboard.

"Did you do this?" she asked.

"No," he said, appearing just as surprised as she was. "Must have been Cook."

A mewling caught her attention, and she noticed a basket with the same little white kitten that Marina had the day before. Grace rushed over to her and picked her up, nuzzling her to her face. "How did you get here?"

She turned to face her husband, who flashed her a wide grin.

"What is going on?" Grace asked, holding the kitten against her while she stroked her back.

"This isn't Marina's kitten, sweetheart," Arthur started. "She's yours. I just had Marina keep her for me until it was time to give her to you. But I can't take credit for this feast before us."

Tears welled in the corners of Grace's eyes, and she threw an arm around her husband's neck, careful not to injure her kitten.

"Thank you, my love. I love her so much already." She didn't know what else to say to such a perfect, wonderful gift.

"I tried to find one that sounded just like how you described Snowball to me."

"You truly are the best of husbands. Do you know that?"

He petted the kitten behind her ear. "I have the joy of being married to you, sweetheart. I am merely just trying to give you all the things you deserve."

"I thought for sure I had outdone you this year. I learned to bake just so I could make you that pie. But I think you have bested me again."

Arthur wrapped his arm around her waist. "I disagree with you there, as I believe your gifts to be the best, and I can't wait to sample what you baked. I still have the letter you wrote me last year in my top desk drawer, and I reread it often."

She did not know he treasured her letter so much, but she supposed it shouldn't surprise her. Her husband was quite the romantic.

"Perhaps we will just have to see what we can come up with next year," Grace said, pressing up onto her toes to kiss his cheek.

Arthur reached for a plate, and Grace noticed a piece of parchment sitting on the corner of the sideboard.

She grabbed it and handed it to Arthur. Then he unfolded it and held it so they could both read the missive.

Grace and Arthur,

I had such a laugh at the two of you working so hard to create the perfect Valentine's gift, unaware that I was in on both of them. I hope you enjoy this Valentine's breakfast I arranged for the both of you, because there is no other dearer to mine and Evan's little family than yours.
So, I also believe that means I win in delivering the best Valentine's surprise!

Love,

Marina and Evan (although he did very little)

P.S. I hope my brother finally bathed.

"You know what this means, don't you?" Grace asked, smirking at her husband.

Arthur kissed Grace's cheek and then nodded. "We are going to have to best her next year."

Grace's kitten, whom she'd mentally decided to name Princess, mewled and she patted her back again. "My thoughts exactly."

About the Author

Christina Diane loves to write super spicy, fast-paced stories set in the Regency era for the modern reader! If you love all the steam, witty banter, spirited heroines, and hot Regency men, then you are in for a treat! She is a hybrid indie and traditionally published author with Dragonblade Publishing. She reads mostly regency and dark romances!

She lives in northern Maine with her husband and two boys, as well as three French bulldogs and two cats. Christina also loves *Bridgerton*, The Grinch, Jessica Rabbit, horror movies, Chucky dolls, cold brew, yoga, *Hamilton*, and the color pink.

You can find Christina on:
Instagram @christinadianeauthor

Visit her website at:
christinadianebooks.com

CONTRIBUTORS' LIBRARY

Please also look for these titles, which were authored by, published by, or feature the authors in this anthology.

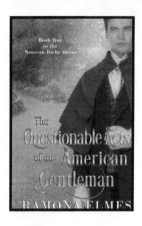

The Questionable Acts of an American Gentleman
Ramona Elmes

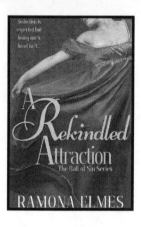

A Rekindled Attraction
Ramona Elmes

A Circle in Seoul
Tamaya Cruz

This Bowl of Stars
Tamaya Cruz

Just Like Christmas
Annabel den Dekker

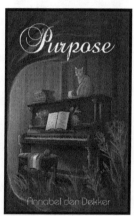

Purpose
Annabel den Dekker

Lady Christmas
Rowen Burrows

The Robin Princess
Rowen Burrows

Sweet Torture
Caz Luan

A Dragon's Tenderness
Rowan Delacroix

Ritual in Ruins
Rowan Delacroix

Northern Woods
Amy Hepp

Ripple Effects
Amy Hepp

The Earl and the Vixen
Christina Diane

The Rake and the Muse
Christina Diane

About the Editor

Courtney Umphress has been a copyeditor and proofreader for over ten years. She has edited for authors all over the world, including several *USA Today* bestselling authors. Although her portfolio includes everything from thrillers to horror to self-help books, she specializes in fantasy and romance.

Courtney has worked for various companies, such as EdiPro, Graphic World, and Skye High Publishing, but she has a soft spot for empowering independent and aspiring authors to fulfill their dreams. Courtney lives in the Panhandle of Texas with her husband, three kids, and two calico cats. You can find her in a coffee shop or a library almost any day of the week, but she also loves traveling, hiking, and playing baseball with her kids.

You can find Courtney Umphress on:

Instagram @courtneyumphress_editor
Facebook @editorcourtneyumphress

And visit her website at www.courtneyumphress.com

Acknowledgments

Of all the people to thank for the creation of this anthology, I must start with the twelve talented authors who contributed so much time, love, and creative energy into their stories. Not only would this anthology not exist without them, but they have also made the experience of compiling and editing an entire collection of stories fun and easy. Ramona Elmes, Tamaya Cruz, Annabel den Dekker, Ann Marie Croft, Nichole Steel, MK Edgley, Rowen Burrows, Carrie Bassen, Caz Luan, Rowan Delacroix, Amy Hepp, and Christina Diane, thank you for your dedication and the wonderful stories you brought to life to share with the world.

I am deeply grateful to Nicole Frail, who bears the motto "Community Over Competition" and spontaneously decided to work with an editor from a different time zone. I'm so proud to have worked for Nicole Frail Books and to continue building up a community of publishing professionals.

Finally, I have to thank my husband and my three children. They have had the utmost patience with me as I've read these stories again and again and again, and they know exactly how much time I mean when I promise them I will help them after three more pages! My husband has been my sounding board as I've bounced ideas off of him and explained plot points that he has absolutely zero interest in. Thank you for being my real-life Valentine!

You've read the spicy stories, now it's time for some sweet! Check out the second part of our Valentine's Day Anthology Duo today!

RECIPES FOR ROMANCE

A Sweet Valentine's Day Anthology

FEATURING SHORT STORIES BY
BJARNE BORRESEN ⬩ MK EDGLEY ⬩ ANNABEL DEN DEKKER
AMY KELLY ⬩ MELISSA MASTRO ⬩ KRISTA RENEE ⬩ KATIE FITZGERALD
AIMEE MOINEAUX ⬩ MEGAN WOOD ⬩ ELISE GILMORE ⬩ DESI STOWE
J.E. SMITH ⬩ MITCHELL S. ELRICK ⬩ CAROLINE BACCENE ⬩ MELISSA CATE
S.B. RIZK ⬩ ELIZABETH BAIZEL ⬩ JESSICA DANILIUK ⬩ HEATHER CULLER

Edited by Nicole Frail

Made in the USA
Middletown, DE
05 February 2025